M. J. Arlidge has worked in television for the last fifteen years specializing in high-end drama production. In the last five years Arlidge has produced a number of prime-time crime serials for ITV including *Torn*, *The Little House* and, most recently, *Undeniable*, broadcast in spring 2015. Currently writing for the hit BBC series *Silent Witness*, Arlidge is also piloting original crime series for both UK and US networks. In 2015 his audio exclusive *Six Degrees of Assassination* was a number one bestseller. His debut thriller, *Eeny Meeny*, which introduces Detective Inspector Helen Grace, has sold to publishers around the world and was the UK's bestselling crime debut of 2014. It was followed by the bestselling *Pop Goes the Weasel* and *The Doll's House*. *Liar Liar* is the fourth DI Helen Grace thriller.

Praise for M. J. Arlidge

'What a great premise! . . . *Eeny Meeny* is a fresh and brilliant departure from the stock serial-killer tale' Jeffery Deaver

'One of the best new series detectives. Determined, tough and damaged, Helen Grace must unravel a terrifying riddle of a killer kidnapping victims in pairs. Mesmerizing' Lisa Gardner

'Dark, twisted, thought-provoking, and I couldn't turn the pages fast enough. Take a ride on this roller coaster from hell – white knuckles guaranteed' Tami Hoag

'Arlidge is the new Jo Nesbø' Judy Finnigan

'DI Helen Grace is fiendishly awesome. It's as scary as hell. And it has a full cast of realistically drawn, interesting characters that make the thing read like a bullet' Will Lavender

'M. J. Arlidge has created a genuinely fresh heroine in DI Helen Grace' *Daily Mail*

'Gruesomely realistic, intriguing and relentless'
Jon Wise, *Sunday Sport*

'A chilling read' *My Weekly*

'A grisly, gripping thriller' *Sunday Mirror*

'A macabre, theatrical thriller that gripped me with every twist'
Woman and Home

'Chilling stuff' *Fabulist*

Liar Liar

M. J. ARLIDGE

PENGUIN BOOKS

PENGUIN BOOKS

UK | USA | Canada | Ireland | Australia
India | New Zealand | South Africa

Penguin Books is part of the Penguin Random House group of companies whose addresses can be found at global.penguinrandomhouse.com

Penguin Random House UK

First published 2015
001

Set in 11/13 pt Garamond MT Std
Typeset by Jouve (UK), Milton Keynes
Printed in Great Britain by Clays Ltd, St Ives plc

A CIP catalogue record for this book is available from the British Library

ISBN: 978–1–405–93204–2

I

Luke scrambled through the open window and on to the narrow ledge outside. Grasping the plastic guttering above his head, he pulled himself upright. The guttering creaked ominously, threatening to give way at any moment, but Luke couldn't risk letting go. He was dizzy, breathless and very, very scared.

A blast of icy wind roared over him, flapping his thin cotton pyjamas like a manic kite. He was already losing the feeling in his feet – the chill from the rough stone creeping up his body – and the sixteen-year-old knew he would have to act quickly, if he was to save his life.

Slowly he inched his way forward, peering over the lip of the ledge. The cars, the people below seemed so small – the hard, unforgiving road so far away. He'd always had a thing about heights and, looking down from this top-floor vantage point, his first instinct was to recoil. To turn back into the house. But he stood firm. He couldn't believe what he was contemplating, but he didn't have a choice, so releasing his grip, he hung his toes over the edge and prepared to jump. He counted down in his head. Three, two, one . . .

Suddenly he lost his nerve, dragging himself back from the brink. His spine connected sharply with the iron window frame and for a moment he rested there, clamping his eyes shut to block out the panic now assailing him. If he jumped, he would die. Surely there had to be another way? Something else he could do? Luke turned back towards the window and looked once more at the horror within.

His attic bedroom was ablaze. It had all happened so quickly that he still couldn't process the sequence of events. He'd gone to bed as usual, but had been wakened shortly afterwards by a chorus of smoke alarms. He'd stumbled out of bed, groggy and confused, waving his arms back and forth in a vain attempt to disperse the thick smoke that filled the room. He'd managed to scramble to the door, but even before he got there, he saw that he was too late. The narrow staircase that led up to his bedroom was consumed by fire, huge flames dancing in through the open doorway.

The shivering teenager now watched as his whole life went up in smoke. His school books, his football kit, his artwork, his beloved Southampton FC posters – all eaten by the flames. With each passing second, the temperature rose still further, the hot smoke and gas gathering in an ominous cloud below the ceiling.

Luke slammed the window shut and for a second the temperature dropped again. But he knew his respite would be brief. When the temperature inside grew too great, the windows would blow out, taking him with them. There *was* no choice. He *had* to be bold, so turning again, he took a step forward and calling out his mother's name, leapt off the ledge.

2

It was almost midnight and the cemetery was deserted, save for a lonely figure picking her way through the gravestones. Simple crosses sat cheek by jowl with ornate family tombs, many of which were decorated with statues and carvings. The weatherworn cherubs and angels of mercy looked lifeless and sinister in the moonlight and Helen Grace hurried past them, pulling her scarf tight around her. The scarf had been a Christmas present from her colleague Charlie Brooks and was a godsend on a night like this, when darkness clung to the hilltop cemetery and the temperature plunged ever lower.

The frost was slowly spreading and Helen's feet crunched quietly on the grass as she left the main path, darting left towards the far corner of the cemetery. Before long she was standing in front of a plain headstone, which bore neither name nor dates, just a simple message: 'Forever in my thoughts'. The rest of the headstone was blank – with no clue as to the deceased's identity, age or even sex. This was how Helen liked it – it was how it had to be – as this was the last resting place of her sister, Marianne.

Many criminals go unclaimed on their death. Others are quickly cremated, their ashes scattered to the winds in an attempt to blot out the very fact of their existence. Others still are buried in faceless HMP cemeteries for the undesirable, but Helen was never going to allow that to happen to her sister. She felt responsible for Marianne's death and was determined not to abandon her.

As she looked down at the simple grave, Helen felt a sharp stab of guilt. The anonymous nature of Marianne's epitaph always got to her – she could feel her sister pointing her finger at her accusingly, chiding Helen for being ashamed of her own flesh and blood. This wasn't true – despite everything Helen still loved Marianne – but such was the notoriety of her sister's crimes that she'd had to be buried without ceremony, to avoid the prurient interest of journalists or the justifiable ire of her victims' relatives. Safety lay in anonymity – there was no telling what some people might do if they found out where this multiple murderer had finally come to rest.

Helen was the only person present at her sister's committal and would be her sole mourner. Marianne's son was still missing and, as nobody else knew of the grave's existence, it fell to Helen to battle the weeds and honour her memory as best she could. She came here once or twice a week – whenever her shift patterns and hectic work schedule allowed – but always in the dead of night, when there was no chance of being followed or surprised. This was a private, painful duty and Helen had no need of an audience.

Replacing the flowers in the urn, she leant forward and kissed Marianne's headstone. Straightening up, she offered a few words of love, then turned and hurried on her way. She had wanted to come here – she never ducked her duty – but the winds were arctic tonight and if she stayed here much longer she would suffer for it. Helen loathed illness – her life never seemed to allow for it anyway – and the thought of being tucked up at home in her flat suddenly seemed very attractive indeed. Hurrying back down the path, she vaulted the locked iron gates and made her way back to the car park, now cheerless and deserted save for Helen's Kawasaki.

Reaching her bike, Helen paused to take in the view. You could see the whole of Southampton from the top of Abbey Hill and this vista always cheered her, especially at night when the lights of the city below twinkled and glistened, full of promise and intrigue.

But not tonight. As Helen looked down at the city that had been her home for so long, she caught her breath. From this high up, she could see not one, not two, but three major fires gripping the city, fierce orange tongues of flame reaching up towards the heavens.

Southampton was ablaze.

3

Thomas Simms slammed the car horn and swore violently. Despite the late hour, the traffic near the airport had been murder, thanks to a lorry shedding its load. Having *eventually* escaped that snarl-up, Thomas had seemed set fair for the short drive back to his home in Millbrook – only to run straight into another jam. It was gone midnight now – where the hell was all this traffic coming from?

He flicked through the local radio stations searching for a traffic bulletin, but, finding nothing save for late-night phone-ins, impatiently switched the radio off. What should he do? There was a shortcut coming up but it would mean diverting through the Empress Road industrial estate, not something he was keen to do, given the prostitutes who'd be there at this time of night. The sight of them, half naked and shivering, always depressed him and he never felt comfortable sitting at the slow-changing traffic lights, eyed up by pimps and working girls alike. Given the choice, he preferred to stick to the main roads, but the sound of approaching sirens made up his mind. A fire engine and an ambulance were trying to bully their way through the traffic. If they were heading in his direction that could only mean that there was trouble ahead.

Slipping into first gear, Thomas mounted the lip of the

pavement and drove for twenty yards before turning sharply left down a dark, one-way street. Suddenly liberated, he drove too fast, speeding past the 30 mph sign as if it didn't exist, before catching himself and lowering his speed to a more sensible level. If he was lucky, he would be home in five minutes – kissing his wife and kids goodnight before flopping into bed. There was no point in getting pulled over by the cops now that the end was so nearly in sight.

He worked sixteen-hour days at his import business near the airport, and he missed his family – but he was no fool. So though he was tempted to run the red light on the Empress Road, to escape the unwanted attentions of the scrawny drug addict in hot pants, he waited patiently for the lights to change, distracting himself from the unpleasant sideshow by thinking of the warm, king-size bed that awaited him at home.

He drove through the city centre, then picked up the West Quay Road, before finally hitting the home straight. Millbrook wasn't a fancy neighbourhood, but the housing was solid Victorian, the neighbours were decent and best of all it was quiet. Or at least normally it was. Tonight there seemed to be a lot of people about, the majority of them making their way to Hillside Crescent – his road.

Thomas muttered to himself. Please God there wasn't some kind of party going on. A couple of the more expensive houses had been occupied by squatters recently and local residents had been kept awake as a result. But things had been quiet of late and, besides, the people hurrying towards Hillside Crescent were not ravers, they were ordinary mums and dads, some of whom he recognized from the morning run.

The expressions on their faces alarmed him, and as he approached the turning into his road he realized why they were looking so concerned. A huge plume of smoke billowed into the night sky, illuminated by the sombre sodium glow of the streetlights. Someone's house was on fire.

No wonder everyone was worried – the housing round here was gentrified Victorian – all scrubbed wooden floorboards and feature staircases. If the fire jumped from one house to the next then who's to say where it would end? Fear gripped him now as he sped down the street, honking his horn aggressively to clear his path of gawpers. What if the fire was close to *his* house? Immediately he clamped down his fear, telling himself not to be stupid. Karen would have called him if she was concerned about anything.

The road was blocked now with ambling pedestrians, so Thomas pulled over to the kerb and climbed out. Locking the door, he started to jog down the street. The fire *was* near his house – it had to be given the direction of the smoke and the concentration of people at the far end of the road. His jog now turned into a full-on sprint, as he barged startled onlookers out of his path.

Breaking through the throng, he found himself at the bottom of his drive. The sight that met him took his breath away and he suddenly ground to a halt. His entire house was ablaze, huge flames issuing from every window. It wasn't a fire, it was an inferno.

He found himself moving forward and turned to find

his neighbour gripping one of his arms, guiding him gently towards the house. The expression on her face was hideous – a toxic mixture of horror and pity – and it chilled him to the bone. Why was she looking at him like that?

Then Thomas saw him. His boy – his beloved son Luke – lying on the grass in the front garden. Shaded by the mulberry bush, he lay with his head on the lap of another neighbour, who was talking to him earnestly. It would have been a touching sight, where it not for the crazy angles of Luke's legs, bent nastily back on themselves, and the blood that clung to his face and hands.

'The ambulance is on its way. He's going to be ok.'

Thomas didn't know whether his neighbour was lying or not, but he wanted to believe her. He didn't care what injuries his son had sustained as long as he *lived*.

'It's ok, mate, Dad's here now,' he said as he knelt down next to his son.

The ground around Luke was covered with leaves and branches from the mulberry bush and in an instant Thomas realized that his son must have jumped. He must have leapt from the house and landed in the bush. It probably broke his fall – may even have saved his life – but why was he jumping at all? Why hadn't he just run out the front door?

'Where's Mum? And Alice? Luke, where are they, mate?'

For a moment, Luke said nothing, the agony racking his body seeming to rob him of the ability to speak.

'Has anyone seen them?' Thomas cried out, panic rendering his voice high and harsh. 'Where the hell are they?'

He looked back at his son, who seemed to be trying to raise himself, in spite of his injuries.

'What is it, Luke?'

Thomas knelt in closer, his ear brushing his son's mouth. Luke struggled for breath, then through gritted teeth finally managed to whisper:

'They're still inside.'

4

Helen Grace flashed her warrant card and slipped under the police cordon, walking fast towards the heart of the chaos. Three fire engines were parked up outside Travell's Timber Yard and over a dozen firefighters were tackling a blaze of monumental proportions. Even from this safe distance, Helen could feel the intense heat – it rolled over her, clinging to her hair, her eyes, her throat, revelling in its power and appetite for destruction.

Travell's Timber Yard was one of the largest in Southampton, a prosperous family business, popular with tradesmen and builders the length of Hampshire. But little or nothing of this successful venture would survive the night. From humble beginnings, this city centre outlet had grown year on year, culminating in the construction of a huge warehouse where timber of every variety, shape and size could be found. Helen watched now as this cavernous building raged in flame, its metal skeleton shrieking in the heat, as the windows shattered and fire rained down like confetti from the disintegrating roof.

'Who the hell are you? You can't be here.'

Helen turned to see a firefighter from the Hampshire Fire and Rescue Service approaching her. His face was caked in dirt and sweat.

'DI Helen Grace, Major Incident Team, and actually I have every right –'

'I don't care if you're Sherlock Holmes. That roof is going to go any second and I don't want anyone standing nearby when it does.'

Helen cast an eye over the roof in question. It was buckling now as the fire ripped through it, seeking new fuel and fresh oxygen. Instinctively she took a step back.

'Keep going. There's nothing for you here.'

'Who's in charge?'

'Sergeant Carter, but he's a bit busy at the moment . . .'

'Who's the Fire Investigation Officer on duty?'

'No idea.'

He walked back towards the fire engines – two of which were now moving *away* from the scene.

'You're leaving?' Helen asked, incredulous.

'Nothing we can do here, except contain it. So we're being sent elsewhere.'

'What are we looking at? Any chance it could have been accidental? An electricity short? Discarded cigarette?'

The exhausted firefighter cast a withering look in her direction.

'Three major fires on the same night. All starting within an hour of each other. This wasn't an accident.' He fixed her with a fierce stare. 'Someone's been having a bit of fun.'

The lead fire engine paused as it passed, allowing the firefighter time to clamber up into the passenger seat. He didn't look back at Helen – she was already forgotten, he and his team discussing the trials that still lay ahead. Helen watched the flashing blue lights disappear down the road, before returning her attention to the huge conflagration behind.

Seconds later, the roof collapsed inwards, sending a vast cloud of hot smoke and ash billowing towards her.

5

Thomas held up his hand to shield his face, then plunged through the front door into the house. Immediately his mouth and lungs filled with a thick, sooty smoke and he began to choke. It was impossible to see – the smoke collecting under the hallway ceiling formed an impenetrable cloud. He had only taken a few steps and already he felt himself succumbing to the foul atmosphere, the carbon monoxide steadily driving out the evaporating oxygen.

Gasping, he fell to the floor. The carpet had already burnt out and though it was agony to touch, the air down here was free of smoke and breathing was a little easier. Scrabbling forward, he made his way to the central staircase. The bedroom he shared with Karen was on the second floor – Alice's bedroom right next to theirs. Somehow he had to get up there. Karen was in sole charge of the kids tonight and there was no way she would have gone out leaving Luke behind. They *had* to be in here somewhere.

His hands were blistering, his clothes starting to smoulder and fizz, but on he went. Eventually he collided with something hard and realized he was at the bottom of the stairs – or what remained of them. The basic shell of the staircase was intact but the whole thing was transformed – instead of a dull, polished brown, the boards now glowed a fierce orange, the burning wood spitting and crackling at him.

'Karen?' His voice was hoarse and weak. In spite of the intense heat that burnt his mouth and throat, he shouted again, louder this time.

'Karen? Alice? Where are you?'

Nothing.

'Please, love. Talk to me. Daddy's her—'

He suddenly petered out, a deep, wretched anxiety paralysing him. He coughed again, more violently this time. Time was running out – he had to do something. Summoning his courage, he moved forward on to the first step. His foot went straight through it as if it were made of dust and he stumbled slightly. Righting himself quickly, he tried the next step up, but this collapsed too. Dear God, what was happening? Could this be real?

He scrambled at the third, fourth, fifth step, but could find no purchase.

'Karen?'

His voice was limp now and drained of hope. He hung his head, overcome and exhausted, his mind starting to spin as the lack of oxygen took hold. As he stood there, not moving, a new smell filled his nostrils. It smelt like burning leather and looking down Thomas was surprised to see that his shoes were on fire. As were his trousers. And his jacket. He was now a walking flame.

Turning, he stumbled back towards the front door. He would never forgive himself for abandoning his wife and his baby girl, but he knew now that he would die if he stayed here a moment longer. He had to get out for Luke's sake, if not his own.

Bursting from the front door, he collapsed upon the soft grass. Before he knew what was happening, he was turning over and over, dozens of hands rolling him on the grass to extinguish the flames. As he lay there, his head hanging upside down, he glimpsed the arriving fire engines and ambulances. The firefighters sprinted past him and moments later Thomas found a paramedic helping him to sit up.

'My son,' Thomas whispered. 'Go to my son.'

The paramedic said something back, but Thomas couldn't hear her. The whole world was strangely muted, though whether this was through injury or shock Thomas couldn't tell. The paramedic was shining a torch into his eyes now, then his throat, assessing the extent of the damage. Thomas didn't care what became of him – were it not for Luke, he'd have happily succumbed to death rather than face the prospect of losing his girls. But even so – even as he dismissed his own existence out of hand – he was still surprised by the sight that greeted him when the attending paramedic lifted his arm to take his pulse. His jacket had burnt clean off, his watch had disappeared and when the paramedic reached over to touch his horribly blistered wrist, the melting skin came away in her hands.

6

The axe connected sharply with the windowpane, sending shards of glass spiralling into the house. With the central stairwell all but destroyed, Fire Officer James Ward and his partner, Danny Brand, had opted for a first-floor entry, heading through one bedroom window, while their colleagues pumped gallons of water in through the other. Time was of the essence – the fire was on the point of going over, after which the house would be unsafe to access.

Brushing the glass aside, James stepped into the house. Immediately the charred boards beneath his feet groaned, threatening to give way. He hesitated, clinging to the window frame for support, before choosing a different route forward. This time the groan was less pronounced and he moved on swiftly but steadily, testing his path as he went. Danny waited for a while before following. This was standard practice – best to lose one officer rather than two, should the flooring give way.

The heat was savage, buffeting his protective suit. James could feel rivulets of sweat pouring down his body. He was uncomfortable and anxious, but he was calm. He had a job to do. It was highly unlikely that anyone had survived, but they had to look. If they were anywhere they would be on this floor, where the main bedrooms were located. James scanned the master bedroom, but there was no sign of the wife or the girl, so he moved forward. As he did so, his foot shot through the floor. Instinctively he grabbed at a light socket and managed to right himself, dragging himself up from the large hole that had opened up in front of him. He could see through now to the ground floor, a smoking mass of burnt furniture and fragmenting walls. Taking a breath, he leapt forward, clearing the hole and landing on the threshold of the landing. For a moment he teetered perilously on the edge, before he gained his balance once more and pressed on.

He moved into what looked like a child's bedroom. The letters that had been stuck to the door – A-L-I-C-E – remained there, oddly unaffected by the fire destroying the rest of the house. James eased the door open to afford himself a proper view of the room beyond. A single bed, a few bits of furniture, a teddy bear on the floor – but no sign of Karen or Alice Simms. His first instinct was to move into the room to conduct a more detailed search, but something made him hesitate. There was a sound, a steady insistent sound, drawing his attention away from the bedroom to the bathroom nearby. It was hard to be sure, but it sounded like a kind of hissing. But not the hissing of burning furniture or a smouldering fire. This was different.

He moved towards the sound, one step at a time. Danny hung back once more, alive to the danger, so James gestured that he intended to check out the bathroom. Danny tapped his wrist, the customary signal that they would need to withdraw in a minute or two – with each passing second the strength of the internal fabric of the house was being degraded. James nodded – he knew that the clock was ticking.

Passing through the doorway, navigating by touch as much as by sight, he was surprised to see that the shower was on in the bathroom. No wonder there was so much smoke, the water vapour being consumed by the flames that raged all around. Dropping down to his hands and knees he crawled forward fast, a sudden thought gripping him.

And there they were, Karen Simms and her six-year-old daughter slumped at the bottom of the shower cubicle, the glass door shut to keep the fire out, the water cascading down on them to keep them from burning to death. James still didn't hold out much hope – they had probably died of smoke inhalation some time ago. Both appeared to be face down in the shower stall, which didn't bode well.

Reaching up, he located the handle of the shower door and pulled it open. A small cascade of water flooded out, creating another hissing burst of boiling steam. He moved closer to the bodies and was surprised to see that both their mouths seemed to be clamped to the shower drain. Suddenly he got it – they were taking in oxygen through the drainpipe.

Hauling Karen over, he looked into her eyes. She was unconscious, but where there was life, there was hope. Beckoning to Danny, he passed the heavy weight of the comatose woman to him. As he did so, the young girl stirred. No more than a small movement, but enough to send a shot of adrenalin through James. Perhaps there *was* a chance they would both survive.

Scooping the girl up into his arms, James turned to follow his colleague. The odds were still in the balance. The building was collapsing around their ears and the extra weight they were carrying would seriously compromise their chances of making it out alive, but they had to try.

It was now or never.

7

'How is she?'

Charlie turned to see Steve silhouetted in the doorway. Jessica, whom Charlie still called her baby despite the fact that she was now sixteen months old, was suffering from a nasty cold. The numerous doses of Calpol and Sudafed had achieved little – Jessica remained resolutely unhappy, her sinuses blocked and painful. Like most small children she had let her parents know that she was suffering – keeping Charlie up into the small hours nursing her.

Charlie raised a finger to her lips and gestured to Steve to stay where he was. Two hours of cuddling and reassuring had *finally* paid dividends and Jessica was asleep once more. Charlie made to leave, then paused to look back at Jessica. There was no sweeter sight for her than that of her little girl slumbering happily in her cot, boxed in by soft toys and her old baby blanket. It always warmed her heart to see her like this and she could have gone on staring at her for hours, but wisdom prevailed. Charlie knew she had better get going while the going was good, so avoiding the creaking floorboards, she tiptoed out of the room, shutting the door quietly behind her.

'Do you want a glass of water?'

Steve was halfway down the stairs, making for the kitchen.

'I might have a hot drink,' Charlie replied, following

him down the stairs. She was wide awake now and, despite the late hour, she would need to decompress a little before she could go to bed. It was amazing how stressful it could be, trying to persuade a toddler that it was in her best interests to go to sleep.

While the kettle boiled, Charlie flicked the TV on. Immediately, the rolling-news channel burst into life – a legacy of Steve's viewing no doubt, as she was more of a Sky Atlantic girl. She was about to flick over to something less real, when she paused. The pictures on the TV surprised and alarmed her. Dominating the screen was live footage from an antiques emporium – a second-hand bric-a-brac-style place on Grosvenor Road. Charlie knew it well – she'd bought a few odds and ends from there in the past; but now the whole place was ablaze, the attending firefighters making little progress in tackling the huge fire. To the right of the screen, in a sidebar, were smaller images from two other incidents – one of a blaze similar in size and scale to the one at the emporium, the other appearing to be a nasty house fire. All of them were in Southampton.

Charlie's mobile rang, loud and shrill, making her jump. Shooting a look at Steve, who'd now joined her, Charlie scooped up her phone and answered it.

'Hi, Charlie. It's DC Lucas here.'

'Hi, Sarah.'

'Sorry to call you in the middle of the night, but you're needed. DI Grace has called everyone in. We've got three serious fires in the city centre –'

'I'm watching them on the TV now.'

'Half an hour, ok?'

Moments later, Charlie was in Jessica's room once more. Now smartly dressed, her hair tied back in an approximation of professionalism, Charlie leant in and risked Steve's wrath by gently kissing her baby girl goodbye. Whenever she went to work she felt guilty – for leaving her baby, for relying so much on Steve to handle things on the domestic front – and the kiss went some way to mitigating those feelings. It was tough and she often felt physically sick leaving the house, but there was nothing else for it. There is one simple rule for working mothers – you have to work harder and longer than everybody else just to be taken seriously. It wasn't fair, it wasn't right, but it was the way of the world, which is why, having kissed Steve goodbye, Charlie unchained the front door and stepped out into the night.

8

Detective Superintendent Jonathan Gardam stood stock still, taking in the scene at Bertrand's Antiques Emporium. He was new to the city – a few months into his tenure as the new station chief at Southampton Central – and if he was honest he was still finding his feet. He had been a front-line officer for so long, a very active and visible DCI in London before his recent promotion, and sitting in meetings all day wasn't his style. He knew it came with the rank, but privately he was pleased for an excuse to be back in the thick of the action.

He walked in the direction of his DI, who was hard at work marshalling the troops. Helen Grace came with a considerable reputation for both brilliance and truculence, but so far Gardam had found her to be both pleasant and professional. She knew how to lead, how to make decisions, and that would prove crucial in what was already gearing up to be a major investigation. As he approached her, she turned and came towards him.

'Do we have any casualties?' Gardam asked.

'No fatalities so far. We have four injured at the house fire in Millbrook, three seriously. There was no one on site here or at the timber yard, so unless the fire team turn up any unpleasant surprises, we should be ok on that front.'

'And it's definitely arson?'

'Looks that way.'

'Any idea why these three sites might have been targeted?'

'We're pulling the owners in and we'll be talking to the family in Millbrook when we get the chance, but there's nothing obvious. Two are commercial, one domestic, they're all in distinctly different parts of town – we can't even be sure yet that the fires were started by the same person, as they started at very similar times. Ever come across anything like this before, sir?'

'Not on this scale,' Gardam replied cautiously. 'This feels . . . organized.'

Helen nodded – she'd had the same unsettling feeling since she'd arrived at the antiques emporium. There'd been no reported incident directly preceding the fire, no witnesses to any unusual activity – the site had just gone up in flames.

'Travell's was the first fire?'

Helen nodded, then continued:

'First 999 calls were at eleven fifteen p.m. This place was next – the calls coming in at around eleven twenty-five p.m. The house in Millbrook about fifteen minutes after that.'

'If the fires *were* set by the same person, it's an interesting escalation,' Gardam continued. 'The first two sites are big and impressive, the third site much smaller, more domestic, yet potentially much more deadly. Whoever set the fire must have assumed there would be people asleep in the house –'

'Which might suggest *they* are the real targets,' Helen interrupted. 'If they were, then what better way to tie up the fire services than by creating two huge fires in other parts of town? We've seen that kind of calculated fire-starting in the States. No reason why it couldn't happen here . . .'

Even as she said it out loud, Helen's mind began to turn. It made sense and would be a good way of disguising the true intent of the crime. There was so much more to learn about tonight, so much evidence to be sifted and questions to be asked, but already Helen's instincts were telling her that this was no ordinary crime. In the sixteen months since the death of Ben Fraser, her life had been pleasantly mundane. But that was all over now.

Once more she was being sucked into someone else's nightmare.

9

The doors swung open and the paramedics raced through, ferrying three hospital trolleys into the bowels of South Hants Hospital. The ambulances transporting the injured family from the Millbrook house fire had radioed ahead and the staff at A&E were standing by to receive them.

At the front of this fast-moving queue was Karen Simms, now in full cardiac arrest. Her brain and body had been starved of oxygen for a long period of time and her body was now reacting. The attending paramedics had used the paddles in the ambulance, but to no effect, so the team now hurried her towards the cardiac unit. Her life was hanging in the balance and every second was vital.

Next came her daughter, Alice. Like her mother she had suffered extensive second- and third-degree burns and was in terrible pain, but she was conscious at least, her young heart seemingly more able to withstand the pressures put on her body by extensive smoke inhalation. Reports from the scene suggested there were no toxic vapours in the house, so if she could survive the next few days, then the young girl had a decent chance. While her mother's trolley veered off left, the young girl was taken straight to the lifts. The burns unit was on the third floor and they were awaiting her arrival.

Behind her came Luke, who had minimal burns but had broken two legs and had significant torso and facial injuries from his fall. He was being taken straight to scans and then to theatre. If he had serious internal bleeding or major head injuries, he stood little chance. But if it was just broken bones, he would be fine. Of the three, he was the one who had been least touched by the blaze.

Bringing up the rear, supported by staff, was Thomas Simms. He watched on as his wife, daughter and son's paths now diverged, all heading in different directions through the hospital. He stood paralysed – like a man frozen in time – suddenly faced with an impossible choice. Who should he go with? Who needed him most? His mind swam, as he processed this dreadful dilemma, but his feet stayed still. There *was* no right choice.

In that moment, Thomas knew that his life had changed irrevocably and for ever. Nothing would ever be the same and much pain and sadness lay ahead. He didn't know how they would get through it or what was the right thing to do. He was lost. And haunting him, like an insistent, nagging ache, was the fear that he would never see *any* of his family again.

10

The imposing Victorian house was now a ruin. The windows had blown out – dirty smears of soot stained the brickwork – and the whole place looked lifeless, haunted and defiled. A family home had become a horrific curiosity, scores of local residents, well-wishers and journalists having turned out to drink in the devastation. Helen Grace struggled to rid herself of the thought that a family had gone to bed here tonight, happy and relaxed, and had woken up to *this*.

The Fire and Rescue Service had secured the site and a local Fire Investigation Officer was on her way. The house was still too dangerous to enter, so Helen had to content herself with a tour of the perimeter of the building, accompanied by DS Sanderson. Sanderson's predecessor, DI Lloyd Fortune, had moved on a few months back, allowing Helen the opportunity to promote her accomplished and loyal DC Sanderson was now her second-in-command and Helen was glad of her company.

'We're looking for signs of an intruder. Anything unusual or suspicious that might explain what happened here.'

The two women walked in silence, the gutted house casting a long shadow over them, affecting their spirits. The ground was frozen tonight, so there would be little chance of finding any useful footprints or tracks. And if a third party *had* been responsible for tonight's blaze, they had obviously been careful. There was no obvious detritus left behind, nothing that could give them a sense of how the fire started.

But there *was* something that was intriguing. The back garden could be accessed via a passage adjacent to the house, the gate to which was unlocked. Someone *could* have entered the garden unseen from the street. Furthermore, the glass in one of the panes of the back door had been broken. It hadn't cracked or blown out like the other windows, perhaps because the fire damage was less severe at the very back of the house. No, this window looked like it had been deliberately broken. More tellingly, the splintered glass from this fracture lay *inside* the house, suggesting the person responsible was standing outside the house when they struck the glass. The resultant hole would have been big enough for someone to put their hand through and turn the key in the lock on the other side. Donning latex gloves, Helen tested the door and was not surprised to find it unlocked.

'I'll get SOC on to this straight away,' Sanderson piped up, following Helen's train of thought, pulling her radio from her jacket.

As Sanderson liaised with her colleagues, Helen returned to the front of the house. The crowd had grown considerably in size. Despite the late hour, there appeared to be a few hundred people gawping now. Helen gestured to DC Edwards, who hurried over.

'Round up a few plain-clothes officers and do a couple of circuits of the crowd. Use your cameras and get what- [illegible] you can. We're looking for any suspicious activity, anyone recording the scene on cameras or phones. Also I want to know if you see anyone masturbating –'

'Excuse me?'

'Anyone masturbating or displaying any overt interest in the fire site. Got it?'

DC Edwards hurried off to find his colleagues. Helen watched him go, momentarily amused by his discomfort. But the request was a serious one. Arson was one of those rare crimes where the perpetrator could return to the scene of the crime to *enjoy* their handiwork. Helen wondered to herself if the person responsible for this awful crime was looking at her right now.

A sound made her turn – DI Sanderson was approaching, her face drained and sombre.

'We just took a call from South Hants Hospital,' she said quickly. 'Karen Simms died just before two a.m. this morning. Cardiac arrest and multiple organ failure.'

'Is anybody down there?'

'DC Brooks is on site.'

'Get in touch. Tell her to stick close to Thomas Simms and offer him whatever support she can.'

Sanderson hurried off, pulling her mobile from her pocket. Helen watched her go, a rising feeling of dread creeping over her. This was no longer a nasty case of arson.

This was now a murder enquiry.

11

The hospital was like a maze and with each wrong turn Charlie's anxiety rose. She hated hospitals. Just the smell of them inspired a deep melancholy in her – a legacy of the many weeks she'd spent in this very hospital, following her abduction three years ago. She should have known the hospital backwards as a result, but every corridor looked the same to her.

She had headed to the fire at Travell's first, but that had proved to be a waste of time. There had been no eyewitnesses to the start of the blaze, the CCTV had been deactivated some time ago and it was too early for any decent forensics. So, having done a fruitless pass in search of secondary evidence, she'd re-routed to the hospital to check on the Simms family.

As she made her way to the burns unit, Charlie felt her pace slowing. She knew that Karen Simms had died on the operating table and that Alice, the six-year-old, was now fighting for her life. This would always have provoked a strong emotional reaction from Charlie, but she felt it even *more* keenly now. Ever since Jessica's birth, she'd been unable to stomach any article or news bulletin that involved children coming to harm. As a copper you had to have a strong stomach and be able to master your emotions, but if she was honest Charlie no longer trusted herself to keep her feelings in check – it was an instinctive and overwhelming reaction for her now.

Pausing outside the entrance to the burns unit, Charlie gave herself a silent talking to. How dare she worry about her own feelings, when this family were in hell? Her job was to help them, not worry about herself.

'Get a grip, girl,' Charlie muttered to herself, before opening the doors and stepping inside.

'DC Charlie Brooks. I'm very sorry for your loss.'

Charlie offered her hand to Thomas Simms, fully aware of the absurdity and pointlessness of the gesture. He looked up and shook her hand before returning his gaze to Alice, who lay beyond the glass in an isolation unit. Her whole body was swathed in surgical bandages and an oxygen mask was secured over her mouth and nose.

'I can't believe that's Alice,' Thomas said suddenly.

It certainly didn't look like her. The photos already making their way on to the news and social media sites showed a smiley, fun-loving girl who liked sports and dancing. The mummified figure in front of them bore no relation to that youthful, vibrant spirit.

'How's she doing?'

Thomas shrugged.

'She's hanging in there. She's a fighter.'

It was said with a smile but tears now filled his eyes, overcome with the desolation that this shocking night had brought.

'I hear encouraging things about Luke. The doctors

said he should be out of theatre soon – he's a brave boy,' Charlie offered.

Thomas nodded, but the smile faded now, as the full cost of the fire made itself felt once more. There was a long silence and Charlie was about to offer Thomas a cup of tea, when he suddenly said:

'What am I going to tell them? About their mum?'

He looked utterly bereft as he turned to Charlie. Quickly she sat down by him, placing an arm on his shoulder. She wanted to comfort him, to reassure him, but there was no easy solace to give.

'The truth. That's all you *can* do. You have to tell them the truth.'

'That's what I'm afraid of,' he replied bleakly, returning his gaze to his daughter.

Charlie left her arm on his shoulder and thought of what to say next. But in truth there was very little to say. She would help him in any way she could of course, would try and lighten the blow felt by Luke and Alice. But how do you dress up something like this? There is no easy way to tell a child that their mother is dead.

12

It was 4 a.m. when Helen finally got back to her flat. Her clothes stank of smoke and her face was coated with a layer of fine ash. She had never felt so beaten up on the first day of an investigation before. The thought that a family had gone through such an ordeal and that the perpetrator was not even *present* at the point of their suffering made her feel very uncomfortable indeed. It was such a callous and premeditated crime and suggested a level of anger and cruelty that was hard to countenance. Who would do such a thing? And why?

Stripping off her clothes, Helen hurried to the shower. More than anything now she wanted to get clean, to wash away the traces of the night's distressing work. The water poured down on her, as she washed her long hair once, twice, three times, but refreshing as it was, she couldn't shift the anxiety and fatigue that gripped her.

Later, swathed in a thick towel, Helen looked out over Southampton from her large bedroom window. Dawn was about to break, heralding a day in which the full reckoning of last night's devastation would become painfully clear. Waiting for the sun to rise, Helen suddenly felt very isolated. In the past, when dark feelings started to assail her, she would seek out her dominator, Jake, but she couldn't do that now. He had started to develop feelings for her, so she'd had to sever their connection, before things became too complicated. She had no family to speak of and she couldn't bother Charlie – she had enough on her plate already – which left Helen feeling very exposed.

Once the fracture in her relationship with Jake had become clear, Helen had considered turning to another dominator. She had always moderated and controlled her emotions through pain – the scars that decorated her torso and arms were a testament to this – and she missed her sessions with Jake. No one was better at driving away her dark thoughts than him. She had gone as far as calling one of his rivals – a dominator who went by the absurd name of Max Paine – but she had hung up before he answered, suddenly unsure about starting the process with a total stranger. With Jake, she could be herself, naked and unadorned. It would take a while before she could let herself be that vulnerable in front of somebody else.

Helen stared out into the night, pondering what the future might hold – for this city, for its inhabitants, for herself – one dark thought tumbling on top of another. Sitting there, framed by the large, picture window and silhouetted by darkness, Helen was the very image of quiet loneliness.

She held this pose for a few minutes then, angered by her self-indulgence, slid off the ledge and walked quickly to her wardrobe, pulling out a fresh set of clothes. Despite the late hour, she'd already resolved to go straight back to base to sift through the latest developments.

There would be no sleep tonight.

13

Blog post by firstpersonsingular.
Wednesday, 9 December, 07.00.

Winter sucks, right?

What else is there to say?

Ok, there is more. Let me try and explain it to you.

Everybody moans. As soon as the Christmas decorations appear in the shops everybody starts whinging: about the cold, how it gets dark early, about snow, about their relations, about their relationships, about how they fucking hate Christmas. But they're lying. They love it. Otherwise they'd have nothing else to talk about, nothing else to <u>do</u>. It's just an act – as predictable as it is false. They have no idea what winter really means. To people like me.

Imagine you're standing on the beach, watching a huge black cloud coming towards you. It's the darkest cloud you've ever seen – it's huge – and it's heading your way. It won't rush – it wants you to know it's coming, to anticipate its horror – but it's moving. Inch by inch, mile by mile – it's coming for **you**.

You feel the sun disappear as the storm blocks out the sun. Soon afterwards you feel the first flecks of rain, as the wind rises, whipping you again and again. Now you're cold, really, really cold. It feels like . . . it feels like all the nice, kind, warm things in the world have been lost for ever. Now the cloud moves over you, surrounding you, stealing you. There's no way out of it now. Even if you wanted to run you wouldn't know which direction to go in. You are powerless. Unable to move. So you sit there. Doing nothing. Hoping for nothing.

It clings to you now, denying you light, hope, warmth. Day after day after day. But you never get used to it. Night and day – it's hard to tell one from the other. Existence seems to stretch out far in front of you – long and pointless. You want to kill yourself but somehow can't muster the energy. You are lost for ever, wandering around and around but always ending up at the same point. And there's no one with you here, no one to guide you to safety. You are all alone. YOU ARE LOST.

THAT'S what winter feels like to me.

But this one is different. A good deal worse and a whole lot better. This year I am taking control of the situation – and the angels are on my side. I saw what people said online about the fire at the Millbrook – they said it was hideous, ugly, an abomination. But not to me. I thought it was beautiful.

14

'Everyone's here now, so let's begin.'

It was only 8 a.m. but already the incident room was packed. Crime scene photos from the three fire sites adorned the walls and data officers were logging and labelling the many hours of footage – both police and amateur – that had been taken from last night's incidents. Nearly everybody present had been up half the night, yet they had all assembled punctually, as Helen had requested.

'I don't have any detailed forensics for you yet,' Helen continued, 'but we are treating all three fires as arson. There was a strong smell of paraffin on the ground floor of the Simms house and at the timber yard. Both Thomas Simms and Dominic Travell have confirmed there was no paraffin stored on site. Presuming the same is true at Bertrand's Emporium, then we can assume that all three fires were started deliberately by a person or persons unknown. CCTV was deactivated at Travell's, Bertrand's didn't have any and of course there wasn't any at the domestic property in Millbrook. We'll see if street cameras picked up anything but it's likely to have been busy at that time – it was kicking-out time from the pubs. The fires were extremely fierce and extensive so it's very likely that any on-site traces of the perpetrator – DNA, hairs, fibres – were destroyed, plus the ground outside was frosty and hard, so we weren't able to find any obvious tyre tracks or footprints. Which means . . . we're going to have to rely on some old-fashioned detective work. I'll pull in as many uniformed officers as I can as we'll need to be knocking on doors, seeing if anyone saw anything out of the ordinary, anything suspicious. DC Edwards, are you ok to coordinate this for me?'

'Yes, ma'am.'

'Anything comes up, feed it straight back in. Someone set three major fires last night and got away with it. They might be shocked by Karen Simms's death or they might be feeling empowered and excited. I want whoever it is to know that we're tearing the city apart, looking for them. So be visible, make some noise.'

'I'll try my best.'

'DC Lucas, I'd like you to handle the PNC checks. See if any local arsonists have been active recently.'

'On it.'

Helen put her file down and addressed the whole team.

'Arson. What are the possible motives?' she asked.

'To cover up a crime?' Charlie offered.

'Good. Anything else?'

'Property crime. To claim on the insurance,' DC Edwards offered.

'What else?'

'Revenge. On a former partner or unfaithful spouse.'

'For the thrill of the fire itself?' Sanderson pitched in.

'Fire gives some people a sexual charge, a feeling of being in control. So we have to put pyromania on the list,' Helen added.

'What if it's something to do with the city itself?

Someone who feels let down in some way? By the people or the place?'

Helen nodded, but before she could reply DC McAndrew jumped in.

'Could there be a financial motive? Two businesses were hit. Plus Thomas Simms runs an import/export business. Might that be a connection?'

'It's certainly possible and in the absence of any hard evidence guiding us towards the perpetrators' motives, we're going to have to focus our initial attention *on the victims*,' Helen responded. 'Why would someone want to attack them? What connects the three attacks? It's not geographical, so there must be another reason why they were chosen. Look at the victims themselves, their spouses, family members, colleagues, lovers. Look at their business affairs, bank accounts, their successes, their failures. McAndrew, I'd like you to coordinate this, paying special attention to the Simms family – they could well be the principal targets of last night's fires.'

Helen paused a second, before concluding:

'Leave no stone unturned. There is a reason why these three sites were targeted. And it's our job to find it.'

15

The Simmses' ruined house was even more sinister in the daylight. It looked hollow – like a skull picked clean of eyeballs, skin and flesh. Deborah Parks, Hampshire Fire and Rescue's most experienced Fire Investigation Officer, was already hard at work when Helen arrived. Helen had crossed paths with Deborah before and knew her to be a determined and incisive investigator. She was hoping Deborah would be able to give them something – anything – to work with in a case that was already extremely light on leads.

Deborah was an attractive and intelligent brunette, but encased in her sterile suit, goggles and mask, she looked like a robot, painstakingly picking over the wreckage, minutely sifting the ash for evidence. Pulling on her suit, Helen quickly joined her and they walked the fire site together, starting their journey at the back door of the house.

'I'd agree that our intruder entered by the back door,' Deborah began in her typically brisk and efficient way. 'The damage to the glass was made by an implement or a fist, not by the fire. Has Meredith found anything useful on the exterior of the door?'

'Nothing yet. We were hoping for a print or something but . . .'

'I'm nearly done now, so I'm happy for her to try

her luck inside. It's perfectly safe now that the struts are up.'

'I'll let her know.'

'I would suggest,' Deborah continued, 'that our arsonist then made his or her way towards the stairs.'

They had reached the ruined stairwell and Deborah now gestured towards what had once been a small understairs cupboard. Helen bent down and was immediately assaulted by a strong scent of paraffin.

'The fire started here, directly beneath the main stairwell. There's no trace of paraffin anywhere else in the house and look there . . .'

Helen followed the line of Deborah's index finger to see a small, black, crumpled box, lying amid the ash on the floor.

'It's a carbonized cigarette packet. It was used to ignite the fire, which then spread upwards – as fire always does – meaning that though the cigarette packet was burnt in the fire, it wasn't destroyed.'

'Why would you use a packet of cigarettes to start a fire, why not a match or a lighter?' Helen responded.

'Look closer.'

As Helen did so, Deborah continued:

'The cigarette packet has something wrapped around it, something which melted in the heat and is now fused to it permanently. My guess is that it was a rubber band. It's a common arsonist's trick. You lay down your accelerant. Then you take a cigarette out and attach it to the packet with a rubber band, not forgetting to stick a few matches under the band for good measure. You lay the box on the accelerant, then light the cigarette. The cigarette burns down until it hits the matches, sparking a fire flare –'

'Which sets the accelerant alight.'

'Exactly.'

'And how long would the cigarette take to burn down to the matches?'

'Ten to fifteen minutes.'

'Leaving our arsonist plenty of time to get away *before* the fire ignites.'

Deborah Parks nodded. Helen digested this development – struck by the care and intelligence of the perpetrator – as the FIO continued:

'There were old cardboard boxes, a couple of brooms, other detritus in the cupboard – plenty of fuel to help the fire grow. If the cupboard door was closed the temperature would have risen quickly. Hot gases would have built up above the flames and when the temperature in the cupboard reached a certain level, the gases themselves would have ignited, causing a flashover. And, of course, the stairs above are made of wood that's over a hundred and fifty years old –'

'So it would have gone up like a candle. And the fact that the stairs would be ablaze before anyone was the wiser, means there would be little chance of escape.'

This crime became more unpleasant the more Helen learnt about it. This was a calculated attempt to kill the Simms family.

'Any room for doubt?' Helen offered, more in hope than expectation.

'No. There are no electrics under the stairs and clear

evidence of paraffin having been poured on the floor. This wasn't accidental or vandalism, it was murder.'

Helen took this in, then:

'What does such a calculated attempt on their lives suggest? In your experience?'

'Well, if you'd wanted to make it look like an accident you would have started the blaze by the fuse box or in the kitchen perhaps, where there are plenty of appliances that could cause a fire. Your arsonist isn't interested in that. He or she doesn't care that people know it's a deliberate act of arson. Perhaps they *want* people to know.'

'So it's an act of hatred? Revenge of some kind?'

'Could be. If I was a betting woman I would wager that the arsonist was known to them. Someone they'd crossed swords with, wronged in some way perhaps.'

Deborah Parks paused before concluding her train of thought.

'This was *personal*.'

16

Luke Simms looked broken in every way. He was putting a brave face on things for his dad's sake, answering Charlie's questions patiently and politely, but his eyes gave the lie to his performance. As he lay with his legs suspended in his hospital bed, he seemed to stare past Charlie to some unspecified spot on the wall, as if he was still struggling to take in what had happened.

By all accounts, Luke was a bright lad with a promising future. He was a pupil at St Michael's Secondary, a prestigious fee-paying school in Millbrook. He was studying for his A-Levels – Maths, Biology and Sports Science – but his real dream was to play football. He practised five times a week and was a key player for a semi-professional team. He had twice been scouted by the Saints and like many local boys harboured hopes of playing for his hometown club. But that seemed a very distant possibility now.

Luke had sustained compound fractures to his legs – both were now encased in plaster and raised on hoists, making it virtually impossible for him to sit up. A dislocated shoulder made matters even more awkward, meaning Luke lay flat on his back hour after hour, supine and defeated. He had a digital radio and a packet of his favourite Percy Pig sweets to cheer him up, but both remained untouched. This young man was thinking only of his mother, his sister and his own broken body. Charlie's instinct was to reach out and comfort him – she couldn't bear the fact that his hopes and dreams had been so brutally shattered – but that wasn't her place, nor her priority. She was here to do a job.

'I'm sorry to have to ask you this, Luke, when you have so much else on your plate, but can you think of anyone who might have wanted to harm you or your family?'

Luke looked at her blankly. For a moment, Charlie thought he hadn't heard the question, but then something changed in his expression. A look of utter incomprehension settled across his features.

'No, of course not.'

'Is there anyone you've argued with? Anyone you've seen threatening your mum or your sister? Do you remember anything that worried you or made you suspicious?'

'No. I . . . I don't pick fights with people. And even if I did, they wouldn't do *this*.'

It was a fair point and the boy's protestations seemed genuine, so Charlie asked a couple more questions, before moving the conversation on. Luke's dad, Thomas, had been present throughout, keeping a watchful eye over his son. He divided his time now between Luke's bedside and the burns unit, where his daughter Alice continued to defy her injuries. There seemed to be no time in this punishing schedule for sleep and Charlie decided to keep her preliminary questions to the point, such was Thomas Simms's exhaustion and desperation.

'So you were heading home around midnight last night, Mr Simms?'

'Yes.'

'Is that normal?'

'It shouldn't be, but it is' was the swift response. 'I import clothes and sell them on. Teenage fashion from China, Hong Kong, Asia. Margins have always been tight but since the recession . . .'

Charlie nodded, but said nothing. The deep worry lines on Thomas Simms's face told their own story.

'I've had to lay off a lot of staff, so most nights I'm there late. I hadn't planned to be packing and unpacking stock at my time of life, but I've invested too much in this business to let it fail.'

'And you had no inkling that there would be trouble last night?'

'No. It was just another day. I'd spoken to Karen earlier in the day and she seemed fine. She was just about to put Alice in the bath when I spoke to her and . . . and she was happy.'

Thomas Simms wept now, holding his face in his hands, as his grief ambushed him once more. Charlie turned away from him only to find that Luke was also crying, tears running down cheeks that were already livid and raw. Charlie felt the emotion rise in her throat and she stared hard at the floor, determined not to give into the tears now pricking *her* eyes. After a moment, Thomas's silent sobbing subsided and Charlie looked up once more, determined not to be weak. She was pleased that her voice didn't betray her as she resumed her questioning:

'And Karen hadn't confided in you about anything – or anyone – that she had concerns about?'

'No.'

'And Alice had seemed ok? Nothing worrying her?'

'Nothing at all.'

Some of the vigour seemed to be returning to Thomas now, as he gathered himself.

'And what about you, Thomas? Can you think of anyone who might have wanted to do this to you and your family?'

For the first time Thomas paused, before replying.

'No. I've no idea who might have done this to us.'

Charlie nodded and moved the conversation on. But she had seen the pause – that brief moment where something might have been said and wasn't – and it left her wondering. What was he about to say? What did he know? And, most importantly, why was he lying to her?

17

An experienced journalist knows when to pounce. Those who've been around the block know not to fight for scraps with the press pack – better to bide your time and hit a police officer once they think they've escaped the mob, when their guard is down.

Helen was just about to climb on her bike, when she saw Emilia Garanita approaching. The Crime Correspondent for the *Southampton Evening News* was no stranger to Helen and they had been through a lot together – some of it good, some of it bad, some of it downright unpleasant. But they were currently enjoying an extended truce, so for once Helen didn't cut and run.

'You've got two minutes, Emilia. I'm needed back at Southampton Central.'

'Same old same old,' Emilia replied, smiling broadly. It never ceased to amaze Helen how brazenly unaffected Garanita was by the things she reported on. A woman had died here, three other family members had been injured, yet still Emilia seemed happy, excited even, about the story that lay ahead.

'What can you tell me? I'm presuming all three fires were arson?'

'They were,' Helen replied quickly. She had already discussed their media strategy with Gardam and they both agreed that there was no point concealing the fact from the press or public, given their need for witnesses and the continuing threat posed by an arsonist at large. 'I'm happy for you to print that, as I want the public to be vigilant and to ask themselves if they saw anything suspicious last night. But . . .' Helen continued, fixing the young woman with a beady eye . . . 'I don't want this arsonist glamorized or sensationalized in any way. I want you to report facts, Emilia, not speculation.'

'That's the creed I live and die by.'

'I'm very glad to hear it.'

'So you think you're after a glory hunter here? Someone who *wants* the headlines?'

'Possibly.'

'Do you think they'll try to contact you? Contact the press?'

'It's happened before, but, like I say, we have no idea what the motivation behind these fires might be. That's why we print the facts, appeal for help and no more, right?'

Helen climbed on to her bike and turned the ignition.

'One last question. Are you expecting more fires?'

As ever, Emilia had saved her best question – her real question – for last.

'I sincerely hope not' was Helen's neutral reply, as she slipped on her helmet and sped away. But she had spent half the night wondering the very same thing. The three fires had been so 'impressive', so devastating, so *newsworthy*, wouldn't the perpetrator feel some sense of triumph now? They had achieved their aims and got away scot free. So what was to stop them doing exactly the same thing again?

18

Denise Roberts stood in front of the full-length mirror. She turned this way, now that, appraising herself. She had spent a small fortune on her new underwear and she wanted to be reassured that it had been money well spent. Tonight was important – she'd been thinking about nothing else for days – and she wanted it to be right. No, she wanted it to be perfect.

Throwing on a dressing gown, she marched down the stairs towards the living room. She lived in a two up, two down in Bevois Mount which was well cared for and pleasant enough – or at least it would have been were it not for the constant presence of her layabout son.

'Get off your arse and tidy this place up,' Denise ordered, as she bustled into the living room. Her son, Callum, a truculent sixteen-year-old, always acted up when she had someone coming round and today was no different. A half-eaten bowl of Cheerios sat next to a mug of coffee, as usual plonked down on the wooden coffee table without a coaster. Magazines and freesheets littered the floor and her son sat beached on the La-Z-Boy, eyes fixed to the large plasma screen on the wall.

For a moment, Denise's eyes strayed from the shambles in the living room to the TV. She was ready to launch another broadside at him for his viewing habits – he could waste a whole day watching *Dog the Bounty Hunter* and *Ice Road Truckers* – but momentarily she paused. He wasn't glued to these staples today – for the first time in living memory he was actually watching the news. The screen was dominated by terrible pictures from last night's fires. There were reporters at each scene relaying the latest news – overnight a mother of two had died – and this was the national news, not local. Southampton was suddenly on the map for all the wrong reasons.

'A change from your usual rubbish,' Denise commented drily, casting an eye in her son's direction. But he seemed not to hear her – his attention was totally fixed on the screen. As was customary now there was endless amateur footage of the fires (not to mention the many eyewitness accounts of publicity-hungry meddlers) being replayed, meaning that the news channels could replay the fires as 'live' hour after hour. It was strangely hypnotic to watch – the huge flames from the timber yard exploding upwards as the warehouse roof collapsed – but still her son's trance annoyed her. She couldn't have him lying about, cluttering the place up. Not today.

She gave him a little kick.

'What the fuck?' he spat out, snarling at his mother.

'You need to shift. I need to be tidying.'

'Big night, is it?'

'Callum . . .'

'Got something nice in store for him, have you?'

'Watch your mouth,' Denise replied, her anger colliding with a strange and unnecessary sense of shame. What did she have to be ashamed about? She was a single woman, with many good years left in her, why shouldn't she seek out a little affection? A little love? She got precious little from her own family.

'Now shift before I say something I regret,' she continued, bending to pick up the discarded magazines. 'Come on, out!'

Still he didn't move. Denise could usually predict his every thought, his every action – he was her only child and she had spent her whole adult life raising him. But something was different about him today. He was unreadable.

'Why do you let him come here?' Callum said suddenly. 'He treats you like shit and still you go back for more.'

'He does not –'

'He's a parasite. He takes what he wants and if you ever stick up for yourself then –'

'That was just the once.'

'Still hurt though, didn't it? If you had any self-respect, you'd shut the door on him.'

'Callum, I'm warning you –'

'It's *him* that needs the warning, not me. Why do you go on protecting him? Why can't you see what he is?'

Denise braced herself for more abuse – there was a fire in her son's eyes today – but Callum just stared at her. Then, dropping his eyes, he said:

'I pity you.'

Hurt now punched through Denise's anger – Callum had never spoken to her like that before, despite their many rows. She didn't know what to say. What was the right way to respond to your son's contempt?

Callum was now marching towards the front door. Denise stood frozen to the spot, but the sound of the latch lifting prompted her to action and she hurried after him.

'Don't you talk to me like that. Don't you ever talk to me like that!' she called after his retreating back. But he was already halfway down the road and didn't look back – her anger had fallen on deaf ears.

Slamming the door shut, she stalked along the corridor into the kitchen. Her nerves were already shattered and it was only mid-morning. Would Callum stay out as she'd requested? Or would he return later to deliberately sabotage her evening? Denise could feel her anxiety rising, so she reached over and looked for her cigarettes in her bag. She pulled out her work pass, her phone, her make-up – but there was no sign of her cigarettes. Little bastard, she thought to herself. It had been virtually a full packet – she'd only bought them yesterday morning. Her son was a thief as well as a slob, it seemed. Muttering to herself, she started tidying and cleaning the house, but her mind continued to turn on the missing cigarettes. Just one more crime to add to her son's growing rap sheet.

19

'For God's sake, do something. There's a little girl in there. Where are those bloody fire engines?'

The woman looked crazed and desperate, scanning the horizon wildly for blue flashing lights. Sanderson paused the footage to study the scene, then wound it forward, stopping at intervals to study faces, expressions and body language. She had been at it for several hours now, trawling through the amateur footage from the fires and it was beginning to get to her. Not just because of fear and anxiety etched on the faces of many of the onlookers, but also because of the blank expressions on many of the others. These gawpers exhibited nothing more than a casual curiosity – as if a dead woman or a family home reduced to rubble might be momentarily diverting.

'Found anything?'

Sanderson turned to see Helen Grace standing next to her. She had an alarming way of approaching without making a noise, leaving you no time to put on your professional face. Sanderson managed to stifle a yawn – the viewing suite was airless and hot – before bringing her boss up to speed.

'Nothing so far. I've done Travell's and I'm halfway through the Millbrook footage. Lots of people keen to have a look but no one displaying any overt signs of excitement. Just the opposite if anything.'

'Recognize any faces?'

Sanderson shook her head.

'What about our local arsonists? Have we run them down?' Helen continued.

'We've got seven on our list – all of whom have committed fire-related offences in the County in the past twelve months. The majority of them did it for insurance fraud and the others are just kids. We've chased down four – verifiable alibis so far – and we're on to the last three. But there's no one on the list who's attempted anything of this magnitude before.'

'Keep trying. Also let's run a national search to see if there have been any other instances of coordinated arson attacks in the last two to three years. This guy's MO is pretty specific, not to mention well executed. I'd say he'd had practice.'

Sanderson nodded, promising to expedite this search, then resumed her viewing. In truth she just wanted to be away from here. She wanted fresh air, light, happiness. She wanted to be away from the stench of death.

Helen strode into the incident room and was pleased to see the team was hard at work. Everyone at Southampton Central had been shocked by last night's crimes – many were fearful of what they might presage – so they were pulling out all the stops. It always cheered Helen to see how her officers were willing to cancel their plans and put their personal lives on hold when the job demanded it. It was inconvenient for family and loved ones, but a woman had died. Karen Simms deserved justice and Helen was hopeful her Major Investigation Team would deliver exactly that.

As she was scrolling through a mental list of important tasks that lay ahead, Helen noticed DC McAndrew approaching. She could tell by her face and the spring in her step that she had something of note to tell her.

'Something for you, boss.'

McAndrew handed Helen a sheaf of papers. They appeared to be a bundle of bank statements and credit card bills.

'I've been running the rule over the Simms family like you suggested. Thomas Simms runs a small business - "AEK trading" – from a warehouse on the Grawston industrial estate. It's a practical spot and the rents are fair –'

'But?' Helen interrupted, keen to get to the point.

'But the business is on the brink of going under. He's been paying staff wages via his credit cards, withdrawing cash on them at extortionate rates.'

'That's crazy.'

'Exactly, but he's just not getting the business any more. He lost a contract with a couple of high street stores twelve months ago and has never managed to find replacements. Bigger players can bring in the clothes cheaper – basically he's too small to get noticed, but too big to stay afloat financially. Just too many outgoings.'

Helen felt a twinge of sympathy for Thomas Simms. His wife didn't work, so the family's financial welfare was down to him. What must it have felt like to watch a business of over ten years' standing slowly dying in front of you?

'And here's the really interesting bit,' McAndrew

continued. 'There seem to be other payments to staff – cash payments again – that don't come from credit card withdrawals.'

Helen looked down a line of payroll transactions that McAndrew was indicating.

'All in all it totals over fifteen thousand pounds.'

'Any invoices? Did he make this from sales?'

'Can't see any. He hasn't taken in that kind of money in ages. He seems to have been buying a new line of clothes from Malaysia –'

'Hoping that something will finally stick.'

McAndrew shrugged.

'Either way, he was heavily in debt. I've checked – the house insurance was renewed three months ago and there's a hefty payout in case of fire.'

'Even so, I can't see it, can you?'

'Stranger things have happened,' McAndrew replied calmly.

'He's got a solid alibi, he'd be a fool to do it when his family were there and, besides, it was so obviously arson – the insurance company would never pay out.'

'Desperate times prompt desperate acts.'

Helen pondered this new line of enquiry. She had seen men lose everything and destroy their families rather than face up to it – one incident particularly was burnt in her memory. If Thomas Simms *was* in the throws of a nervous breakdown, it was possible he might have done something desperate and foolhardy. He seemed so smitten with his family though and so devastated by the loss of his wife. Had a crazy plan gone badly wrong somehow? Had an accomplice set the fire and messed it up?

As Helen thanked McAndrew and headed for the exit, she knew there was no point speculating about it. There was only one way to find out the truth about Thomas Simms.

Ask him.

20

'I don't see what this has to do with Karen's death. I'm sorry, but I really don't.'

Thomas Simms was hostile and defensive. He had been since the moment they'd suggested it would be best to conduct their interview away from the wards in a private room. His evident frustration could be down to his anger at having been pulled away from Alice's bedside or it might be something else. Helen was determined to find out which.

She was flanked by Charlie, who already seemed to have a good rapport with the family. This was her forte – the human side of an investigation – and Helen was glad to have her here. It had been a while since they'd worked so closely together on a case.

'We're just trying to establish a full and accurate picture of the family situation.'

'The family situation?' Thomas countered incredulously.

'So we can ascertain why your house was targeted,' Helen continued unabashed. 'We're not judging anyone or prying, but we do need to know what was happening in your lives.'

'Best do this now, Thomas,' Charlie interjected softly, 'then we can leave you alone to support your family. If there was any reason why someone might have targete—'

'What makes you think it wasn't random?' was the

assertive response. 'You see it all the time on the news. Messed-up kids, setting things alight because they've had a rough time or are bored or –'

'That may well be the case, but there are several aspects of this attack which suggest otherwise. Petty acts of vandalism are seldom carried out on residential properties. It's nearly always derelict buildings, playgrounds, schools – somewhere out of the way where there's no CCTV, no possible witnesses. Family homes are very rarely targeted randomly.'

For once Thomas Simms had no comeback.

'Furthermore, whoever attacked your house broke in. They had to access your garden first – which presented a risk – then they had to break the glass in the back door, while people were at home. In setting the fire centrally within the house, they took another risk – all of which indicates that this was not a random crime. Whoever did this was organized and determined, and I would suggest had probably scoped out the house beforehand. They appear to have been very committed to targeting your house, despite the very real possibility of discovery and apprehension.'

Helen let her words settle. The strain was showing now on Thomas and Helen didn't want to break him with a barrage of questions or insinuations. She had to proceed but needed to do so cautiously – it was horrifying to have to process the idea that someone had gone to such effort to decimate your family. Simms sat silent now, rubbing his face with his hands. Already the fight had gone out of him and Helen knew from many years of interrogating suspects that this was her opportunity.

'We've discussed the difficulties your business faced – none of them of your own making – and the way you maximized your credit to stay afloat.'

'We know you took your responsibilities to your staff very seriously,' Charlie said, overlapping. 'Many of them had families just like you and they needed to be paid. But the money just wasn't there, was it?'

A beat, then Thomas nodded.

'What were you going to do?' Charlie continued softly. 'How were you going to keep going?'

There was a long pause as Thomas Simms struggled for an answer. Then:

'Keep digging.'

'I'm sorry.'

'Keep digging myself a bigger fucking hole to jump into.'

'I don't follow, Thomas. What do you mean by that?' Charlie prompted. She could tell Helen was following the conversation intently, waiting for Thomas Simms's next move.

Another long pause. A furious internal debate seemed to be taking place within the bereaved husband. Charlie half expected a bitter 'No comment' but then suddenly Thomas blurted out:

'I kept borrowing, didn't I?'

'More credit cards?' Helen replied.

'No. I . . . I couldn't get any more. Too many unpaid bills. Bad credit history.'

The bitterness oozed from him. Helen could tell he blamed the moneymen for his current predicament.

'Who did you borrow from, Thomas?' Helen pressed

gently but insistently. 'Those unaccounted-for cash payments – where did they –'

'A loan shark,' Thomas interrupted. 'A bloody loan shark.'

His face was turned to the floor – the full extent of his shame was now becoming clear.

'We'll need a name,' Helen said as neutrally as she could. The mere mention of loan sharks had her alarm bells ringing.

'I can't give you a name.'

'Why not?'

'I just can't.'

'Not good enough, Thomas,' Helen replied. 'If you've borrowed money from an unregistered lender, then we *need* to know. If you've been threatened, we can offer you protection –'

'I think it's a little late for that, don't you?' was the bitter response.

'What do you mean by that?'

'Nothing,' he replied after a brief pause. 'Nothing at all.'

'*Were* you threatened?' Helen persisted.

Still nothing from Thomas Simms.

'Give us a name and we can help you. If there's been any harassment or threats, we can have them for intimidation. We have the powers to deal with these people. Please, Thomas. Tell us what happened.'

'I . . . I borrowed five grand from a guy – just to tide me over. The business was in trouble, Luke's school fees are astronomical, then there's Karen, Alice . . . I thought it would be a one-off. But then I borrowed another five. Then another.'

He paused, but neither woman felt the need to jump in. Whatever was coming was coming now – he needed to confess.

'I tried to pay him back but suddenly the interest payments went up. I couldn't meet them. And . . .'

His voice caught as a deep misery stole over him. Charlie could feel her heart pounding inside her chest, her anxiety rising in sympathy with each word.

'And he came to the house one night. When I was out. He . . . he threatened Karen. She didn't know anything about my . . . problems. I'd kept all that crap from her and the kids. And now . . . and now this.'

Thomas Simms buried his face in his hands, overwhelmed.

'Dear God,' he whispered suddenly. 'Is this my fault?'

Helen watched him as he wept, nodding to Charlie who extended a hand to comfort him. Helen had never really bought Thomas Simms as a suspect for the arson attack, but it was clear now that he still might be responsible for the attacks. It was their best lead and he had kept it from them. Helen knew that if that meant Karen's killer escaped justice, it would go hard with him. As Helen knew herself, your soul is never at ease when you have another person's death on your conscience.

21

'The loan shark's name is Gary Spence.'

Helen was marching away from the hospital, her phone clamped to her ear. She'd opted to bring Gardam up to speed immediately – knowing the kind of character he was, she was sure he'd expect nothing less.

'What do we know about him?'

'Nasty piece of work,' Helen went on. 'Convictions for ABH, GBH, extortion, extracting money with menaces. He also escaped a possible conviction for attempted murder – because of an eyewitness pulling out at the last minute.'

'Any history of firestarting?'

'A couple of juvenile offences, plus an insurance fraud five years ago. Burnt down a warehouse he owned to cash in on the £150,000 policy on it.'

Gardam digested this but said nothing. Helen was still making up her mind about her new boss. He was less political than his predecessor, but that didn't mean he wouldn't be trouble. Some bosses were lazy, some too concerned with self-promotion, others were micro-managers. Helen had already filed Jonathan Gardam in the latter camp. He wanted to be *fully* involved in investigations. Was he a control freak? Did he miss life on the front line? Or did he not trust his new colleagues?

'He's obviously not above this kind of thing, but does he fit the MO?' Gardam finally replied.

'MOs develop over time,' Helen responded, 'so we can't rule it out. And we know for a fact that Spence had also lent money to Bertrand's Antiques Emporium. It's a very hand-to-mouth business. It's dressed up as antiques but actually it's a glorified rag and bone shop. Bertrand Senior operates on the edge of legality – he's had problems with HMRC and others – and on a few occasions he's borrowed money from Spence. He swears he paid the last lot back –'

'But he might be lying to avoid trouble with his insurance company,' Gardam interjected.

'Precisely. Spence is our best bet, so I've scrambled the team to his home, office, known associates, mistresses – everything. We'll have him in custody before the day's out.'

'See that we do. We've already had a sustained assault by the press on this one and we owe it to the family to solve this brutal crime quickly. So no excuses from your team. We need to bring him in.'

Helen agreed and, ringing off, climbed on to her bike. Gardam had tactfully aimed his warning at her team, but really it was aimed at her. It had taken a while to come, but her new chief had finally bared his teeth.

22

Sanderson sipped her drink and cast a discreet look at her watch. She had been here for over an hour now and she had the distinct impression she was starting to arouse the regulars' curiosity. The Hope and Anchor was a pub on the edges of Millbrook that had seen better days. The wallpaper was bubbling, the carpets were worn and the whole place had the feel – and smell – of a waterhole gone to seed. The lager was cheap and the clientele cheaper, so it still attracted a certain type of crowd. Sanderson had dressed down to try and fit in with the ex-cons and wannabe villains who patronized this establishment, but she had the feeling she still stood out too much. Her clothes were a bit too new, a bit too clean in comparison to the stained tracksuits and hoodies worn by the other drinkers. Moreover, she'd washed her hair last night, which couldn't be said for the gaggle of girls touting for free drinks and cigarettes at the bar. Their lank hair and scruffy appearance suggested they didn't think much of other people's opinions and probably not much of themselves either.

Sanderson picked at one of the corners of her coaster and cursed her luck. What was the point in her arranging dates? Something always seemed to come up to put the kibosh on it. It wasn't Helen's fault – someone senior needed to be running the stakeout and her boss didn't know she had dinner plans – but still. The simple truth of it was that she was tired of being single and irritated by the fact that work always got in the way. Before she'd joined the Force she'd had a run of boyfriends – handsome, fun, likeable guys whose company she'd enjoyed. But as soon as you put on the uniform, something changes. It's not just that your life is not your own any more or that you often work nights. It's something to do with being a copper. Women are supposed to like men in uniform, but it doesn't work the other way round. Are men intimidated by female police officers? Are they uncomfortable with the authority they have over them? Are they worried that they will be pulled up for every minor vice or misdemeanour? Whatever the reason, they seem to back off. No doubt about it, the uniform was a massive turnoff.

Sanderson finished her drink and returned to the bar for a refill. She chided herself for being so negative. Surely it was possible to find someone – Charlie and many others like her had managed it. Privately, Sanderson rather envied Charlie – her happy home, her baby girl. She knew it meant sacrifices on a personal and professional level, but at least it *meant* something. Charlie's life seemed very grounded compared to hers. But she was never going to get there unless she tried and she had been looking forward to meeting Will tonight. He sounded fun from his emails, had an interesting job and he was certainly easy on the eye.

The question was whether she would make it. Helen had told the team that finding Gary Spence was their top priority and a number of his known haunts were now under surveillance. His home, his mates, a couple of snooker halls and this pub – a place he liked to frequent at the end of stressful day, extorting money from desperate debtors who hadn't read the small print properly. As Sanderson returned to her seat in the corner, she felt several sets of eyes following her progress. Did they suspect her? Or did they just like the look of her? It was feasible that they had already called Spence and warned him not to come. It was impossible to tell and as with all stakeouts there was only one way to find out.

Watch and wait.

23

He recognized her immediately. As she put on her protective suit, mask and goggles, he took in her trim figure. She was pretty and well groomed, her glossy chestnut hair always secure in a very professional-looking bun. He had observed her at a number of burnt-out properties over the past year, diligently carrying out her work, and had even looked her up on Facebook. Her name was Deborah Parks and he always felt a little charge when looking at her.

She had been working at Travell's Timber Yard since lunchtime. The massive site looked like a war zone – the main warehouse had burnt to the ground, as had most of the stock, temporarily turning the skies over this part of town black. It'd been an amazing thing to witness and had drawn big crowds, but now they had all disappeared. Back to *X Factor* and *Celebrity BB*. They thought the show was over. They didn't value what was right in front of them. They couldn't see what he could *see*.

Deborah Parks was on the move now, entering the shell of the warehouse and temporarily out of view. A couple of uniformed officers guarded the main gate, but the site was huge and the chain link fence had not been well maintained – they obviously didn't get too many timber thieves round here. It was a matter of a few seconds to haul up the bottom of the fence and roll underneath.

Dusting himself down, he surveyed the scene, pausing for a moment to breathe in the strong aroma of carbonized wood that rose from the ashes of this once-vibrant business. Moving out of sight, he began filming. A slow panorama at first, taking in the full devastation of the scene, then a series of zoomed-in close-ups. The devil is in the detail at fire sites – the small remnants of the conflagration, the things that survived, tell the story best. A successful family business that had taken years to build – destroyed in less than an hour. Such was the power of fire.

The sound of a voice nearby made him look up from his recording. He had been so wrapped up in his work that he'd failed to notice Deborah Parks leaving the warehouse to make a phone call. Berating himself for his carelessness, he ducked behind the remnants of a timber stack and scuttled along the perimeter fence away from danger.

Finding a new place of safety towards the back of the site, he rested for a minute – to catch his breath and reassure himself that he hadn't been spotted – putting his camera back in his rucksack. Now he got on with the real business. Crawling on his hands and knees, his eyes darting this way and that, searching, searching, searching. You never knew what you were going to find in these situations – sometimes it took ages to find anything decent – but today fate was smiling on him. Near the fence edge was a fire-damaged sign. As soon as he picked it up and turned it over, he broke into a broad smile. 'Travell's Timber Yard', it proudly announced, but this boastful sign was now smeared with soot and violated by fire. It was ideal. The perfect souvenir of a memorable night.

It was too big to fit in his rucksack, but if he held it to him with the writing facing inwards he would be ok. He didn't have far to go. Lifting the fence, he slipped it under, then followed himself. Picking it up, he got to his feet and, having checked that there were no police officers about, hurried off down the street.

As he went, he chuckled to himself. It had been a very satisfactory day's work.

24

When would he ever escape this place?

Luke Simms had only been in hospital for a day, but already it felt like a lifetime. When you cannot move, when there's nothing you can do for yourself, time passes very slowly. Luke had hardly slept – kept awake by the pain in his shoulder and legs and the dull ache of his loss. But at least at night he had been left alone.

During visiting hours today, he had been besieged – inundated with teary visitors who lavished him with affection or urged him to 'stay strong'. They left flowers, chocolates, books, DVDs – already his room was a riot of colour. It was like an Aladdin's cave and, though he was grateful for their kindness and concern, he hated it all. Some people he was glad to see of course, but his misfortune now seemed to be a magnet for anyone who'd ever known him. So in addition to family and close friends, he'd been visited by football mates and their parents, ex-girlfriends, godparents, guys from school, cousins several times removed. Some of them barely knew him, some of them he thought actively disliked him, but suddenly they all wanted a piece of him. Wanted to tell him how brave he was. Wanted to offer their sympathy to him and, worse than that, their praise.

It was all so inappropriate. What had he actually done? He had jumped from a building and broken his legs. In a stroke his home, his life, his future had been shattered – so what exactly was there to be happy or hopeful about? He was always polite, but when they geed him up by telling him how quick-thinking he'd been, how courageous, he wanted to tell them all to go Hell. He hadn't jumped because he was brave. He had jumped because he was scared.

Had he been a proper son and brother, he would have braved the flames. He would have charged through them to find his mother and sister. He could have got them out of the house ten, twenty minutes earlier perhaps, but he didn't. Because he was scared by the awful chorus of smoke alarms and the flames devouring the stairs, he had turned and fled, climbing out of his window and jumping to safety.

Because of that his mother had died. His mother who had given up work to raise him. Who had taken him to football practice three times a week. Who had always called him her 'special one'. He'd abandoned her – as he had abandoned his little sister – to her fate. And for that he would never forgive himself.

Which is why all the bouquets and cards with messages of good will and praise seemed completely obscene. If he had his way, they would all have been thrown straight in the bin.

25

Sanderson punched the button and the wheels spun in front of her. She wasn't a gambler – didn't play fruit machines and wasn't sure what tactics you were supposed to employ – but it passed the time and gave her something to do. Were some of the regulars laughing at her amateur efforts, wasting pound after pound on ill-judged spins? She thought so, but as long as they put her lack of prowess down to her stupidity or her sex, then that was ok. She was happy to live with their casual sexism if it meant they didn't question her presence here.

Another two hours had passed. She had drained a couple of pints, faked a few phone calls, even smoked a couple of cigarettes in the freezing yard out back. She hated cigarettes and had only managed to get halfway through both of them, taking very intermittent puffs. But she needed to do something and there were no freesheets left to read and no more phone calls she could legitimately fake. Which is why she now found herself at the fruit machine, cherries and bananas spinning in front of her in some strange, surreal dance.

'All right, Gary, what can I get you?'

Sanderson froze, her finger hovering over the Play button. A voice answered the barman's jovial welcome – the accent was local and rough – and the conversation carried on in a pleasant enough vein. But there was something in the barman's tone that intrigued Sanderson. It sounded very much like fear.

She continued playing the machine, trying to get a sight of 'Gary' in the reflection on the machine's glass front. But there was a post in the way and she couldn't make out the face. Whoever it was, he was now talking in low tones to his fellow drinkers, wry, humourless chuckles occasionally punctuating the conversation. Why had he dropped his voice? Was this normal or had he already clocked the tall woman by the fruit machine whom no one could vouch for?

Perhaps he was watching her right now. If she turned, would she find him staring right at her? Sanderson knew from experience that a quick, darted look over the shoulder was the most suspicious move you could make and that in situations like this it paid to be up front and bold. So abandoning the fruit machine, she picked up her half-drunk pint and marched over to the bar.

'This lager tastes like cat's piss. Got anything better?'

The barman broke off his conversation, eyeballing her unpleasantly.

'We don't hand out freebies in this pub. That'll be three pounds.'

'Daylight robbery,' she replied, casting an eye towards the other drinkers in search of support. But they weren't interested in her, still deeply involved in their murmured conversations. Sanderson however was *very* interested in them and caught a good side view of Gary Spence. She had memorized his mugshot and there was no doubt about it. It was him. He was unshaven and shabbily dressed in old, stained clothes.

Tossing three coins on to the moist beer towel, she said:

'Fill her up then. And don't spit in it when I'm gone, eh?'

With that, she turned and headed through the bar door and down the corridor to the Ladies. Pushing inside, she counted to twenty, listening sharply for any signs of pursuit. Then, hearing nothing, she pulled her phone from her pocket and dialled Helen Grace's number.

26

The car sped through the streets, bullying the traffic out of its way. The sirens weren't on, but the flashing blue light was having the desired effect. The roads were clogged today – it was less than three weeks until Christmas and Southampton was full of out-of-town shoppers – but their progress was swift nevertheless. It was almost as if people knew how important this was and made way accordingly.

Helen always felt more comfortable on two wheels than four, so she'd let Charlie drive. There were three other cars making their way to the scene – Helen wanted to create a secure perimeter around the pub – meaning that for once Charlie and Helen were travelling alone. The road had opened up now and they were finally entering Millbrook. Helen could see the police incident boards on the pavement, appealing for witnesses to the Simms house fire and it refocused her mind on what lay ahead.

Pulling up around the corner from the Hope and Anchor, Helen took out her police radio. She could see one unmarked car in place and wanted to check that the other two were in their positions. A swift radio round established that they were.

'Right, let's do this. Ready?'

Charlie nodded, so they climbed out of the car and hurried round the corner to the pub. Some officers – mostly male – would have advocated a mob-handed approach, going through the front door with a phalanx of uniformed officers in body armour. They thought this was a safer, more effective approach to bringing crooks in than the traditional tap on the shoulder. But Helen didn't agree. Often you gave the game away before you'd even begun. The people in these sorts of places drink with their eyes and ears open. They are likely to spot a group of coppers gathering in the street. Moreover, such a clumsy approach was, in Helen's view, *more* likely to lead to trouble, the disturbed criminals reacting violently to such a sudden and heavy-handed intrusion.

As they stood on the threshold, Helen looked to Charlie once more – a silent nod returned – then she pushed the door firmly and went inside. The pub was filling up now – scallywags drinking a 'well-earned' pint at the end of another day of ducking and diving – and was noisy and lively as a result. As soon as the two smartly dressed women stepped into the pub, however, the atmosphere changed. Heads turned, voices were lowered – everyone present wondering who had done something wrong.

Gary Spence hadn't looked to see who these intruders were, but Helen could tell by his body language that he had tensed up. Was he expecting them?

'Gary Spence?'

There was long pause – nobody was talking now – before Gary slowly put down his pint and turned to face her.

'Have we met, darling?'

'I'm DI Grace, this is DC Brooks. We'd like a word with you, please.'

Gary stared at her, saying nothing. He took a slow, deliberate sip of his pint, then said:

'Fire away.'

'Not here. We've got a car outside.'

'Serious, is it?'

'I'd prefer to do this at the station, so when you're ready.'

Gary looked at her once more. A thin smile spread across his mouth.

'Have it your way.'

At which he flung his pint in Helen's face and bolted for the back of the pub. Helen was too startled to react and Charlie a nanosecond too slow. He brushed past her outstretched hand and sprinted for the saloon door. Immediately he came face to face with Sanderson who had sprung from her position.

'Police. You are –'

But she didn't get any further. Spence launched himself at her, his beefy shoulder connecting with her head on, sending them both reeling backwards through the door and into the dingy passage outside. Sanderson tried to get up first but felt an elbow slam into her stomach, knocking the wind from her. She was left clutching at thin air as the escaping Spence raced away towards the emergency exit nearby.

Before Sanderson could rise, Helen Grace sped through, hurdling her grounded officer and setting off after the fleeing crook. Charlie paused momentarily to check Sanderson was ok, before following suit. Moments later they were both in the freezing courtyard outside. Spence was nowhere to be seen but the fixed gaze of a couple of startled smokers now revealed his position. He was climbing the fire escape – Helen had expected him to head out and away, but actually he was heading *up*.

Helen turned to Charlie.

'Tell the others he's making for the roof.'

As Charlie radioed this in, Helen ran up the fire escape, taking the steps two at a time. Spence had a head start on her, but carried considerably more weight than Helen and she was hopeful of hunting him down.

One flight, two, three, then finally Helen crested the fire escape, spilling out on to the gravel roof. Immediately she spotted Spence sprinting towards the far edge. She gave chase but he was thirty feet ahead and as he came to the edge of the roof, leapt from it, straining every sinew to get across the large gap that separated the pub from its nearest neighbour. He made the other side, but only just, his right foot sliding off the slippery ledge, threatening to unbalance him, before he righted himself and raced on.

Despite the forty-foot fall that awaited her if she misjudged the jump, Helen didn't hesitate. The buildings round here were detached, flat-roofed commercial properties. If Spence was quick and lucky he could escape their net altogether via the rooftops. Helen launched herself across the divide, landing safely on the other side. But as she landed, she skidded on the scattered gravel, her legs giving out from underneath her. Feeling herself go, she wrenched her torso round, rolling swiftly and elegantly on the ground, before flipping back up on to her feet.

She was slowly gaining on Spence, those many hours spent busting her lungs round Southampton Common finally paying off. She was lean and agile, cresting the next gap with ease, landing safely on the other side. Spence was visibly tiring now – he was full of cheap lager and had been expecting an easy night – so Helen upped her speed.

Then suddenly Spence ground to a halt. Helen did likewise, keeping herself at a safe distance. She could see why Spence was hesitating. The next gap was wider – nearly ten feet – and he lacked the puff to be confident of making it. Slowly he turned. As he did so, she cast an eye over her shoulder. Charlie was a couple of properties back – Helen couldn't rely on help from that quarter in time, so she would have to handle Spence alone.

As he stared at her, reeking anger, she pulled out her baton and extended it.

'Well, that's hardly a fair fight, is it?'

'Needs must, Gary. Shall we call time on this one?'

'Fuck you' was the terse reply as Spence burst forward, trying to dodge past Helen, back in the direction of Charlie.

He had a nanosecond's advantage, but Helen had been expecting this move. She lunged left to stop him, bringing her baton down hard on his kneecap. Spence yelped in pain, stumbling forward and into Helen's shoulder, which was braced low against him. For a moment, he took off then landed flat and hard on the roof floor, the gravel scraping the skin off his cheeks. Helen was on top of him in a flash and before he could rise, she had her knee in his back and the cuffs on. As Spence swore and spat gravel from his bleeding lips, Helen afforded herself a brief smile.

'I think it's time we had a little chat, don't you?'

27

'So, how's business?'

Helen was back in the interview suite at Southampton Central opposite a deeply hostile Gary Spence. He had been seen by a doctor, given time to shower and change and consult with his lawyer – but none of this had improved his mood. He scowled and swore at every opportunity – making a point of firing personal insults at Helen and DI Sanderson whenever he could.

'You know this will go a lot easier if you just answer the questions, Gary,' Helen continued. 'How is the loan shark business?'

'My client provides credit –' his lawyer interjected, but Helen wasn't in the mood to split hairs.

'Whatever you want to call it,' she interjected. 'Is it treating you well?'

'Keeps the wolf from the door,' Spence eventually replied.

'I'd say it's more than that,' Sanderson responded. 'You've got a nice big house in Merry Oak. And rumour has it you're in the market for a place in the New Forest. Business must be good.'

Spence just shrugged, then looked at his watch theatrically.

'What happens when they don't pay back what they owe you, Gary? When they can't pay?'

'My client will always attempt to renegotiate any problem loan, change the sums or intervals of payment if necessary –'

'But if they default, then what? I'd like your client to answer that, not you, Ms Fielding.'

Spence's brief said nothing, but Helen knew she'd antagonized her. She was a young and intelligent brief, keen to flex her muscles against a renowned DI. Helen only wished she'd found a more worthwhile cause on which to bestow her undoubted talents. Spence had four grams of cocaine on him when arrested. He swore blind that this was why he'd done a runner – but Helen wasn't convinced.

'They lose their collateral,' Spence said evenly.

'Meaning you take their car, their property –'

'Whatever the money is secured against.'

'And what about for smaller, unsecured loans? A few grand, ten maybe. What happens if they borrow that from you, then can't – or won't – pay it back?'

Spence shrugged – seeming to imply that such sums were beneath him.

'What about Thomas Simms for example?'

'Jesus Christ, is that what all this is about?'

'He borrowed money from you and when he couldn't pay it back, you threatened his family.'

'Whoa, whoa. You're going to have to rewind a bit there. Who says my client threatened the Simms family?'

It was offered aggressively, but Helen could see Fielding hadn't been expecting this line of questioning and was rattled as a result.

'Your client came to the door and told Karen Simms

that if he had to come back again, she would regret it. Sounds pretty much like a threat to me, wouldn't you say?'

'That's bullshit,' Spence barked back, earning a silent but pointed look from his lawyer. But Spence didn't seem to be care. 'I never went near that bloody house,' he continued, 'and anybody who says I did is lying out their arse.'

'We have the date when you visited – November 30th. Around nine p.m. apparently. What's the betting that street cameras and your phone signal put you there around that time, Gary?'

For a moment, Spence said nothing.

'Ok, maybe I went round there for a quick word,' he offered finally, earning yet another look from his lawyer, 'but I was looking for Thomas Simms. I never threatened no one.'

'Of course not. You're good as gold, aren't you?' DI Sanderson said, picking up the baton. 'Not that you'd know it from your record. ABH, GBH, attempted murder –'

'I was never convicted of that!' Spence protested.

'Lucky break then, because you did throw a live grenade into the property of one of your particularly troublesome debtors, didn't you?'

'Don't answer that,' Spence's brief cut in.

'And you've got a bit of form with fire, haven't you?' Helen persevered, keeping the pressure on.

'A one-off mistake,' Spence dead-batted in return.

'Is that what you'd call it? I think you like to teach people who won't pay a lesson,' Helen continued. 'I think you like people to know that no one, absolutely no one, gets away with ripping you off. Am I right?'

Spence said nothing in response. Neither did his lawyer.

'The attack on the Simmses' house was determined, organized and *personal*. Let me tell you what I think happened. I think you threatened Simms and when he didn't pay you, you went *back* to his house. We've applied for a warrant to check your phone records – it won't take long to find out where you were, Gary.'

Spence just scowled, so Helen carried on:

'We know you'd had words with Bertrand Senior. Had you also lent money to Travell's? Was this payback? A one-night spectacular to punish Thomas Simms? A warning to keep all your other debtors in line? I must say, Gary, I admire your style. You think big.'

Spence breathed out slowly. He looked weary and angry now.

'Keep talking, Inspector. But know this. I was in bed last night. With my wife. And if my Pug could talk he'd tell you he was there too, sitting on the end of my bed from nine p.m. till six a.m. the following morning. I didn't do it and you can't say I did. So do your work, run down your dead ends and then let me go. Interview over.'

28

'What do you think?'

Helen had gone straight to Gardam's office, only to be told he was in the viewing suite with McAndrew, casting an eye over the latest batch of amateur footage from the fires. Instinctively this made Helen feel uncomfortable – officers of his rank usually steered well clear of the coalface and she didn't appreciate him overseeing her team's work. She resolved to ask Gardam why he felt the need to impose himself on her investigation but wasn't given the chance. Having dismissed McAndrew from the viewing suite, her superior cut straight to the chase.

'Is he our man?'

'Hard to say,' Helen replied. 'His alibi is hardly rock solid, but even if he *is* telling the truth, that still doesn't mean he didn't do it.'

'Because he's got associates?'

'Precisely. Spence likes to throw his weight around, but he's not stupid. He could have told one of his cronies to start the fires. If he did, then he reduces the personal risk but ups the chances of one of them talking – so our next move is to round up as many of his known associates as we can. They've all got mothers, so perhaps Karen Simms's death will persuade them to help us.'

'Good.'

'We're also going to look into Spence's finances,' Helen

continued. 'I want to see if anyone's putting the squeeze on him or if there's any reason why he might want to lay down a marker in this way. I've got the team on it and I should have more shortly. We're throwing everything we can at this.'

'Well, it sounds like you've got everything in hand. Keep me posted.'

'Of course.'

A brief silence followed. Helen had expected the conclusion of her update to prompt Gardam's departure, but he made no move to leave. Instead, he leant back against the desk, staring right at her, as if trying to read her mind.

'What's your feeling on this one, Helen?'

'My feeling is that I'd like to link Spence to Travell's Timber Yard. If we can prove that they owed him money or that they'd had a disagree—'

'But what's your *instinct*?'

'My instinct is not to trust my instincts. I prefer to deal in facts.'

'That's a politician's answer.'

'Forgive me, sir, but I'm not quite sure I understand the qu—'

'I'm only putting you on the spot,' Gardam interrupted, 'because I value your opinion. You're unique, Helen – both at Southampton Central and in the Force. No one's got your track record when it comes to bringing these complex investigations to a successful conclusion. You did it with Ben Fraser, with Ella Matthews and more besides . . .'

Gardam had tactfully not mentioned Helen's sister, but it was clear that she was included in this list of Helen's 'achievements'. Her new boss had clearly done his homework on her.

'So I'm interested to find out how your mind works,' Gardam said, not missing a beat. 'I want to know if your gut is telling you that Spence is capable of these crimes.'

Gardam's gaze never wavered for a second. His eyes were fixed on her, as if she were a rare breed or curiosity. In the hushed, darkened interior of the viewing suite, his close attention made her feel distinctly uncomfortable.

'He's certainly capable of it,' Helen replied evenly. 'The question is whether he has the imagination to pull off this sort of crime. And, in the absence of a confession, only patient and diligent detection will tell us that.'

It was a polite but firm full stop to the conversation. Helen had had a long day – with the scrapes and bruises to prove it – and she had no appetite to undergo an interrogation of her own.

'We'll just have to wait and see then, won't we?' Gardam said, rising finally, a relaxed smile spreading across his face. 'Let me know what you find out.'

'Straight away.'

'Now, it's late, so why don't you get off home?' Gardam said, crossing to her. 'Can I give you a lift anywhere? I'm heading your way –'

'Thank you, but I've got my bike, so . . .'

'Of course, the famous bike. Solo traveller, eh?'

'Something like that,' Helen replied.

'Well, I won't keep you then,' Gardam finished, laying his hand gently on her arm, 'and my thanks again. You did well today, Helen.'

Helen acknowledged the compliment and departed

quickly. As she opened the door, she caught McAndrew staring right at her – her junior was clearly intrigued by the interview from which she'd been so pointedly excluded. Helen nodded at her, then hurried off down the corridor. She could feel the colour rising in her face, which made her feel foolish and flustered, like she'd been caught out in some way. She walked on purposefully, keen to escape into the anonymity of the night. But all the while she could feel McAndrew's eyes on her, which made her wonder: was Gardam watching her too?

29

Charlie crept into the darkened room, taking care not to make a sound. Jessica was breathing heavily, her little sinuses still blocked with cold, and she had only just gone down, despite the late hour. Secretly, Charlie had hoped she would be up when she arrived home, so she could say goodnight to her properly, but Steve had done his job well, stroking and singing her to sleep. Despite her tossing and turning, she looked content now, blissfully unaware of the world around her.

'How long did it take you?' Charlie whispered.

Steve had joined her and both were now gazing down at their slumbering daughter.

'Two to three hours,' Steve answered evenly. 'She was pretty cross.'

'Sorry.'

'It was ok. Though I must have gone through my whole repertoire of nursery rhymes at least three times.'

'I'm glad I was out then,' Charlie replied, teasing. Steve raised an eyebrow, but didn't respond. Then he crossed the room, and having doused a tissue with a generous measure of Olbas oil, laid it gently in Jessica's cot. Immediately, the room was filled with the comforting scent of eucalyptus.

'Come on, we'd better hit the hay,' Steve whispered. 'There's no telling when she's going to be up again.'

Charlie nodded. He was right of course but she hadn't seen her all day and suddenly she didn't want to leave. Steve moved to the doorway but lingered on the threshold, waiting for Charlie to follow. A brief flash of irritation shot through her – it seemed she wasn't in control at work or at home now – but then common sense prevailed. She was knackered and needed a shower, so, relenting, she bent down to kiss her goodnight.

'Don't.'

Charlie stopped, hovering inches from Jessica's soft face, taken aback by the sharp tone of Steve's voice. She turned to him, surprised.

'She needs to sleep and if you wake her, it'll take hours to get her dow—'

'All right, all right' Charlie responded, straightening up and brushing past Steve without another word. It was a childish response and she knew it. She had no cause to be shirty with Steve, whatever she felt about missing out on quality time with Jessica – but still his chiding irritated her. She was fed up with compromise and making do. She wanted her life to be simple, straightforward and satisfactory – but in reality it was none of these things. These days she seemed to lurch from one mini-crisis to the next, achieving little, pleasing no one, forever facing choices that left her the loser whichever way she jumped. Would she get better at this? Or was this how it would always be? Perhaps the brutal truth was that, whatever she did and whatever she tried, this was one circle that Charlie would never be able to square.

30

The noise assaulted you as soon as you stepped inside. Helen let it roar over her, enjoying the sensation, as she stood in the doorway of the bar. It was close to last orders now and the place was packed. There didn't seem to be a quiet night in the city centre any more – Southampton was full of young people who wanted to chat, flirt and drink – and as soon as you stepped inside you were struck by the warmth, energy and excitement of the place.

'Tonic over ice, please,' Helen shouted at the barman, as she pushed her way to the bar. As he obliged, she took in the scene, her eye wandering over the first daters, the groups of friends, the hangovers-in-waiting and more besides. Helen didn't drink – hadn't done for years – but she liked these places. Things could turn ugly where drink was concerned and Helen had had to intervene on a couple of occasions to defuse unpleasant situations, but young people as a rule seemed to be drinking rather less than previous generations – the whole scene was more a social thing than an excuse for binge-drinking. That was especially the case around here, so close to Southampton University, where the pubs and bars were full of twenty-somethings who couldn't afford vast rounds of drinks even if they'd wanted to.

Helen had come here straight from work as she couldn't face going back to her flat. Her meeting with Gardam was still bothering her and if she went home she would only obsess about it further. Better to be here, enjoying the buzz, than stewing alone.

As her eyes swept the crowds, she became aware of someone waving sheepishly to her from a table on the other side of the room. It took her eyes, her brain, a couple of seconds to process the sight, but there was no doubt about it.

Jake. Helen had never seen him in a social context – barring one exception, she had only ever encountered him in his workplace, where he played the role of dominator to perfection, never letting the real Jake through. He was on his way over now and for a second Helen was surprised to find that she was panicking, wondering what to say to him in a conversation that she hadn't paid for.

'I thought it was you.'

He leant in and kissed her gently on the cheek. Unlike her, he seemed completely at ease. More than that, he seemed happy.

'I didn't expect to find you somewhere like this,' he continued lightly.

'Neither did I, but it's been a tough day, so I thought I'd come and inhale a bit of youthful optimism.'

Jake smiled, but the accidental subtext of Helen's reply was lost on neither of them. Previously Helen had run to Jake when work had got to her, but not now.

'How about you?' Helen continued quickly.

'I'm on a date,' Jake said, pretending to be embarrassed, as he nodded towards a handsome young man, who smiled awkwardly back at them from across the crowded room.

'Good for you,' Helen responded, though her brain was still playing catch-up. She knew that Jake was bisexual, but such was his interest in her that she'd always assumed he was more romantically attracted to women.

'Is this a new thing . . . ?' she went on.

'Not really,' Jake answered, diplomatically.

'And it's going well?'

'Well tonight is our sixth date, so . . .'

'Wow.'

'Yes. Wow.' Jake laughed at himself easily and confidently.

Helen smiled, but couldn't think of the appropriate way to respond, so said nothing. She knew so little of Jake's romantic history that she didn't really know if this was a big development or not. She suspected it might be.

'And you're ok?' Jake queried.

'Oh you know. Same old same old.'

Jake smiled and nodded. Conversely he knew an awful lot about Helen and understood exactly what she went through during a major investigation. For a moment, the conversation lapsed into a comfortable silence, then Helen said:

'Don't let me keep you, Jake. I'd hate to sabotage young love . . .'

'You're right, I'd better go. Take care of yourself, Helen.'

He leant in and kissed her once more, this time giving her a brief hug with it. She responded, but felt a sharp and sudden stab of sadness as she did so. This felt very much like Jake finally cutting loose.

She watched him return to his date and hung around for another ten minutes, not wanting Jake to think he'd driven her out by his presence. But as soon as he and his boyfriend were once more engaged in happy, tactile conversation, Helen slipped out into the night.

Walking back to the flat, she reflected on her strange evening. She had gone to the bar seeking solace, but had found something else instead. She had the strange feeling that her life was changing for ever, moving past her in a way that she could neither prevent nor control. Worse still was the fact that Jake's happiness made her miserable. She pushed the thought away – it was so unpleasant to feel sad about someone else's joy and yet there it was. Deny it though she might, the truth was that she had never felt so alone as she did tonight.

31

Blog post by firstpersonsingular.
Wednesday, 9 December, 23.30

More bullshit today. Where do these people get off? With their half-arsed statements and brain-dead journalism. Why does everything have to end up being a fucking soap opera?

Know what I mean?!?☹☹☹☹

She could have written about anything. She could have written about it. But instead she wrote about them. Not many pictures of the fire and even those were blurred. It's not hard, people . . .

Lots of pictures of the dad though. And his poor ickle son. So brave. Both of them. Really. I mean it.

They may have suffered, but here's the thing. At least someone cares. At least their pain registers.

You must know what I mean. And before you dismiss me as just another troll, think about it.

Because it's not the pain that matters. It's the context of that pain. Do you follow?

People give a shit. The dad. The son. Even the crispy sister. They've lost their momma, their anchor/rock/mainstay (delete as appropriate), but they've got each other. In a fucked-up way, they're closer now than they ever were.

So before you expend all your sympathy on them, think. Do they need it? Do they want it? No, they have everything right there in their tight little family.

They are the lucky ones. I've been alone from the moment I was conceived.

32

'Nice to meet you, Eleanor. I don't usually accept spur-of-the-moment clients, but just this once I'll make an exception.'

It was said pleasantly enough, making it hard for Helen to tell whether there was innuendo lying beneath it or not.

'So, why don't you tell me what I can do for you tonight?'

The final sentence was loaded with possibility. With Jake sex was never part of the deal – he was a dominator pure and simple – but she got the distinct impression that Max Paine was a very different animal. He was incredibly well built and seemed to take pride in displaying as much of his body as possible. Was that to impress or intimidate? Helen couldn't tell.

'Let's keep it simple to start with. I don't want to be touched, I don't want to be teased. I just want you to do what I ask and nothing more.'

'You're in charge.'

'Exactly. A leather riding crop should do us fine. Twenty minutes max. My safe word is "release". If you hear tha—'

'Then everything stops. I have done this before, Eleanor.'

'Of course. I'm sorry.'

Helen stared at him, refusing to show that she was

embarrassed or nervous. But she was both – unsure of her footing in this strange, new environment. Jake's room had had a bizarre cosiness to it – which matched his personality. This place was something different – bigger, more elaborate. Helen wondered what secrets these walls could reveal.

'That's pretty clear, so shall we get started?' Max continued, pointing Helen towards a small, curtained, changing area. Helen obliged, removing her coat and scarf and stepping inside. She undressed quickly, but her fingers fumbled over the buttons of her blouse, gripped by a sudden anxiety. Had she made a mistake coming here? She didn't know who he was, hadn't checked him out at all. She had been stupid and reckless. And yet the alternative – sitting at home trying to resist the temptation to hurt herself – seemed even worse.

Now in her underwear, she stepped out of the changing area. Max was waiting for her by the restraint wall, which was decorated with an assortment of chains, clasps and cuffs. Helen moved swiftly over to him, choosing a fairly normal-looking pair of restraints in the centre of the wall. Max snapped her wrists into them, then bent down.

'Not the legs,' Helen said quickly.

'You're the boss,' Max replied with a broad smile. 'Ready?'

Helen nodded and turned her head to the wall.

Moments later, the first blow struck. Then the second, harder this time. A brief pause and Helen whispered:

'Again.'

The blows rained down now, each impact jarring Helen's body, causing her to cry out. And slowly she started to relax, the pain taking her away to another place, away from life, away from herself. The tension that had been building up inside her for weeks was already receding, replaced by a relaxed exhaustion that was familiar and comforting. Perhaps it hadn't been a mistake to come here after all.

33

At first, she wasn't sure if she was dreaming. Someone – or something – was pressing down hard on her, depriving her of breath. She lashed out with her arm, expecting to meet resistance, but connected with . . . nothing. Now she started to cough – savage and harsh – and rousing herself, slowly opened her eyes.

She *wasn't* dreaming – but still none of this made sense. She'd had a good night with Darren and they'd come upstairs together around 10 p.m. He said he'd stay the night with her, so why was her bed now empty? He'd done a bunk before, broken his promises, but still it must be the middle of the night, given how dark it was. Denise fumbled for the clock radio, but couldn't find it. Why was it so bloody dark in here?

She coughed some more. Painful, rasping, insistent coughs. Suddenly Denise couldn't stop coughing, bringing up great clods of mucus and even a little of tonight's dinner. She swallowed it back down, but the acidic taste of vomit lingered in her mouth, along with something else. The taste of smoke.

Now Denise was wide awake. Why hadn't she noticed this before? The whole place stank of smoke. The whole place was *full* of smoke. A horrible fear now gripped Denise and her mind immediately whirled back to a promise she'd made to herself some weeks back to replace the batteries in her smoke alarms. Why hadn't she done it? Why was she such a lazy cow?

Her hand fumbled its way to the bedside light and she clicked it on. As she did so, her free hand shot to her mouth. Black smoke was pouring in under the closed bedroom door, invading the room and claiming it as its own.

Throwing off the duvet, Denise stumbled towards the door. Grogginess was making her clumsy, while her rising panic made breathing hard. Was Callum in? Had he come home or stayed out with friends? Denise grabbed the door handle, determined to run straight to his bedroom – then pulled her hand away sharply. The cheap metal handle was red hot. Looking down she saw a long livid line forming on the palm of her hand, as a biting pain took hold. Whimpering now, Denise stood stock still, the horrible craziness of this situation temporarily paralysing her. Then thoughts of her son forced their way back into her consciousness, spurring her on. Grabbing a drying vest from the radiator, she wrapped it round her good hand and worked the handle again.

It wouldn't move. This made no sense – there was no lock on this door. She tried again harder, yanking the handle back and forth, and this time she became aware of a noise. It was the sound of the wooden doorframe bending and buckling in the intense heat.

'Please God, no. I can't die here. I don't want to die here,' Denise muttered to herself through tears as she pulled and pulled to no avail. Suddenly she let go of the handle, fear and exhaustion robbing her of her conviction. Sweat was pouring off her now, but it evaporated almost as quickly as it appeared, leaving a sticky, salty residue clinging to her body. She was finding it harder and harder to breathe – she would only last another minute at best – so summoning what courage remained, Denise grabbed the door handle and pulled it for all she was worth.

This time the door gave, swinging violently and unexpectedly towards her. It all happened so quickly thereafter that Denise only had a moment to react to what she saw, a second in which to throw up her arms to her face in horror. A vast wall of flame was charging directly towards her, destroying everything in its path.

34

Callum Roberts took a big drag, inhaling the smoke slowly and letting it hang in his mouth, before exhaling. He felt the rush immediately and drew heavily on the joint again, before offering it to Dave, who was waiting impatiently for it. As his friend reached over to take it, Callum pulled it away again, having one last toke from it and earning himself a punch on the shoulder for his cheek.

Slowly his mood was lifting. He hated it when his mum had that man over. It was bad enough just thinking about what they got up to. It was even worse having to listen to it through the paper-thin walls. His own mother giving it away to someone who wouldn't hang around once he'd got what he came for. Callum could always tell when her date nights were coming up – a sudden burst of cheerfulness, followed by steadily rising anxiety as the day approached, punctuated all the while by endless trips to buy perfume, dresses, new underwear. The whole thing made him sick to the stomach.

Marching to the fridge, Callum pulled out a can of beer and drank half of it down in one go. He always made himself scarce when his mum had company, seeking refuge with whichever of his mates would have him. As it turned out, Dave's parents were away for the night, meaning Callum could stay over without having to face their sly looks and whispered, disapproving comments. Strange really how Dave could be so sound, yet they were such total dicks.

Quite a few people had come round to Dave's now, word having spread of an impromptu party. With the new arrivals had come booze, dope and more besides, all of which Callum helped himself to, despite the fact that he had arrived empty-handed. To his mind, he deserved it after his shitty day.

He felt pleasantly light-headed as he made his way across the room towards the balcony. Dave lived on the top floor of a sixties apartment block. All the flats here were originally council-owned, but were later snapped up by smug homemakers like Dave's folks. Now they were pretty plush and every flat came with a small balcony, commanding decent views over Southampton.

From across the room, Callum spotted the pretty blonde again – what was her name? Kerry? Carrie? She had been round Dave's on previous occasions and, even though she was a stunner, she never seemed to have a boyfriend in tow. Callum had a mind to do something about that, given half a chance.

When he stepped out on to the balcony, he was immediately struck by the noise and energy of the banter – unusual for these potheads. He'd planned to sidle up to the blonde and get to work on her straight away, but everyone seemed to be staring out from the flat towards something that lay beyond. There was a definite charge and excitement to their chat and curiosity now got the better of Callum – he brushed past his intended target in the hope of getting a better view.

There was a fire. Smoke was billowing into the sky nearby, and if you stood on tiptoe, you could just make out the tops of the flames leaping into the night sky. Sirens could be heard in the distance and closer there was a strange buzz, as the fire drew local residents out on to the street. What was that buzz? Fear? Or excitement?

Already a disquieting thought was starting to arrow its way through Callum's brain and he pushed his way further forward, straining to get a better sense of the exact location of the fire. He got a few muttered *Fuck's sake*s from the people he barged aside, but he didn't care. Sweat was breaking out on his forehead now, despite the bitter cold, as dread slowly crept over him.

He suddenly realized Dave was at his side – he too had been drawn out by the sight of the fire. And he seemed to echo Callum's growing fears, as he turned hesitantly to his friend and muttered:

'Looks like it's over your neck of the woods, mate.'

35

A large crowd had gathered already and Helen had to shout to be heard, as she barged her way to the front. The burning house was a detached two up, two down on a run-down housing estate. The front garden wasn't well kept and the house was little better. But whatever unsightliness it offered was now obscured – the whole house was ablaze, huge flames punching out of the shattered windows.

Helen had made it across town in record time, kicking herself all the way for taking her eye off the ball at such a crucial time. Her blood had run cold when Sanderson called her with the news – three more fires had broken out. Helen had detailed other officers to investigate the first two, a furniture showroom in Bitterne Park and an outdoor car park in Nicholstown, while she'd biked straight to the residential blaze in Bevois Mount. This was the third fire that had been called in and instinct drew Helen to it.

Firefighters were battling to get into the property, but the fire was at its peak now. Stalking round the house to see if the crews on the other side were faring any better, Helen was alarmed to see how completely the fire had taken hold. Cheap plywood walls, synthetic flooring, worn-down carpeting – the whole place was a fire hazard. Helen prayed that there was no one left inside it when it went up.

The firefighters at the back were having no more joy than their colleagues. They battled manfully, but it seemed hopeless and Helen could see the weariness on the faces of many of them – they probably hadn't had any rest since last night's fires.

Making her way back towards the uniformed officers who were keeping the crowd at bay, Helen's mind turned on these latest disturbing developments. This was an impoverished part of Southampton – which could provide some sort of link to Gary Spence and the loan sharks who preyed on desperate people. The furniture showroom currently burning in Bitterne Park might also be connected if they had borrowed unwisely, but an outdoor car park? That would be council-owned and the cars there would presumably have been parked at random – no, that smacked of being a diversionary fire. Already Helen had a nasty feeling that both the larger fires were simply there to draw resources away from this smaller, potentially more catastrophic blaze.

'We've got a name, ma'am,' one of the uniformed officers was now saying.

'Go on,' Helen replied, snapping out of her thoughts.

'The house is owned by a Denise Roberts, forty-two years old, single mother to a teenage boy, Callum Roberts. We know him – he's got form for possession, a bit of shoplifting – but we've nothing on her. Just your average single mum.'

Helen thanked the officer and turned back to the house. If there was anyone in there, they stood little chance of survival. The fire had been going for thirty minutes or more now and still the fire crews hadn't been able to gain access. It was a bleak scene to behold.

A second spate of arson attacks in twenty-four hours. It was bold to be sure, but did something else lie behind it? Was their arsonist on a mission? Did they feel compelled to start these fires? If not, why the hurry? What alarmed Helen most was the realization that the perpetrator of these attacks was committed, precise and well organized. The three fires were all in different parts of town, yet tightly timed to make fighting them near impossible. Whoever did this was intent on creating death and destruction on a scale Helen had never seen before.

It was as if they wanted to raze Southampton to the ground.

36

The heat was so intense, the smoke so dense, that for a brief moment Denise thought she had died and gone to Hell. Having blacked out as the wall of fire swept over her, she now came to on the floor, stunned, confused and ripped through with pain. But she was alive. Against the odds, she was still alive.

She tried to raise her head from the floor, but immediately felt so faint that she let it drop once more. What was happening? Where was Callum? Why wasn't anyone coming to help her? Closing her eyes, she gingerly raised her head once more, working herself up on to her elbows. A wave of nausea swept over her, her vision swam, but she could support herself now and, feeling a little more confident, slowly opened her eyes.

Darkness surrounded her. It was as if she was at the centre of some terrible storm cloud that had blocked out the sun. Pushing herself up further, she looked around her, but she couldn't find her bearings. Was she still in her bedroom? She assumed she was, but how could she tell?

Looking down, she could just make out that she was naked. Lifting her arm, she ran her hand over her body. There was no sign of her night clothes – they must have burnt clean off. Her skin felt mottled and unfamiliar and as she ran her fingers over her torso, caressing the fresh burns, a huge spasm of pain ran through her. This time she was sick, bringing up the whole contents of her stomach on the floor next to her. It fizzed as it hit the surface.

Denise knew in that instant that she had to move. She was dying by degrees, her body slowly cooking, while her lungs filled with thick sooty smoke. Coughing violently, she brought up another heave of watery bile, then slowly, agonizingly, pushed herself up on to her knees. She had to get out. If not for herself, at least for Callum.

She reached out for something to support herself, but could find nothing. So closing her eyes, she willed herself upright and staggered forwards on to her feet. The searing heat immediately claimed her, crawling over her face, her neck, her hair. It was impossible to breathe up here – every second counted now – so she opened her eyes, searching for something familiar. The outline of the window, the door, anything to help her find a way out.

But she couldn't see a single thing. The black smoke had consumed everything and she was lost in the centre of her own nightmare. She took three steps forward. The disintegrating boards groaned, her feet picked up fresh blisters with each painful step but on she went. One step, two, three. Her arms swung around wildly expecting – hoping – to connect with something solid, something familiar. But she found only smoke.

Crying now, she turned and went hard the other way. Surely this must be right. Her right foot caught on something and she fell to one knee, but on she went, dragging herself up, driving herself forward. She cannoned off something solid and suddenly filled with hope ran her hands over the surface. Was it a door? A window? She scraped at it, but it came away in her hand. Clawing harder, she now came up against solid brick. Jesus Christ, it was one of the walls. She was in the wrong place. The door must be . . .

She turned and moved randomly forward, no idea now which way was which. Her head swam wildly and she stumbled again. Which way was left? Which right? Which direction should she go in?

Denise stood still, paralysed by fear, as the fire raged around her and the smoke enveloped her. The decision she was about to make would either cost her her life or save it. So crying quietly and praying to God for help, she picked a direction, swallowed her fears and stumbled slowly forward.

37

Charlie clamped her hand over her mouth, as the bitter fumes filled her nose and throat. Instinctively she recoiled, struggling to breathe. She had never smelt anything like this before – and she hoped she never would have to again. Turning away quickly, she rejoined DI Sanderson, who was marshalling the uniformed officers, attempting to create a secure perimeter around the burning building. Above them a helicopter circled – it wasn't one of theirs, so presumably was press, no doubt beaming live pictures into homes all round the country. Was this what their arsonist wanted? Charlie rather suspected it was.

This was the biggest blaze yet. A plush furniture showroom stocked to the rafters with foam-filled sofas, raffia tables, wooden dining tables and chairs – the fire wasn't starved for fuel and the flames now leapt fifty, sixty feet into the air. You could tell from the firefighters' body language that this was already about containment.

Set against the dark night sky, the fire was an awesome sight, towering over the ghouls who'd come to witness the excitement. Bitterne Park was a nondescript part of town with little to set the pulse racing, hence the heavy crowd of locals. Adults, teenagers, even little kids were braving the heat to take photos and videos, edging dangerously close to the blaze. What the hell were they thinking? Were they really that desperate for entertainment that they would risk their lives and those of their children for a cheap thrill?

'Back. I want everyone back,' Charlie barked loudly, corralling the uniformed officers to push the throng away, scooping up any daredevils who seemed minded to ignore their advice. 'It's not safe for you here. Move back, back, back.' Police tape was now being rolled out and looped around the site, distancing the public from the blaze, but Charlie wouldn't put it past some of them to sneak under it and chance their arm once more. What was it with modern folk that everything – however unpleasant and depressing – has to be recorded and repackaged for others on social media? Charlie had no doubt that Twitter and Instagram would be going nuts tonight, ordinary punters snatching a bit of reflected glory from the arsonist's work.

Charlie walked the perimeter, her eyes flitting over the faces in front of her. Many were openly awestruck, others were joking and laughing, but hardly a single person there didn't have some kind of recording device. Were they all there for the fun of it or was there someone among them with more malign intent? Was one of these onlookers responsible for all this? On and on she went, looking for signs of guilt, but she knew she was looking for a needle in a haystack. Even if she alighted on someone who was unnaturally excited by the blaze, that didn't necessarily prefigure guilt and, besides, something told Charlie that their perpetrator was far too clever and cautious to be caught out so easily.

To her surprise, Charlie now felt an icy chill crawl up her neck. The wind had changed direction and was growing in strength, fanning the flames of the burning superstore. Acrid, green fumes now billowed towards the crowd, stinging eyes and throats as they swept over the onlookers. Suddenly Charlie picked out Sanderson racing towards her.

'We need to get everyone out of here,' she half gasped as she gestured to uniform to push the crowd back still further. 'I need a loudhailer. Has anyone got a loudhailer?' she shouted half to Charlie, half to the assembled officers.

'What's going on?' Charlie replied, suddenly alarmed.

'Polyurethane foam in the sofas. When it burns it creates cyanide oxide. These fumes are bloody poisonous. They can't stay here,' she continued, gesturing at the crowds, 'and neither can we.'

Clamping her scarf over her mouth, Charlie surged towards the crowd, grabbing recalcitrant kids by the arms as she went. Strange to think that a few hours ago she was at home, safe and sound with Jessica, and now here she was, hauling small children and grown men to safety in the shadow of an inferno. Suddenly energized, Charlie now took the lead, marshalling her fellow officers, driving the onlookers away from the reach of the bitter fumes. It was punishing physical work, especially in such an unpleasant atmosphere. Was that the arsonist's intention all along? To put police officers and firefighters in jeopardy even as they battled the flames? It was impossible to tell and there was no time to speculate now. So Charlie fought on, working tirelessly to save the people she was bound to protect, all the while engulfed by the toxic cloud of death.

38

It was only a small movement in the corner of her eye, but Helen spotted him before anyone else did. He was just a blur, speeding towards the fire, running straight through anything that stood in his path. Helen was already on the move, and as the young man hurdled the police cordon she was on to him. She only had a second before he would be past her, so she dived at his legs, clamping her arms tight around them.

He hit the deck hard, but seemed to bounce off it, the scrubby grass breaking his fall. Despite Helen's best efforts to restrain him, he was already clambering to his feet. Shouting at him to stop, Helen got a solid grip on his jacket and pulled sharply down. Immediately she felt something connect with her chest, temporarily knocking the wind out of her. The man lashed out again, but this time Helen dodged the blow, using his movement to unbalance him, sending him spiralling to the floor once more. She had caught him off guard and was quickly on top of him, pinning him firmly down.

'Get off me. Get the fuck off me,' the young man roared, struggling violently.

'Not until you calm down.'

'Get OFF!' he shouted back, twisting again.

'If I have to restrain you, I will.'

'My mum's in there. Please, she's still in there.'

So this was Callum Roberts. Even now, Helen refused to relinquish her grip. Denise's son was desperate with worry, consumed by the idea that his mother was alone in that terrible fire, but there was nothing he could do and Helen couldn't risk further injuries or fatalities by letting him go.

'The firefighters are doing everything they can, Callum. Jesus –'

The young man had sunk his teeth into Helen's hand and was bucking violently once more. Helen removed her hand quickly, but as she did so brought Callum's right arm up sharply behind his back. He screamed out in pain.

'I'm not letting you go, so unless you want to be charged with assaulting a police officer, I suggest you calm down. Ok?'

Finally the fight seemed to go out of him.

'Where is she? Is she ok?' he begged.

'We don't know, but we're doing everything we can, believe me.'

She tried to sound upbeat, but Helen already feared the worst. There had been no sign of Denise Roberts since the fire was reported and neighbours said she was very much a homebody. Even more concerning was the fact that when the firefighters *had* managed to gain entry to the house through the front door – not three minutes ago – the chain and deadlock had been secured from the inside. They had had to barrel charge their way in. It looked very much like someone had been in the house when the blaze started.

'Jesus Christ, what have I done?'

'What do you mean, Callum?'

'Oh God . . .'

'Talk to me. What's worrying you?'

'I . . . I told her I pitied her. That was the last thing I said to her. Jesus Christ, she must have thought I fucking hated her . . .'

Now the floodgates opened, the devastated young man sobbing on to the dusty ground beneath him. Finally, Helen relinquished her grip, helping the young man up on to his haunches and wrapping her arms around him. He refused to look at the fire and seemed powerless to move now, so he just sat there, sobbing into his hands. Helen gave what comfort she could, but he barely seemed to register her presence. So they sat there silently, entwined together in desperation and sadness, their faces illuminated by the dancing flames that continued to consume his home.

39

Ensuring the car was centrally placed in his viewfinder, he gently pressed Record. The little red dot appeared at the side of the screen and a small smile spread across his face. There it was – in perfect definition. If he did his job right, if he got all the footage he needed, he'd be able to enjoy this little baby for many years to come. His smile stretched wider, then as quickly as it had appeared, he swallowed it back down. No point drawing attention to himself. So flattening his expression into one of general concern he carried on recording.

The vehicles were parked cheek by jowl in this lonely outdoor car park. Eight separate vehicles were now ablaze, the fire having spread from one to another, fanned by the rising wind. A sign claimed that the site was owned and maintained by Southampton City Council, but it was nothing of the sort. It was just a dusty piece of wasteland. Parking was so expensive in the city centre that those in the know came here. It was dirt cheap by day and at night the wardens weren't around to enforce payment, so if you were smart you could park up here and head into the city, saving yourself a parking fee. Security was non-existent, but that didn't seem to deter people. Perhaps this fire would.

A sudden jolt from the side nearly knocked the camera from his hand – some oaf pushing his way to the front of the crowd. In a flash, he'd turned on him, spitting bile in his direction – but the idiot didn't even notice, too caught up in his own pathetic universe. Firing a parting shot of abuse, the man moved on, seeking a better vantage point from which to view this event.

Skirting the perimeter, he found a decent spot and once more pressed the little red button. He had a good shot of three different cars here, nicely positioned at intervals, their interweaving flames creating pretty patterns in the sky. This was more like it.

Relaxing, he started to rotate the camera, taking in the full panorama of the scene – the cars, the coppers, the rubberneckers, the paramedics, TV journalists, press photographers and local hacks. So much activity, so many people, all drawn here by the flames. It was strangely moving to behold.

Panning still further, he came to rest on the face of a young, pretty woman. Dressed in a smart suit, with her hair neatly tied up in a bun, she was bossing the uniformed coppers about. CID obviously, though he didn't recognize her. It wasn't Grace or the other one, but she would do. He drank in the anxiety on her face, the stress crumpling her pretty brow and making her voice tight and strangulated. Already he could feel his arousal growing, there was something about the way fire changed people that always provoked a physical reaction. This officer – whoever she may be – had had no idea that she would be here tonight, doing this, dancing to somebody else's tune.

He realized he was smiling again. Shaking his head at his stupidity, he rubbed his tired eyes and looked into the viewfinder again – only to find that the female officer was staring straight at him. Immediately his body froze, all thoughts of arousal evaporating. Had she spotted him smiling? Was there something in his body language which had given him away? She was looking directly at him, her eyes seeming to bore into his brain, his soul. Now she was taking a step towards him. Should he turn and run? Or bluff it out? He suddenly felt tongue-tied, sweat dotting his back, unsure what to say or how to say it. The officer took another step, then suddenly darted off in another direction, having been hailed by a fellow officer.

In a flash, he had finished his recording and stowed the camera back in his rucksack. Now he was walking away at pace. He half expected her to cry out, to call him back, but no cry came.

He had been stupid to linger. Excited as he was, he must learn to be disciplined – to take what he needed and no more. If he was lucky he would be able to return tomorrow to garner some souvenirs, but for now he had other things to do. The Roberts house fire would probably be extinguished soon and he'd have to move quickly if he didn't want to miss it. Checking once more that he had escaped undetected, he pulled his hood up on to his head and disappeared into the night.

40

He stared at the floor, refusing to look at her. Helen was well aware that she had just shattered this poor boy's world, but she'd had no choice. She owed him the truth. When the firefighters had finally worked their way up to the first floor of the Roberts residence, they'd found a woman's body in the main bedroom. She was curled up in the classic pugilist pose you so often see with fire victims. Oddly she was found plum in the middle of the room, seemingly having made no concerted move towards the windows or the door. There was precious little else Helen could pass on at the moment – Deborah Parks would have to wait until the site cooled before she could do her work. They hadn't even managed to formally ID the body yet – that would happen later – but it seemed highly unlikely that another, unknown female had made her way into Denise's bedroom and perished in the blaze. It looked for all the world like Callum's mum was the arsonist's second victim.

They were holed up together in a relatives' room at Southampton Central police station. It hadn't taken long for the press to gather outside the burning house and they soon zeroed in on Helen and the weeping boy, hoping for a photo and some good copy. Helen had bustled Callum to the nearest police vehicle and got him back to base safe and sound. He obviously couldn't go home and, until they unearthed some friends or relatives to take him, it was down to Helen and her colleagues at Hampshire Social Services to ensure that he was ok.

A cup of tea and a Wagon Wheel sat untouched on the table. Callum had barely said a word since they'd got here, resisting the overtures of both Helen and the Family Liaison Officer she'd tasked with babysitting him. Helen would have to return to operational duties – there was much to do now – and she didn't want Callum palmed off on a total stranger once she did.

The young man stared at his feet, occasionally biting his nails in aggressive little bursts. He was clearly still trying to process the awful events of the last few hours and this made it all the harder for Helen to have to probe him for information now, but she had no alternative. Two devastating attacks on consecutive nights. Two people dead. Several more injured. Hundreds of thousands of pounds' worth of damage to property and possessions. And still not a single eyewitness to point them towards the perpetrator. Gary Spence had been in police custody when the second set of fires began. True, he had associates to do his bidding, but surely he wouldn't be so foolish as to carry out more attacks when the police spotlight was so firmly on him?

'You said your mother had company tonight, Callum. Can you tell me who that might have been?'

The boy flinched slightly but said nothing.

'Callum?' Helen continued gently. 'I know you don't want to talk right now, but we really need your help. I want to find out what happened so anything you can tell me –'

'Darren something. I don't know his surname,' he said abruptly.

'Was he your mum's boyfriend?'

'Just someone who comes round now and again.'

'She didn't have a long-term partner.'

'No.'

'So you just got out of the house?'

Callum nodded.

'Where did you go?'

'To Dave's – I've told you. Dave Spalding, right? Lives in the Lynwood flats?'

'What time did you go there?'

'Around four p.m.?'

'And you stayed there until you noticed the fire? Around midnight?'

Callum nodded.

'And someone can vouch for your presence there for all of that time?'

'What's that supposed to mean?'

'I have to ask these questions, Callum.'

Helen's tone was gentle but firm and Callum quickly backed down, shrugging his shoulders as he replied:

'Dave was there and a few others. You can ask them.'

Helen nodded and jotted a note to herself to do just that.

'What about your father? Where's he at the moment?'

A long, heavy silence ensued.

'It's really important we find him, Callum. He's probably very worried about –'

'I don't know who my father is. She never told me.'

It was muttered quickly, but landed heavily with Helen

nevertheless. This poor kid only had his mother. Despite all the rows and problems, they were everything to each other. His mother had sought affection elsewhere to quell her loneliness and Callum had a loose collection of acquaintances to distract him from his empty existence. But at the end of the day it was mother and son alone against the world. And now she was gone.

Helen made a mental note to follow up on the issue of paternity. Could an estranged father have done this to this family? It seemed unlikely given the other fires but every angle had to be investigated.

'And was there anyone who'd threatened your mum? A former lover? Someone she'd borrowed money from?'

'No one gave a shit about us and if she borrowed any money . . . well, I never saw any of it. We had the benefits and that was it. If we'd had a bit more money, we might have been able to stick the bloody heating on.'

He buried his head in his hands once more and sobbed. Memories of domestic privation only made his plight worse – he'd clearly give anything to be back there now, nagging his mum to loosen the reins and put the heating on. Helen watched him, saddened and frustrated in equal measure. Perhaps he would be more forthcoming as time passed, but there seemed to be no obvious suspect for this callous and deadly attack.

Helen probed a bit more, asking Callum if he or his mum had friends in Millbrook or if he'd ever heard of the Simms family, but he knocked her back on each count. He and his mum had no cause to be in Millbrook – far too posh for the likes of them. As he did so, Helen glanced at the clock. It was nearly 4.30 a.m. now and Callum looked just about as exhausted as she felt. It was time to wind things up now – long, dark days lay ahead for them both.

'I'm going to suggest we pause there so you can get some rest.'

The young man said nothing, biting his nails feverishy once more, before hanging his head between his knees.

'Callum, can you hear what I'm say—'

'Did she suffer?' he interrupted suddenly. 'Did she suffer before she . . .'

'I don't think so. Chances are the smoke would have got to her long before the fire did,' Helen replied. 'It would have been quick.'

Callum nodded but didn't look up, thankful at least for one tiny shard of good news. He had obviously been imagining the worst and wanted to dispel those hideous images from his mind. Helen was happy to oblige, knowing from her own personal experience how devastating the loss of close family members is. If it helped him find his feet in the short term, Helen was happy to soft-soap the details of his mother's death – there was much he would learn over the next few days that would rock him back on his heels. Like the fact that the fire site reeked of paraffin. And the fact that the central stairwell had again been deliberately targeted. And the fact that his mother's body was so badly burnt that she would have to be identified from her dental records.

41

It was early morning, but already the hospital corridors were packed with people. The breakfast rounds were about to begin and the night shift was just handing over to the day workers, so it was always busy at this time – but still today was different. The hospital had received more walking wounded as a result of last night's fires – one firefighter, two members of the public and even a foolhardy journalist who'd been hit by falling debris – and everywhere you went concerned health workers were discussing this sudden spate of arson attacks. Six fires in two nights was unheard of in Southampton – everyone was clearly wondering what the next twenty-four hours would bring.

Charlie didn't linger, ignoring the hopeful looks from staff and patients hoping for titbits from one of the investigating officers. She wasn't here to gossip. Stepping out of the lift on the third floor, she presented her credentials to the ward nurse, then made her way into the burns unit. As expected, Thomas Simms was sitting where Charlie had seen him so often, keeping a silent watch over his daughter, Alice.

The six-year-old girl was still in a critical condition, but she was stable and with each passing day her chances of survival increased. She had a long road ahead of her and who could predict what kind of life awaited her at the end of it, but there were grounds now for cautious optimism.

Thomas Simms looked up as Charlie approached, offering her a brief wan smile, before returning his gaze to his daughter.

'How's she doing?' Charlie asked, as brightly as she could.

'Up and down. But more up than down. She has her mother's spirit.'

Charlie nodded and looked at the little girl. She looked so fragile there, wrapped in bandages, her breathing and heart rate controlled by machines – Charlie hoped Thomas Simms was right.

'And how are you?' Charlie asked.

Thomas Simms just shrugged, but said nothing in reply.

'It's tough, I know,' Charlie continued and was immediately aware of how hopelessly inadequate her response was. What did she know of what he was going through? Charlie was thinking what to say next – and coming up blank – when Thomas suddenly said:

'I heard about last night's fires.'

Once more, Charlie kicked herself. This was why she was here, to make sure Thomas and his family were up to speed with developments and yet in her own blundering way she had left it to Thomas to bring it up.

'Of course. That's why I wanted to see you – to answer any questions you may have about them.'

'Are they connected?'

'It's a bit early to say. We'll know more later when we have the forensics reports. But the MO appears to be similar.'

Everyone at Southampton Central was assuming the perpetrator was the same, but no one would say it publicly.

'Is there any connection to Spence? With these latest . . .'

'Nothing so far. There's nothing in his accounts to suggest he'd lent to any of last night's victims and the individuals concerned don't appear to have heard of him.'

'So this is something else then?'

Charlie paused, uncertain how best to respond, and before she could do so, Thomas Simms added:

'Karen's death and Alice and Luke . . . they're all part of something . . . bigger?'

'That's what we're trying to find out.'

'Well perhaps you could fucking hurry up.'

It was spat at her with such venom that Charlie was struck dumb.

'I don't think you get it, do you? Any of you. You come in here with your platitudes and good wishes, but I'm dealing with a terrified sixteen-year-old boy whose whole life has been crushed and who is looking to *me* for answers as to *why his mother is dead*. Is it something he did? Is it something I did? Or is it because some crazy fucking psychopath wants to burn down the whole city?'

'Believe me we're pulling out all the stops –'

'Well it doesn't look that way to me. So stop mollycoddling me and do something. Get *out there* and do your bloody job.'

With that he turned back to Alice, dismissing Charlie once and for all.

On her way out, Charlie kept her head down once more. But this time it wasn't to avoid entreating glances. It was to hide her shame.

42

Helen awoke with a start. For a moment, she had no idea where she was or how she'd got there. Then slowly the pieces started to fall into place and, taking in the familiar surroundings, she recollected her decision to sleep in her office. There had seemed little point going home given the late finish, and she'd had a day bed installed some time ago for such eventualities.

'Helen?'

It was softly spoken but still made her jump. Someone was in the room with her. The voice wasn't familiar or at least not in this context. Straightening up, she was surprised to find Gardam standing in the doorway.

'Sorry, I did knock three times, but you didn't seem to hear me.'

His eyes were cast down as he spoke and Helen realized that she was still half dressed. Torn between sitting like an idiot with a sheet pulled across her chest or getting dressed, she chose the latter – scurrying across to the wardrobe and rifling through it for a fresh blouse and suit. As she pulled her clothes on, Gardam carried on speaking, his eyes still fixed to the floor to spare her blushes.

'I know the team's due in shortly and I wanted to catch you before your briefing, so we can talk about our media strategy. The press conference is scheduled for eleven a.m.'

Smoothing down her clothes, Helen emerged from her

impromptu changing area. She had her professional face on now, but felt embarrassed at having been caught out in this way.

'I meant to talk to you about that,' she replied evenly. 'Press liaison isn't really my thing –'

'It's ok. I'm happy to field them if you want, but if you change your mind –'

'Thank you, sir. I think it's important that I stay with the team.'

'I agree. So what have we got for them?'

'Well, we're still sifting the intel from last night, but we do have one interesting lead – CCTV footage of a man running away from the house in Bevois Mount shortly before the blaze began. I've run off stills that we should share with the media – see if anyone recognizes him. I'm also going to show them to Gary Spence – I'd like to see his reaction, in case the man turns out to be one of his lackeys. But in truth I'm not holding out much hope. We've yet to establish any link between Spence and the properties targeted last night and I'm just not sure it's his style – it's a very public and messy way to conduct business.'

'So what are we looking at?'

'Well, they could be personally motivated attacks, given the concerted effort to kill. Or they could be about the fires themselves – somebody enjoying the chaos they've created, without a thought for the human cost.'

'So what line do we want to take with the press?'

'We appeal for witnesses, stress the need for vigilance and bring them up to speed with our progress.'

Helen continued in this vein, trying to sound upbeat

about their ongoing searches, but truth be told – CCTV aside – there was nothing 'juicy' for the press to get their teeth into yet. Helen wasn't sure how Gardam would react to this. Some station chiefs seemed to relish disappointing the fourth estate – depriving them of sensational titbits they craved – others panicked if they didn't have anything substantial to lay before them. Helen despised these appeasers, but Gardam didn't appear to be one of them. He seemed supremely relaxed about the grilling he was about to undergo.

'How is the team?' he continued, changing the subject without warning.

'Tired but determined.'

'And you?'

'I'm fine.'

'I'm sure you are, but don't feel you have to take the weight of the world on your shoulders, Helen. I know you like to lead from the front, but we're a team – or at least we should be.'

'Of course.'

'Which is a roundabout way of saying that my door's always open. It's important that senior officers have someone they can talk to.'

'Thank you, sir.'

'Speaking of which, I was going to ask you if you would like to come round to dinner at our place one evening? Sarah and I would love to get to know you a little better, in less formal surroundings.'

'That's very kind of you.'

'We'll make a date, then. And of course you should feel free to bring someone with you, if you want.'

It was said in an open, friendly manner, but Helen could sense that a question lay beneath Gardam's amiable offer.

'Just me, I'm afraid,' Helen replied.

'And are you ok with that?'

For a moment, Helen was silent – surprised by the bluntness of the question.

'I don't mean to pry,' Gardam continued. 'But I'm aware that you don't have any family locally and I've seen talented officers get eaten up by the pressures of the job, simply because they don't have anyone to share their burden with. I'd hate to see that happen to you. *Do* you have someone you can talk to?'

'I have a very supportive team,' Helen replied cautiously.

'And outside of that?'

'Really I'm fine. But if it ever gets too much, I'll be sure to let you know.'

'I'll hold you to that. And I meant what I said. I'm happy to talk any time – I don't want there to be any barriers between us. It's not in your best interests and it's certainly not in mine.'

Smiling, he patted her on the shoulder and took his leave, bestowing his cheery optimism on the officers who were starting to gather in the incident room as he left. It had been a pleasant enough encounter, but it left Helen with many questions. Why had be been probing her for information? Why was he so interested in her personal life?

And how long had he been standing there before she woke up?

43

'We're still waiting on DNA results to confirm the identity of our victim, but we're assuming for now that it is Denise Roberts. She's a single mum who lives with her son at the address that was targeted last night. I've already spoken to Callum Roberts and got a pretty clear idea of the family situation and her lifestyle. We also have CCTV footage which may be helpful.'

Helen hit the remote control and some grainy footage came up on the screen behind her. The officers shuffled forward, all hoping to see something significant.

'This was taken from a security camera above a lock-up on Ramsbury Road, which can be reached in under a minute via a cut-through from Denise's house. The time code shows that it's around eleven twenty-three p.m. The first 999 call reporting a fire at Denise Roberts's was logged at just after eleven thirty-five p.m., so who is this man?'

The team watched intently as a tall figure jogged past the camera and away down the street.

'He's got his back to us, so we can't see his face, but we can tell that he is white, about six foot tall with dark hair. He wears heavy boots, dark jeans and a puffa waistcoat, so why was he going for a jog? It was pushing midnight, he wasn't dressed for it, he doesn't seem to be running away from anyone, so what's the hurry?'

'Perhaps he was just late for something?' DC Lucas chipped in.

'Maybe, but I'd like to know for sure. Run the rule over Spence's associates, but let's start from the top on this one. Clear minds, ok?'

The team nodded. They all knew that Helen was considering releasing Gary Spence on police bail, pending further investigations.

'Denise's son confirmed that she was expecting male company that night,' Helen continued. 'There were two pizza boxes and an empty bottle of wine in a Tesco's bag in the outside bin. The receipt in the bag suggests she bought these items yesterday, so let's assume for now he showed up as planned.'

'Are we sure he didn't just have his dinner and go?' Charlie asked.

'No, we're not, but, according to Callum, Denise liked to have someone to warm her bed and was very accommodating in that regard.'

A few wry smiles from the team, but Helen pressed on.

'DC Brooks and DC Lucas will run with this,' she said, turning to Charlie. 'Corral as many uniforms as you can and find out if anyone saw this man last night. I want people on the street within the hour, ok?'

Charlie nodded, catching Lucas doing likewise out of the corner of her eye. Lucas was a young fast-streamer who appeared to have had a sense of humour bypass at birth. Great company for the arduous task that lay ahead.

'DC McAndrew will look a little deeper into Denise's private life. She is rumoured to have had a few boyfriends who came and went. I want to know who they are and where they were last night.'

'Could this guy have any connection to the Millbrook house fire?' DI Sanderson asked. 'We know Thomas Simms was working all the hours God sent. Perhaps his wife got lonely and sought other company. Perhaps she and Denise shared a lover? Maybe they thought better of it eventually, kicked him out –'

'We'd be stupid to rule anything out at this stage, so check it out, but do it *tactfully*. If we can find a connection between the two principal victims – Karen Simms and Denise Roberts – then we're halfway towards identifying the perpetrator. In the meantime, let's think about other possibilities.'

Immediately DC Edwards piped up.

'The MO seems to be identical. Two diversionary fires to tie up the emergency services, then an attack on a residential property. Very calculated, very precise.'

'But in a very different part of town,' DC McAndrew added. 'Millbrook is aspirational, lower-middle class and upwards. Denise's housing estate in Bevois Mount isn't. High unemployment and crime rates, people living off benefits and the black market, very little spare cash to throw around.'

'So is there a financial motive?' Lucas asked. 'Thomas Simms could certainly do with the insurance money and I presume Denise Roberts could too.'

'Denise Roberts let her home insurance lapse some time ago,' Sanderson said quickly. 'And the attacks seemed designed to kill, so I think we can rule that out.'

'Perhaps there is no connection then,' DC Lucas

returned a little tartly. 'Perhaps our arsonist is showing us that he can strike whenever and wherever he likes.'

It wasn't a pleasant thought but Helen knew Lucas might be right.

'We have to consider that possibility,' Helen responded. 'There's no evidence suggesting these fires were started to conceal a previous crime or to profit financially. They could be personally motivated against the victims but, equally, they could be random acts of arson whose significance lies in the feelings they afford the arsonist. A sexual charge, a God complex, a desire to expel anxiety, to exert control: there are many different ways in which arson can satisfy.'

Helen had done plenty of academic research on serial offenders during her time in the States, knowledge she would now bring to the fore in their hunt for a home-grown offender. She pulled up the bullet point profile on the screen.

'Your typical arsonist is white and male – over ninety per cent of all arson-related crimes are committed by Caucasian men. He is normally aged between twenty-one and thirty-five, unemployed or in a badly paid job, with low self-esteem and few prospects. He is very likely to exhibit paranoia and is quick to take offence. He may be living at home or in shared, hostel-type accommodation, or may even be homeless. Often the choice of fire site relates to a desire to strike at authority figures, at people or institutions that have wronged them. That doesn't seem to be the case here, but we ought to be alive to the possibility.'

Several of the team nodded – they seemed to be hanging on Helen's every word.

'Our perpetrator is obviously feeling confident, having committed major acts of arson on consecutive nights. They are clearly not panicked by Karen Simms's death – they haven't contacted any media outlets expressing remorse for their actions. They may even be enjoying themselves. A large percentage of arsonists try to insert themselves into the narratives of their crime, so let's compare all the footage from last night's fire with that from the night before. See if there's anyone present on both nights who's making themselves especially visible, trying to help in the rescue effort, playing the hero, what-have-you. It may be they were tucked up safely in bed by the time the fire reached its peak, but somehow I doubt it.'

Helen was in her element now – this was why people were queuing up to join her team.

'Let's keep an eye out for self-aggrandizing statements on social media, the internet. Also anyone talking repeatedly to journalists or the TV. But let's not forget about the basics too. Many a killer has been caught through mundane slip-ups. So talk to local businesses – find out if anyone has been stockpiling paraffin or washing smoke-damaged clothes in the laundrette. Any unusual behaviour or tiny changes in someone's routine could be significant, so remember to ask the small questions as well as the big ones.'

More nods from the team.

'Admin support have run off print-outs of the best

CCTV image we have of our fleeing male, complete with time code, so get out there and jog some memories. You can't commit crimes of this scale and just vanish into thin air. So let's find someone who saw our perpetrator.'

Within five minutes, the incident room was clear. As Helen strode out herself, shutting the door, she felt a quiet surge of satisfaction. The hunt was on.

44

All around him people were screaming and crying. 'There's someone in there, there's someone in there,' a woman shrieked nearby, as if the repetition of the bloody obvious could somehow affect her rescue. Satisfyingly, her bleating was suddenly cut short by a huge boom, as the front bedroom flashed over, blasting the main window from its casing and sending hot splinters of glass flying towards the crowd. Many present now turned and ran, bumping into him and disturbing his framing. That had pissed him off. Up until then, his recording had been perfect.

Watching the footage from last night's fires was proving to be a pleasurable experience. He had over an hour's worth of material from each fire and over time he would edit them into tight, dramatic narratives. But for now he was content to enjoy the raw, uncut recordings.

He had had a busy night, so could afford himself a little R'n'R now. He'd returned home just after midnight and, having changed his clothes and picked up the camera, went straight out again. Meticulous as always, he visited the sites in order, culminating with the smoking house in Bevois Mount. He had lingered there the longest, drinking in the reactions of the shocked neighbours, enjoying the moment.

As dawn broke, he'd chanced his arm. The fire crew

had done all they could do – it was the arson investigator's scene now – and they departed in short order. The site was roped off and a uniformed police officer was standing guard, but there were enough local gossips and journalists to distract him, so slipping round the back, he vaulted the fence and approached the back of the house.

It was a stupid, reckless thing to do, but somehow he knew he wouldn't get caught. He'd filmed his approach. It looked like a trick from a cheap horror film and he smiled now as he watched it back. Teasing the fire-damaged back door open, he'd slipped inside.

He knew that Deborah Parks would be on site first thing, so pocketing the camera, he'd set to work, searching for suitable souvenirs. He could hear the chatter at the front of the house. The earnest enquiries of local residents, the pushy questions from the hacks and the self-important PC ordering them to move back. Walking through the living room, he found only devastation, so darting across the hall, he investigated the box room-cum-study.

There had obviously been piles of stuff stored in here – he could see the charred remnants of cardboard boxes – which provided the spreading fire with plenty of fuel. Fortunately – depending on your point of view – the linoleum floor in the hall had delayed the fire reaching this room and the firefighters had managed to extinguish the blaze before the whole room went up. The trinkets of a life half lived now littered this small space and, among the burnt manuals, books and shoeboxes, he'd found a framed photo. The glass was cracked and black with soot, the metal frame bent and awkward, but the photo inside had survived. Burnt at the edges and buckled with the heat, but you could still make out mother and son smiling awkwardly at the camera. Slipping it into his rucksack he hurried out and across the hall. He'd paused briefly as he departed. There was something strangely moving about standing in the smouldering ruins of the house. Smoke and steam still rose from the floor – hence the need for his work boots – and the whole place reeked of fire. Breathing in the sharp odour one last time, he'd turned and headed for the back door.

The footage was coming to an end now, but his pleasure was not. So flipping the footage back to the start, he settled back in his easy chair, undid his fly and slipped his hand inside his trousers.

45

'Do you have *any* leads?'

Detective Superintendent Jonathan Gardam had not met Emilia Garanita before. But he had heard a lot about her. Helen Grace had given him chapter and verse, as had Hampshire Fire and Rescue's Chief Officer, Adam Latham, who now sat beside him, fielding questions from the press. The major tabloids were represented at their briefing today, but Emilia Garanita was not going to let them bully her or hold her back. Watching her as she tried to lead the questioning, Gardam had the distinct impression that this represented an opportunity for the ambitious young journalist to shine on a bigger stage.

'Are you making any progress?' Garanita persisted. Gardam paused, taking a moment to drink in all the small details of this local curiosity – the facial scarring, the dyed hair, the fuck-you attitude – before replying:

'DI Grace and her team are pursuing a number of leads and we have pulled in every officer available to help with our enquiries. There is currently a greater police presence on the street than at any time in the last five years.'

Gardam let this register. He wanted every journalist to note this surge in manpower. Moreover, he wanted their arsonist to take heed of this when it was reported later today. When you're struggling for concrete leads, prevention is often as good as detection. He wanted to make the arsonist think twice before carrying out further attacks.

'And we're confident that progress in the investigation *will* be swift. Alongside this, we have been liaising with our colleagues in the Fire and Rescue Service who have now drafted in extra fire response vehicles as well as additional firefighters from neighbouring forces.'

'We are now confident,' Adam Latham added, overlapping with his police colleague, 'that we can deal with any emergency quickly and effectively, however complicated the situation may be.'

Another tacit warning to the arsonist. They had more police, more firefighters, more resources. Diversionary fires would be of little help to him now. Privately Gardam wondered how he would react to this challenge. Would he back down or respond in kind – upping his game as they upped theirs?

'I'll ask the question again – do you have any suspects?'

Garanita was a dog with a bone, revelling in her self-appointed duty of holding the police to account. Gardam had heard that the *Southampton Evening News* had been going gently on them for a while – thanks in part to a temporary truce between Garanita and Helen Grace – but that respite appeared to be over now, as Southampton's pre-eminent crime reporter sniffed a juicy new story.

'There are several persons of interest whom we are trying to trace, but chief among them is a man seen running from the scene of the Bevois Mount house fire at around eleven twenty-five p.m. last night. You are being handed printed images of the CCTV still now and we would urge your readers, your viewers, to take a good look at it. Do they recognize this man? If so, we would ask them to get in touch via the special incident hotline, which is manned twenty-four hours a day, so we can eliminate him from our enquiries. In the meantime, I would ask the public to remain calm and take sensible precautions, especially after dark.'

'So lock your doors and sit tight. Is that the best you can do?'

'It's the *sensible* thing to do. I appreciate that these attacks have caused alarm, but the best thing the public can do is be vigilant, be sensible and let us go about our business.'

'In the police we trust?'

'Exactly, Emilia. As you know, DI Grace has an exemplary record in running investigations of this scale and complexity. And I have every confidence in her,' Gardam responded forcefully, pausing a little for effect before concluding:

'She's delivered before and I'm sure she'll do so again.'

46

Enveloped in a sterile suit, Helen climbed the ladder to the first floor. The fabric of the house was so unstable that a temporary scaffold and gantry had been erected to help the fire investigation officers navigate the gutted property safely. Cresting the ladder, Helen found Deborah Parks already hard at work in what had once been the master bedroom. It was a profoundly depressing site – the place looked like it had been bombed – and Helen's feelings of anxiety were only amplified by the insistent thrumming noise of the plastic sheeting which now covered the shattered main window. The wind was strong today, rattling the temporary covering vigorously and ensuring that everyone working on site was chilled to the bone. Last night temperatures in here would have topped 600 degrees Celsius, now it was touching freezing.

Swallowing down her anxiety, Helen navigated her way along the walkway of planks towards Deborah. The Fire Investigation Officer rose as she approached, nodding soberly at her. Deborah was a scientist first and foremost, but she was also a mum to three boys and Helen knew from experience that she always felt the human cost of the tragedies she investigated. In many ways their lives were pretty similar – both spent their working lives immersed in the worst things that human beings could imagine or endure.

'Your victim was found here, bang in the middle of the room. It's very likely the smoke and the panic got to her and she just froze. You often see that in these situations. House fires are things that happen to *other* people. When it happens to you, people lose their wits, their sense of direction, everything.'

'It must have been terrifying.'

'The smoke would have been so thick in here that she wouldn't have known which way was up.'

It was a horrific way to die. Terror, confusion and horror all colliding at the same time. Was this what their killer intended?

'Any thoughts on why her body was so . . .' Helen paused, not quite finding the appropriate word.

'Carbonized?'

Helen smiled a brief thanks. It was hard to put into words what Denise's body had looked like.

'Oxygen basically,' Deborah Parks continued. 'There are massive scorch marks around the border of the bedroom door. The fire was started downstairs, rising upwards, consuming whatever it could. It met an obstacle at the door, which is solid and fire-resistant to a basic level. The heat built up –'

'And then Denise opened the door as she tried to escape?' Helen asked.

'Probably. The frustrated fire would have gobbled up the fresh oxygen in the bedroom – these marks here show how the fire literally exploded into the new space.'

Deborah pointed to a number of long, livid scorch marks across the ceiling.

'Denise may or may not have regained consciousness

after that initial explosion. Either way, if she was motionless in the middle of the room, the fire would have consumed her, setting light to her nightclothes, her hair . . . If she was still conscious at this point, her body would have gone into a massive state of shock. Cardiac arrest, smoke inhalation, there are many things that might have spared her the worst.'

'Please God.'

Deborah was already making her way across the gantry and down the ladder to the ground floor. Helen was glad of a moment's respite from this narrative of destruction. She was used to being at crime scenes, of seeing unspeakable things, but this was different to anything she'd experienced before. Denise Roberts's attacker was not human and there was no opportunity to escape, defend herself or fight back, as there would have been in a common murder scenario. Hers was an enemy that could not be beaten. Helen, who feared nobody, shivered slightly at the thought of what Denise had faced last night.

Descending the ladder, Helen found Deborah Parks crouching down by the bottom of the stairs. Helen joined her.

'Your arsonist's MO is pretty similar,' Deborah outlined. 'You can smell the paraffin for yourself and I found a charred packet of Marlboro Gold here. There's no understairs cupboard, so the arsonist went directly for the stairs themselves, soaking the bottom three steps in paraffin before presumably lighting the delay device and leaving.'

Helen nodded, then said:

'What are these things here?'

She was pointing at a handful of numbered forensic markers laid out by Deborah around the foot of the stairs.

'Sodium flares,' Deborah replied.

'Matches?' Helen queried.

'Exactly. I'd expect to find them on the bottom step, where the delay timer was positioned, but there seem to have been a number of other matches scattered around the base of the stairs and on the floor.'

'Was that to amplify the spread of the initial fire?'

'Unlikely. There would be no point putting matches on carpet already soaked in paraffin – our arsonist would know that.'

'So he or she was just clumsy?'

'Or in a hurry. We think of these guys as being ice-cool, but they are human beings. Their victim was asleep upstairs but could have woken up at any moment. The arsonist would have wanted to be in and out of the house as soon as possible and when you rush . . .'

Helen nodded. It was a disturbingly human moment in the midst of a horribly premeditated crime.

'Other than that it's pretty much a carbon copy of Tuesday night's fires. There's more work to do, but I'm ninety-nine per cent certain it's the same perpetrator.'

'Any idea how they gained access?'

'Looks likely it was via the back door. The front door had the chain on and as yet I've found no broken windows or other obvious means of access. The back door was unlocked when we arrived. You'd have to ask family members if the back door was left unlocked as a rule –'

'Or whether someone unlocked it on their way out.'

If the fire had been started by whoever shared Denise's

bed last night, then it would make sense that he would exit via the more hidden back door to effect his escape. But they were still no nearer finding her mystery lover, so it was all supposition. Perhaps she was just careless of domestic security? Or perhaps just this one time she forgot?

'Anything else that leaps out at you?' Helen said, as she made her way to the back door.

'Nothing tangible yet in terms of our perpetrator. The safety boys putting up the scaffolding disturbed the site anyway, so it would be hard to prove in court that any evidence hadn't been cross-contaminated or brought in by them.'

Helen swore – that was all they needed.

'My feelings exactly,' Deborah returned before moving off to continue her work. 'I'll call you when I'm done.'

Helen thanked Deborah and went out through the back door. She did a quick tour of the garden, but, finding nothing of interest on the hard ground, turned to look back at the house. She shivered as she took it in – a modest, family home had been desecrated by fire, turned into a grim curiosity for local youths who lined the streets now, camera phones raised in approval. Denise Roberts hadn't had many breaks in life, but the cruellest blow had been saved for the very end.

There was only one, tiny glimmer of light in this whole awful story. She had argued with her son and had probably regretted it subsequently, as parents were wont to do. But in doing so she had done him the greatest service a mother can do for her child. She had booted him out of the house to serve her own interests last night, but in doing so she had ended up saving his life.

47

Callum Roberts stared straight ahead as he walked along the gloomy, forbidding corridor. He refused to look at the police officer – DS Sanderson – who kept pace with him. He knew that if he did so, she would start to work on him again, trying to dissuade him from doing this. This was hard enough as it was without her chipping away at him, eroding his determination and preying on his fears. And he knew that if he allowed himself to falter, then he wouldn't take another step.

They had all urged him not to view his mother's body. They had identified her from DNA and dental records, so there was no need for him to be here in this sterile, lifeless place. Callum had seen police mortuaries on TV crime shows but he now realized how fake those versions were. The real deal was washed out, soulless and just . . . dead.

Sanderson seemed to have given up trying to talk him down now and walked mutely beside him. Which was fine by him. He had been irritated by her presence at first, but as they approached the doors to the body storage area, he was suddenly glad to have her with him. He had no idea how he would react once he was in there.

Why *was* he here? Did he really believe that it *wasn't* his mum in there? The DNA tests had proved it was her and yet he still had to see. He couldn't logically say why, but he did.

They had euphemistically hinted at the state of his mother's body, then when he'd refused to play ball, the gloves had come off and they'd described in concise but graphic detail what remained of his mother. Even so he'd refused to be put off. He knew instinctively that refusing to see her now would be the grossest betrayal of all.

Why had he been such an idiot? So ungrateful? So hostile? Sure his mum had messed up plenty of times and was a doormat, with terrible taste in men. But she had raised him single-handedly when other lesser women might have abandoned him to his fate, fobbing him off on a relative or putting him into care. And in the early years they had got on well. She was a relaxed parent, happy to have a laugh and a joke. And she doted on him, often going without so that he could go on school trips, have birthday parties, even the odd holiday. He had never missed having a dad, which had to mean something, didn't it? She even came with him when he got his first tattoo, advising him on where to have it and what to go for. She looked after him afterwards, making sure that the tattoo didn't get infected, giving him hot Ribena and powdered paracetamol to dull the pain in his throbbing arm. She wasn't the best of mums, but she was very far from being the worst.

'This is Jim Grieves. He's our Senior Pathologist.'

Callum suddenly found himself shaking hands with yet another stranger. He never shook hands – who the fuck did? – and yet he seemed to have been doing nothing else for the past few hours. Shaking hands with medics, police officers, fire investigators and now the pathologist who'd been prodding and probing his mother's body.

'I'm very sorry for your loss,' the man was saying. He was a big guy with a gruff manner but kind eyes. Callum couldn't think of what to say in reply, so nodded briefly. He wasn't here to chat.

They walked on to the body storage area. 'Body storage area' – how the hell had he ended up here? It was a nightmare, a living bloody nightmare. The man was talking again, but he couldn't hear a single word, his conversation drowned out by the clamouring panic within him. Suddenly he wanted to be anywhere but here. He wanted to turn and run, run, run . . .

'Are you ready?' the pathologist said, sounding like he was repeating the question for a second time. Callum snapped out of it, nodding and smiling at his interrogator. Why had he smiled? What was there to smile about?

They were standing by a long metal table – he knew they called them 'slabs' but couldn't bear to think of them like that. With one last look at him, the pathologist leant forward and lifted the sheet.

Immediately, Callum's arm shot out, grabbing at the sleeve of the policewoman who still flanked him. He didn't know what he had been expecting, but not this. This wasn't his mum. She didn't even look human. This was an abomination.

Letting go his grip, he turned and ran to a nearby sink, vomiting hard into it. Once, twice, three times as the horror of what he'd just seen forced its way out. Afterwards, gripping the cold metal rim, he hung his head, trying to steady his breathing, to calm his thundering heart. Up until now it had seemed horrific but unreal. Now the full devastation of last night was making itself felt. And he knew in that moment, with piercing clarity, that his whole life had been reduced to ashes.

48

Blog post by firstpersonsingular.
Thursday, 10 December, 15.00

Have you ever burnt yourself? I mean properly. Like holding the palm of your hand over a flame and letting the fire eat your flesh. You should, it's good.

I guess like me that you've probably been on suicide websites. I look at those things for hours. Always something interesting in the details and I just love the tone of those sites, don't you? So sombre, so serious and so fucking DULL?!? Like it's a training manual or textbook. This isn't homework, friend, this is the final frontier. Not that I haven't been tempted, but I wonder how many people would stop short if they just learnt to use their pain. Like I say, it's good.

I first burnt myself when I was six. I stole my mother's lighter, which made it all the sweeter. She thought I was trying to interfere with her smoking or just being a little shit, but I wanted something of hers to make its mark. Somehow it felt twice as good holding her lighter – with its stupid engraving – in my hand as I lowered my palm down, down, down on to the flame. I held it there, refusing to move. Exercising my power over it. Over my pain. Over my life.

A lot has happened since then. But the lesson I learnt stayed with me. There is so much that is random and cruel and pointless in life. So much shit to wade through, so many small indignities marching side by side with gross injustices. So much darkness that visits itself on you whether you want it to or not. But there are some things you can control. You can control you. You can control your feelings. And if you're bright, you can control other people.

That is when you come out of yourself. When you become more

than yourself. They thought you were worthless. You thought you were worthless. But then suddenly it all makes sense, you take control and for a brief tantalizing moment you know what it means to look God in the face.

49

It was time to call off the dogs. They had knocked on every door, canvassed every potential witness and passer-by within a mile radius of Denise Roberts's house and had come up empty-handed. Charlie checked with Sarah Lucas that she was happy to move on, redeploying their manpower to the nearby high street in the hope of richer pickings, then called it in, galvanizing the uniformed sergeants into action. It had been a dispiriting few hours and Charlie wasn't looking forward to telling Helen that their massive deployment of resources had yielded precisely nothing.

She was standing by the police cordon at the fire site. Last night and this morning there had been large crowds, but even these were starting to diminish now. This should have cheered Charlie – who needs these rubberneckers? – but in fact its effect was quite the opposite. Seemingly this terrible tragedy was worthy of a few hours' attention, then the world moved on, seeking fresh entertainment. If only it was so easy for those left behind.

'All right, girls, move along now. You've all got homes to go to.'

A small knot of teenage girls lingered by the police tape, chattering, shouting and occasionally taking snaps of the house. As Charlie called over to them, they turned, but made no move to leave. They went back to their chat, keeping a wary eye on the smartly dressed officer who seemed intent on intruding on their day. Watching them, Charlie felt a sudden spike of irritation and anger. This was somebody's home, not a bloody shopping mall.

'*Now*, girls. It's getting dark and there's no reason for you to be hanging around here.'

Charlie had a sudden flash forward to what she would be like when Jessie was a teenager. Would Charlie have any credibility in her eyes as a successful career woman and authority figure? Or would having a policewoman for a mother be the ultimate disaster, a kind of social death that kept friends and boyfriends at a remove. Charlie was surprised to find that she was suddenly worried about this and chided herself for being foolish. There were bigger fish to fry right now.

'Girls, I'm going to ask you for the last time to move on. I'm happy to drop you home in a police van, but I don't think that would do you any favours, do you?'

Charlie was upon them now, raising her voice as she pointed them in the direction she wanted them to head in. There were a lot of cut-throughs and alleyways round here – even though there was safety in numbers, she would rather they made their way home along the high street.

'She saw him,' one of the girls replied tartly, her attitude to coppers shining through clearly.

'Saw who?'

'The guy what did this,' the teenager answered, nodding towards the fire site.

'Who saw him?' Charlie asked, trying to keep the desperation from her voice.

'Naomie,' she said, pointing to another of her group. Naomie was mixed race, a little overweight and blushing to her roots. Blocking the others out, Charlie approached her.

'Tell me what you saw, Naomie.'

The blushing girl seemed not to hear her, so Charlie pulled out her warrant card.

'I'm DC Brooks. I'm working on this case and anything you can tell me would be very helpful.'

'Tell her, girl. Tell the pig what you saw,' the leader said, laughing.

In another situation, Charlie would have cautioned the little shit for that alone, but today she had to let it go.

'Who did you see, Naomie?' Charlie pressed. 'I really don't want to have to make this official, but I will if I have to. Please – tell me what you saw.'

Finally the gravity of the situation seemed to land home and the girl looked up. And as she did so, Charlie was surprised to see fear in her eyes.

'I saw *him*.'

50

'I know you've been over this with DC Brooks, but I'm going to need you to walk me through it again, ok?'

Helen looked across the table at Naomie Jackson, wondering if even at this late hour she might refuse to help them. According to Charlie, it had taken a lot of persuasion to get her to the police station at all. Now that she was here, ensconced in an interview suite with them, the nervous teenager seemed even *less* convinced of the wisdom of assisting them.

Naomie fiddled with her empty bottle of Sprite, spinning it round and round in her hands. To Helen's eyes, she seemed a nice enough girl, but there was a massive hole where her self-esteem should have been. Her scruffy appearance, monosyllabic conversation and inability to look grown-ups in the eye were all testament to that. She was a follower, not a leader, and was no doubt cursing her mate for dumping her in it. But there was no time for mollycoddling – if Naomie had important information about the fires, Helen needed to have it.

'We don't want to cause you any trouble, Naomie. We won't contact your mother if you don't want us to. And DC Brooks will drop you anywhere you need to go when we're done. She will be your point of contact from now on and any worries or concerns you have – about any of this – well, you can call her directly and she will be straight round to help. So please tell me what you saw.'

Naomie spun the bottle one more time, then said:

'I saw a guy running down the cut-through.'

'To be clear, this is the cut-through that leads on to Ramsbury Road?'

'S'right.'

'When was this?'

'Just before closing time. I'd left the pub and was going home.'

Helen nodded, not reacting. Charlie shot a look at her, but Helen ignored it. Right place, right time for the CCTV – but Helen wasn't getting her hopes up yet.

'Where had you been?'

'At a pub near the Common. I live in St Mary's, so was walking back this way.'

'And what did you see?'

'This guy came up behind me real fast. Scared me half to death. I was on my own and that and it was dark and you hear all sorts happening to girls –'

'And what was he doing?' Charlie interrupted, anxious to keep the girl on track.

'Running. Running real fast. He ran straight past me, never seemed to clock me at all.'

'What was he wearing?'

'Dark trousers and boots, I think.'

'Any coat?'

'Yeah, maybe. But his arms weren't covered.'

Helen nodded. The details of the man they were after hadn't appeared in the media yet, so unless this girl was lying or had seen the stills, then this was the lead they'd been searching for.

'Did you see his face?' Charlie asked gently.

Naomie shook her head.

'He went by too fast.'

'What about his hair colour?'

'Brownish, I think.'

'Height?'

''Bout six foot maybe.'

'Anything else?'

The girl shook her head.

'Anything at all?' Helen repeated, trying not to sound as anxious as she felt. There was hardly anything in this description that they didn't already know.

There was a long pause, before Naomie finally replied:

'There was one other thing. He had a tattoo. On his arm.'

'What did it look like, this tattoo?

'It was a star, a big one.'

'Anything else?'

'The star had a crown and a flower in it. Kind of weird, you get me.'

Helen's heart was beating faster now. Without looking, she could tell Charlie was feeling the same way.

'What kind of flower was it, Naomie?'

Naomie thought hard, then finally said:

'A red rose.'

'You're sure about that?'

'Yeah, for real. Big one, it was.'

Helen nodded and thanked Naomie for her time. Leaving Charlie to run over the written statement with her,

Helen hurried from the room. Already her mind was racing ahead, trying to see a way through the shit storm that now lay before her. Truth be told, there *was* no simple or obvious way forward. The case had just taken a decisive and unwelcome turn.

For in her own faltering way Naomie had perfectly described the crest of Hampshire's Fire and Rescue Service.

51

'This is complete bullshit.'

Adam Latham's eyes were blazing and tiny flecks of spit shot from his mouth as he spoke. He was known to be a bullish, uncompromising guy, never more so than when he was defending his beloved Fire and Rescue Service.

'There is no way that one of my guys would do something like that,' he said. 'I know each and every one of the men and women who serve under my command. I trained most of them, for God's sake, and well . . . it's just not possible.'

Helen was about to respond, when Gardam cut in. The three of them were gathered in his office for what had been billed as 'a chat'.

'I hear where you're coming from, Adam,' Gardam soothed. 'And I sympathize. But you'll appreciate that we have to follow up every lead and the witness gave a very precise description of the tattoo.'

'She's lying then.'

'And what grounds do you have for saying that?' Helen interjected.

'Well, it's obvious, isn't it. She's after attention, you know what teenage girls are like.'

This last comment was addressed to Gardam and Helen was about to interject, when her boss once more intervened.

'Well, I'm not sure I share the sentiment, but we're both saying the same thing. We must investigate this lead quickly and discreetly. If there is nothing in it, we can all move on.'

Helen let Gardam take the lead, but inside she bridled at his constant interventions. It had been her idea to contact Latham in advance to secure his cooperation and she would have happily handled the difficult meeting herself, but Gardam had insisted on hosting it, hoping perhaps that his superior rank and masculine mateyness might help persuade Latham. Perhaps Helen should have felt grateful for his support, but she didn't. She had never needed or asked for the protection of a man. She didn't do white knights.

'And you think that's possible, do you? That this little line of investigation can be kept under wraps?' Latham's tone was witheringly sarcastic. 'Your station is as leaky as they come – as soon as you start interviewing my officers the press will know about it and then what happens? The public stop cooperating with us. They start impeding our work, abusing our officers, attacking them even. Something like this can cost lives. Is that what you want?'

'We want to catch the person responsible,' Helen shot back before Gardam could step in. 'I cannot let any other considerations distract me from that goal. But there is no need for anyone to get overexcited. We're not going to go around kicking in doors –'

'No? I rather thought that was your speciality.'

'Only when it's warranted. For now we're just making enquiries.'

'I'll remember that when I'm visiting my officers in

hospital, once you've whipped up the mob with your half-baked accusations –'

'I believe you're the one jumping to conclusions here, not me. We've no reason to believe this girl is lying –'

'I'm wasting my time, here. Jonathan, can you talk to her?'

Now Helen really wanted to smack him. She hated nothing more than being talked about as if she weren't in the room. Gardam saw the flash of anger and stepped in decisively.

'I'm not going to overrule my best officer, Adam. DI Grace must pursue every avenue of investigation. History won't thank us if we fail to catch our man because of political sensitivities. We've heard your concerns and noted them. We will do everything in our power to stop this rebounding on your officers, but we are going to pursue this lead, so I suggest we all start cooperating on the best way to do that, ok?'

There was nowhere for Latham to go now – Gardam held the whip hand in this situation – so very begrudgingly Latham conceded the point, marching from the room without a single look at Helen. Gardam waited until his counterpart was well out of earshot before turning to Helen.

'At least that's cleared up,' he said.

Helen nodded. Gardam was looking at her, but said nothing. Was he waiting for some kind of thanks, for her to congratulate him on rescuing the situation? If so, she wasn't going to give him the pleasure. She was used to handling worse dinosaurs than Adam Latham.

'I'll get on, sir.'

'You do that, Helen,' Gardam responded evenly. 'These sorts of situations require multi-agency cooperation and we've just lost the support of one of our key players here. So let's make the most of it, eh?'

Helen hurried down the corridor towards the incident room, less certain now than ever about her standing with the new station chief. Did he like her? Or dislike her? Was he as progressive as he seemed or an old sexist in sheep's clothing? Helen had the distinct impression that he wanted to protect her. But to what end? To safeguard the reputation of Southampton Central or for some other reason? Helen's gut instinct – usually so reliable – was letting her down this time.

Pushing through the door, Helen was immediately assaulted by a wall of noise. They had had to draft in more phone operators to deal with the flood of leads to their incident hotline. Nothing significant had come out of this so far, but it showed the public were engaged with the issue and remaining vigilant, which might make their arsonist think twice. It was already mid-afternoon – not long now until darkness stole over Southampton once more. In reality, they were still no nearer to apprehending a suspect and the nagging question of what he might do next was forever at the front of Helen's mind.

Spurred on by this fear, Helen waved Sanderson into her office. Shutting the door gently but firmly, Helen asked her deputy to sit. Already Sanderson had a pen and pad poised, which cheered Helen – they had a lot to do today.

'So we need staff rotas and post-incident reports from

Hants Fire and Rescue for the last few days. They won't like it but they'll have to play ball, so don't be coy in asking.'

Sanderson suppressed a small smile. She always looked forward to squeezing the pen pushers and bureaucrats who delighted in trying to hold up vital investigative work.

'Once you've got them, pull in McAndrew – just McAndrew, no one else – and quietly go through the staff lists, rota patterns, etc. and find out who was working the last couple of nights and just as importantly *who wasn't.* Prioritize male officers for now. We are looking for opportunity and motive. Focus specifically on those who are young, single, possibly isolated. Anyone who's had disciplinary problems, or been turned down for a promotion recently, or had marital or family problems. Whoever is doing this is angry, they want to make a point to the world, but perhaps also to someone closer to home – to colleagues, family, their ex. Go over it once, twice, however many times you have to, then give me some names. I need this done quickly and discreetly, ok. You can use my office for now.'

Sanderson was already on the phone before Helen was out of the door. They had achieved nothing concrete yet, but they had the first major lead now and Helen was determined to make the most of it. Having been on the back foot so far, it was time to wrest back the initiative.

52

She padded softly behind them without being seen. She had followed them halfway across Southampton – her red Fiat tucked three cars back from the dark Megane, hidden by the heavy rush hour traffic – but this was the most dangerous bit, now that they were on foot. If they were going to spot her, they would spot her here, when she was out in the open and exposed.

They were heading deep into St Mary's now. People who'd never been to the city had heard of St Mary's thanks to Southampton Football Club, who'd moved to a swanky new stadium there in 2001. The move was supposed to be part of big regeneration for the area, but truth be told nothing much had changed. The streets flanking the giant stadium seemed to be somehow in its shadow – neglected, forgotten and more than a little depressed.

It was a description that could have aptly fitted Emilia Garanita over the past year or two. She was a talented and ambitious reporter who had underachieved so far. There was no point dressing it up as anything else. She had overplayed her hand during previous investigations and ended up back at the bottom of the heap, the victim of a particularly unscrupulous game of snakes and ladders.

Many held her responsible for this, but Emilia never had. She had been made promises, promises that hadn't been kept. This was the story of her life in many ways and in this particular instance the irony wasn't lost on her. She had trusted a journalist and look where it had got her.

The pair she was following slowed now. The woman was instantly recognizable – DC Charlene 'Charlie' Brooks – an honest and determined copper whom Emilia had crossed swords with many times. The girl she didn't know, but Charlie Brooks had been incredibly solicitous to her since leaving the police station – driving her home, buying her drinks and magazines, pep talking her every step of the way. This girl wasn't some truant or teen runaway – she was someone *important*.

Emilia snuck into a greasy spoon and found a table by the window. Ignoring the unfriendly assertion by the owner that she couldn't sit there without buying anything, Emilia kept her eyes glued on the dumb show playing out opposite. The girl looked nervous, even a little anxious, but Brooks was working hard to soothe her. Emilia couldn't hear the words but the body language – the hand gently squeezing the girl's arm – spoke volumes.

Removing her tablet from her bag, Emilia pulled up the link for the electoral register. She shouldn't have it of course – it was for internal Council use only – but no self-respecting local journalist could do without it. She'd already clocked the road name as they turned into it, now she added the house number. Instantly she had her answer. Two people registered to the address: Sharon Jackson, aged forty-two, and Naomie Jackson, aged seventeen.

Slipping her tablet away, Emilia was pleased to see that Brooks was taking her leave. Rising, she allowed her to turn the corner, before hurrying from the café and straight across the road. Once on the doorstep she paused for a second – to smooth her hair and reapply her lipstick – before confidently ringing the doorbell.

Naomie must have been expecting Brooks again, because her face fell when she saw a stranger standing on the doorstep.

'Naomie? It is Naomie Jackson, isn't it?'

The girl nodded cautiously.

'I was given your name by DI Grace at Southampton Central. She says you're assisting them with their enquiries?'

Another tiny nod.

'Well, as you know, the *News* always plays an active role in keeping the wider public informed about matters affecting their safety and well-being. I understand you have new information which is proving very helpful to the police in their hunt for this terrible arsonist and I was wondering if I might come in for two minutes to chat about it?'

The girl was clearly unsure, so Emilia followed up quickly.

'We don't have to use your name, anything you tell me is in confidence and, yes, we do pay. So what do you say?'

Moments later, Emilia was settled in the girl's dreary living room prising information from the monosyllabic teen. She kept her eyes locked on the girl, but her hand worked overtime, scribbling down every tiny detail of her testimony. Already Emilia had the feeling that this was going to play well for her – that this latest case would finally allow Emilia to write her own happy ending.

53

Deborah Parks marched across the café, turning heads as she went. Out of her work scrubs she was quite something – her svelte figure and flowing hair released from the baggy, sexless suit to impressive effect. Helen was not surprised to see more than one man pause in his conversation as she glided past their tables.

Kissing Helen hello, she sat down and gestured to the waiter for a cappuccino. It was always strange – and refreshing – to meet colleagues away from the workplace. Interaction at crime scenes and on disaster sites was necessarily sombre and professional, but this didn't really suit Deborah or do justice to her bubbly, optimistic personality. They chatted happily, then Helen elegantly moved the conversation on to more serious matters. This wasn't a social call – Helen was here to dig for dirt.

Sanderson's first pass on the Fire and Rescue staff rotas had thrown up six preliminary names. Six men whose shift patterns could have allowed them to start the fires and who fitted the profile in terms of age, marital status and disciplinary history. Helen had already dispatched officers from her team to do the preliminary checks, asking these six individuals standard, routine questions about their movements, their take on the fires and any suspicions they might have – all in the interest of sniffing out small discrepancies in their alibis or something unusual in their behaviour. These conversations were necessarily anodyne and often brief, but it was surprising what they sometimes threw up. A family member listening in, a girlfriend uncomfortable at providing a false alibi – these visits often served to undermine the perpetrator in unexpected ways.

'So are you going to tell me what this cloak and dagger stuff is all about?' Deborah enquired. It was said pleasantly, but was shot through with curiosity. Helen had had no choice but to do this discreetly, given the earlier altercation with Latham, and she knew that if she'd dragged the diligent Deborah away from her work in person, then tongues would have wagged. So she'd asked her to meet in a Caffè Nero near the fire site and suggested she invent a reason for her absence.

'I told the boys that I had a doctor's appointment,' Deborah continued, 'which set the cat among the pigeons. You wouldn't believe the stuff that lot come up with.'

'I appreciate that and I know your time is not your own, so I'll cut to the chase. I need to talk to you off the record about some of your colleagues. None of it will come back to you – it's just to help me get some background on them.'

Deborah Parks nodded, then replied:

'Strictly off the record?'

'Of course.'

Deborah nodded, a little less convincingly this time, then said:

'Ok, shoot.'

Helen delved into the folder that lay in front of her. Deborah was Southampton born and bred and had served at stations all over the city. Attractive, popular and ambitious as she was, every budding firefighter made a friend of her – a fact that Helen now hoped would stand her in good stead.

'I'm going to show you a list of six names. All male colleagues of yours. I know little more than their ages and job titles at present. I need you to fill me in on the detail – what they're like, whether you trust them, whether it's possible,' Helen went on, lowering her voice, 'that they could be our arsonist.'

Deborah nodded soberly as Helen slipped the piece of paper across the table towards her. There they were in black and white:

Alan Jackson, John Foley, Trevor Robinson, Simon Duggan, Martin Hughes and Richard Ford.

Was one of these six men their killer?

54

Lifting the police cordon, he entered the site, his boots crunching satisfyingly on the charred bits of wood that littered the former showroom. Just a day ago, this place had been a popular destination for couples and families seeking a new sofa, dining table or king-size bed. The guys who ran this place must have been making money hand over fist, but not any more. The vast building had gone up in flames and in the early hours of this morning the roof had eventually come down – the final majestic act of destruction ensuring that everything below would be consumed as well.

He had chosen his moment carefully. Deborah Parks had left the site rather suddenly following a phone call and the rest of her team had taken advantage of this to nip off for a cup of tea. There was only one uniformed police officer and he was soon talked round. This was too good an opportunity to miss.

He felt his heart beating faster as he made his way across the deserted space. It looked otherworldly, like a scene of devastation on another planet – you seldom got to see fires on this scale. Pulling the camera from his bag, he executed a slow pan. Right to left, then back again, slow and steady, missing nothing.

Clicking it off, he stowed it back in his bag and pulled a bin liner from his pocket. Encasing his hands in sterile gloves, he bent down, sifting through the burnt detritus on the surface, looking for the good stuff. Truth be told, it wasn't such fertile ground as a domestic property, with all the family photos and trinkets, but these larger sites could sometimes surprise you and it obliged now. Buried beneath the ash and protected by a solid metal door were the remnants of a banner poster, advertising a recent flash sale. You could still make out 'Everything must go' plumb in the centre. He liked that, given the context, and slipped it quickly in his bag.

'Can I help you?'

He hadn't heard anyone approaching and froze momentarily – his adrenaline spiking – before he gathered himself and rose to face his interrogator. It was one of Parks's crew – where the bloody hell had he sprung from?

'This is a sealed site. Members of the public are not allowed in here.'

'It's ok, mate,' he replied calmly. 'I'm the advance guard. I was told you needed some help, shifting fire-damaged obstacles.'

'And you are?'

'Hants Fire and Rescue,' he said confidently, holding up his ID for inspection. 'It's supposed to be my day off, but you know firemen . . .' He paused briefly before concluding:

'We're always happy to help.'

55

He'd visited this place a dozen times and it was fast becoming his own personal Hell. Initially he had hoped it might be a sanctuary – somewhere to get a moment's respite from the horror of everyday life. Later still, he'd imagined it might be the place to buy something nice for Luke, a token of some kind that would offset the terrible guilt he felt about his many failings as a dad. But it was none of these things. It was just a simple shop, staffed by hospital volunteers, and as he stood still, staring at the modest selection of chocolate bars in front of him, he felt so empty, so helpless that for a second he thought he might cry.

'I wouldn't buy the chocolate from here, it's always past its sell-by date,' a voice next to him whispered. Thomas Simms turned to find a young woman next to him, clutching a copy of *Grazia*. She had nice eyes and a pleasant smile but the historic scarring down one side of her face was what really grabbed your attention. She was probably a patient-turned-volunteer and Thomas was struck by the serendipity of this moment. Here he was, lost in self-pitying introspection, forgetful of the fact that everyone suffers and somehow they get through it.

'I'm Emilia,' the woman said, extending her hand.

'Thomas,' he replied, shaking hers. Oddly her name

seemed to fit her perfectly, as if that was what he'd been expecting her to say. Did he recognize her from somewhere?

'Do you have a minute to talk?' she continued, her smile never faltering as she subtly changed tack.

'You're a journalist?' he replied sharply, removing his hand from hers.

'Emilia Garanita, *Southampton Evening News*.'

'Look, I know you're doing your job but I've said everything I'm going to say. We've issued a statement this morning asking for some space –'

'I respect that, Thomas. As you can see, I've had troubles of my own. I know what it feels like when life stabs you in the back. I've no interest in making your life harder.'

'I wish I could believe that –'

'In fact, I'd like to help you.'

Thomas paused for the first time in their conversation. He could usually tell when people were beaten. He'd knocked back dozens of journalists and ghouls in the last couple of days. But this one looked utterly unrepentant and totally confident, as if she *did* have something up her sleeve.

'There have been some developments. In my experience the FLOs are terrible at keeping the family informed of these things, they don't tell you a single thing until it's all done and dusted and tied up with a bow on top. Which is fine – they're covering their arse – but it doesn't help you or Luke or Alice. You need to know *now*. It's the not knowing that's torture, right?'

Thomas said nothing. His first instinct had been to tell her to go to Hell, but now he wasn't so sure.

'So I am very willing to help you. I'd like to *help* you. But I need something in return.'

Thomas suddenly felt his temper flare again. What the hell was he doing bartering with a bloody journalist in a hospital shop. His son was waiting for him upstairs. His daughter was still fighting for her life. What was he doing *here*? Sensing his anger, his pursuer reached out her hand and laid it on his arm, gently arresting his departure.

'They are going to arrest a firefighter. One of Hampshire's own,' she whispered, looking him dead in the eye. Thomas suddenly felt breathless and dizzy. He had wanted the police to make progress desperately, but now a part of him wanted it all just to go away. He was scared to think what the next chapter of their life might hold.

'I can't give you his name yet, but I should know more in the next twenty-four hours. I'll tell you, I'll tell you as soon as I have it, I swear. Unlike the police, I'll hide nothing from you.'

Thomas looked at her, but didn't know what to say. Should he believe her?

'A witness saw the suspect running from the scene of last night's fire and picked out the crest of the Hants Fire Service tattooed on his arm. I can give you her name too, if you want.'

But she wouldn't give it yet – that was clear. Thomas hung his head and once more tears threatened. Everything was telling him not to do this, not to get caught up in this game, but how could he brush her off and go back upstairs now? Knowing that she knew more about his wife's killer than he did. So after a long pause, he raised his head, looked her dead in the eye and said:

'What do you want?'

56

'Simon Duggan wouldn't have the brains for it. You can definitely rule him out.'

'How certain are you?' Helen responded. They had already ruled out three possibles – Duggan was the fourth that seemed to be going the same way – and they were fast running out of options.

'Look, I know he fits the profile. Bit of a loner, lives at home with his mum and so forth, but he's a follower. He wouldn't go to the toilet without someone's permission. He doesn't have the nerve or intelligence to pull off something on this scale, nor does he have the anger. He's a simple soul.'

'Ok, what about Martin Hughes?' Helen replied, trying to keep the strain out of her voice.

For the first time, Deborah paused. She rolled this possibility round her brain a few times, then said:

'Better, but still not right.'

'How so?'

'He's quick to anger and has fallen out with pretty much everyone at one time or another. It's cost him career-wise, no question, younger guys have progressed faster than he has, he's divorced . . .'

'All of which fits the profile,' Helen said.

'But he's not a young man –'

'Profiles are just guides, they're not blueprints.'

'And he loves his family. They may have split up, but he still loves his ex to bits and dotes on his son. He's a fuck-up for sure, but his temper blows out as quickly as it comes and the rest of the time he's a pretty sound bloke. I'm sorry, Helen, but I just can't see it.'

'Which leaves Richard Ford,' Helen replied, more in hope than expectation. But this time, there was genuine hesitation from Deborah. Prior to this, she'd been assertive, confident even, knocking back Helen's suspicions about her colleagues. But now she seemed troubled.

'Talk to me, Deborah. What's he like?'

'I don't really know him that well . . .' she answered.

'But what you do know gives you doubts?' Helen asked. She didn't want to lead Deborah to any conclusions, but she had something for her here – Helen was sure of it.

'Yes,' she eventually said. 'He's one of those guys that as a woman you just steer clear of. Something about the way he looks at you. Like you're some sort of foreign species.'

'Does he have friends?'

'Not within the team. He avoids crowds, pubs, that kind of thing. He doesn't take part in all the usual macho posturing you get from fire guys, he doesn't really take part in anything at work, except . . . work.'

'How long's he been working for the Fire and Rescue service?'

'Since leaving school, I think.'

'Does he have a tattoo – with the Hants Fire crest?'

'Sure – a lot of the guys do.'

'Is he a hard worker?'

'Very. Happy to come in on his days off to help out. I don't think he has a girlfriend.'

'Boyfriend?'

'Not that I know of.'

'What about family?'

'He's never mentioned anyone. He's a loner. New guys try to engage with him, then give up after a while. That's the way he wants it, so . . .'

'And if he's so diligent and experienced, why is he still at a relatively junior rank?'

'Can't do the exams. He's great on all the practical stuff, but the theory, the homework . . . And as for his interview technique . . .'

'Has he been passed over for promotion?'

Another moment of hesitation, then:

'Yes. He failed his fire sergeant's interview for the third time recently. Which means . . . that he can't apply again.'

Helen tried to suppress the excitement growing within her, as she asked the next question.

'And when was this?'

All Deborah's confidence – her resistance – seemed to have deserted now as she replied.

'A month ago.'

Helen marched away from the café, her phone clamped to her ear. As soon as Sanderson answered, she launched in without introduction.

'We need to check out Richard Ford. Who was doing the initial chat with him?'

There was the briefest intake of breath from Sanderson, before she replied.

'Charlie. She's with him right now.'

57

Something was wrong in this house. Charlie had felt it the moment she stepped inside. Everything was in the right place, there were no obvious signs of anything amiss, but the whole place felt unused, like a museum. It looked – and smelt – stale.

Richard Ford had been less than pleased to find Charlie waiting for him on his doorstep. He had been helping out at one of the fire sites, he'd told her, shifting some of the detritus, so the arson team could do their work. He was dirty and sweaty and stank of smoke – clearly he had been looking forward to getting a shower. But instead he found himself answering the gentle questions of a DC, probing him about his work patterns and movements over the last couple of days. Charlie didn't blame him for being irritated and yet that wasn't quite it. He seemed to be giving off something else. Suspicion? Anxiety? Something else? Charlie couldn't put her finger on it.

He'd been carrying a black bin liner, which he made no reference to, stowing it in the hall cupboard, before shepherding Charlie into the old kitchen. He'd put the kettle on for tea, but it laboured to work up a head of steam. It was as if everything was slightly *off* here – the slow tick-tock of the dusty carriage clock on the mantelpiece giving the dated kitchen the washed-out feel of yesteryear.

'Do you live alone?' she asked.

'Yup. Mum died a few years back. Got a sister, but she didn't want any of this,' he replied gesturing to the house. 'She emigrated to Oz.'

Charlie could hardly blame her. As Ford now made the tea in what looked very much like two dirty cups, Charlie's eye ran over the Hants Fire and Rescue tattoo that graced his left bicep. The sight set her nerves jangling, but when Ford turned to her, Charlie was all smiles once more.

'And last night you were home alone?'

'That's right.'

'You didn't go out at any time? To the shops? Anything?'

'No. Why?'

'These are just standard questions. We've been asked to verify the movements of everyone on the fire team . . . So what about Tuesday night? The night of the first fires –'

But Charlie got no further. Her mobile rang out, disturbing the eerie quiet of the house.

'I'd better take this. Sorry,' Charlie said as she hurried out into the hall. Ford watched her go, seemingly neither surprised by nor interested in her sudden departure.

'Charlie Brooks,' she said cheerily, as she scuttled into the small parlour opposite. It was even more forgotten than the kitchen, and Charlie's eyes flicked over the dusty surfaces, as Helen filled her in on the latest developments. Charlie responded steadily, giving affirmatives where necessary, keeping calm, but she could feel the hairs on the back of her neck starting to rise. When she rang off, she hesitated for a moment to quieten her breathing. If she played it cool, this would probably work out fine. Helen was on her way, so summoning up her courage, Charlie marched back into the kitchen.

'Sorry about that. Normal nonsense about being in two places at –'

Then Charlie stopped dead. Richard Ford was nowhere to be seen.

58

Helen shot past the red light without hesitation. It was a risky manoeuvre given the heavy rush hour traffic, but Helen felt she could make it. She knew the sequences of every set of lights in this city and judged she would make it across the junction without getting caught by oncoming vehicles. The pursuing squad cars hung back, despite the flashing lights and sirens that should have cleared the way – they were junior officers with their whole careers ahead of them and were not in the business of taking unnecessary risks.

Helen had only one thing on her mind, however, and that was to get to Charlie as quickly as she could. She was across the junction in a flash and now ratcheted up her speed, pulling away from the city centre and blasting into the open road beyond. More vehicles were attending from Southampton Central, but no one would be as fast as Helen on her bike, which is how she liked it. If Ford was dangerous – as he surely must be – then she wanted to be first in line to get her friend out of trouble and resolve the situation swiftly and decisively.

Charlie seemed to have a knack for these things, Helen thought to herself as she leant into a sharp corner, dropping her speed a notch, before pulling the throttle back hard once more. She was a very diligent and able copper, yet she seemed to have the most amazing nose for trouble.

Forever going where angels fear to tread. Helen had every confidence that Charlie could handle herself, but you could never predict how a situation would pan out and everybody's luck has to run out sometime.

Helen's knee found the road as she bent in hard to another tight right-hander. The leather that encased her legs protested slightly then sighed as she straightened up. She was driving aggressively but felt completely in control, eating up the miles to Ford's house in Midanbury. She was only a few minutes away now – minutes away from delivering Charlie and apprehending their man. But minutes could be costly, as Helen knew all too well, and she prayed that she wouldn't be too late.

59

'Mr Ford?'

Charlie's cry echoed through the house, but remained unanswered.

'Mr Ford? I have a few more questions for you, so . . .'

Nothing. Instinctively, Charlie's hand reached out for her baton, which was holstered discreetly inside her jacket. She half expected Ford to emerge from the toilet, apologetic and contrite. But the other half of her knew he had fled. But where to? The house was a tall, rickety property which backed on to open scrubland. There might be numerous hidey-holes and avenues of escape in houses like these.

'Mr Ford. I'm going to ask you for the last time to join me. Otherwise I will have to assume –'

Bugger it, Charlie thought, pulling her radio from her pocket. She called for back-up, then moved quickly through the kitchen to the back of the house. There was a small pantry off the kitchen, which was empty save for discarded work clothes, so she moved on to the back door. This would have been Ford's quickest means of escape, but it was locked from the inside, the key still in place.

Charlie turned quickly. Experience had taught her never to have her back turned for too long – in these situations you had to stay alert to any possible angle of attack.

But there was no one there and the only sound she could hear was the sober tick, tock, of the clock.

Extending her baton now, she marched through the kitchen, towards the parlour, pausing only to tease open the front door. It might facilitate his escape, but it would allow her back-up to get in quicker when they arrived. Charlie hoped they would come sooner rather than later. She had a nasty feeling about this place.

The parlour was empty, so turning she mounted the main staircase. This was one of many dilapidated Georgian houses in this part of town. They had been grand once but decades of neglect had taken their toll and now they were just old and rotten. The boards creaked noisily as she climbed, announcing her presence as if screaming to their master.

She crested the stairs on to the first-floor landing.

'Mr Ford? Back-up is on its way, so it's in your best interests to talk to me.'

Still nothing. Charlie pressed on. The master bedroom was straight ahead of her, its contents obscured by the door, which stood ajar. Charlie took a deep breath, darted a look over her shoulder, then nudged the door gently open with her foot. It swung round lazily, coming to an ungainly halt against the edge of the bedstead. Charlie scanned the interior as best she could, then stepped inside.

The whole place stank. It was piled high with newspapers and magazines and seemed to be more of a dumping ground than a night-time retreat. Clothes had been left abandoned on the ground and Charlie could see the remains of past meals, some of which now bloomed with fungus. Charlie heard a skittering behind her and spun round. But it was just vermin, fleeing the scene of their crimes.

There was a hefty wardrobe placed between two large casement windows. Having checked under the bed, Charlie hurried over to it and, counting to three, yanked it open, her baton raised. Just more papers and old, mouldering clothes.

Leaving the main bedroom, she darted left into a small side bedroom, but she could barely gain access. It was stacked to the ceiling with boxes marked 'Mum' and the window appeared to be totally inaccessible. There was no means of escape from here, so Charlie crossed the landing to the other bedroom. This had clearly once belonged to a child. It was full of *Beano* annuals, rolled-up posters and a rocking horse, damaged by years of hard toil. Its lifeless eye seemed to stare at Charlie as she entered. But there was nobody here. Which only left one place to look.

Back on the landing, Charlie looked up the stairwell to the top floor of the house. She couldn't hear anything, but was that smoke she could smell? Alarmed by this thought, Charlie walked quickly up the steps. Creak, creak, creak. She was careless now as there was no chance of ambush and nowhere left for Ford to run.

Reaching the top of the stairs, she grasped the door handle and wrenched it round, flinging the door open. A small attic room lay in front of her. Like the other rooms, it was piled high with junk, but this room had a small sofa, an easy chair and an old coffee table, on which sat a couple of mugs. This cramped, remote room looked the most lived in of the house.

The smell of smoke was stronger now and stepping inside Charlie spotted its source. A small wood-burning stove stood in the corner, connected directly to a flue which pierced the roof. And in front of it was Richard Ford. The doors to the stove were open and to her horror Charlie realized that Ford was now feeding the blaze – with pieces of paper, videotapes, photos. He scrabbled through a cardboard box, pulling out anything he could find and throwing it into the fire.

Charlie charged towards him. He turned as she approached but too late. Charlie brought her baton down and it connected hard with his collar bone. He staggered back, howling in pain, so Charlie followed up with a huge arcing cut to the back of his legs. He seemed to take off briefly, hanging in the air, before crashing to the ground, sending up a thick cloud of choking dust.

As he lay there groaning, Charlie spun and raced to the fire. Pulling her jacket off, she encased her hand in it, then delved into the open furnace, flicking whatever she could out of the flames. A videotape and some books fell to the floor. But there was more in there, so Charlie delved deeper –

She cannoned sideways away from the fire, surprised by Ford's sudden charge. He had rugby tackled her at speed and she crashed hard to the ground now. Winded, she tried to rise, but he was quickly upon her now. A fist seemed to come out of nowhere, connecting with her jaw – she felt the back of her head hit the floor with a crack that went right through her. Now his hands were seeking out her throat, wrapping themselves around, squeezing, squeezing, squeezing. She tried to shake him, but his knees were pinning her down and he tightened his grip now, his eyes bulging with fury and hatred. He meant to kill her and Charlie knew in an instant that this time there would be no escape.

60

Helen dumped her bike and sprinted up the path. The back-up vehicles were only a few moments behind but something told Helen that she couldn't afford to waste a minute. Seeing the front door ajar, Helen paused to remove her baton, then kicked the door open and ran inside. The hallway was deserted and Helen stood stock still, her senses primed for danger.

But there was nothing. The whole place was deathly quiet.

'Charlie?'

Helen strained, listening for a response, but none was forthcoming.

'CHARLIE?'

Helen stalked forward, darting her head first into the pantry, then the parlour as she charged towards the back door. The place was deserted, the door locked, so turning on her heel, Helen sprinted back towards the small parlour across the way. Her disquiet was growing with each passing second – the absence of both Charlie and Richard Ford couldn't be explained in a way that augured well. Why was the front door open? Had Ford fled and Charlie followed in pursuit? Surely not – she would have radioed in in that case? So what had happened here?

Helen took the stairs two at a time and was soon on the landing above. She explored the side rooms first, wary of ambush, but found only the detritus of Ford's sorry life, so she pushed into the front bedroom. The room was gloomy and unloved, reeking of mould and rotten food and Helen yanked the heavy curtains open. As she did so, she saw the squad cars pull up outside, sirens blaring and lights flashing. The cavalry had arrived, but to what end? They'd be able to do nothing for Charlie if they couldn't find her. Where the hell was she?

Turning once more, Helen sprinted from the room. Every second counted now.

61

Stars studded her vision, as the fight went out of her. Charlie had struggled for all she was worth, but he was too strong, too determined to crush the life out of her. The lack of oxygen was having an effect now, waves of darkness washing over her – she knew she was close to losing consciousness for good. She could smell the smoke on his hands, could feel flecks of his spit landing on her face, as he shouted and screamed at her. Was this it then? Would his livid face be the last thing she saw?

As her eyes slowly closed, his grip seemed to loosen slightly and suddenly Charlie rolled hard to the right. Where this resistance had come from she couldn't say. One last instinctive attempt to save herself perhaps, some innate desire to live. Surprised, Ford tried to steady himself, but now off balance toppled over, landing heavily on the floor. Rolling in the dirt, he was on his feet quickly, charging back towards her. He almost left the floor as he virtually leapt at her. Charlie could only hope to defend herself now – her throat raged and she couldn't breathe properly – so she raised her knee and braced herself for impact. The point of her knee now connected sharply with Ford's groin, bucking him off balance once more. He half fell, half stumbled to the ground, his chin connecting savagely with the wooden floor, tearing the skin. He tried to rise and couldn't – he appeared to be gagging – and suddenly Charlie found herself crawling towards him fast.

Now she was on top of him. He flung an arm back at her, but she had been expecting that and grasped it gratefully, twisting it hard and fast all the way up his back. He screamed in agony, but Charlie didn't hesitate, drawing her cuffs from her belt and binding both his hands together. Ford writhed underneath her, trying to throw her off, but pressing her knees into the small of his back, she pinned him down, determined to deny him any purchase. After a few moments, the struggle went out of him.

Charlie now became aware of someone else in the room – it was Helen calling to her, approaching fast – but there was no need of reinforcements now. Against all the odds, and somewhat to her surprise, Charlie had carried the day.

62

'Drop whatever you're doing and listen to this.'

Emilia Garanita had a flair for the dramatic and enjoyed bossing people around, but she seldom got the chance these days. The roll call of crime in Southampton usually extended from shoplifting in Tesco's through drunk-driving offences to a bit of Class B possession – hardly the stuff of banner headlines. But today was different. She wouldn't normally talk to her editor in this way, but she was on the cusp of a big one here and felt some of her old confidence returning.

She had arrived at the address in Midanbury fifteen minutes after the squad cars. Flashing her press card, she immediately sought out PC Alan Stark, her favourite mole in Hants Police. He was a young man with a fairly serious gambling problem and always welcomed the extra funds Emilia provided. Checking they weren't overlooked, Emilia had crushed three £50 notes into his hand and as he pocketed them, quizzed him for the details. As he'd relayed his info to her, Emilia had spotted a young man being led from the house in cuffs. From her discreet vantage point, Emilia had fired off a series of headshots with her Nikon SLR – and was pretty pleased with the results.

'For God's sake, Emilia, I've promised you the centre spread for your Simms piece! Could you please stop chewing my balls for one minute –' her beleaguered editor replied. He had given up punishing her for her previous disloyalty some time back and Emilia sensed he now regretted it, as it allowed her to harangue him night and day, pushing for more, more, more.

'Forget that,' Emilia interrupted. 'This is better.'

'Go on.'

'I'm currently watching Hampshire's finest drag a young man from his house in cuffs. According to my source, police think he's our serial arsonist.'

Silence on the other end, but she could hear him breathing. There was nothing better than having your editor hanging on your every word.

'Better still, he's a firefighter. His name is Richard Ford and he's been with Hants Fire and Rescue Service for most of his life. Bit of a fire nut apparently, but that's as much as I know. I need people to get on to his colleagues, family, ex-girlfriends, plus I need a bio for him. I'm going to stay at the house and see what I can glean.'

It was the editor's call as to how he deployed his reporters. They only numbered a handful and most were more used to covering school fetes and Council meetings – Emilia was their only full-time crime reporter. But Emilia knew Gary Rowlands loved the big stories – it reminded him of the good old days when he was a proper editor at Wapping – and she was sure he would throw the scant resources they had at this one. Stories like this didn't come around very often.

'I'm going to go big on the hero turned villain, firefighter who became a firestarter, so anything in his private life that might explain this, any past offences, would be really useful as context,' Emilia continued, slipping under the police cordon and scurrying towards the house. Stark had turned a convenient blind eye and Emilia was keen to get a few shots of the interior before she was discovered.

'I'm going to have to go now, but let me know how you get on.'

'As I have it. Stay in touch, ok? No going AWOL on me.'

'Absolutely, boss. Oh and one last thing . . .' Emilia teased, a smile breaking out over her face.

'Hold the front page for me, will you?'

63

Helen crouched over Charlie as the paramedics gave her the once over in the back of the ambulance. Charlie was insisting she didn't need to go to hospital, but Helen wasn't convinced. She had a large bruise rising on her chin, several more on her neck and, though she could walk and appeared compos mentis, her eyes had a strangely glazed look. She was still in shock – as she had every right to be, given what she'd just been through.

'I'm ok,' Charlie protested, as the medics shined a torch into her eyes. 'I know it looks bad but, really, I'm fine.'

'Let the medics be the judge of that,' Helen replied calmly.

She had been in this position herself and she knew that one's first instinct in these situations was denial, batting away concern while attempting to minimize the nature of the trauma you'd been through. It made sense – if you said it wasn't that bad, then maybe it wasn't – but it wasn't rational or truthful. Charlie had been through a terrifying ordeal – she just wasn't able to admit it to herself yet.

'She has extensive bruising to the neck, though there's no sign of fracture. Cuts to the back of the head, facial bruising and mild concussion, I would suggest. She'll need several days' bed rest at the very least.'

'For God's sake, I've said I'm fine,' Charlie said angrily, trying to rise. But Helen stopped her with a gentle hand.

She could see tears pricking Charlie's defiant eyes now so, having thanked the paramedics for their work, asked them to give her five minutes alone with Charlie.

'Honestly, boss, I'm . . .' but Charlie didn't have the energy or conviction to finish the sentence now that it was just her and Helen.

'Listen to me, Charlie. I know Ford was your collar. I know you want to help. But I would be a terrible team leader if I didn't ask you to heed the medics' advice and step back from this. I know a few days in bed isn't realistic, but I want you to stand down for today. I'll get uniform to take you home. Freshen up, talk to Steve, get some rest and we'll talk in the morning. Please don't fight me on this one, Charlie. It's for your own good.'

Charlie's body was starting to shake now, as the fear and emotion of the day's events started to register. She could have been killed today. That would take a while to sink in but when it did it would be hard to shake off. Charlie had responsibilities, loved ones who depended on her. The selfishness of life in a dangerous, front-line job was something you dealt with day after day, but it was hard when you had a nice family to go home to, when events forced you to confront the prospect of your own mortality. Helen didn't really expect to see Charlie back tomorrow, but she had to offer her that carrot for now, to ensure that she did the right thing in going home to rest.

Charlie nodded gently but said nothing. Helen could tell she was trying not to sob and laid a gentle arm around her shoulder.

'Don't worry, Charlie. You made it.'

Charlie leant in closer, seeking Helen's warmth and

support. Helen squeezed her a little tighter in response. Then, having gestured to a uniformed officer to bring a car round, said:

'Now go home and give that beautiful daughter of yours a big kiss.'

64

'Tell me exactly what you said to her.'

Deborah Parks stared at her boss, refusing to be intimidated by his aggressive manner.

'She's an old friend and she asked me to talk to her off the record. She wanted some background info on certain members of the team, that's all.'

'Your team said you were away from duties for over an hour. You must have been in a very talkative mood.'

'It wasn't like that!'

'So what was it like?'

Deborah squirmed in her seat, privately cursing whichever colleague of hers had dobbed her in. Adam Latham was a canny operator, very political and extremely sensitive about both his reputation and that of the Service. He actively encouraged internal gossip and whistleblowing, as long as the matters arising could be dealt with discreetly. He prided himself on being too smart to be duped and his little network of informers helped him justify that bold claim.

'You left your designated work to sit down with Helen Grace and within the hour one of our own officers is in cuffs. One of *your* colleagues. What did you say to her?'

'She asked me a direct question about Richard Ford. And I answered as honestly as I could.'

'Saying what?'

'That he was a good officer, but was socially isolated.'

'And?'

'And that he'd failed to make promotion.'

'Jesus Christ.'

'I couldn't lie, Adam. She's a Detective Inspector investigating a double murder and she asked me a direct question.'

'And what would she have done if you'd refused? Arrested you?'

'That's hardly the point. I'm loyal to this place, of course I am, but *someone* is doing this and we all have a moral duty to help find out who.'

Adam Latham eyeballed Deborah silently, while chewing on his biro. She refused to blink, refused to bow her head in contrition – she had to front this out. But already she could feel the ground shifting beneath her feet. Latham was an old-fashioned guy who prized loyalty and solidarity above all things, and she knew that in talking to the 'enemy' she had committed a cardinal sin. There was only one way for Latham – *his* way – and Deborah knew that she would suffer for her close association with Helen Grace.

'Grace is clutching at straws,' Latham said suddenly, jolting Deborah out of her thoughts. 'Time will show that. For now, we'll take the line that Ford is just helping the police with their enquiries and that we fully expect him to be back at work protecting the people of Southampton in the very near future. I have talked to our press people and they are drafting a statement, which I expect everybody to read and follow to the letter. Is that clear?'

'Of course.'

'No more talking out of school. It's time for the wagon train to circle, Deborah. If you get my drift.'

'Yes, sir.'

'Good, that's settled then. Now fuck off.'

It was said with such contempt that for a moment Deborah froze, uncertain if she had heard him correctly. But the way Latham ignored her presence, as he picked up the phone, left her in no doubt as to his opinion of her. She stood quickly and walked out and away down the corridor. With each step, her heart slid a little further into her boots. She had done nothing wrong, but she would be punished nevertheless. Latham would no doubt let it be known that she couldn't be trusted, that she was a turncoat. Through no fault of her own, she would pay the price for somebody else's crimes.

65

Helen stood quietly as Meredith Walker went about her work. The stove fire had been extinguished, but the claustrophobic attic room still reeked of smoke, rendering the atmosphere close and unpleasant. There were no windows or vents in this place, the open door was the only means of expelling the pungent smoke that danced around the naked bulb in this strange cocoon.

Emotions swirled through Helen as she took in the scene. Concern for Charlie, irritation at Emilia Garanita, whom she'd had to forcibly eject from the crime scene, but also disquiet at what she now saw. Every room in the house was packed to the rafters – Ford was clearly a hoarder – but the attic was different. This seemed to be a more ordered chaos, a kind of nerve centre, a shrine almost and the object of Ford's worship was clear.

The walls, the roof, every joint and joist were covered with photos of fire. The floor and every available surface were piled high with boxes overflowing with clippings, while the rickety shelves erected on two of the walls groaned with first-hand accounts of history's deadliest blazes. The whole room felt like a brain bursting with one man's obsession. A dark, secret place where he could revel in his private passion.

Helen immediately wondered how long Ford had been living alone in this house. His mother had passed away a few years back, though exactly how long ago she wasn't sure. Did all this start then? Had he kept it buried inside while she was alive, only to give in to his obsession once there was no one to rein him in? Had his loneliness, his isolation, contributed to the feelings that had pushed him over the edge?

Ford was now in custody at Southampton Central. He'd been passed fit for questioning by their medics, but Helen had decided to let him stew for a while yet. She wanted him to feel the confines of the holding cell, to witness the whispered comments of the screws – she wanted his fear and paranoia to grow. It wasn't a pleasant way to treat someone, but it often worked. A brief taste of incarceration – and the promise of more to come if convicted – often prompted suspects to confess quickly in the hope of making a deal.

There was another reason Helen wanted to buy some time. His attic was a veritable treasure trove of evidence and she wanted to be fully armed when she sat down opposite Ford. She would never forgive herself if he managed to wriggle off the hook because of a procedural error or some omission in the narrative she presented. It was obvious that some of the photos on the wall were of the fires in Millbrook, Bevois Mount and elsewhere. No doubt the dozens of mini-cam tapes now being bagged by Meredith and her officers would yield similar evidence of an unhealthy interest in these terrible attacks. Everywhere you looked you saw recent events reflected back at you – Helen had only been here an hour but already her unusual surroundings were starting to affect her, seeming to suggest that the world was made of fire and fire alone.

There was one thing that was missing, however, and that was any imprint of Ford himself. No photos, no possessions, no sign of *him*. It was as if his whole identity had been subsumed by a greater master.

'Any personal mementoes? Any family snaps? Passing-out parades?' Helen asked.

'Only this,' Meredith replied, scooping an evidence bag from the floor and passing it to her. 'Found it down the back of a chest of drawers.'

It was a clipping for the local paper showing a fire crew visiting a school. Two officers were featured in the large photo, surrounded by adoring, curious kids. One of them was a female officer whom Helen didn't recognize. The other one, as the caption beneath confirmed, was Richard Ford.

Helen froze as she looked at the picture. She hadn't really taken Ford in properly when arresting him. She was more concerned with Charlie's well-being and had passed the shell-shocked Ford on to her colleagues quickly. But there could be no doubt about it now – she had met Ford before.

Helen was still processing this development when her phone buzzed loudly. Her mind was elsewhere, but somehow she knew exactly who it would be.

Jonathan Gardam.

66

Helen threw her coat and scarf down on the chair and turned to face her boss, who reclined on the sofa in her office.

'DS Sanderson's waiting for me in the interview suite, so I'm going to have to be relatively brief, I'm afraid.'

Gardam either missed or ignored the note of irritation in Helen's voice. When he replied it was in an open and friendly manner.

'Of course. Questioning Ford has to be our top priority. How sure are you that he's our man?'

'Pretty sure,' Helen replied, without elaborating further.

'Why?'

'Because he's in love with fire. Because he'd know what to do. Because he was there. I think these fires have been fuelling his fantasies.'

Gardam nodded.

'Do you think he'll talk to you?'

'Doubt it, but you never know how people will react under interview. Thanks to Meredith we've got a lot of evidence to lay before him and his lawyer.'

'You heard about that. The Fire Service have paid for the best, so expect a rough ride.'

'I can handle myself. I've done a few rounds with Ms Shapiro before now.'

'I dare say you have,' Gardam answered, once more

breaking out into a broad smile. 'Well, let me know how you get on. If she is being deliberately obstructive, I can have another word with Latham. Though the gloves might come off a bit now that we've got one of theirs in custody. Do the press know about it?'

'Garanita was there ten minutes after we were.'

Gardam nodded as if he weren't in the least bit surprised, then made to leave:

'Let me know what you get out of him.'

'Before you go, sir . . .'

Gardam stopped and, turning, walked back towards Helen. They were separated now only by the battered desk which Helen had come to know well over the last few years.

'May I speak freely?'

'Of course, Helen, say whatever you want,' Gardam replied, a cloud of concern creasing his features now.

'Well, you seem to be rather . . . present at the moment. And I was wondering why that was.'

'Present?'

'You're on my shoulder, sir. If you have any concerns about my work, then I'd rather you were up front about it –'

'Of course not. You know I have a high opinion of you. This is a tricky case, but we're making progress, so . . .'

He petered out and the pair of them stood there, framed by Helen's drab office. Gardam was looking at Helen quizzically as if trying to fathom her, the ghost of a smile tugging at the corner of his mouth.

'Is it something else then?' Helen found herself saying.

'I don't follow . . .'

'Well, I mean that you seem to be very interested in my personal life – my relationship status and so on – and I'm not sure what I'm supposed to infer from that . . .'

There was a brief silence, then Gardam half laughed as the import of Helen's words dawned on him.

'You think I'm *attracted* to you?' he said. 'Dear God, Helen, is that what's been worrying you? I'm a happily married man and, believe me, I wouldn't betray Sarah for all the tea in China.'

'Right,' said Helen, trying to stem the colour that was fast rising to her face.

'I'm sure you're a lovely person, Helen, but it would be grossly unprofessional of me to think of you in that light and I can assure you that I don't. The only reason I have been so . . . present . . . is because I'm trying to be supportive. This is a big case for you, for the team, and it's my first major investigation as station chief, so . . .'

'Enough said,' Helen replied. 'I'm sorry I raised it.'

'That's quite all right. You must never feel concerned about being open and honest with me. Trust is a two-way street, Helen.'

'Of course. I'll endeavour to remember that,' Helen said quickly. 'Now, if you'll excuse me, I'd better . . .'

Helen didn't wait to be dismissed, marching from her office and across the incident room as fast as she could. She just wanted to be *away*. She had embarrassed herself in front of her new boss, looking like a foolish schoolgirl in the process. But she had to put that behind her and gather herself. The investigation now stood at a vital crossroads and she had important work to do.

Richard Ford was waiting for her.

67

Charlie clutched Steve's hand tightly as they approached the nursery. He had urged her to stay at home and rest up, but Charlie had insisted on picking up Jessica today. Pick-up time at Grasshoppers Nursery was 6 p.m. sharp and this was usually Steve's duty, as the garage he worked at always shut before then. In the face of his resistance, Charlie had argued that she seldom got the chance to see Jessie properly at the end of the day and wanted to take advantage of her 'early finish' today. But they both knew this was a lie. In reality, she just wanted to hold her husband and her little girl close and prove to them – and to herself – that she hadn't gone anywhere.

Charlie had put on a polo neck jumper and woolly hat and smothered her chin in as much foundation as she dared, but she still looked terrible. The colour had not returned to her face and she looked like death. Was Steve worrying that her appearance would alarm Jessica? Possibly. And who's to say he was wrong?

Nevertheless, she had to be here. Being a loving and attentive mum. A *good* Mum. Lord knows she seldom felt like that, but today she had to at least pretend that things were normal, that she and Steve had a normal life and were making a go of things.

Steve remained silent as they walked up the pretty, picket-fenced path to the nursery. Truth be told, he didn't need to say anything – it was clear they were both thinking the same thing.

Had Charlie made a mistake returning to the Force? And, if so, what were they going to do about it?

68

'We've met before, haven't we?'

Helen didn't believe in soft-soaping suspects and, having consulted with Sanderson, decided to go straight for the jugular. There would be plenty of time later to talk about his unhappy childhood or low self-esteem.

'At Travell's Timber Yard. We had quite a long chat, didn't we?'

Richard Ford looked at her blankly, while his lawyer, Hannah Shapiro, just seemed puzzled, wrong-footed by this opening salvo from Helen.

'I don't recall,' Ford finally said, his voice listless and monotone.

'Oh come on, you can do better than that,' Helen countered. 'I turned up at Travell's and you told me to leave.'

'I'm sure my client was just concerned for your safety,' Shapiro interrupted.

'Too right he was,' Helen replied. 'The roof was about to give, he had other fires to be at and he didn't want my death on his conscience. That's right, isn't it, Richard?'

Ford looked at her suspiciously, then shrugged.

'You seem a bit uncertain,' Helen continued, keeping the pressure up. 'But you were very sure of yourself that night. You certainly seemed to know a lot about the fires.'

'Inspector . . .' Shapiro intoned, the warning note in her voice clear.

'What was it you said to me? You said to me that the fires weren't an accident. You seemed sure on that point, despite the fact that, at that stage, you'd only been to one of them. Why was that, Richard? Why were you so sure?'

Shapiro shot a look at her client and, when it was clear he wasn't going to reply, waded in on his behalf.

'My client is an extremely experienced firefighter. He has attended numerous scenes of arson in the course of his duties and, besides, it was the assumption of pretty much everyone in Southampton that night that three major fires in under an hour was suspicious.'

'And while we're reminiscing,' Helen went on, ignoring Shapiro's speech, 'let me remind you of the final words you said to me. You said: "Someone's been having a bit of fun." Why do you think you used those words, Richard?'

'Can you prove my client actually said any of this?' Shapiro interrupted.

'Why, Richard?'

'Because it was obvious. Like she said, three fires in under an hour . . .'

'Were you supposed to be working that night?'

A little pause, then Ford answered:

'No.'

'Like many other off-duty firefighters, he volunteered as soon as he became aware of the scale of the problems facing the emergency services that night,' his lawyer elaborated.

Helen looked at her blankly, then turned her gaze back to Ford. She really was a piece of work, determined not to let her client speak if she could possibly prevent it. Helen could understand why. Close up he was not an attractive specimen. He had a shaved head, bad skin and teeth that could have done with more regular brushing. But more than his physical appearance, it was his demeanour that was offputting. He refused to look you in the eye, his gaze seeking out the farthest corners of the room – when he wasn't staring at his feet. He spoke in a gruff whisper and his whole manner was furtive, secretive and suspicious. Had he ever had a girlfriend? Did his mother love him? He gave off the distinct vibe of having turned against the world, having found it not to his liking.

'So according to your watch captain you arrived at Travell's at just after midnight,' Helen said. She was pleased to see that Ford flinched at this. Perhaps he'd thought that this was going to be a cosy chat. The fact that Helen had already grilled his boss for the particulars of his movements showed that it would be anything but.

'That's right.'

'Other volunteers met at the station but you turned up at the scene by yourself in full battle dress. Why was that?'

'Because I live nearby. I had the uniform at home –'

'So you live near to the first fire site? It's convenient for you?'

'Come off it, Inspector . . .' Shapiro interjected.

'It's a perfectly reasonable question,' Helen asserted, refusing to be knocked off course.

Ford thought for a moment, then nodded.

'For the benefit of the tape, Mr Ford is nodding. Let me ask you about your uniform. You're not supposed to take it home, are you? But you do.'

'Yes.'

'But technically it is breaking the rules?'

'Suppose.'

'Then again, there's a lot of stuff in your house that you're not supposed to have, isn't there?'

Ford briefly met Helen's gaze, then resumed staring at his feet.

'How many tours of the fires did you do that night?'

'Just the one.'

'You absolutely sure about that?'

'Course.'

'The fires at both Bertrand's Emporium and the Simmses' residence started well *before* midnight. I would estimate it's only a fifteen-minute journey back to your house from Millbrook, allowing you plenty of time to change into your uniform and head back to the site of the first fire.'

'No.'

'It would have got going nicely by then, wouldn't it?'

'I don't know.'

'Oh, I think you do, because you caught it on camera.'

'No law against that,' Ford shot back.

'But it's not your job, is it? That's the work of fire investigators. You're job is to *fight* the fire. Yet we found footage of your house of all three fires that night. According to the time code on the tapes, this footage was recorded around two thirty a.m., well *after* you and the other volunteers had left the scene of the fire in Millbrook. The others went home to clean up presumably, but you went back.'

Ford said nothing.

'So that makes at least two tours of the sites. And I'd like to suggest that actually you made three tours – if you include the one where you set the fires.'

'No way.'

'Do you smoke, Richard?'

'Sometimes.'

'Which brand?'

'Don't answer that,' Shapiro said quickly.

'We'll come back to that,' Helen continued.

'I'd like to talk to you a little bit more about that footage, if I may?' DS Sanderson piped up. It had been pre-agreed that she would wade in at the appropriate point, to keep the opposition on their toes. 'Can you confirm that the recordings – of all six recent fires – were made by you personally?'

Ford shrugged.

'Yes or no?'

'Yes.'

'Why did you record the fires?'

'For professional purposes,' Shapiro intervened.

'I'm asking Mr Ford, not you,' Sanderson said brusquely.

'It's my job. I'm interested in it, like.'

'Fire interests you?'

Ford said nothing.

'I'd say it interests you very much,' Sanderson suggested, unabashed. 'I think you spent most of your time in that little room at the top of the house. You wouldn't believe the amount of newspapers, empty pizza boxes, cans and so on we found up there. Have you been living in that room? Do you *sleep* in that room?'

'Sometimes.'

'Yet there's no bed. No TV. No heating except a small stove. There's very little in the way of home comforts in fact, but . . . there *is* your collection, isn't there?'

As the words hung in the air, Helen took over.

'We've bagged every last item. The books, the DVDs, the clippings, the recordings, everything.'

Helen watched Ford closely – how would he react to knowing that his precious haul was now in the hands of strangers? And worse than strangers, the police.

'We found a lot of souvenirs, Richard. A fire-damaged sign from Travell's, a cash box from Bertrand's, family photos from the Bevois Mount fire. You went back to these sites – returned to the scene of the crime – and took things that didn't belong to you. Your little trophies . . .'

Ford gave Helen a look then dropped his gaze. Was that anger Helen saw?

'You took them because you wanted to revel in your crimes. In the wanton destruction and loss of life that *you* have caused. And when DC Brooks came to talk to you yesterday, you tried to destroy the evidence.'

'It's her word against his –'

'Are you kidding me?' Helen replied angrily. 'We pulled tapes, clippings and more from that stove. Your client was destroying the evidence because he's guilty, because he'd been caught red-handed. Two people are dead, two more are grievously injured and I would suggest that unless your client wants to spend the rest of his life behind bars, then he'd better start talking.'

Helen turned, fixing Ford in the eye.

'So what's it going to be, Richard? Are you going to play ball or shall I charge you with a double murder here and now?'

69

The wheels squeaked noisily as they slid over the tired linoleum floor. Thomas Simms cursed under his breath – he already felt as if the eyes of everyone in the hospital were glued to him and his son. He didn't need the ancient hospital wheelchair trumpeting their presence to one and all.

It was a long journey from Luke's ward to the main exit and each step of the way Thomas questioned the wisdom of what he was doing. He hated being away from Alice and it was convenient to have Luke in the same place, being looked after by the attentive nurses. But his son had begged to be discharged and in the end Thomas had relented. There was little more that the surgeons or doctors could do – Luke's legs were set in heavy plaster after the operation, his shoulder was in a sling – now there was nothing to do but rest up and wait. And Luke clearly didn't want to do that here.

Here he couldn't hide from the visitors, journalists or prurient well-wishers, so Thomas had arranged that they would go and stay with his sister, Mary, who had a big place in Upper Shirley. They obviously couldn't go back to their own house – Thomas privately wondered if they would ever return there again – and he couldn't face staying in a hotel, so Mary's had seemed a good bet. He and his older sister hadn't always got on, but it was the best he could do in a no-win situation.

'How you doing, mate? Not hurting you, am I?'

'No, you're all right,' his son lied bravely, each bump on their journey clearly going right through him.

Thomas immediately felt the emotion rise in him once more. His son had been so brave throughout, facing up to his injuries, his grief, his fractured future, with admirable stoicism. When the real reckoning of recent events would finally land on him, Thomas couldn't tell. He both hoped and feared he would be on hand when it did.

They had reached the main atrium now and the exit was just ahead of them. The taxi wasn't due for another ten minutes or so, so Thomas dived into the nearby shop to buy a can of Coke for them both. Karen had never been keen on the kids drinking it, but Luke had developed a taste for it while in hospital and Thomas was happy to indulge him. As he queued to pay, his eye fell on the stack of local papers nearby.

'SUSPECT ARRESTED!' the headline screamed. And beneath it more details, including the fact that the suspect worked for Hants Fire and Rescue. The paper didn't reveal his identity, but Thomas knew his name. He knew because he had made a deal with the devil. He had nodded and thanked the FLO who'd come to the hospital to keep him up to date on developments later, failing to admit that he already knew the man in question was Richard Ford. Thanks to his deal with Emilia Garanita – the fruits of which were spread over the centrefold as well as the front six pages – he knew where Ford lived, what his family history was and some details of what the police had found when they'd raided his house.

Garanita had called him from outside Ford's house.

He had had to stand in a corridor out of view, given the ban on mobile phones in wards, and had listened, speechless, to her summary of developments. She had excitement in her voice as she relayed her news and for a moment Thomas had hated her for that – for enjoying this experience – but as the hours passed afterwards, he'd hated Richard Ford more. Thomas was by nature a peaceful guy, but he felt in himself now an anger that was strange and fierce. That guy, that shaven-headed little shit, had destroyed their lives. Taken his beautiful wife, scarred his daughter and broken his son – all to satisfy his thirst for fire. He had crept into his house, set fire to his stairs and shattered his family.

The shopkeeper was offering Thomas his change now, but he wandered off without collecting it. He walked back to his son, a rictus smile plastered on his face, but his thoughts were miles away. In a small room across town, his wife's killer was sitting, safe and well, fighting his corner, while he was here, wheeling his injured son through a lobby, watched every step of the way. Where was the justice in that? Could there ever be justice for something like this?

Thomas Simms had never wanted to harm anybody before, but suddenly he yearned to be in that room, face to face with Ford. He would show him what he'd done – to Thomas, to his family – and then he would see that justice was done. He knew there and then, with absolute certainty, that if he ever found himself alone with Richard Ford he would kill him.

70

'My client has protested his innocence – repeatedly – and has said all he's going to say on the matter. We are going round in circles, Inspector, so can I suggest –'

'We'll stop when I say so, not before,' Helen replied sternly. She had had enough of Shapiro's constant interruptions.

'I'm not sure I like your tone,' said Hannah Shapiro.

'Then find alternative employment.'

Shapiro glared at Helen, but said nothing, so Helen resumed.

'I've given you the chance to come clean, Richard. To help us to help you. But you've refused to cooperate. So we're going to have to keep going, I'm afraid. It's six fifteen p.m., so I make it that we have at least another two hours to go.'

Helen paused to let Ford take this in, before she said:

'We've established that you had footage of the six recent fires. But your collection goes back a bit further than that, doesn't it?'

A moment's hesitation, then:

'Yes.'

'The labels on the tapes cover pretty much every year since you joined the Fire Service. That's over fifteen years' worth of footage. I take it this is all your own work?'

'Yes,' Ford answered quietly.

'We had a little look at some of them. I recognized the fire at the WestQuay in 2010, the fire at Garton NCP in 2006, even the fire at the Tetherton Ballroom on Millennium night.'

'I've already said they were for professional purposes. I wanted to learn how fire behaves –'

'Well then, you must have been a very diligent student, because the tape boxes are covered in your prints and often cracked and the tapes themselves are well worn. You've watched them over and over again, haven't you?'

'We've already established that my client has no family to speak of and a limited circle of friends –'

'Spare me the violins. I don't think you watch them because you're lonely, Richard, I think you watch them because you want to. Because you like fire. Because it turns you on.'

'You've got it all wrong,' Ford responded quickly.

'We found a bin which was overflowing with tissues,' Sanderson butted in. 'We've had a few of them analysed and guess what. There's semen on every one. And, hey, I'm no prude. I know what boys get up to. But here's the thing. There's no pornographic material in your little attic, no web history of porn surfing either, so exactly what is it that gets you so excited?'

Silence in the room now. For the first time, Helen thought she saw doubt in Hannah Shapiro's eyes.

'I was wrong earlier,' Helen said. 'You don't like fire, do you? You love fire.'

Ford shook his head unconvincingly, so Helen stepped up her attack.

'You like the way it dances, don't you? What do you

think it's saying to you when it does that? Is it calling to you? Asking you to come closer? Or is it *performing* for you? Dancing to its master's tune? Is that what you like? The feeling of power it gives you? The knowledge that all this chaos, all this fear, all this beauty was created by you? I don't blame you for that. I can see the attraction.'

Ford closed his eyes.

'I think your curiosity about fire goes way beyond professional interest. I think it's an obsession. And I think that's why you started these fires. I don't know yet if you meant to kill anyone – but I know that you wanted these fires to be big, for people to take notice of them and, through them, you. This was your moment, wasn't it, the moment you finally became what you were meant to be? But it's over now, Richard, so for your sake as well as for the sake of your victims, it's time to tell us what you know.'

A long, pregnant pause. All eyes were now on Ford. He stared at the ground for what seemed like an eternity, then slowly he looked up. He half turned to Shapiro and shook his head slowly. His lawyer didn't miss her opportunity.

'We'll take that as a "No comment." My client *has* said everything he's going to, so it's shit or get off the pot time, Inspector. Either you charge my client now or you release him without delay. It's really very simple.'

That cocky smile returned to her features once more.

'So what's it going to be, DI Grace?'

71

'Come on, cheeky girl, it's time for you to go to sleep.'

Jessica Brooks giggled, picked up one of the many fluffy toys that filled her cot and threw it at her mother. It was the third projectile that Jessica had had aimed at her in the last minute. She was trying to be stern, but privately loved this little game. Jessie seemed to enjoy it so much, displaying a vivacity, cheekiness and sense of humour which Charlie found irresistible. She fervently hoped that her daughter would never lose that aspect of her personality. She was a little girl who seemed to enjoy life and Charlie hoped she always would.

'Now, don't you do that again.' She wagged her finger at her daughter in a pantomime gesture. Jessica's hand was already stretching towards a cuddly panda and seconds later it flew at Charlie. Quickly Charlie caught and threw it back, causing more peals of giggles from Jessica.

Charlie could hear the landline ringing elsewhere in the house and she prayed it wasn't for her. She loved her time with her daughter and the couple of hours spent in her company tonight had made her feel normal again. Or as normal as could be expected. Her voice was still hoarse, her throat hurt like hell, but the shock had worn off, her hands no longer shook and each minute spent in Jessica's joyful company was a powerful tonic.

The phone had stopped ringing and she could hear Steve talking. She breathed a sigh of relief, then turned to her daughter once more.

'Ok, you. How are we going to get you to sleep? It's past your bedtime and you know you'll be a grouch in the morning if you're tired. So how about we put Brown Bear, Teddy, Snoopy and Fred *back* in your cot and think about closing our eyes.'

Jessica didn't seem particularly keen on this plan, defiantly kicking away the descending mass of soft toys. Charlie realized Steve was now in the doorway and, smiling, gestured towards Jessie.

'Do you want to have a go? I don't seem to be having much joy.'

But the look on Steve's face stopped her in her tracks. He looked sombre and very pale.

'It's for you,' he said simply, holding up the cordless phone.

Charlie suddenly felt sick, though she didn't know why. Steve never let things get to him, so it must be bad.

'Charlie?' he reiterated, offering the phone to her. Now she didn't hesitate, plucking it from him and walking from the room.

'Charlie Brooks,' she said quickly into the receiver.

'It's Susan Roberts, Charlie.'

Susan was one of the Force's most experienced Family Liaison Officers. Charlie knew her to be a cheery, redoubtable character but her tone only served to spike her anxiety still further.

'What's the matter, Susan? What's happened?'

There was a long pause. To Charlie's surprise, she

realized that Susan was trying not to cry. She had an inkling now of what was coming, but still it rocked her backwards when Susan finally said:

'Alice Simms is dead.'

72

Helen and Sanderson stood in Helen's office, neither saying a word. Outside, Helen could see news of Alice's death rippling round the incident room. Several members of the team were fighting back tears, others just looked blank with shock. Everybody had been knocked for six by this terrible, sudden tragedy.

'What did they say?' Sanderson asked.

Helen had only just got off the phone from the hospital and was still trying to process what they'd told her.

'She'd been stable since the fire but they never managed to get her to regain consciousness. It seems . . . that her injuries were just too profound and in the end . . . her heart gave up fighting.'

Tears pricked Sanderson's eyes and Helen felt her desolation. They had all been so convinced that this brave little girl would pull through. Had this just been wishful thinking? The doctors had seemed hopeful, but in the end it was a terrible trauma for a little girl to endure. Despite her mother's very best efforts to save her, it hadn't been enough. Which meant that Richard Ford was now facing a triple-murder charge.

'What do you want to do?' Sanderson asked.

They had been discussing how to respond to Shapiro's ultimatum when the call had come through. Helen knew she had to keep calm and avoid getting caught up in the emotion of the moment. It was very tempting to charge Ford right now, to seek some immediate justice for Alice and her mum, but they had to be able to make the charges stick.

'Well, he's got motive and opportunity in abundance. Not to mention the expertise. We know he's lied to us under caution already on a number of occasions, but he's not going to confess, so –'

'He might if we charge him. If he thinks he can wriggle out of it by pleading diminished responsibility –'

'But if he doesn't and ends up beating the rap, it'll be our fault. We need to link him to the site of the fire itself –'

'What about Deborah Parks's findings? She said she found a boot print at the Roberts house which matched the sole of Ford's fire boots –'

'But that print was made post fire, we need evidence of him setting them. We need paraffin in the house, on his clothes, a print on the residual evidence, footage of him buying cigarettes . . .'

'What if we ask Naomie Jackson to ID him? Put him in the frame for the Roberts fire at least.'

'Wouldn't stand up. She was clear that she didn't see his face and it would be easy to disprove. It was dark, she'd had a drink and so on . . .'

'So what then?'

Sanderson's tone was a little too strident for Helen's liking, but she let it go. They were all wound tight today.

'I'm going to let him go.'

Sanderson looked so shocked, so disbelieving, that Helen followed up quickly. She didn't have the time or the headspace for a row with her deputy.

'We can hold him here, but he's not going to say anything. I want to get him away from Shapiro. While she's in play, he'll keep his head down and do what he's told. But once he's out there, isolated and scared, then we'll see the real Richard Ford. He'll need to be tailed 24/7 of course and we'll have to keep an eye out for have-a-go heroes wanting a piece of him. If Meredith or Deborah turns up anything, we'll pull him straight back in, but until then I think his isolation and paranoia could be our best friends. If there is a site where he's keeping the paraffin and his tools of the trade, then he may well be tempted to try and destroy it now. If he does, we'll be waiting for him.'

Sanderson nodded, begrudgingly seeing the wisdom of Helen's words. Helen knew, were she younger, that she would have been tempted to push Ford through another round of questioning, to try and bulldoze a confession out of him. In some situations this might have worked, but this was different. The Hants Fire and Rescue Service had paid for one of the best legal brains on the South Coast to chaperone their man, so they had to play this smart. Releasing him might destabilize him. He couldn't return to work while he was still under investigation, so he'd have plenty of time to think. And Helen wanted to see what he would do next.

So, calling McAndrew into her office, she set the plan in motion. She prayed it was the right move. The team were baying for blood now, they wanted justice, and Helen knew they would never forgive her if the killer slipped through their fingers now.

73

Emilia Garanita jogged up and down, trying to keep warm. The temperature was dropping fast and, despite the many layers she'd put on, she was frozen to the bone. She had always felt the cold – a legacy perhaps of her Portuguese heritage – and had never acclimatized to the raw winter winds that swept up the Solent into Southampton.

This was the part of the job she enjoyed least. Hanging out in doorways, on street corners, outside police stations and courtrooms, waiting and hoping for the story to come to her. Sometimes you got lucky, most of the time you did not. The knowledge that her siblings – all seven of them – were currently at home tucking into a takeaway in front of *Gogglebox* only made matters worse. She would give anything to be there with them now, enjoying the warmth and banter of a family evening in, rather than here, freezing her arse off in the vain hope of a break.

She would give it another hour or so. Her friendly PC had told her to expect developments but so far there had been no signs of movement. She had been posted in a doorway opposite the discreet back entrance of Southampton Central for nearly three hours now. For the first two of those she'd managed to amuse herself tweeting and surfing for info on Richard Ford. But his Facebook page had been shut down – his lawyer's work no doubt – and the rest of his digital footprint was very limited indeed. This was a guy who seemed to exist in his own world and was thus a journalist's worst nightmare. No easy copy, no creepy photos to use, no easy inferences to make and no way to damn him with his own words. Garanita hoped he was guilty just for the trouble he was causing her.

A sound made her look up and suddenly her heart beat a little faster. There was his lawyer, Hannah Shapiro. Normally she would stride out the front, bold as brass. If she was coming out the back, it could only mean . . .

There he was. He was hard to miss, the severe buzz cut failing to hide the fierce orange tone to his hair. If Ed Sheeran joined the army this is what he'd look like, Emilia chuckled to herself as she raised her camera. To her frustration, Shapiro's blonde bob popped into view, blocking her shot. Nothing for it, Emilia thought, but the direct approach.

Striding towards him, she called out:

'Richard? Richard Ford?'

He turned quickly, confused and alarmed by her sudden intrusion. Immediately Emilia fired off three shots. To her surprise, Ford now started marching directly towards her. She backed off, but was too slow – now he was grabbing at her, trying to tear the camera from her. She lashed out with the heel of her boot and prepared to defend herself, but suddenly Ford lurched backwards, dragged away by his irate lawyer.

'You use any of those and we'll sue,' she shouted as she marched her client away to safety.

Like hell you will, Emilia thought to herself, smiling. She had every right to be here and she was very glad she had been.

She had been hoping to hang Richard Ford out to dry and now she had exactly the pictures she needed to do just that.

74

'I can't do anything with her.'

Steve let Helen in, shutting the front door quietly behind her. Jessica was asleep and the last thing they needed now was an inconsolable toddler.

'I've tried to talk to her. To get her to eat something, but . . .'

'It's ok. I'll take it from here.' Helen laid a comforting arm on his shoulder and quietly mounted the stairs.

Helen had been to Charlie's house many times and knew exactly where to go. Ford had been released and had an eight-strong team tracking his every move, so once Helen had checked in with Meredith Walker, her first thought had been for Charlie. She had been keeping a close eye on the Simms family and, knowing her, would take the little girl's death harder than most.

Charlie was lying on the bed with her face to the wall. She stirred briefly as Helen entered and, on realizing it was her boss, smiled a brave but washed-out smile. Helen smiled back, sitting on the bed next to her and pushing the door to. The pair of them sat in darkness for a second. Helen sought the right words to begin, but before she could do so, Charlie blurted out:

'I'm not sure I can do this any more. I don't think I've got the strength.'

Tears threatened. Helen let her finish, then said:

'You've had a shock today. We all have. It's horrible, too horrible, what's happened. And there's nothing wrong with feeling like you're feeling now.'

'She was doing so well, I was so convinced she was going to make it . . . What's going to happen to the rest of them now?'

'They've got a very long road ahead of them,' Helen agreed. 'But they have each other. And things will never look as black for them as they do tonight.'

There was another pause, then Charlie said:

'I really wanted to come back to work. I wanted to *contribute*, but I don't think I'm up to it. I could just about handle what happened today, but this? I'm a bloody mess. I can't bear it for them . . .'

'I know.'

'I came back too early. I'm not ready . . .'

'Do you think you ever would be ready for something like this?'

It was a good question and for a moment Charlie said nothing.

'You can't prepare yourself for tragedies like this, nor is there an easy way to deal with them. I'd be very worried if you *were* able to just shrug them off.'

Charlie looked up at Helen as she continued:

'You're a good officer *because* you care Charlie, not in spite of it. You're the most determined, committed, honest copper I know. You won't believe me, I know, but you are and that is why whatever you feel now, you mustn't give up. Because you're going to be one of the best police officers this Force has seen.'

'Please –'

'I mean it, so cry your heart out, cry all night if you want to, but I want to see you back in tomorrow fighting fit. The Simms family will need you and we will need you if we're going to get justice for them. We *have* to bring their killer to book now.'

Charlie lowered her head, but didn't fight back.

'So please don't give up on me, Charlie.'

75

Luke Simms lay in bed, listening intently to the voices in the hall downstairs. He'd heard the key turn in the door, then earnest, fast conversation – he could tell by the deep tone of one of the voices that his father had returned from the hospital. He had rushed off there as soon as he got the call. None of them could believe the news and Luke knew that his father would have to see Alice before he could accept that it was true.

There was no way Luke could accompany him, so he'd had to stay where he was, laid up in his aunt's spare room. Mary and her husband had popped in intermittently to check up on him and to offer him some consoling words, but they didn't really know him and were tongue-tied anyway. So, after a while, he said he'd try to sleep and they'd left him alone.

But he couldn't sleep of course. All he could think of was Alice. The games they used to play, the languages they invented, the way she used to fight dirty when they scrapped. She was so much younger than him but had always been mature beyond her years. She often came across as the more sensible of the two – the Grade A student to his football obsessive. She was also a brilliant manipulator, able to wrap their father round her little finger whenever she chose to. Luke had never had that gift and he envied her. For it was just him and his dad now.

He heard the landing creaking and immediately closed his eyes. Moments later, his door opened gently and he heard his father creep in. He had wanted his father to stay, so he could talk to him, be with him, but now he was back he suddenly felt overwhelmed with the misery of their situation. He didn't want to add to his dad's worries so, keeping his eyes closed, he pretended to sleep, working hard to calm his breathing to complete the fiction.

His father hovered above him, then suddenly leant in, planting a gentle kiss on Luke's cheek.

'Love you,' he whispered, his voice quivering as he spoke.

He rose and Luke heard his footsteps receding as he crept from the room. His father hesitated in the doorway and Luke kept stock still, willing himself not to blow it now. Then his father pulled the door to and Luke was alone once more. He lay there staring at the ceiling, wondering if Alice was at peace.

As his thoughts turned on his beloved sister, he was startled by a new noise. Something he'd not heard before in his short life.

His father, in the room next door, crying his heart out.

76

Helen walked briskly away from Charlie's house. She had left her old friend in a decent place, despite the traumas of the day. Charlie had agreed to rest up and think about things – Helen didn't want her making any snap decisions that she would come to regret. It was very easy in the heat of the moment to make the wrong call. Better to sleep on it and come again at the problem the following day. Helen hoped she would return to help the team, but she couldn't be sure. It was a long time since she'd seen Charlie as shaken as this.

It was all a far cry from the happiness that she, Steve and Helen too had enjoyed in their cosy family home. Jessica's arrival had transformed all their lives and Helen had enjoyed her role as godparent. She didn't really do the religious side of things – she had long since given up believing in anything like that – but she took the rest of her duties seriously – buying her toys and books and spoiling her with treats when her parents weren't looking.

Helen had no children of her own, had never had younger siblings or nephews and nieces to care for and she had found it an oddly moving experience holding the tiny little girl in her arms. Helen had taken delight in watching Jessica blossom into a cheeky little girl, marvelling at her ability to walk and 'talk'. Human beings really were little miracles when you thought about it. She had taken plenty of snaps of the growing girl, many of which now decorated her flat, giving the formerly sterile space a sense of life and hope. But the joy they all felt towards her, towards life in general, had been tarnished by recent events. The death of little Alice would stay with them all for a long time.

A bitter wind was ripping through the city tonight and Helen realized she didn't have her scarf. Charlie had given it to her this time last year and Helen was vexed now to think that she couldn't remember where she'd left it. She'd kick herself if she'd lost it for good. She would need it in the days that lay ahead.

Southampton was now swathed in darkness. Night had settled upon it, bringing with it a distinct air of menace. Helen felt it keenly, as did the many officers who were out on the streets now, keeping a watchful eye for fresh trouble. Helen had pulled every uniformed officer back from leave and even requested auxiliary numbers from neighbouring Forces. Along with the extra fire service resources, it was a big show of strength and Helen hoped that it would be enough to prevent more devastation. Ford was under surveillance, the city was on red alert, everything should be ok.

So why did Helen feel so anxious? Under the cover of darkness, terrible things had happened. Three lives had been taken and many more touched by these awful fires and somehow Helen knew in her gut that it wouldn't end here. Was she missing something? Was there more she could yet do? Helen sensed those familiar feelings creeping up on her again. She didn't seem to be in control of this situation, she felt hopeless and helpless, and, in spite of everything she'd done, her instincts now told her that more people would die before this thing was over.

77

DC Lucas pulled up Google and typed in 'Kardashian'. Immediately, dozens of links offered themselves, an endless array of portals inviting further dissection of the celebrity family. Lucas didn't really do reality TV, nor was she a big Kanye West fan, but she thought this was a decent cover. She was dressed in casual clothes, hair down and untethered – she could pass as a bored, lonely twenty-something with nothing to do but stalk the rich and famous.

She had chosen her position in the café carefully. In the reflection of her screen, she could see Richard Ford at his terminal, tapping away intently. He had been here for a couple of hours now. Lucas, McAndrew and Edwards were in charge of surveillance and had done a decent job so far, dovetailing neatly as they rotated to avoid detection. Shapiro had dropped him off near his home in Midanbury, but as Ford turned the corner to his road, it became clear that going home was not a viable option. The police forensics team had departed, but a small knot of journalists were trawling the street, tapping up neighbours and searching for dirt – sent no doubt by Emilia Garanita, who had aggressively doorstepped Ford as he'd left Southampton Central earlier. Ford wisely thought better of another confrontation with the press and turned on his heel, walking straight past McAndrew, who carried off her role well, seeming to struggle with heavy Lidl bags which were in fact full of empty cereal packets.

Ford didn't seem to smell a rat and hurried away, ending up at Al's Internet Shack ten minutes later. He had been holed up here ever since, barely moving from his seat. What was he up to? Why was he typing so furiously? What was he planning?

Lucas had been tempted on more than one occasion to get up and pass behind him. She couldn't see his screen from her seated position – he had chosen a terminal in the far corner of the room – and would only be able to do so by inventing an excuse to pass by. But there was no toilet here, no drinks machine, nothing that could legitimately take her in his direction. She had considered talking to him – asking him for a pen – but had chickened out. If there was any hint in her manner that she was not what she seemed, if she gave herself away by even the briefest of glances at his screen, then she would have blown their cover. They had all worked too hard and too well for her to allow that to happen and, besides, she wouldn't fancy facing DI Grace to explain that, so she stayed where she was, scrolling through yet more pictures of Kim Kardashian's backside, wondering to herself what was going through the mind of Richard Ford.

78

Blog post by firstpersonsingular.
Thursday, 10 December, 21.00

When people come to judge me, they will see that none of this is my fault. Some people have addictive personalities. If you've experienced that sense of compulsion, you'll know what I'm talking about. I'm not in control of this thing any more.

Just stop.

Well, I would, but that would hardly be fair. Who would I stop for? There's no one out there who gives a shit and now that I'm on the side of the angels, why should I stop? Too much has already been done and the road ahead is long. There is so much more to do. It makes me feel funny just thinking about it.

More boots on the street. As if that can stop this thing. It just gives me more puppets to play with. Do you ever step outside yourself and look down? I do all the time. What do I see? Ants, loads of tiny little ants, scurrying around, crawling all over each other. Panic, panic, panic. And what do you do with ants? You tread on them. Tread on them until they don't move any more.

I read an e-book recently called 'Footprints in History'. By an American dude who took out his entire class with a Mac-10. He was a smart guy with a bitch of a mother and a dad who liked to hold his son's head to the stove. They told him he was a worm, a germ, a piece of shit who should never have existed. But he did more than any of them. He did something, then wrote a book about it. He's going to be as famous as Hitler or Jeffrey Dahmer.

I don't have a book in me, not got the patience. And my hands get tired with all the typing. Perhaps I should get a speech recognition program??? I would but I can't say out loud what I'm thinking. I'd say ***LOL*** if it wasn't so dated. Anyway, I'm rambling now, so I'll sign off. You can talk all you want, but it's actions that count and I can't sit here gossiping all day.

I have work to do.

79

'So, what's she like?'

'Strange.'

'Strange good or strange bad?'

Jonathan Gardam sat back in his chair and considered Sarah's question. They had just finished a late dinner – an exquisitely prepared Dover sole – and were now working their way through what remained of the wine. This was their customary end-of-the-day routine – they weren't great box set people, nor were they devotees of Facebook. They liked to sit and talk.

'Good mostly. She's very talented. Very committed and the most fearless officer I've met.'

'Probably because she doesn't have a family to go home to.'

'Perhaps, but, whatever, it works.'

'So why do you say she's strange?'

'Because she's so hard to read. She's a great team leader, good at inspiring the troops, but she's determined to keep everyone at arm's length.'

'Some people are like that,' Sarah said, shrugging.

'But how does she do it? How does she take the hits and then go back to an empty flat?'

'That's for her to know. It's not your place to ask.'

'But I'm curious. I know *I* couldn't do it. You need

someone to come home to, someone to change the mood music in your life, to distract you from yourself.'

'You say the sweetest things, honey,' Sarah mocked as she rose, taking their plates to the sink. 'Now finish up that wine and come upstairs. I'm going to run a bath and there's room for two if you're interested . . .'

Jonathan did as he was told, placing his empty glass on the marble top. Upstairs, he could hear the hot water thundering into the tub and it made him think. Here he had warmth, love and more besides. Out there in the dark somewhere was Helen Grace. What did she have? Who did she have? How did she make her world work? Their discussion earlier had been embarrassing but also illuminating. Brilliant as she was, she was terribly alone and who could say what the eventual cost of that might be? He never felt paternalistic towards his staff but he did worry about *her*. She was the bedrock of Southampton Central, if she broke they would all suffer.

Sarah was calling for him now, so turning he headed upstairs. He wondered if Helen had ever enjoyed such simple pleasures. Who was out there for her?

80

Helen cried out in pain and her body slumped forward. The impact of the blow had temporarily winded her and for a moment she struggled to breathe. But then the feeling subsided, though her heart was already thundering out a terrifying rhythm.

Max Paine raised the paddle and brought it down hard on her back. Helen bucked fiercely but straight away ordered him to strike again. He obliged, harder this time and Helen felt it go right through, piercing pain from her temples to her feet and back again. But still it wasn't enough.

She couldn't dispel those familiar feelings of hopelessness tonight. Was this because Max was new to her? That she wasn't comfortable in his presence? There was an edge to things tonight for sure. He seemed in a heightened, energized mood, barely bothering to conceal the lines of cocaine he took in the back room before their session, and Helen's instincts told her that he enjoyed looking at her. He kept a professional face on at all times, playing the role he was paid for, but she could feel his eyes on her nevertheless, tracing the contours of her body, no doubt asking himself questions about the many abrasions and scars that covered her.

'Again.'

Why couldn't she stop *thinking* tonight? Why couldn't

she relax into it, as she had with Jake so many times previously? Why did she suddenly feel self-conscious and stupid, parading herself in her underwear for a man she neither knew nor cared for? Was she really that *lost*?

The paddle slammed into her back once more, pushing her hard against the wall. Max seemed not to be waiting for instructions any more and, as Helen regained her footing, the paddle struck again. Helen closed her eyes and swallowed the pain. She wanted this to work. So gritting her teeth, she took the beating, hoping that Max could drive her dark thoughts away. For an hour or two at least, she needed to be free of the world and, more importantly, free of herself.

81

It was raining. The sun was high in the sky, beating down on her, yet still she was getting *soaked*. The rain swirled around her, saturating her clothes, getting in her ears and eyes, dripping from her hair. Where had this sudden storm come from? And why was she the only one getting wet? None of it made any sense.

The cloud seemed to be hovering directly above her, shadowing her every move. It was as if it had been created just for her. She tried to run away from it but now realized she was horizontal, her legs moving ineffectually back and forth in thick, heavy mud where she lay. The more it rained, the more the mud clung to her. Her legs felt so heavy. Soon she wouldn't have the strength to move at all.

Then as suddenly as it had started, the rain stopped. And in the aftermath she drank in that smell – the bitter, dank aroma that storms leave before the ground dries off and the deluge is forgotten. But this rain smelt different. What was it that made it smell so odd? It smelt like petrol or . . .

Now Agnieszka knew she was dreaming. She had kind of known it all along, but it had been so vivid that for a while she had gone with it, indulging herself in the harmless craziness of it all. She didn't want to remain in this space any more, but part of her didn't want to wake either. She had had a hard day – there was precious little respite in this job – and she didn't want to be back in the real world just yet. But something was tugging at her now, forcing her awake. It was that smell, so strong, so suffocating, so sharp . . .

And a noise too now. Like an overflowing water pipe dropping its load on concrete paving. Splatter, splatter, splatter. No, not that. It was liquid bouncing off leather. The leather she was lying on.

Through her grogginess, she remembered now that she had been watching *Breaking Bad* on the TV. She remembered the episode finishing but little after that – she must have fallen asleep on the old leather sofa. Sitting up, she shook her head, trying to dispel her curious dream. And, as she did so, she felt her wet hair swing round, sticking to her face. Opening her eyes, she realized that she was saturated. But not with water. With something much worse. The smell of paraffin was overpowering, filling the small room completely.

Blinking furiously, she tried to make sense of what was happening. The paraffin ran off her, off the sofa on to the floor below. Across the room there was a figure. In the gloom she couldn't make out his face, his head shrouded in a dark hoodie. She tried to call to him but no words came out. And now she saw something in his hand. She blinked again and looked closer. And as he came towards her, she saw it. It was a match. He had a lit match in his hand.

She watched it leave his hand, somersaulting slowly through the air on its way towards the sofa. She could see it but was powerless to stop it. And as it made contact with the soft leather, the entire room seemed to burst into flames.

82

She couldn't breathe now. The blows were raining down on her, faster and faster, depriving her of the time to recover and robbing her of oxygen.

'Stop.'

It came out as no more than a whisper – that was all she could muster. Max Paine raised the paddle and brought it down again. Helen's whole body swung forward with the impact, her chest crunching into the wall.

'STOP!' she repeated, finding the breath from somewhere to raise her volume.

'You don't want me to stop,' Max called back, delivering another duo of heavy blows.

This had stopped being enjoyable some time ago. Helen had come here for relief but had found none and their encounter was now turning into a beating.

'Stop *right now*,' she gasped.

'Beg me,' he replied aggressively. 'Beg me to stop.'

'I want you to stop.'

'BEG ME!' he screamed, raising the paddle threateningly.

'Release,' Helen finally gasped. This was their code word for a full cessation of their session. In a pursuit where consent can be a grey area, where people sometimes protest in the hope of incurring *more* punishment, it was vital to have a code word that would bring proceedings to a sudden close. It was standard practice in any S&M scenario and Helen was glad to have uttered it.

The next blow caught her completely by surprise and she cannoned into the wall at speed.

'Release,' she cried as she rebounded, but another blow caught her between the shoulder blades. She looked up just as he brought the paddle down again and was horrified to see that Max had no intention of stopping. He looked like he was *enjoying* himself.

Helen lurched to the left, but she was still shackled to the wall and the blow connected as it glanced off her, jarring her rib cage. Helen tugged hard at the shackles, suddenly alive to the danger she was in.

'Stop, God damn y—'

The next blow cut her off. She tugged harder – her body was slumping now under the weight of the blows and she wasn't sure how long she could go on. She had already taken terrible punishment.

As the next blow descended, her right arm suddenly came free. A split second before the paddle landed, she flung her elbow backwards. It connected sharply with Max's chin. Stunned, he rocked for a moment, then stumbled forward. With one hand still tethered, Helen's options were limited, but she twisted quickly, ramming her knee into his groin. It struck home and he collapsed to the floor gasping. Helen tugged her other hand free now and before she knew it was holding his discarded paddle. Max was trying to rise now and Helen was quickly upon him, bringing her weapon down hard on the back of his neck. He slumped once more but Helen's blood was up and she hit him once, twice, a third time. Still he wouldn't lie down, so she hit him again and again.

Helen swung freely, driven by anger and fear, determined to break this man who'd tried to hurt her. But as she raised her hand to strike him again, a strange noise startled her. Something familiar, but strange. Something unexpected and oddly jaunty. It was a ring tone – her ring tone. She must have forgotten to turn her phone off.

The phone rang on, bringing her to her senses. Dropping the paddle like a hot coal, she ran to her clothes, tugging them on roughly as she answered the phone.

'Yes?' Her voice was cracked and weak.

'It's Sanderson, boss. We've got three more fires.'

Helen's head spun. Could this be happening?

'Text me the details,' she replied and rang off. Seconds later, she was out of the door. Max Paine lay on the floor where she left him, silent and still.

83

Helen sprinted to her bike, berating herself every step of the way. Why, why, why was she such an enormous fuck-up? Was her loneliness so severe that she would willingly take her eye off the ball at such a crucial moment in the investigation? What the hell was she *doing*?

Her mind was already scrolling forward. If Paine reported her assault on him, then she would be off the investigation and probably out of the Force too. Given her good track record, she could possibly ride out the disciplinary proceedings if she was contrite, agreeing to a demotion, community service and a large helping of humble pie. But would it be worth it? Once her extracurricular activities became common knowledge, she would be a dead woman walking as far as top brass were concerned. They would correctly surmise that it would be impossible for her to maintain authority over her unit, when everyone would be cracking ribald jokes about what she got up to after hours. Some would be repelled by her activities, others still might be attracted to her because of them – either way it would be an impossible circle to square and she would be put under heavy pressure to step down.

It seemed as though Helen had been walking a tightrope for years. Keeping her private and professional lives totally separate, hoping in her own muddled way that she could find the strength to keep doing what she did.

Suddenly a crushing wave of sadness swept over her. This was all she'd ever done, all she'd ever been good at. And she *was* good it – she had saved numerous lives, ended a number of brutal killing sprees. She loved her job and felt she made a difference to people's lives. Was all that about to be taken away from her?

Brushing these thoughts aside, Helen climbed on to her bike and fired it up. Her fate would have to be addressed later, there was important work for her to do now and she had to focus. Three more fires had been set. One at a nursery, one at a cash and carry and the third at a terraced house in nearby Lower Shirley. It wasn't hard to work out the exact location of the last fire. Not half a mile away, a giant plume of black smoke climbed ever higher, blocking out the moon's gaze and casting a shadow over Southampton.

Helen raced towards it now, all thoughts of her own future temporarily forgotten. Their killer was at play once more.

84

Buzz, buzz, buzz. The phone was on silent mode and appeared aggrieved to be neutered in this way, buzzing its irritation angrily over and over again. It lay in a Marc Jacobs bag underneath the small table, temporarily forgotten by its owner.

Jacqueline Harris drained her glass and reached over towards the bottle. She pulled it out of the ice bucket, a few drops of icy water spilling on to the white tablecloth, and was aggrieved to find that it was empty. She cast a suspicious glance at her husband, Michael. He had been in ebullient mood, telling stories, joking and refilling his companions' glasses at every opportunity. Wouldn't it be like him to finish the bottle without ordering another – he wouldn't want to break the flow of his delivery, now that he had a captive audience.

Signalling to the waiter, Jacqueline sat back in her chair and let out a heavy sigh. It had been a pig of a day – a day when every one of her pet projects had taken a step backwards. She had lost the pitch for the new building at Solent University, a client had complained about rising costs on another project and, to top it all off, she'd run into more planning problems on her luxury flats overlooking Ocean Village. She'd get over them, of course, it was too big a development to be stymied and she was a big enough name locally to cut through the red tape, but still it was irritating. Sometimes it seemed to her as if the world delighted in throwing small-minded pettifogging bureaucrats into her path just to see how she would react. By now it should have known – she reacted *badly*.

The waiter was on his way over now and Jacqueline relaxed a little. Her eye wandered to Michael, who was building to the end of another of his stories – adventures from the front line of psychiatry. He would never tell stories of current patients of course, but when it came to serving up the gory details of past fruitcakes he'd treated he was utterly shameless. He was currently dissecting the neuroses of a former patient – Katie B – who'd suffered from a condition called Objectum Sexuality, in which the victim became sexually obsessed with inanimate objects. Washing machines, car bonnets and the like were common, but Katie seemed to have a particular flair for her condition, having developed an unhealthy and somewhat unnerving obsession with Ferris wheels. She had been arrested in various states of undress at funfairs up and down the land and seemed to have no desire or ability to combat her addiction, despite the best efforts of her family and Michael too.

Jacqueline regarded her husband – he was expanding his theme now to bring in the real-life cases of two other female sufferers who'd married the Eiffel Tower and Berlin Wall, respectively. Despite her mild irritation with him and her high stress level, she couldn't help smiling. When he was in this mood he was kind of irresistible – he would happily entertain their large party deep into the small hours if given the chance.

Jacqueline ordered another bottle of Sancerre and gave

in to the flow of the evening. As the crisp white wine hit the back of her throat, she felt her whole body relax. She'd only had a couple of glasses and they hadn't done much, but this one landed. It was late and they should probably be getting home, as they both had hectic days tomorrow, but somehow she knew they wouldn't. They were night birds and didn't really do sleep – they were never happier than when entertaining together. So she refilled her glass, launched herself into the conversation and forgot all about the woes of her day.

All the while, her phone buzzed violently underneath the table, out of sight and out of mind.

85

Adam Latham stood in front of the blaze, trying to stem the fierce anger rising inside him. Ever since his crew had arrived on the scene – their third fire of the night – they had been on the receiving end of catcalls and abuse. A knot of young lads hung on the cordon, swearing at them and accusing them of being killers, firestarters and more besides. A plastic bottle had been thrown at one of his officers, at which point the police had finally done their job, dragging the offender away for a night in the cells. But in general the boys in blue had done nothing to protect his team. No doubt they were in thrall to DI Grace, believing every ugly lie that came out of her mouth.

Every instinct was urging him to charge over to those scrawny kids and teach them a lesson they'd never forget. But he wasn't an excitable rookie any more, he was Southampton's Chief Fire Officer, which meant that though it stuck in his craw, he had to suck it up for now. They had more urgent priorities as the imposing house in Lower Shirley continued to rage, but he made a private vow to himself that if *any* of his officers were harmed or hampered in fulfilling their duties tonight, he would have Grace's head on his wall before the month was out.

'What shall we do, boss?'

Simon Cannon, the team captain, hurried up to him. His face was smeared with dirt and riven with tension.

'Have we had any joy reaching the parents?'

Cannon shook his head.

'Their car's not here and Mrs Harris's PA confirmed that she and her husband have gone out to dinner tonight. But we've got no way of knowing if they've got their son with them or not.'

'How mobile is he? Could he get out himself? Call for help?'

'Hard to say. He's epileptic and has some physical disabilities according to the neighbours. He can get around, but he might have been asleep when this started. Even if he was awake, the stress of the situation might get to him and . . .'

'Jesus Christ.'

Adam Latham had recurring nightmares about moments like these. He had faced enough of them over the years but they still haunted him – those moments when you had to make the big calls, when innocent lives were at stake and it was down to you to decide which way to jump. His team had already been in the building for upwards of ten minutes and it was touch and go as to how much longer the structure would hold. The fire appeared to have started in the basement and ripped through the old terraced house – it was a very real risk that the flooring would collapse, sending four officers to their deaths. He couldn't have that on his conscience, but if they pulled out too early and allowed a disabled boy to die in the conflagration, they'd be slaughtered. And rightly so.

'What are the boys saying? What's it like in there?'

His deputy pulled a face.

'They're getting barbecued. They've got three or four minutes at best.'

Cannon paused and looked at his boss. Latham looked at him, then up at the house, before saying:

'Give them two more minutes. If they haven't found the boy by then, tell them to pull out.'

Cannon was immediately on his radio, as he hurried back towards the house. Adam Latham watched him go, hoping and praying that he'd just made the right call – and that he'd be able to live with the consequences.

86

The fire swirled around him, but still he pushed on. He had to keep going. The temperature in the house was savage now – it wouldn't be long before his protective suit started to melt – but he had no choice. The intelligence was that there was a teenage boy in the house and he was damned if he was leaving without him. The order to pull out could only be seconds away – their bosses were very cautious when it came to officer safety and he was profoundly grateful for that.

Yet still Leroy Friend marched on, climbing the stairs to the top of the house, despite fully expecting them to give out at any moment. He was recently married with a young baby – if there was a child in here, he would move heaven and earth to get him out. But this place no longer resembled either of those – it looked like more like hell. Everything was ablaze, coming at them from below, from the sides and even more alarmingly from above. The roof had caught, was weakening and might come down at any second.

Distracted by this alarming sight, Leroy missed his step and stumbled as he moved forward. His arm shot out to right himself but the weakened bannister came away in his hand. Suddenly he was pitching forward, his heart skipping a beat as he sailed through the air, powerless to stop himself. He collided hard with the staircase and to his horror part of it gave way. Lying spread-eagled on his front, he could look through the stairs now to the inferno awaiting him below. And in that moment, he knew he had to turn back.

Levering himself up cautiously, he called it in and turned to retrace his steps. It would be hard going – he would have to resist the temptation to run despite the intense heat, testing each foothold before he put his weight on it. If he brought the whole staircase down, he'd not only put his own life in jeopardy, but the lives of the rest of the team too.

Tentatively he moved his right foot forward, hoping to jam it into the corner of the staircase which still seemed solid. But halfway to his foothold, he paused. He could hear something. Something that frightened and alarmed him.

You hear all sorts of things when you're in the midst of a fire and you become attuned to what each sound means, used to processing every small noise in case it poses a danger or a threat. And these sounds become your friends, the soundscape of emergencies that become familiar through repetition. But this sound he didn't recognize. It wasn't the usual roar or crackle or shriek. This sounded more like a wounded animal. Like some kind of keening.

Cursing himself for his stupidity and calling on all the saints he could think of, Leroy turned and continued to climb. Immediately his radio crackled and nearby he could hear the rest of the team calling to him. He gestured for them to get out, but didn't turn or engage them in conversation – he didn't want to drag them into his madness.

The sound was getting louder now as he mounted the stairs. Was it to the left or the right? As he stood, straining to hear, a roar above him made him dive to the left. A flaming wooden beam came crashing down where he'd just been standing, sending a vast column of white hot sparks leaping up into the air.

Now he was scrambling to his feet, racing to his left. There was no time to hesitate and think, he just had to act. In front of him was a door. He turned the handle and pushed with all his might, but immediately he met resistance. Was it fallen debris behind there or something else?

His head was beginning to throb, the oxygen in his tank draining fast. Muttering his baby son's name, he shouldered the door once, twice, three times. And now finally it did move. Pushing it roughly open he stepped inside. There on the floor in front of him was a teenage boy in the midst of a full-blown seizure.

It was what Leroy had been hoping to find, but still this discovery filled him with dread. There was precious little chance of him getting out now, let alone two of them. But there was no time to hesitate, so scooping the quivering boy up, he placed him over his shoulder and strode back to the stairs.

Time was against them, there was little hope for either, but Leroy Friend had to try. If this boy was *his* boy, he would expect nothing less.

87

Charlie lay in bed and listened to the sirens. Another night, another set of fires. It was unbelievable but it was true. She had tried to avoid anything work-related given the horrific day she'd endured, but Southampton's news was now national news, so even though she'd flicked her DAB radio to a classical station in an effort to relax, the news bulletins still brought real life crashing back into her world. In the end, she'd turned the radio off, pulling the duvet up around her chin, hoping against hope that she could block out the madness and get some sleep.

But old habits died hard. And even as she lay there tossing and turning, there was a part of Charlie that wanted to text Sanderson or McAndrew to find out what was going on. In normal circumstances she would have done so already, probably while driving to the station to pitch in, regardless of whether it was her shift or not. As a police officer you just want to know the details – to find out if you can help, if there is anything that can be done. Even now, with Steve counselling her not to dwell on recent events, with Charlie herself trying to wrench her mind towards more mundane, domestic matters, there was a part of her that craved the detail. What was happening out there?

When you're wallowing in ignorance, your mind conjures up the very worst kind of images. Who's to say that their arsonist hadn't exceeded himself tonight, visiting his most serious night of chaos on Southampton? Charlie shook her head to ward off such morbid thoughts, but suddenly all sorts of nightmarish images presented themselves. Charlie knew she was disturbing Steve and didn't want to have to explain why, so she fled their room, heading past Jessica's bedroom and downstairs to the kitchen.

She poured herself a cool glass of water from the jug in the fridge and, having downed half the glass, held it to her forehead. She was surprised to find that she was sweating and for a moment the cold glass soothed her. Draining the glass, she refilled it and drained it again. She seemed to be locked into some kind of panic now. She felt dizzy and, steadying herself with a hand on the kitchen island, lowered herself to the floor. It was cool down here, the quarry tiles radiating a wintery chill from the frozen ground below, but Charlie liked the sensation, so slowly spread herself out, feeling the coolness seep into her chest, her stomach, her thighs. If Steve found her like this he'd probably ship her straight off to the funny farm, but Charlie didn't care. She just wanted to be calm, cool and quiet for a moment.

Lying in the darkened kitchen, Charlie felt invisible and momentarily safe from the world. Perhaps this could be her sanctuary for the night, a place where she could process the terrible tragedy of little Alice's death without disturbing Steve or Jessica. But to do so she'd have to ignore the sirens that wailed outside, ebbing and flowing, but never truly going away. It was as if every emergency vehicle in Southampton was out there right now, chasing shadows. And each time they neared her house, they seemed to accuse Charlie directly, shaming her for her absence. And tonight she felt every bit of that shame. They were right to lambast her – she deserved no mercy from them.

She'd always thought of herself as a dedicated and diligent officer, but tonight she felt nothing of the sort. Tonight she knew in her heart that she was nothing but a coward and a fraud.

88

The house fire in Lower Shirley had attracted so much interest that the roads surrounding the blaze were clogged with emergency workers, journalists and onlookers – so much so that Helen had had to abandon her bike in an alleyway and carry on on foot. She had no worries about doing so: this was an expensive neighbourhood and her bike would still be there in the morning, but it slowed her progress considerably. She was curt with idlers and aggressive in her tactics as she bullied her way to the police cordon.

Swinging underneath it, she made her way towards Adam Latham. He was the last person she wanted to see right now, but she had no choice. She needed to know what they were dealing with here. As soon as Latham turned to her, she could tell it was bad news. He usually had a rosy, corpulent complexion, he was one of those desk jockeys who had happily let himself go since retiring from front-line action, but tonight his face was ashen. He looked sick with worry and more than a little scared.

'I was wondering if you'd show your face,' he said, failing to disguise his contempt for her. 'But I'm glad you're here. Now you can see what your baseless allegations mean to officers on the ground. The shit that they have to put up with because of *you*.'

He turned towards the fire, offering Helen his back.

Helen's eyes flitted across the scene, taking in the kids idly abusing the fire crew, the journalists taking photos, no doubt wondering if any of the men in uniform was responsible for tonight's blaze, before they came to rest on Latham once more.

'What's happening?' she asked, drawing level with Latham, refusing to be dismissed.

'What's happening is that four of my best officers are in that inferno attempting to save a boy who may – or may not – be in there. Trying to pull innocent people from a blaze that you and your lot are solely responsible for. Have you got even a single *genuine* lead? Anything that might bring this guy to book?'

'This isn't helping, Adam.'

'Fuck you. If the truth hurts, then don't ask the question.'

'Where are your team, Adam?'

She said it as gently as she could – she didn't want to provoke him further – and finally Latham seemed to soften a little. A dinosaur he may be, but he did care about his team and would be devastated if anything happened to them.

'Last we heard they were on the second floor. But that was over five minutes ago and we've lost radio contact with them. I can't risk sending any more of them in until we put this thing out. We're doing everything we can . . .'

Helen was suddenly struck by how conversational and intimate his tone was. It was as if he wanted to talk to her – to talk to someone – to alleviate the tension that gripped him.

'You have to trust in their training. These guys know what they're doing and if anyone can make it out of there, they can. You have them well drilled – there are no better officers in the country.'

Adam nodded, but said nothing, his eyes still fixed on the blazing house. Helen wasn't sure if she believed it either – they were good, no question, but the five-storey house was *consumed* with fire. Could anyone survive an inferno like that?

The pair of them stood there, scanning the scene, as Latham's deputy repeatedly tried to restore radio contact. The tension was almost too much to bear, then suddenly there was movement from the front of the house. The front door barrelled open, collapsing off its hinges, and the first two men in the team hurried out. Suddenly the whole scene came to life, as paramedics, colleagues and more hurried over to them. The escaping firefighters were already signalling for an ambulance and now Helen saw why. The third and fourth men in the team had now followed their colleagues out of the house, carrying someone in their arms.

The house belonged to Jacqueline and Michael Harris and they shared it with their son, Ethan, and a nanny. The parents were out tonight but the other two were thought to be home. Helen could see the boy was now in the firefighters' arms and though there was much concern for him – paramedics now rushing him towards the awaiting ambulance – at least he could be accounted for. Of the nanny, Agnieska Jarosik, there was no sign.

Helen stepped aside as the boy was wheeled past. He looked in a terrible state, covered in dirt and blood and in the grip of some kind of fit. As he sped by, Helen was suddenly struck by the diabolical nature of this latest crime. Their arsonist presumably knew who lived here, knew that a vulnerable boy like Ethan would struggle to escape such a savage fire. And yet this thought hadn't stilled his hand, hadn't occasioned any second thoughts. It almost beggared belief, but it was true. If she hadn't known it before, Helen knew it then – this killer's cruelty knew no bounds.

89

Her heels made a harsh, repetitive clicking sound as she ran towards the hospital entrance. Michael was paying the cabbie, but she hadn't waited for him. Her head was spinning, her mind full of awful possibilities, and now she just wanted to *know*.

Without thinking, she ran straight into the A&E department. The automatic doors opened obligingly for her and as she hurried inside, that familiar hospital smell hit her. Disinfectant warmed up by the overactive heating system and sprinkled with a little urine. She hated that smell and she hated hospitals. God knows she'd spent enough time in them and more than enough time in A&E over the last few years. Because of his condition, Ethan was clumsy and accident-prone so Jacqueline had spent too many hours slumped on these grim plastic seats, surrounded by the drunk and the disorderly.

She generally forced Michael to accompany her on these visits – scared of the shambling drunks and paranoid care-in-the-community types that littered the emergency department – and she was glad when she found him by her side now. Her nerves were spiking wildly, as they had been since she'd pulled out her phone to call a cab, only to find she'd missed numerous calls. She'd only made it through the first two messages, before she'd grabbed Michael and sprinted from the restaurant, leaving the bill unpaid. Their first instinct had been to head home, but, on hearing that Ethan had been taken to South Hants Hospital, they diverted there instead. There was still no word as to the fate of Agnieszka – that was something Jacqueline didn't even want to think about.

Gripping her husband's hand, Jacqueline marched up to the first nurse she could see and collared him.

'Our son was brought in this evening. Ethan Harris.'

For a moment, the nurse looked blank.

'You'll need to go to reception. All admissions –'

'There was a fire. At our house in Lower Shirley. My son was there – they just brought him in.'

Immediately, she saw the nurse's expression change and it made her feel sick. Suddenly he knew exactly what she was talking about and looked worried and concerned.

'Of course. You'll need the burns unit. Let me take you there now.'

He walked briskly and they matched his pace, though Jacqueline felt nauseous and short of breath. Both she and Michael must have had the best part of a bottle of wine each and the alcohol was now making its presence felt. All pleasure had evaporated long ago: now she felt dehydrated and washed out. What on earth were they doing, drinking, laughing, joking, when their bloody house was on fire?

She looked at her husband, but his gaze was fixed resolutely forward. She had heard about the recent fires of course, but to her shame had thought they were other people's problems – people with less money and more issues perhaps. It was embarrassing to admit that, but it was true. Even now, she hoped and prayed that *their* fire had nothing to do with these arson attacks. Faulty wiring perhaps, a hob left on. It wouldn't be excusable, especially if it turned out to be Agnieszka's fault, but she didn't want to be part of that other thing. She and Michael didn't have any enemies, there was no one out there who would want to harm them. He was a psychiatrist and she was a bloody architect, for God's sake.

And yet something inside her *knew*. Knew that they were getting sucked into something bigger than them. And that this was just the start of their misery.

90

'Are you absolutely sure?'

Helen's tone was abrasive and aggressive. She would never usually talk to one of her officers in that way, but she forgave herself tonight. Too much had happened tonight for her to pussyfoot around important issues.

'One hundred per cent,' DC Lucas replied evenly, choosing to ignore Helen's rudeness. 'He hasn't moved a muscle.'

Helen stepped forward and looked through the grimy windows of the internet café. She had hung back out of sight, not wanting to compromise Lucas's surveillance operation, but now she had to see for herself if he was really in there. Her heart sunk when she saw that he was. According to Lucas, Richard Ford hadn't once got up from his monitor, tapping away on the keyboard as though his life depended upon it.

'What time did you both arrive here?' Helen continued.

'Around eight p.m.?'

'And he was never out of your sight? You didn't go to the loo, for a cigarette . . .'

'Come on, boss.' Lucas's tone was less forgiving this time – she clearly didn't enjoy having her professional competency called into question.

'So what's he been doing?'

'See for yourself,' Lucas replied. 'Just . . . that. I wanted to get round the back of him to see what he was typing, what he was looking at, but I couldn't without massively flagging my interest in him, so . . .'

Helen nodded at Lucas and considered her next move. Richard Ford was such a good suspect – he fitted the general profile in almost every way. And yet he hadn't moved a muscle tonight. A thought suddenly grabbed her and Helen now found herself striding past her colleague and into the café. Lucas was unsure whether to stay outside or follow, but in the end chose the latter. She wasn't sure what was about to happen, but she knew she didn't want to miss it.

Helen was making straight for Ford. Such was the speed of her approach that he barely looked up until she was upon him.

'What the hell do you want?'

His right hand moved quickly towards the keyboard but Helen grabbed it, twisting it sharply, pulling Ford away from the terminal. He yelped in pain and stumbled backwards off his chair, Helen's sudden momentum catching him completely by surprise.

'What are you doing, you mad bitch?' Ford said, picking himself up off the floor.

It was a rash move, especially in front of the handful of witnesses who were still haunting the internet café at his late hour, but Helen knew she had no choice. She had to see what he'd been doing.

To her surprise, the website for Sussex Fire and Rescue Service was up on his screen.

'What's this?'

'What do you think it is? I've got to work, haven't I?'

Ignoring him, Helen pulled up his recent search history. Kent Fire and Rescue, Devon and Cornwall Fire and Rescue, job vacancies, training opportunities, nothing incriminating at all. Then she noticed a minimized Word document at the bottom of the screen and pulled it up. Immediately, Richard Ford lunged forward, trying to wrestle the mouse from her grasp.

'Can't you give me a moment's peace?' he pleaded. 'Can't you leave me a shred of dignity?'

It was his resignation letter.

'You don't let up, do you?' Ford continued, incandescent with rage and embarrassment now. 'My life is in bloody tatters and even now you won't just . . . let me be. I'm finished in this town and you want me tarred and feathered. You won't be happy until you've set the lynch mob on me, will you?'

His Southampton accent pinged through loud and clear as his voice rose, which made Helen feel all the more ashamed. Ford was clearly a strange, unpleasant man, with a peculiar fascination with fire and yet . . . he was also a successful, well-trained firefighter who'd been helping keep his home town safe since the day he was old enough to join the Service. And Helen had effectively exiled him from Southampton. In some ways she'd had no choice, she'd had to pursue every lead with the utmost vigour, but it was still a bad outcome for everyone concerned.

'I thought . . .'

'We all know what you thought,' he spat back, his face puce with anger and shame. 'But I've done nothing wrong.'

Helen suddenly became aware of the other people in the café – their faces turned towards her, drinking in the drama.

'I'm sorry,' she repeated and headed for the exit.

It was an ignominious retreat, with Lucas scurrying to keep up with her, but there was no point making the situation worse by arguing further. The damage had been done. Helen had never felt so foolish or misguided, ruining an innocent man's life while letting the real perpetrator continue his reign of terror unchecked. Where, Helen wondered, would this end? And what would it take to stop their perpetrator killing again?

91

Emilia had been up all night and she was dog-tired. This story was a good one, but did this guy really have to strike every night? Getting testimony from witnesses and emergency service personnel at one major fire was hard enough, but to have to do so from *three* fires, in the small hours, three nights running? This guy just didn't let up.

Emilia drained her last drop of coffee. It was 7 a.m. and the office was starting to fill up. Her colleagues all stopped to chat, aware that Emilia had been at her desk since 4 a.m. working up her copy for the next day's edition. Emilia was a child of the Twitter generation – her live feed keeping colleagues, fans and friends bang up to speed with what she was doing at any given moment. It was a brilliant way to disseminate breaking news, but also a fabulous vehicle for self-promotion. As she'd sat in the lonely office through the night, she'd made sure to keep the Twittersphere in the loop about developments, so the world could marvel at her investigative zeal and her bosses (and more besides) could see how committed she was. Privately, she hoped that someone in London might take notice and drop her a line.

But that was the future. Her priority now was creating a detailed four-page spread about the Southampton arsonist's 'Reign of Terror'. The police hadn't confirmed it yet, but it was strongly rumoured that a young woman had died in tonight's fires, bringing the killer's total to four victims in three nights. That was pretty good going by anyone's standards and confirmed his status as a prolific serial killer. If he kept going at this pace, he might exceed them all.

Reading between the lines, the police still had no clue who their arsonist was. Everyone – police, public, even Emilia herself – had expected this guy to slow down, but he hadn't and it now prompted an interesting question. If they couldn't catch him, then how could they stop him? Her editor had leapt on the idea of a city-wide curfew and Emilia had been happy to run with it. She didn't necessarily believe it would happen, but it raised some concerns about human rights while simultaneously highlighting the police's lack of progress. Secretly, Emilia hoped the city authorities would go for it – it would be incredibly dramatic and would ensure that the world's attention would be on Southampton for a short period of time. Not since the Boston manhunt had anything so draconian been floated.

She had almost finished typing when her mobile rang. She always put her number and Twitter handle by her byline, so was constantly receiving phone calls from snitches, crooks and chancers on the make. The caller ID flagged the number as 'withheld', suggesting the caller was either important or very shady, so scooping up her phone Emilia hurried to the ladies' loo – it was the only spot in this place where you could get a modicum of privacy.

'Emilia Garanita.'

'Emilia, it's Adam Latham. I'm the Chief Fire Offi—'

'I know who you are, Adam. What can I do for you?'

'I hear you've been talking to a number of my officers tonight. About the latest fires –'

'Everything I did was strictly legal and above board and I don't appreciate being call—'

'I haven't called to bollock you, Emilia. I've called to help you.'

There was a pause, as Emilia took this in. Behind her, the ancient cisterns murmured quietly to themselves.

'Go on.'

'I want to talk to you off the record about Helen Grace. I can trust you to be objective in your attitude to her, can't I?'

'We only print the facts here, Adam.'

'I'm very glad to hear it. I obviously don't want to be named or quoted, but I want to give you the inside track on Grace's handling of this case. It's my firm belief that her bungled approach has endangered the public and cost lives. And I'd like to give you the details.'

Emilia sat down on the nearest loo seat and pulled the door to. So Latham wanted to do a hatchet job on Helen. She was happy to listen – finally she would have the inside track on the investigation and potentially a scapegoat too.

Emilia smiled to herself. This juicy story had just got a lot juicier.

92

Jacqueline Harris stared through the glass window at her son and felt a sharp stab of guilt. Ethan had never been an easy child and she had spent less time with him than she should have – hiring help to allow Michael and her to pursue their professional lives unchecked. But now, when she really wanted to be with her son, to reassure him that everything was going to be fine, she couldn't.

The doctors had asked her to leave the room while they carried out further tests. Why hadn't she spent more time with him? Why had she been so preoccupied by work? If she had lost him, she would never have forgiven herself. Things would be different now, she vowed.

In some ways, they had been extremely lucky. Ethan's room was at the top of the house and though he had sustained scrapes and minor burns while being dragged from the blaze, they were superficial and would heal in time. He had of course inhaled a significant amount of smoke and that was what doctors were really concerned about, given that he already suffered from a mild form of brain damage, present since birth. Could this boy, who'd already been dealt a fairly tough hand, suffer yet more indignities? For all his physical problems, he was still bright and articulate – please, God, don't let that be taken away from him too, Jacqueline prayed.

Jacqueline heard steps behind her and turned to see a

young woman in a smart suit approaching, a police warrant card held out for inspection.

'Mr and Mrs Harris? I'm DS Sanderson.'

'Jacqueline. And this is my husband, Michael.'

They shook hands.

'How's he doing?'

'Good, I think. He's awake, and alert, and seems to be passing all the tests fine. We want to get him discharged as soon as we can, but obviously that's in the hands of the doctors.'

'That's great news.'

Jacqueline nodded, suddenly ambushed by emotion. Had things turned out differently, she would have been at the police mortuary today.

'We'll need to ask Ethan a few questions.'

'Of course.'

'You're welcome to be present and if it gets too much for him at any point, we'll call a halt. But he could be a vital witness to last night's events, so . . .'

'That's fine,' Michael Harris chipped in. 'We understand. Can I ask about Agnieszka Jarosik? I'd like to be able to tell Ethan what her condition is.'

Jacqueline Harris watched DS Sanderson closely. She saw a cloud pass across her face and knew immediately what the officer was about to say.

'I'm very sorry, but she died of her injuries last night. The fire was too fierce in the basement for the emergency services to get to her.'

Jacqueline turned to Michael. He looked as sick as she felt, but reached out his hand to take hers.

'Will you need us to identify her? She's from Poland

and doesn't have any family over here,' Michael said, trying to sound as business-like as possible.

'Thank you, but that won't be necessary. We have other ways in which we can identify her without putting you through that.'

Jacqueline shut her eyes. That could only mean one thing – that Agnieszka had been so badly burnt that a visual identification was impossible. An image of her charred corpse now shot into Jacqueline's mind, turning her stomach. None of this felt real but it was happening nevertheless. As Jacqueline stood there, dutifully answering the officer's polite questions, she had the feeling that the axis of their world was shifting. Their home had been destroyed, their son injured, their nanny murdered. *They* had now become the news story – the collateral damage of someone else's insanity.

93

Smoke rose gently from the ashes. Only the shell of the building now remained – everything inside it had been consumed by the fire. Twenty-four hours ago this had been an expensive terraced house in the one of the most desirable parts of the city. Now it was a smouldering wreck and, worse still, a murder scene.

The body of a young woman had only recently been removed from the scorched basement flat. The fabric of the building was still impressively hot and Helen had to wear protective boots, as she carefully traversed the site with Deborah Parks. The latter had been on site for a couple of hours already, braving the unpleasant atmosphere and risk of falling debris, in order to try and gain an understanding of what had happened last night.

'Our arsonist is developing his or her MO,' Deborah said, after the formalities had been concluded.

'In what way?' Helen asked, alarmed by Deborah's concerned expression.

'The seat of the fire was here,' Deborah answered, gesturing towards an area in the middle of the small, basement living room. A partially melted TV stood nearby, surrounded by the remnants of charred furniture. 'The smell has cleared now that we've ventilated the site, but when we first arrived, we had to wear these,' she explained, tapping her mask. 'The aroma of cyanide oxide was still very strong.'

'Burning foam?'

'This leather sofa – or what remains of it – would have been stuffed with polyurethane foam. Highly flammable and highly toxic.'

'Is that what would have killed Agnieszka?'

'Nothing so pleasant, I'm afraid,' Deborah said, pulling a face. 'We found a melted paraffin container about five yards from the sofa. My suspicion is that your arsonist entered via the back door and poured the paraffin directly on to the sofa before setting light to it.'

'No delay timer?'

'I haven't found any evidence of one and, believe me, I've looked.'

'And you think Agnieszka Jarosik was on the sofa when this happened?'

'Best guess is that the fire started just before midnight. If Agnieszka was on the sofa, we can guess she didn't fight back because she didn't have time or –'

'Or because she was asleep,' Helen interrupted, earning a measured nod from Deborah. 'She'd had a busy day, sticks the TV on, falls asleep on the sofa. And the next thing she knows she's being doused in paraffin . . .'

'It's all supposition,' Deborah replied. 'But it's our best guess. The body was directly over the seat of the fire. She never moved.'

'She burnt to death,' Helen said, her heart sinking even as she said it.

'Jim Grieves will be able to tell you more,' Deborah added, 'but if you were an optimist you might think that she died of shock. When an individual is set on fire like that, their heart often gives out straight away, the initial conflagration proving too much for them.'

'What a way to die.'

There was silence for a moment, then Helen continued:

'What makes you think the arsonist came in through the back?'

Deborah gestured at the back door and the pair of them picked their way cautiously through the wreckage towards it.

'It's an old-fashioned wood and glass door with a solid, traditional lock. The bolts weren't across, but when we turned up this morning, the door was locked – from the outside. Look, the key is as we found it.'

Helen peered through the devastated door and sure enough the key was poking out of the heavy iron lock on the wrong side of the door.

'Our arsonist was taking no chances,' she muttered. 'So why the change in MO? Why not carry on as before?'

'Who's to know? We've a different house layout here. No cupboard under the stairs, plus the stairs down to the basement do not link up to the main staircase. That could be relevant or it could be there was some other factor driving such a direct attack.'

'A particular hatred for the victim?'

'Or some kind of time pressure. Perhaps the extra boots on the street have made him nervous. Perhaps he was worried about getting caught and wanted to get this one done as fast as possible.'

'Perhaps they'd had a close shave earlier in the night?' Helen offered.

'Very possibly. Either way, dousing another human being in paraffin and then discarding the empty bottle nearby represents a definite escalation. Whether it's fear, desperation or sadism driving them, I really couldn't say.'

And Deborah wasn't *saying* it, but the implication was clear. It was down to Helen to answer this. She thanked Deborah and picked her way towards the front door, her mind whirling. The nation's press were camped outside waiting for a statement, but what was she supposed to say about a case that still had far more questions than answers?

Helen had never felt under so much pressure, but there was no point putting these things off. When you're leading an investigation of such magnitude and complexity there always comes a point when you are called to account. So, summoning her courage, Helen put on her most authoritative face and walked out of the house towards the awaiting press pack.

It was time to face the music.

94

'Can you give us an update on the number of casualties?'

The first question was from the BBC's South of England correspondent. Helen was surprised that she couldn't see Emilia Garanita present. This was her patch – she was adept at elbowing her way to the front of the pack and always asked the first question. Detective Superintendent Jonathan Gardam flanked Helen, as did the station's media liaison officer, but apart from that there were a lot of unfamiliar faces in the crowd today.

'I am sorry to have to report that a young woman died in last night's fire. She has yet to be identified formally. Beyond that we only had minor injuries at this site and those of the other fires. The fire at the PlayTime Nursery was contained very effectively by the fire services but the blaze at the First Buy cash and carry was extremely severe, gutting most of the property.'

'Do we take it from that that you are critical of the way the fire services have dealt with these blazes?' the correspondent continued.

'Not at all,' Helen replied calmly. 'This is a unique set of circumstances and very challenging for us all.'

'Do you have a suspect in custody?' Sky's reporter piped up. It was said innocently, but everybody knew that Richard Ford had been released.

'We have several active lines of enquiry, but no suspect in custody currently.'

'Have the extra boots on the street made any difference at all?'

'We're still evaluating that –'

'Can the public be assured that they are safe?' A journalist from *The Times* was now attempting to get in on the act.

'We're reiterating the advice we gave to the public earlier. Which is to make sure all windows and locks are secure at night and to remain vigilant at all times.'

'Are you any closer to catching the perpetrator?'

'Our understanding of this individual is growing day by day.' Helen knew it was baseless flannel and got the response it deserved.

'I'll ask again, are you any closer to catching the perpetrator?'

'We're doing everything we can –'

'Would you consider a curfew?'

From the *Telegraph* this time and the question Helen had been dreading.

'We're ruling nothing out at this point.'

'You're that worried that you would consider imposing a curfew in Southampton?'

The gloves were off and the questions rained down now. There was a reason they called it the press pack. Once one became emboldened to attack, then they all piled in. It was a relentless assault, calling into question Helen's competency, Southampton Central's reputation, the course of the investigation. No stone was left unturned as they hunted for a scapegoat. When people are scared, they look for someone to blame and Helen had the distinct impression that it was going to be her. This was not surprising and in some ways was justified, but as Helen defended herself and her colleagues as best she could, one thing puzzled and worried her. There was one person who should be here and wasn't and this could only mean trouble.

Where *was* Emilia Garanita?

95

Emilia's finger hovered over the Send button. She had been on the job since the moment Latham ended their call. His testimony was incendiary stuff, a chapter and verse evisceration of Helen Grace both as a human being and as a police officer. He had accused her of gross incompetency and blind prejudice in pursuing members of Hampshire's Fire and Rescue Service who were – and always had been – innocent of any wrongdoing. In the process, much damage had been done and the real perpetrator had been left alone to *kill* again. According to Latham, the death of the Harrises' nanny, Agnieszka Jarosik, was on Helen's conscience and she would have to answer for it.

Emilia had had one ear on the live TV feed from the police statement outside the Harrises' house in Lower Shirley, but her mind was really on her own copy. In the background she could hear the aggressive questioning, could hear the mood turning against the police, and it chimed with the mood of her piece. There *were* legitimate questions to be asked about the way Hampshire Police, and Helen in particular, had run this investigation. Hundreds of thousands of pounds of damage, four people dead, several others injured. For the first time that Emilia could remember it appeared that Helen was struggling – from an outsider's point of view the investigation seemed unfocused and floundering with no real handle on the how, why or who of these terrible crimes.

Normally, Emilia would have pounced on the populist bandwagon. Fear, confusion and a good scapegoat – all of these things sold newspapers. These crimes were not isolated, they appeared to threaten anyone and everyone. For that reason, copies of the *Southampton Evening News* were flying off the shelves. Everything was pushing Emilia to print Latham's allegations, to do a hatchet job on Helen Grace and yet still Emilia hesitated. She had taken on Helen before and lost, narrowly escaping prosecution for illegally tracking the celebrated officer's movements. Since then, the former enemies had enjoyed an extended truce, managing to work together, helping one another to do their jobs to the best of their respective abilities.

But that seemed to Emilia like the cosy collaboration of peacetime and there was a war raging now. A war in which there would be winners and losers. Emilia could tell which way the wind was blowing and had never been the sentimental type, so really there was only one thing to do. Taking a breath, she scanned her copy once more then hit the Send key.

Let the games begin.

96

He had never felt this bad in his life. The pain was unremitting, surging through his body from his battered torso to his pulsing head. Sleep was impossible, the super-strength painkillers had no effect and he looked a total mess. He had lost a tooth, had deep, purple bruises on his face, neck and chest and was as white as a sheet. He'd had to cancel his appointments for the entire week – inventing a plausible excuse – and now lay on his bed, moaning quietly and cursing his fate.

He had considered getting a cab to A&E, then thought better of it. He had contemplated phoning a friend, even his sister at one point, but in the end had decided against that too. He couldn't face the welter of questions. Max Paine knew his family disapproved of his lifestyle. An attack such as the one he had endured last night would give his parents the perfect excuse to stage another of their crude 'interventions', in a vain and self-serving attempt to save Max from himself. He didn't want to be saved – though he could have done with their help last night.

There was one point during the attack on him when he really thought she was going to kill him. He realized now that even as he was taking the blows, he wasn't unduly alarmed – initially at least. The tables had turned and he was expecting a beating as his due. It wasn't the first time that had happened and he rather feared it wouldn't be the last. But this time it had been different. She had been so unrelenting, so fired up by her violence, that a part of him had already started to resign himself to death. He had always had a premonition that he would end his days like this, in some after-hours encounter gone badly wrong. He had just never pictured it as being at the hands of a woman.

He wasn't ashamed that he lost out in the fight – she was a fit, strong and aggressive character who was clearly no stranger to violence – but he was unnerved by it. He had always traded on misanthropy, flaunting his disgust at the vulgar parade of a pointless existence in front of his disapproving parents, teachers, girlfriends and more. And, of course, the more they chided him, the more he hammed it up, venting his anger on them, lacerating them for their petty-minded and bourgeois attitudes. But now, faced with a sudden and violent end, he realized that he actually valued life. Parts of it at least.

As he lay in his sick bed, drifting between watching the TV and trying to sleep, his mind had turned slowly on *her*. She had booked in under a false name: Eleanor Noel. Subsequent attempts to google that name, looking for local connections, had come up with a complete blank. Perhaps she was married? Or in an important job? Or perhaps there was another less savoury reason why she concealed her identity?

Round and round he went, remembering her voice, her face, the way she held herself, the clothes she wore. He was searching for clues, anything however small that might give him a steer as to who this weird angel of violence was. Occasionally he laughed at the absurdity of it – beaten black and blue by a female client – but he knew that this was a defence mechanism, trying to rob the situation of its seriousness and the fear it engendered. What would he do if he ever came face to face with her again? He had no idea, but he desperately wanted to know more, wanted to put a name to the face that dominated and bullied him the night before. He wanted her to know what she'd done and call her to account for it.

As he half slumbered, the voices from the TV intruded on his thoughts. There had been more fires last night and people were wringing their hands about it as usual. Same old same old. Yet this time something was different about the reports. Something about them was . . . familiar. Yes, the voice, that was it. It was *her* voice.

Max's eyes shot open and he sat up in bed. Immediately he was assaulted by a wave of unbearable agony, but he managed to stay upright. He blinked hard, trying to focus on the TV. The news channel was replaying an earlier press briefing, which had been staged outside one of the fire-damaged houses. And, in the midst of it, there she was. For a moment, he sat transfixed, barely taking in what she was saying, his eyes glued to her face. She looked very different with her hair down, with her professional face on, but there was no question it was her. And as she spoke, his gaze drifted towards the caption on the screen beneath her. He nearly choked when he saw it, but in some ways it made perfect sense. He had long ago learnt not to be surprised by the secrets people hold deep and hers was a good one.

The woman who paid for his services, then violently assaulted him, was a police officer.

97

Encouraged by his parents, Ethan Harris leant forward and took the plastic spoon in his mouth. He had been officially released from the burns unit two hours previously and was now tucked away in a private room, where he would remain until a car came to pick him up. He had come off the drip now since dehydration was no longer a concern, but he needed to build his strength up again – he needed to eat – and milky Weetabix was all he could face. His throat had been irritated and inflamed by the hot smoke, so taking anything more solid was out of the question.

The seventeen-year-old had tried to feed himself but his hand shook too much to guide the spoon properly. This was partly a result of his medical condition – he had suffered from cerebral palsy since birth – but partly due to the shock of his experience. The boy could barely keep still, the rhythm of his trauma seeming to resonate through his shaking body. He had come very close to death last night, and even though in the end he'd had a very lucky escape, the legacy of his experience would linger for years to come.

Helen knew how he must be feeling. She had stared death in the face, had found herself in situations that took her beyond ordinary fear to a much darker place. So she let the boy take his time, helped and guided by his parents. At least he had his mother and father to support him, Helen thought. Others, such as Luke Simms and Callum Roberts, were not so lucky.

After a few mouthfuls, Ethan decided that he'd had enough. His parents took the bowl from him and placed it on the side table, then turned to face Helen. They weren't exactly hostile, but they didn't seem keen to encourage questions either, which Helen understood. In their shoes, she'd have felt exactly the same.

'I know you need to take it very easy, so I'll keep this brief. If at any time you want me to stop just say so, ok?'

Ethan nodded, so she continued.

'According to your parents, you usually turn the light out at around ten thirty p.m. on a school night. Is that what happened last night?'

'Yes,' Ethan croaked, immediately wincing as he did so. The smoke damage to his larynx and throat was not severe, but it was painful. He had a small burn on his left palm and some abrasions on his face – but overall he'd been remarkably fortunate, given the intensity of the blaze.

'What happened after that? Did you read at all?'

'Yes.'

'Until what time?'

'Eleven p.m.' he replied.

'And then you went to sleep?'

'Yes.'

'Did you hear or see anything after that which alarmed or surprised you? Anything out of the ordinary?'

Ethan shook his head.

'You don't remember the doorbell ringing? Or a phone

call or anything between your turning the light out and discovering the fire?'

'No.'

Helen took this in.

'How had Agnieszka been with you that evening? Was she ok in herself? Normal?'

'She was good. Fine.'

'She hadn't been having any problems recently?' Helen said, now addressing herself to Jacqueline and Michael Harris. 'Any boyfriend problems? Money worries?'

'Not that she told us of,' Michael responded. 'She seemed very steady. Then again, she'd only been with us for three months, so whether she would have felt comfortable coming to us, I don't know.'

'So the first thing you encountered that was out of the ordinary was your discovery of the fire?' she said, turning back to Ethan once more.

'Yes.'

'Can you describe to me what happened?'

Ethan took a deep breath. Whether this was to brace himself for the physical pain that was to come or because of the emotions his memories aroused, Helen wasn't sure.

'I was in bed. The smell of smoke was very strong and . . . when I switched on the bedside light, I still couldn't see anything.'

'What then?'

'I called for Agnieszka but . . . I didn't hear anything. I was panicking – I knew what was happening. So I got out of bed and walked to the door and then I felt it . . .'

He paused, asking his parents for some water, which he

drank down greedily, the cool liquid soothing his parched throat.

'Felt?'

'I could tell a seizure was coming on. I get a tingling feeling in my hands and feet first and then my vision goes. Everything takes on a kind of glow and well . . . I guess I knew I had to try to get out before it came on properly.'

Helen nodded but said nothing. She could see his parents were affected by his description. It must have been terrifying trying to escape the fire with that kind of time pressure hanging over you.

'Next thing I know, someone's carrying me. And it's hot, hotter than I could ever have imagined. Did Agnieszka get out ok?'

Helen glanced quickly at Ethan's parents. She had thought they might have broken the news to their son, but they'd obviously decided he wasn't ready for it yet. They gave Helen a small nod to proceed.

'I'm afraid she didn't make it. I'm very sorry.'

Ethan took this in, shaking his head slightly.

'How did she die?'

It was a tough question to answer, especially to a kid.

'The fire started in the basement. It would have been very quick – she wouldn't have suffered.'

Ethan nodded, then turned to his parents. They were quick to comfort him. Everyone present was thinking that Ethan could have ended up the same way.

'That's enough for now. I'm going to leave my card with your parents. If you think of anything else that might be relevant, please do get in touch. In the meantime, rest up and try not to worry. We'll get whoever did this to you – you have my word.'

Helen took her leave. She walked down the corridor fast, her thoughts tumbling over each other. So far they had no real witnesses, nothing tangible from CCTV and still no clear motive. Helen had resisted the idea of a curfew when it had been mooted – it seemed a gross overreaction – but given the proficiency and determination of their killer, it was beginning to feel like they no longer had a choice.

98

Helen was half the way down the corridor when she spotted her. Helen had biked straight from the hospital to Southampton Central and was now striding along the seventh floor. She had called the team in for an early briefing and was surprised and relieved to see Charlie, smartly dressed and looking a little refreshed, bending her steps towards the incident room. After a terrible night, it was a boost to see her old friend and colleague back on the case.

'Everything ok?' Helen asked as they walked.

'As ok as it'll ever be. Thank you for coming round last –'

'Don't mention it. I hope you'd do the same for me.'

An unwelcome memory of last night's violence shot into Helen's mind, but she pushed it away. She'd have to deal with that later.

'Of course,' Charlie replied, 'though I doubt I'll ever need to.'

That was nonsense, naturally, but it was said with a smile. It was the first time Helen had seen Charlie smile in some time and it buoyed her up as they pushed through the double doors and into the throng.

'As DS Sanderson has just pointed out, we're going to have to disregard previous witness statements and start again. This is a ground-up job, so we need open minds, ok?'

The team nodded, but Helen could sense the deflation among them. So much devastation, so many deaths and still no progress. Helen knew that it was Karen and Alice Simms's funeral today – this was preying on everyone's mind, affecting their mood. Helen had to drive the team forward, had to keep them focused, had to convince them that this guy *could* be caught.

'I've got uniform doing house-to-house near last night's sites. They will feed any intelligence they gather straight back to the incident room and I've asked DCs Lucas and McAndrew to collate and sift the witness statements from all the incidents. Who called the fires in, who was passing by, who'd seen unfamiliar characters hanging around – let's double-check we've not missed anything important.'

'Yes, boss,' DC Lucas piped up.

'And I know it's laborious, but I'd like DC Edwards and DC Marnie to go over the footage from the fires again, looking for faces in the crowds. Our perpetrator is a superstar now – he's viral on the internet, he's made the *New York Times*, the *Sydney Herald* – he must be enjoying himself. There's no way he isn't forcing himself into the story somehow, so let's see if we can find him. I know we've done it before, I know it can seem like a waste of time, but the small things matter.'

'No problem,' DC Marnie acknowledged.

'DS Sanderson is coordinating a survey of recent police incidents involving psychiatric patients to see if there are any leads there, anyone with a grievance against the city, or a predilection for pyromania –'

'So we think our perpetrator is crazy now?' DC Edwards asked.

'That's not a word I'd use, but our killer is certainly very driven, very focused. He's clearly obsessed by fire – or the consequences of fire – and has no regard for human life. The direct nature of the attack on Agnieszka Jarosik suggests that our arsonist is upping his game, becoming less cautious and more aggressive. This might be the end product of his sadism or it might be that he's feeling under pressure. Either way it's not good news for us.'

The team digested this, then Helen carried on.

'There will be a reason why he's doing this, something that's driving him, so let's focus on that.'

'So we're now saying the attacks aren't random?' McAndrew asked.

'It was a valid theory – initially at least – but this is too well planned to be random. The commercial sites targeted have their similarities – all small businesses without expensive security in place – but the domestic properties couldn't be more different in terms of geography, price tag or social class. They were, however, easily accessible, the attacks were methodically executed and even when our perpetrator rushed things – for example, in the attack on Agnieszka Jarosik – he still took the time to lock the door from the outside before leaving. He must have known these people or these properties well, so in addition to witness statements, let's take an interest in people who knew the families and would have walked past these sites every day. Is there a particular job that would take someone there regularly? Posties, refuse collection, social workers, cold callers – anyone who would know the houses and would have come into contact with these families. It's very likely our arsonist is hiding in plain sight, so disregard no one, however respectable or stable they might appear on the surface.'

'We should also look at break-ins,' Charlie offered. 'We had a break-in at the Simms residence and, at the others he walked in bold as brass. He is confident at what he's doing.'

'Good,' Helen responded. 'Let's also look at stalking incidents – any recent reports that might link the three sites. There *has* to be a connection.'

Helen nodded at the nearest DC, who hurried off to set this in train.

'In the meantime,' Helen resumed, 'let's look again at motive.'

'Could he have a thing against women?' Sanderson asked. 'All the murder victims so far have been female. And the attack on Agnieszka was pretty direct. Does he hate women for some reason?'

'Did he know the husbands would be out? That the boys lived on the top floors and were less at risk?' DC Lucas said, overlapping. 'We've had two mothers die, one nanny. Is this about kids and their guardians?'

'Maybe,' Charlie interrupted. 'But it was sheer good fortune that Luke Simms and Ethan Harris survived. Both probably should have died. And what about Alice? The arsonist must have known a young girl would be in bed at the time – so why was she targeted?'

A long silence, which Helen leapt to fill.

'I think we can rule out a financial motive, as the killer has not tried to make contact or issued any demands. Also, it doesn't appear that there is a professional connection – Denise was on benefits and among the others we have an architect, a small businessman and a psychiatrist. So for me the motivation has got to be personal. We know that Agnieszka Jarosik was internet dating, had seen a few guys. Denise might well have been doing likewise. Had Karen Simms been in touch with any old flames however innocently? Unwittingly raised anyone's hopes? This killer wants to destroy these people, destroy these families, so let's climb inside their lives. Everyone has enemies and if we find a link between them, then we have our man.'

There was a brief pause as everyone took this in.

'Now get on with it,' Helen urged them. 'Let's bring this guy in.'

99

Luke Simms stared at himself in the mirror and felt nothing but shame. He had tried his best for his mum and his sister, but to his eyes he still looked ridiculous. His hair had been cut and styled, and make-up applied to conceal his bruises, and his dad had bought him a smart jacket, shirt and tie. But all he could see was his two preposterous legs, cased in plaster and hoisted up in the air on the end of long metal arms. If he wanted to go to his family's funeral, this was how it had to be – his father pushing him along in a specially adapted wheelchair – but it didn't make it any better. He looked comic and it felt as if he was mocking proceedings, rather than paying his respects.

The funeral was only a few hours away now. Luke knew this moment had to come, but now it was here he didn't feel ready. It still didn't seem *real*. His mum and Alice – he had taken their goodness, love and humour for granted, he had taken their presence for granted – and now they were gone. Just like that. Today they would bury them. As if it was all done and dusted. As if they could close that chapter and move on.

They had no home now and only half a family. If Luke was honest, he wasn't even sure he had that. He had asked his dad to stay with him this morning, but something had come up and he'd had to head into town. Where he was going, he wouldn't say. He didn't seem to say much to

Luke since they'd moved in here. He looked after him, dressed his wounds, helped him to the toilet, in and out of bed, did everything that could be expected of him. But he didn't *talk*. Luke wanted to, wanted to find out if his father felt the same sense of emptiness and desolation, the same sense that this was . . . a bad dream with no ending. But his dad never gave him the opportunity. He was so caught up in the business of death.

He didn't really understand how you went about these things. How *did* you organize a funeral? Perhaps in later life, when he was older, he would reflect that he had judged his father harshly. But he nevertheless felt his father was avoiding him. He didn't look him in the eye, didn't engage him in conversations of any length. Was Luke harsh to blame him? Probably. But the truth was Luke missed him. He really missed him. He had lost his beloved mother and sister and now he felt that he was losing his father too.

100

He felt like a marked man.

It wasn't enough that Helen Grace had ruined his career, destroyed his piece of mind and shredded the last vestiges of his self-respect. No, she had left him with a stain – a stain that everyone could see.

He had been exonerated, for God's sake. The police *knew* he wasn't responsible for any of the attacks, yet what did they do about it? Did they trumpet his release as they had his initial arrest? Did they let the world know that he was innocent? No, they put out a two-line statement confirming he'd been released from custody and left it at that.

To the wider world, Richard Ford was still the face in the frame. The hero firefighter turned villain, betraying his colleagues and his calling, revelling in the destruction of his hometown. He was a pariah in Southampton and wherever he went he sensed people's hatred. He had lasted all of an hour in the hotel, hiding in a small room that reeked of bleach, unable to venture out for fear of the abuse and insults that the staff, guests and passers-by were happy to heap on him. One of the cleaners actually spat at him in the corridor. He didn't respond or turn back to seek sanctuary in his room. Instead he broke into a run, sprinting back home.

His house had been defaced of course. Graffiti on the walls and windows, dog shit smeared on the door. But he didn't care. He knew he would be safe here. Having done a quick recce of the interior, he made a list of all the things he would need: padlocks, chains, a crowbar, perhaps a hammer for good measure. He had no idea what the future held, what he would do with his life, but he had resolved to hunker down in his home until he could see a way out of all the darkness.

The guy in Robert Dyas had been surly and hostile. He obviously recognized him from the papers, as did the halfwit in Tesco's who glared at him as she bagged his food. Richard could have sworn he heard her mutter: 'I hope it chokes you' as he left, but he didn't care. He was looking forward to getting home and shutting out the world.

Pushing open the garden gate, he hurried up the path towards the front door. Putting down his shopping, he reached into his pocket to pull out his key. Then suddenly he felt himself flying sideways, careering off the steps and landing hard on the paved path. The right side of his head felt strange – numb and tingling – and he raised his hand to it now, but it was wrenched away roughly.

This time he saw the fist coming. He turned his head to avoid it, but too late, the balled fist crunching into his jaw. His head kicked back, connecting sharply with the hard ground. Suddenly everything went quiet – he couldn't hear properly and his vision was swimming. He tried to wriggle free, but the fist came again. This time he felt two teeth go – though whether he'd swallowed them or they'd fallen out he couldn't say.

Now the rough hands were circling his throat, squeezing hard. And his attacker seemed to be shouting – coarse, violent words tumbling over one another. Richard Ford swung out a fist, but it was hopeless. He was already beaten and he knew it.

Then as suddenly as it started, it stopped. In his confusion and shock, Richard could see a man being dragged away. His attacker tried to escape the hands that now restrained him, lurching back towards him, but he couldn't break free. And now he seemed to give up the fight, slumping to the floor, as those who'd intervened stood guard. And as the passers-by who'd saved his life punched numbers into their mobile phones, Richard Ford tried to focus on his attacker. The man was breathing heavily but now looked up. For a second their eyes met and suddenly Richard knew exactly who he was.

And why he'd come for him.

101

Thomas Simms looked up as Charlie entered the room. He stared at her briefly, then dropped his gaze to the floor, unable or unwilling to look at her.

Charlie had run down to the custody area as soon as she'd heard that Simms had been brought in. Her first reaction to news of the attack on Richard Ford had been shock – it was Karen and Alice's funeral today – then as it became clear that Ford's injuries were superficial and that he had no desire to press charges, her anxiety was tempered with some relief. Ford's desire to avoid any further involvement with the police would save Thomas Simms a day in court.

'Thomas?'

He didn't look up, his face now pressed into his hands. He looked wrung out, exhausted, his dirty, blood-flecked clothes hanging off his thin frame.

'Thomas, you're going to have to talk to me.'

'I don't need to be lectured by you,' he replied suddenly. His tone was abrasive and harsh.

'I'm not going to lecture you, but we need to talk. I know you're upset, I know you're angry, but you can't go around doing things like *this*.'

'Don't tell me what I can and can't do,' Simms replied, now raising his eyes to Charlie. 'He deserved it for what he did to my girls and as soon as I'm out of here I'll be straight back round to finish the jo—'

'He's innocent, Thomas.'

'Bullshit. You had him and you let him go. This is on your head, not mi—'

'He didn't start the fires. *Any* of them.'

'Then who did?'

Charlie hesitated – unsure how best to respond – so Simms renewed his attack.

'You haven't got a clue, have you? You've been chasing your tails since day one.'

'We're doing everything in our power to catch the person responsible,' Charlie countered. 'But believe me when I tell you that you have just attacked an innocent man.'

Finally Charlie's words seemed to land. Thomas Simms glared at her, but said nothing in response.

'You could have killed him and where would that have left Luke? What would you have said to him when you were in the dock? When you were behind bars?'

Thomas stared at the floor once more. Charlie softened her tone:

'I know what you're going through, I know you have doubts about whether we can bring this guy in, but Luke *has* to be your number one priority now. You will have justice, I promise you that, but that is *our* job. Yours is to be with your son.'

Charlie braced herself for an angry comeback, but it never came. Thomas looked up at her sharply, but some of the fire seemed to have gone out of him now.

'Don't abandon him, Thomas. Don't let your anger or your desire for revenge drive a wedge between you. Luke doesn't want any of that. He just wants you.'

Thomas stared at her and then, from nowhere, tears

came, running down his cheeks in thick streams. He wiped them away, but a dam had broken now and he crouched down on the floor, all the tension and misery of the last few days escaping, as his body shook with quiet sobs.

Kneeling down, Charlie put a comforting arm around him.

'Go to him, Thomas. He needs you now more than ever and if you can help him through the days, weeks and months ahead, then you will have done your job. You're all he has.'

Charlie had leads to chase and duties to fulfil but these were forgotten now as she held on to the man who thought he'd lost everything, but still had one very valuable prize to fight for.

102

It all felt alien and wrong. The last few hours had been a grotesque caricature of their ordered, settled lives, and try as they might to regain some kind of normality, life continued to frustrate them.

Jacqueline Harris's nerves were shot. She was of course relieved that Ethan was largely unharmed, but their home was a smoking ruin, their nanny was dead and they now found themselves here – in a hastily rented apartment in Upper Shirley. They had taken it because it was large, available and close to their former neighbourhood, but standing here now in the bland, sterile space, Jacqueline suddenly felt they'd made a mistake. The whole place felt cold and unwelcoming.

Ethan had gone to bed to rest – he had a nice enough bedroom out the back with a good view – and Michael had stepped outside to call the nanny agency. She didn't know whether it would fall to them or the agency to inform Agnieszka's relatives of her death, but she had ducked the issue anyway, landing that one on Michael. She had enough on her plate already – dealing with Ethan, liaising with the insurance company, organizing a new home help, not to mention fielding the endless press calls and follow-up questions from the police. How had their life suddenly become *this*?

She'd tried to engage Ethan in conversation, thinking

it was better for him to be occupied, but he'd only managed five minutes before flaking out. Leaving her alone in this horrible, unfamiliar place. She hoped that Michael would hurry up and come back. She'd never been very good at being on her own. She checked her emails again – a deluge of sympathy messages – and her BlackBerry for a third time. But it was all just distraction – an attempt to pretend that life was going on as normal. But who was she kidding? Someone had tried to kill their son last night, had razed their house to the ground, and she had no idea why. Would they strike again? Or had they achieved all that they hoped for last night?

Not for the first time today, Jacqueline craved a drink. She knew she shouldn't – couldn't – but she longed for one nevertheless. She was lonely, miserable and scared – and terrified of what was still to come.

103

Mandy Blayne was smiling, but it was all an act.

She had cooked Darren a full English as usual and he was wolfing it down opposite her. He never left a scrap and always said it was the best breakfast in Southampton. But that never made him stay. He had dropped several hints during the course of last night that he'd be moving on in the morning – he said it was work, but Mandy was sure that was a lie. She knew he had other women on the go. He always denied it of course, angered by the suggestion, but she could smell it on him when he arrived.

He often turned up unannounced, knowing he'd always get a warm welcome. Mandy was a fool to herself, she knew that, but she loved him. Pure and simple. She shouldn't but she did. And when he did come, when he was here with her, things always seemed better. They'd have a few beers, watch a bit of TV, then go upstairs for a cuddle. And that's where they'd stay – often spending a whole weekend in bed. Darren always joked that he needed a good breakfast in the morning to regain his strength after what they got up to.

This time had been different of course. She'd been building herself up to telling him she was pregnant since the moment he turned up on her door with a bunch of roses in his hand. He'd been away from her for nearly seven weeks and her depression this time round was compounded by the realization that she'd missed her period. She had put off buying a pregnancy test, hoping against hope that she was just late, but in the end she had to know. The positive result sent her mood plunging still further, then later when she'd had time to think, she'd half wondered if it might be a good thing. Was this the start of a different future for Mandy?

She'd meant to tell him before they had dinner. Then, having failed to do that, she vowed to tell him before they went upstairs. But when it came to it, she didn't want to tell him, didn't want to risk spoiling the evening, so they'd tumbled into bed together as usual. He never used protection, it never seemed to enter his head to do so. She thought she'd had this covered, but obviously she hadn't.

After that the moment had passed. If she told him now, it would be like she'd sprung it on him. Accepted the flowers, the booze, the company and then handed him an unpleasant bill for his services. All her fond hopes that he might actually be pleased evaporated and she knew instinctively that he would run a mile if he thought she was trying to tie him down. She couldn't risk that, so she said nothing.

She had decided to get it dealt with. She would go to the doctor and see what he could give her. He'd try to talk through the options, but she had made up her mind. She wasn't ready to be a mother. Wouldn't wish it on the poor kid anyway.

There'd be no one to comfort her afterwards. She'd come back to her little two up, two down, in St Denys, shut the door and hear the silence. Maybe she'd cry for a bit. Or have a smoke. Either way she'd end up spending the night alone, clutching a mug of tea and watching the TV. And that would be her lot.

Nothing interesting ever happened in her life.

104

'I'd like to start by apologizing.'

Helen was anxious to get this over with so came straight to the point. So much had happened since her awkward interview with Gardam last night that for a while she had put it from her mind. But there was too much going on in the investigation, too much overlap between her and her boss, for the issue not to be addressed.

'I'm sorry if I embarrassed you last night. That was never my intention.'

'It's fine, Helen. There's no need to apologize.'

'There is and I've done so, so I hope we can move on –'

'And not mention it again. It was just a misunderstanding, nothing more.'

'I'm glad you see it that way. Thank you.'

'Of course and the offer still stands. Sarah and I *would* like to have you round at some point, so we can get to know you in a less formal environment.'

'That sounds very pleasant. We'll find a date.'

Helen tried to sound upbeat and enthusiastic, though in truth she had no desire to be given a tour of Gardam's home and marriage. There seemed no way she could wriggle out of it now, however, so it was probably best to bite the bullet and follow through on her promise.

'Good. Well that was all I came to say, so I'd better –'

'Is everything ok, Helen? I don't mean between us,

I mean more generally. I noticed you wincing just now, when you sat down. Have you hurt yourself in some way?'

Helen said nothing, ambushed by Gardam's question. The truth was she ached all over today. Her back and shoulders were black and blue and her neck felt like it had seized up completely. It was excruciatingly painful and though her stash of painkillers had taken the edge off it, she wasn't moving any more freely.

'I know you're the sort to put a brave face on it,' Gardam continued. 'But it's my job to make sure my best officers are fit and happy. You always put your body on the line, for which I know you receive very little gratitude from the public or indeed our friends in the fourth estate.'

'I know we're under scrutiny, sir, but you don't need to worry about me.'

Gardam was referring to the latest edition of the *Southampton Evening News*, a copy of which languished in his bin. Pretty much the entire paper was a hatchet job on Helen's handing of the investigation. It had riled Helen when she first saw it – Emilia Garanita revealing her true colours by choosing the very worst moment to break their truce – but she had put it from her mind now. There was too much going on to worry about tomorrow's chip paper.

'I'm not concerned about what the papers say,' Gardam assured her, 'or what our two-faced MP is accusing us of on the phone-ins. What I *do* care about is the smooth and effective running of our investigations and hand in hand with that the health and well-being of my best officer.'

Helen nodded, as Gardam asked:

'So is everything ok? I don't want to overstep the mark

here, but is anything bothering you? Is there anything I can do to help?'

Helen looked at Gardam, knowing she had to make a split-second decision. The right thing to do was to tell Gardam about her confrontation with Max Paine and let him decide what to do about it. If she didn't and her leadership of their present investigation was compromised by subsequent revelations, then he would have to suspend or sack her – and rightly so. It wouldn't be fair on him, the investigation or the victims' families to lie about her actions, but even as she opened her mouth to begin, she found herself saying:

'Old war wound. I'll be better in a day or so.'

Gardam asked her a few more questions – he seemed to be genuinely concerned for her – but eventually appeared satisfied with her explanation. As Helen left she knew that whatever the rights and wrongs of it, she didn't feel able to let someone else into her own private – largely dysfunctional – world. She knew that she would have to deal with Paine herself and already had a sense of what needed to be done. She was so deep in thought, turning the various possibilities over in her mind, that she initially didn't realize McAndrew was standing in front of her, blocking her path.

'Sorry to disturb you, boss. But I think I may have found something.'

105

Helen and McAndrew were closeted away in Helen's office, a list of dates and times in front of them. The door was closed, the blind down – this was a private conversation for now.

'So I went back over the witness statements, the call operator logs, emergency service reports, and I found something interesting about the most recent fire. Agnieszka Jarosik crashed out on her sofa after a busy day's work and while she was watching TV sent a few texts, posted a little on Facebook. The last text was sent at eleven fourteen p.m. The text looks genuine, so we can assume that she was still awake at that point. She probably fell asleep soon afterwards. Not long after that our arsonist entered the house.'

Helen nodded – so far nothing unexpected. They had found partial footprints outside the back door, but nothing that was of any tangible use.

'Several people called the fire in. They were mostly neighbours who saw the smoke and flames and were worried that their own million-pound houses were about to go up.'

Helen let that one go – she knew McAndrew lived in a one-bed flat and was vocally bitter about it.

'These calls came in in a flurry. Call operator logs show

that they came in at 11.50, two at 11.51, 11.53, 11.54 – pretty much the whole street got in on the act.'

'I'm sure they did.'

'But one call came significantly earlier than that. At eleven thirty-eight – a full twelve minutes before the others.'

Now McAndrew had Helen's attention.

'Interestingly, this call didn't come from a neighbour, it came from a payphone. And here's the thing. It came from a payphone two streets away – there's no way the caller could have seen the fire from there.'

'So they saw the fire and ran to the nearest payphone?'

'Possibly, but how come they saw this fire a full twelve minutes before anyone else? And why didn't they stick around to help? If Agnieszka stopped texting at eleven fifteen p.m., she probably didn't go to sleep immediately, so the arsonist gained entry at, what, eleven twenty-five p.m.? Eleven thirty? The fire was initially contained in the basement. The sofa burnt well, but it took a while for the fire to spread upwards as the basement stairwell did not connect with the main stairs.'

'So on that basis,' Helen said, picking up McAndrew's thread, 'the most likely explanation is that the arsonist set the fire at around eleven thirty p.m., left and walked the five-minute walk to the nearest payphone and called it in.'

'It's a theory,' McAndrew replied calmly.

'Ok, get me the audio from every fire over the last few days. I want to see if our arsonist has been in on the act from day one.'

McAndrew was halfway to the door when Helen called out:

'One other thing. You didn't say if the caller was male or female?'

There was a small pause, before McAndrew looked up at her and said:

'Female.'

106

Thomas knelt down, so that he was at eye level with his son. Luke smiled awkwardly at him and in that moment Thomas saw that Charlie Brooks had been right. He had been guilty of neglecting his son, just when he needed his father most. He felt deep shame and sadness rise up in him and, not trusting himself to speak, simply stroked his son's cheek. Tears immediately appeared in his son's eyes, mirrored now in his own and he dropped his gaze to his son's tie, which was characteristically askew. Gently, he straightened it for him.

'I messed up today, son,' Thomas said eventually. 'I should have been here with you, but I wasn't. Instead I let my emotions get the better of me and well . . . this is the result.'

He grimaced ruefully, as he gestured to the scratches on his face.

Luke returned the smile, but it was unconvincing – riven with anxiety and fear. Once again Thomas felt deep guilt at having put his own needs – his own anger – before his son's happiness.

'We'll need to be off in a little while, so I wanted to have a little chat with you first.'

Luke nodded cautiously, so Thomas proceeded:

'I . . . I haven't been a very good dad the last few days. I won't try to excuse my behaviour, all I will say is that I've been struggling a bit. I never prepared for . . . this.'

Luke stared at him, but Thomas was pleased to see there was no judgement in his expression.

'So we're going to have to find our way together, if that's ok. Starting with today. You'll never have to face anything as hard as what you're about to do. There will be a lot of people at the funeral, there will be others – journalists, well-wishers – on the periphery. They will all want to talk to you, they'll all want to offer you support, to ask you questions, to check that you're ok. The answer is of course not, but they'll ask anyway. And in the middle of all that, we're going to have to . . . to say goodbye to Mum and Ali. A boy your age should never have to face something like this and I'm so, so sorry that you have to now. But – and this is the important bit – you won't have to face it alone, ok? I'm going to be by your side every step of the way. Everything we face from now on, we face together.'

Luke said nothing, simply folding his father into an embrace and nestling his wet face into his shoulder. Thomas held him as he cried and for the first time since that awful night felt some strength returning to him.

As he hugged his son tight, he said a silent prayer for his wife and daughter. For his lovely son. And for the sage counsel of Charlie Brooks.

107

The pair of them sat in total silence.

Helen had commandeered an interview suite and asked McAndrew to join her. The table was covered with tapes from the call operators from the fire, police and ambulance services. The simple tape player in the centre of the table had been connected to speakers and McAndrew had turned the volume up high as they listened to the recordings.

There had been several female callers during the course of the three nights who'd reported the fires. Some sounded scared, others sounded panicked, all sounded breathless.

'There – it's the same one,' Helen said, pausing the tape.

They had been listening to the calls from the first night. At around 11.50 p.m., a young woman had called 999, reporting a fire at a house in Millbrook – the Simms residence. And the voice on the tape sounded virtually identical to the early caller from the most recent blaze in Lower Shirley.

'Do you agree that it's the same caller?' Helen asked, turning to McAndrew. A brief pause, then her junior nodded. Helen was pleased – she felt likewise and had a feeling they were about to catch a major break in the case.

They moved straight on to the tapes from the second night of fires. Here they hit a blank, however. There were thirteen female callers. The quality on some of the recordings was better than others, because of bad mobile reception and background noise, so it was hard to say for certain – but neither of them could divine their mystery caller among the collage of anguished voices.

Then suddenly Helen leant forward with purpose, scooping up the recording from the first night. She played their female caller once, then again, listening intently each time. The woman's voice was clear and authoritative.

'There's a fire, like, a big one on Hillside Crescent. You need to get here now.'

'Are you able to see the fire from where you are?'

'For real. And there are people *in* there. So hurry up.'

'Ok, I need you to step away from the fire now . . .'

Helen stopped the tape without warning and, flipping open the tape recorder, started to play the woman's recording from the third night again. McAndrew made no attempt to interrupt her – she could tell Helen was utterly focused on the task in hand, scenting something.

The recording finished. Helen clicked it off, then sat back in her chair.

'I think I know who it is.'

McAndrew looked up at her.

'It's the way she says "For real", and the accent. I knew I'd heard it before.'

'Who is it?' McAndrew asked urgently.

Helen paused for a moment, before replying.

'It's Naomie Jackson.'

108

Sharon Jackson's face turned pale the minute she opened the door. Helen and DS Sanderson had left Southampton Central straight away and raced over to Naomie's home in the cheaper part of St Mary's. The look on the officers' faces betrayed the seriousness of their visit. Normally Sharon would have fobbed them off – she was experienced at dealing with the law – but there was no wriggling off the hook today.

She sat on the sofa, a look of blank incomprehension on her face, as Helen informed her that Naomie was now a person of interest in their investigation. Sanderson had gone upstairs in order to verify Sharon's assertion that her daughter was not at home. She had not yet returned, but Helen had pressed on nevertheless. For her part, Sharon Jackson was shocked by Helen's line of questioning and pushed back hard.

'You're barking up the wrong tree. My Naomie would never do something like that. She *loves* kids.'

Helen let that non sequitur go and continued with her questions.

'Where is Naomie now, Sharon?'

'I've told you I'm expecting her back later, but it's Friday, isn't it . . . I don't keep tabs on her.'

'Clearly not. I'm going to need you to account for her movements on Tuesday, Wednesday and Thursday nights.'

Sharon suddenly looked less bullish, so Helen was quick to follow up.

'Where were you? And where was Naomie?'

'Tuesday night I was in and so was Naomie. Then we had a bit of a falling out and she left for a bit.'

'What time?'

'Around nine p.m.'

'When did she return?'

'Late. I'd gone to bed. I heard her come in, but I don't know what time it was.'

'And the other nights?'

'I was out.'

'Both nights?'

'That's not a crime, is it? I can't spend my life here, I've got things to do, friends and that.'

'And Naomie was here?'

'She was when I left. We weren't really speaking, so I don't know if she stayed in or not. She said she was going to bed . . .'

Helen made a mental note to check for signs of internet use at the property, phone calls and so on – it wouldn't be too hard to work out if Naomie had been at home or not.

'Why weren't you talking?'

Once again, Sharon suddenly looked coy.

'We had a row.'

'About?'

'Man trouble.'

'Hers or yours?'

'Hers. She's a moaning little brat. But that's all she is, I swear. She's had run-ins with the police before. A bit of shoplifting, but just kids' stuff. She could never do something like this. She doesn't have the balls.'

'Has Naomie mentioned the fires to you?' Helen continued.

'No' was the swift reply.

'Did that strike you as odd? Everybody else in Southampton is talking about them.'

Sharon shrugged then said:

'Naomie doesn't follow the news, she's not that kind of kid. Probably wouldn't talk to me about it even if she did. We've never been . . . a good fit.'

It was said so matter-of-factly that for a moment Helen was speechless.

'Who would she talk to?' Helen said eventually. 'Does she have friends? Anyone she hangs out with?'

Sharon thought about it, then said:

'She doesn't really have mates, she's always been a bit of a loner, y'know.'

'Where does she hang out, then?' Helen repeated, insistent.

'She goes to the library sometimes when it's cold. Other than that she goes where she can get up to mischief. The pubs on Oakland Street, the Common, the skateboard park, the WestQuay centre, the parade . . .'

The list went on. Clearly Naomie wanted to be anywhere but home. Helen noted down the many locations down – intending to pass them on to the rest of the team at the earliest opportunity – but before she had finished Sanderson returned, clutching several different copies of the *Southampton Evening News*.

'Found these in a plastic bag under her bed. A copy of

this week's editions which lead on the fires. There's also cuttings from several of the national dailies about the attacks as well. I guess Naomie's a bit more interested in these fires than she lets on.'

Helen was already on her feet and heading for the front door. At long last, they had a prime suspect.

109

'Do you want to go public with this?'

Helen was on her phone, pacing back and forth outside Sharon Jackson's house. Gardam was back at base, supervising the investigation into Naomie's call history, digital footprint, police records, known associates and more. It was important they worked closely together on this one, so Helen had stepped outside and called him straight away.

'I don't think we have a choice,' Helen replied. 'It's already gone lunchtime. If she's planning another attack tonight, then we've only got a few hours to stop her. The eyes and ears of the public are our best resource at this point.'

'Have we got a decent photo?'

'I'm sending one through to you now. If we can line up media liaison, so they're ready to go public with it immediately –'

'I've got McAndrew drafting a press release now.'

'Good.'

Helen took a breath. The last couple of hours seemed to have passed in a flash and she suddenly felt tired.

'How sure are you? That it's her.'

'She's our best bet. She has deliberately inserted herself into the investigation on three separate occasions. Two phone calls, plus a positive ID after the second fire, which succeeded in sending us off on a wild goose chase with Richard Ford. She may not come across as capable of much, but she's been instrumental in how this thing has played out. I think there's a lot more going on under the surface than we give her credit for.'

'Ok, let's do it then and see if we can bring her in before nightfall.'

Helen rang off and, gathering herself, marched back towards Sharon Jackson's house. Finally, the net was closing.

110

'Twenty Marlboro Gold, please.'

The Asian guy behind the counter barely looked up from his newspaper. Reaching behind him, he pulled a pack of cigarettes from the shelves behind him and tossed them on to the counter.

'Nine pounds fifty.'

It was daylight robbery, but that was hardly the point. The shopkeeper took the ten-pound note, handed over the change and resumed reading the cricket reports. It was all so easy – no suspicions, no interest, nothing. Just a simple exchange, so ordinary in its execution, but presaging so much.

Turning to leave, the hooded figure suddenly stopped. The yawning shopkeeper continued to turn the pages, blissfully unaware of who he'd just come into contact with. But the TV on the wall behind him was better informed.

> Breaking News: Police name suspect in Southampton arson attack.

The caption was brief and to the point, but it was what was beneath that was more alarming. An extreme close-up of a family snap in which all Naomie's imperfections – as well as her crooked smile – were revealed in perfect definition. Turning quickly, the figure fled, before the owner even looked up.

III

All was quiet in Mandy Blayne's house, except for the TV news, which played quietly in the living room. Naomie Jackson's face stared out from the screen, but looked on to an empty room. Mandy Blayne had briefly vacated the sofa to make herself a much needed cup of tea.

As she stared out of the window into the scrubby garden, Mandy could feel her mood edging ever lower. She had made the call to the doctor's surgery and booked an appointment for next week, but even now she wondered if she would actually go. She had to get rid of this baby, obviously. What would she do with it? How would she support it? And yet suddenly the thought of disposing of it so casually filled her with sadness and doubt. What if this was her only chance of having a baby? What if she never found someone to be with and ended up alone? She didn't want either outcome and the choice made her miserable. Why did her life always seem to end up in no-win situations?

She poured the boiling water into the cup and grabbed the milk from the fridge. She had bought value teabags to save a few pennies, but it had been a mistake. They were weak and the resulting tea was bland and milky. Another small disappointment to add to her larger reversals. Odd to think though that there was a small thing inside her that would feed off the food and drink she took in tonight.

Strange to imagine that it was already dependent on her. It was getting dark outside now, but she could still make out the small strip of grass, bordered by neat beds, and for a moment had a vision of a small child playing outside. Hands covered in sand, face sticky with dirt, a broad smile on its face. Like she had been, when she was a child. An outdoors kid never happier than when dirty and pleasantly exhausted. Mandy found herself smiling at the thought. It would be crazy to keep the baby, wouldn't it?

Cradling her cup of tea, Mandy walked through the hall and into the lounge. Picking up the remote, she flicked the TV off and went upstairs. She couldn't be bothered to watch the news – she just wanted to relax in a bath and switch off for a while. She would read a book, disengage her brain, and try and con herself into feeling tired. Pretend that this was just another cosy Friday night in. But, for all her efforts, Mandy couldn't rid of herself of the feeling that – however hard she tried to distract herself – she was in store for a sleepless night.

112

'I'm getting tired of this game. So either you answer me now, or I drag you out of here in cuffs.'

Helen didn't like threatening people, but she had had her fill of Sharon Jackson's lies and obfuscations. Sharon had finally confessed that her daughter had taken to doing her own laundry of late, wasting unnecessary amounts of fabric conditioner in washing a single hooded top and a pair of trousers. Add this to the number of newspaper cuttings Sanderson had found stored under her bed and the fact that Sharon couldn't find a packet of matches she'd only bought last week and a clear picture was starting to emerge.

But Naomie's motive remained unclear, which concerned Helen. Sharon Jackson insisted her daughter didn't know any of the victims, but Helen could tell she was lying and was determined to find out why.

'Don't push me on this. I'm more than happy to do it, but it wouldn't look too good in tomorrow's newspapers.'

Sharon finally looked up at her.

'Take a peek out of your front curtains, Sharon.'

Unnerved, Sharon did as instructed. Helen had heard the press trucks start to pull up outside a few minutes ago. She knew they'd be here within the hour, once Naomie's name was released.

'They won't be going anywhere until this is over. So we

have three choices. I can lead you out in front of them. I can leave here and let them loose on you. Or I can get a uniformed officer on the door, so there's a chance you might get a moment's peace. The choice is yours.'

Sharon sat down hard on the nearest armchair and ran her fingers through her long, lank hair. She seemed to be ageing in front of Helen, as if buried fears were now burrowing their way to the surface.

'She's never met Denise Roberts but she might know *of* her,' she said finally and with great reluctance.

'How?'

There was another long pause, and then:

'Naomie's father. His name's Darren Betts. I was at school with him and we've been knocking around on and off for twenty years now.'

'He's your boyfriend?'

Sharon snorted, then said:

'When he feels like it.'

'He has other girlfriends?'

Sharon nodded.

'Denise Roberts,' Helen asked, suddenly making the connection. Callum Roberts had mentioned a 'Darren' too.

'When he's not here, Darren sometimes goes . . . there.'

Sharon Jackson said the last word with utter disdain, as if Roberts were shit on her shoe. Sanderson was sure Roberts probably felt the same way about her.

'Is that what your row with Naomie was about?'

'Guess so.'

'What happened?'

'Nothing. We argued, that's all.'

'What happened, Sharon?'

'She drove Darren away, didn't she,' Sharon responded, her tone suddenly plaintive and self-pitying. 'She fusses around him, trying to get him to do stuff he doesn't want to do, gets in his face, you know?'

'What did you do?'

'I shouted at her a bit.'

'And?'

Sharon said nothing, staring at the floor.

'AND?'

'I gave her a bit of a slap, all right.'

'You *hit* her?'

'I shouldn't have, but she's just so fucking clingy . . . and sometimes I lose it. I hit her a bit –'

'More than once? Did you *beat* her? Sharon, I'm asking you a question –'

'Yes, I've told you. I took a belt to her, but I didn't do any permanent harm. It's no more than what I had done to me when I was a kid –'

'And she knew this Denise Roberts, she knew that her father went there when he wasn't here?'

'Yes, she heard me and Darren talking about it. She's not stupid.'

'Jesus Christ. What about the other places? The Simms house in Millbrook or the Harris place in Shirley? Does he go there?'

Sharon suddenly laughed.

'Are you crazy? Folk like that wouldn't let him in the front door. He wouldn't be knocking around in *those* parts of town.'

'You're sure?'

'Be sensible, will you?'

Helen didn't like her tone, but let it go.

'Do you have any other boyfriends?'

'No.'

'Sharon –'

'I don't, ok, I'm not like that. Darren . . . well, he's all I've got. And I've only got him part-time.'

Her bitterness and loneliness shone through clearly now. Though Helen didn't want to believe her – didn't want to lose the connection between Naomie and her victims – what she said seemed genuine and made sense. The worlds inhabited by the various victims were all so different.

Helen stared at Sharon, her mind whirring. Then suddenly she said:

'Is there anywhere else Darren goes? You said he had other girlfriends on the go.'

This time Sharon hesitated and Helen knew immediately that she'd hit a nerve.

'I know this isn't nice, but I need to know. It's the last thing I'll ask you.'

'There's one other girl that I know of. Lives over in St Denys.'

'What's her name?'

There was another long pause, then, as Sharon debated how to respond:

'What's her name, Sharon?'

'Her name is Mandy Blayne.'

113

She had been in the bathroom for over twenty minutes now. Was she having a bath? The lights were all off downstairs and she'd drawn the bathroom curtains, so it seemed a safe assumption. Normally it would be better to wait until she'd definitely gone to bed, but there was no time for that now and this seemed like too good an opportunity to miss.

Crossing the road quickly, the hooded figure pushed the side gate open and made its way towards the back of the house. There was no hesitation – the house had been recced a number of times and there was one obvious entry point. The French doors that opened on to the garden were old and flimsy, made of decrepit wood and glass. Mandy liked her gardening and often left the doors open. Today they were closed and locked, but it was still only a couple of moments' work to put an elbow through one of the panes and release the latch from the other side.

Stepping inside, the hooded figure paused. Upstairs, music played on the radio – a cheesy power ballad designed to uplift and inspire – and accompanying it was the distinct sound of someone bathing, water splashing on plastic as Mandy Blayne tried to wash away her mediocrity. If she were clever Mandy would stay in the bath once she smelt the fire, but even that wouldn't save her – she would just be cooked alive rather than burnt to death.

Teasing open the understairs cupboard, the figure bent down to examine the contents. It was depressingly empty – like Mandy's life – but there were a few wooden garden chairs that would do the job. Dragging them together into a pile, the figure pulled a bottle of paraffin from a side pocket and emptied the whole contents over the wood. No point in caution or finesse now.

Retrieving the pack of Marlboro Gold, the figure removed a single cigarette and bound it to the pack with a pink rubber band. Moments later, the matches were out. The match head was soon poised against the rough side of the box, ready for ignition, when suddenly the landline rang out, shrill and loud. Startled, the figure dropped the match and in bending down to retrieve it succeeded in spilling the entire contents of the box on to the floor.

'Shit.'

The phone continued to ring and for a moment the intruder stood stock still, straining to hear if Mandy would leave the bath to answer it. The volume of the radio was suddenly turned down, as the phone rang on. The figure tensed, turning its body in the direction of the back of the house, ready to run if need be. Still the phone rang on – it must have been twenty-five, possibly thirty rings already. Someone was clearly very keen to get hold of Mandy.

Then suddenly the ringing stopped. The figure could hear its own breathing, could feel the blood pounding in its ears. Backing out now was unthinkable – Blayne had it coming to her – but there was no virtue in getting caught either. What would Mandy do now? It felt as if the whole enterprise had come down to this moment.

Would Mandy mess everything up by coming down the stairs? Or would the stupid whore stay put?

The music rose in volume again and now the figure didn't hesitate, grabbing at the matches. They were wet and sticky, clinging doggedly to the floor that was now saturated with paraffin. It was hard to get any purchase on them with gloves, so throwing caution to the wind, the figure pulled the gloves off and picked up a match. Even now, though, the match seemed determined to resist, falling to the floor once more from the figure's unsteady hand.

Now Mandy's mobile started ringing, urgent and insistent. It was on the hall table not five feet away. Would this finally pique Mandy's curiosity? There was no point hanging around to find out so, snatching up the match, the figure dragged it down the side of the box. It flared up impressively, thanks to its soaking in paraffin, and the figure suddenly found itself laughing – with relief as much as joy. Seconds later, the match hit the pile of chairs and instantly they were consumed by flames. This had been an amateur performance, a travesty of all the careful planning and preparation – the Marlboro pack tossed in casually as an afterthought – but the job had finally been done.

RIP Mandy Blayne.

114

How do you sum up a life?

It was a question Thomas Simms had asked himself repeatedly as he'd made plans for the girls' funeral. When you're deep in shock and assaulted by grief, how do you find the right way to pay tribute to someone – to two people – whom you loved more than life itself? It was an impossible task, but it had to be done – the thought of drying up while making the funeral oration was too horrific for words.

For a long time the answer had eluded him. There were so many amazing things he could say about Karen and Alice, but each time he gathered their many virtues – the many happy memories – together, he was crippled by his sense of loss, unable to think or say anything that wasn't steeped in bitterness and regret. And nobody wanted to hear that.

But now, as Thomas pushed his son up the church aisle in a wheelchair, he suddenly knew what he would say. There was one thing that had struck him with real force this morning as he'd straightened his son's tie and wiped the tears from his freckled face. And that was that Karen and Alice, though gone, *would* live on – through Luke. They all had the same colouring and shared many of the same mannerisms. His hazel eyes were identical to Alice's and when he laughed his nose crinkled up – that was pure

Karen. They had similar beliefs and shared the same daft sense of humour – many was the time they had all been reduced to hysterics by the *Airplane* movies. They were so similar in so many ways and Thomas was surprised at how much comfort that now gave him.

He felt himself start to smile, then immediately swallowed it back down. People wouldn't understand and he couldn't be bothered to explain himself to disapproving relatives. But the feeling was real and Thomas clung to it now as he prepared himself for the most difficult two hours of his life.

'Dad?'

Thomas looked down to find Luke's eyes fixed on him.

'Can you hear that?'

Thomas had been so lost in his own thoughts that he hadn't heard a thing. But he knew instantly what his son was referring to. Even above the sombre tones of the organ, loud sirens could now be heard. One, two, three emergency vehicles, maybe more, racing past the church on their way somewhere fast.

'Do you think it's . . . ?' Luke began.

'No, son. It's probably just a false alarm. Nothing to do with us, so don't worry.'

Thomas was determined that his son would not be ruled by fear. There were still many questions to be answered, many painful discoveries to make perhaps, but he refused to let his son spend his life jumping at shadows. Someone had tried to destroy his family and they had failed – Luke's happiness and confidence would be Thomas's riposte to the person who had tried to break them. Though his son was still working his way through his injuries, both mental and physical, it was Thomas's job to see that he made it out the other side in one piece. As he pushed Luke to his place next to the front-row pews, Thomas knew that this was it for him now – his job was to guide his son safely through the next few years until he could stand on his own two feet. And that, Thomas reflected, was something that *he* shared with Karen. Had she been in his shoes, she would have done exactly the same.

115

She jumped from plank to plank, enjoying the simple pleasure of the game. When she'd been little, she'd played it with other truants, pretending that if you misjudged your jump and landed on the stones that separated the railway sleepers, then you'd fall through the tracks and straight down to Hell.

Later, when Naomie was older, the game had taken a more sinister turn. She would walk the railway track alone, challenging a train to appear in front of her. To alleviate her boredom she would set herself challenges, determining to walk to a certain point on the track, regardless of whether a train appeared or not. No train ever did, so she'd never had the chance to test her courage, to see whether she would have held her nerve. But she always thought she would've seen it through, if the cards had fallen that way.

But now things were going her way and suddenly she felt the vibrations on the tracks and, moments later, the unmistakable growl of a train approaching. It was like she could do no wrong at the moment and she laughed out loud – had *she* summoned the train? Was the world finally dancing to her tune? This was nonsense of course but it was a nice fantasy to indulge in. She paused to listen, revelling in the slow but steady growth in volume, as the train hastened towards her.

Now it was coming into view, arcing round the curved

track a hundred feet ahead, before straightening up to charge directly at her. Still she didn't move. She felt in control of the situation, as if the train were just a character in her movie. Her feet were glued to the tracks as they had been so many times before. But she felt no fear now, only exhilaration and joy.

A sharp blast of the train's horn made her look up. The driver had spotted her and was sounding his horn frantically. She made no attempt to move, so now he applied the emergency brake, metal colliding with metal in a hideous scream. But it was too little, too late. Naomie had chosen her spot well and there was no way he would be able to stop in time.

So many times she'd dreamt of this moment, had seen her own destruction in a shattering explosion of blood and bone. Whenever the world was black and her bruises smarted, she had *longed* for this moment. But things were different now so even as the train careered towards her, as the driver repeatedly gestured to her to move, she simply smiled, raised her middle finger and stepped out of the way of the screeching train, before calmly walking away.

Things *were* different now. Now she had something to live for.

116

'They'll be here in five minutes. What do you want to do?'

Sanderson's voice was as tense as her expression. Following Sharon Jackson's tipoff, she and Helen had raced over to Mandy Blayne's house, gaining a head start on the emergency services. Helen had called them in as a precaution, but as reports of a house fire in St Denys began to filter through via police radio, it became clear to both of them that they had been too slow to stop Naomie's latest attack.

Helen paused, before responding to Sanderson's question. Mandy's house was ablaze and there was no sign of its unfortunate owner. Smoke billowed out of the windows on both floors, but more so on the lower level suggesting the fire had not fully taken hold yet. Was Mandy even in there? Helen couldn't be sure, but Naomie hadn't put a foot wrong so far, so they had to assume the worst. Waiting for the emergency services to arrive was the sensible thing to do, but the whole house might have gone up by then, by which point any chance of rescuing Mandy would have passed.

'We've got to go in,' Helen replied, already marching towards the back of the house. The front door was locked from the inside and Helen felt sure that Naomie would have entered the house from the rear, where her trespassing would go undetected. 'But I'm going in alone. You wait here and –'

'No chance,' Sanderson replied firmly. She had let Helen go into a fire on her own before and the memory still haunted her. 'If you're going in, so am I.'

Helen nodded her assent – there was no time to argue now – and they marched round to the back door. As Helen expected, one of the panes had been broken and the open door lolled on his hinges. Helen hurried inside, Sanderson close behind. Immediately, they were assaulted by an intense heat and smothered by a cloud of thick smoke that made it impossible to see each other, let alone the geography of the room. Grabbing Sanderson before she lost sight of her completely, Helen dragged her junior officer back out of the house to safety.

'What now?' Sanderson barked through a coughing fit.

Helen was already casting her eyes over the back of the house for another means of entry. There was no shed, no sign of anything that might contain a ladder, so acting on instinct Helen grabbed a wheelie bin and rammed it up against the wall.

'Climb on and give me a hand up,' she said quickly.

Before she had finished her sentence, Sanderson was on top of it, holding out her hand to pull Helen up. Helen climbed up and pressing her heel into Sanderson's interlinked hands made a sudden, upwards lunge for the first-floor windowsill. Her fingers scrambled up the rough brickwork and just as she felt her body begin to fall again after its swift ascent, she caught hold of the windowsill with three fingers of her left hand. She hung there for a moment, out of Sanderson's reach now and suddenly exposed, before, swinging her body to the right, she managed to get some purchase with her other hand. Now the momentum was with her and, using her legs to push herself up the brickwork, she jammed first one elbow, then the other on to the narrow sill.

The window was a cheap double-glazed unit and Helen was relieved to see that the small ventilation window at the top was ajar. Manoeuvring her right knee on to the sill, Helen pushed upwards and, catching hold of the lip of the open window, hauled herself upright. Reaching down inside, she levered the main window open and seconds later she was crawling along the floor of what appeared to be the spare bedroom, keeping her head as low as possible and her eyes pointed down, moving in the thin layer of clear air underneath the blanket of smoke.

'Mandy?'

Her shout was loud, but seemed to rebound off the dense smoke. There was no reply. Crawling out on to the landing, Helen made to move towards what she assumed was the master bedroom, then stopped in her tracks, her eyes drawn to another door which remained firmly shut. Instinct now guided her towards it and as she neared it she heard a strange noise from inside. Signs of life? It was the most unnatural, animalistic noise she had ever heard, but as she reached the door Helen realized that the sounds emanating from behind the door were *human* – a grotesque mixture of coughing, gasping and crying.

'Mandy?'

Still no reply, so moving up into a crouched position, Helen covered her hand with her sleeve and forced the handle down. Pushing inside, she was relieved to see a young woman cowering in the bathtub in front of her.

She had made the right call in coming here, but their escape now depended on swift and decisive action. Helen was already beginning to feel light-headed as the smoke crept into her mouth and nose, despite her attempts to shield herself from its effects. It took her back to her last major case and a scene she'd rather forget.

'Mandy, I'm a police officer. I'm here to help you, but we need to go now.'

The naked woman in the bathtub looked at her as if she was mad. She stared at Helen uncomprehendingly, stunned by this sudden apparition in her bathroom.

'Mandy, *please*.'

Helen took another step towards her, offering her hand. But to Helen's alarm, Mandy backed away, crouching down into the water, raising her arms to fight off her attacker. She was screaming now, high and keening, her whole body trapped in a suffocating panic that would be the death of her – and possibly Helen too.

Helen reached forward but was beaten back. Flicking Mandy's flailing arm aside, Helen lunged for her now, but as she did so felt the woman's teeth sinking into her arm. Withdrawing her arm sharply, she now feinted to the left, drawing Mandy's defence that way, before slamming the open palm of her right hand on to her antagonist's face.

The connection was hard and true and for a moment Mandy just blinked at Helen, rocked by the severity of the blow. Helen seized the moment, leaning in to grasp the woman under both arms.

'If you want to live, Mandy, you need to come with me. But you need to do it quickly and you need to do it *now*.'

And with that she hauled the young woman up and out of the bath. Seconds later the pair stumbled back into the inferno, disappearing into the thick, black smoke.

117

Everybody loves a love rat.

The journalist in Emilia bridled at that sentence – the use of the word 'love' twice in quick succession – but it was true nevertheless. Love rats made good copy, offering up plenty of salacious material while playing on the fears of their female readers. Throw a series of major crimes into the mix and the story becomes irresistible.

Helen Grace had kept the fourth estate away from Sharon Jackson for now, posting uniformed coppers front and back to keep the hacks away. Emilia hadn't wasted any time there, taking off immediately to do door-to-doors in the neighbourhood, before visiting the local GP's surgery, as well as Naomie's former school. In Emilia's experience, the professionals – head teachers, doctors, social workers – always remained tight-lipped, but those who assisted them were more willing to talk. Many a story had been culled from the loose lips of a PA, receptionist, nurse or even school caretaker, especially when flattery and a few free drinks were offered. And so it proved now as Emilia quickly put together a picture of a lonely, disenfranchised young woman who had often arrived at school with unexplained bruises. She would never point the finger at her mother, but, then again, why would she? The poor kid had nowhere else to go.

And when she was at home, what did she find? Her

mother fawning over a man who just wanted to get his leg over without offering anything in return. The other mothers on Sharon Jackson's estate had been only too glad to talk about their neighbour, who it now turned out had been harbouring a serial killer – painting a picture of her as an insecure, needy woman who had never managed to hold on to a man and took what pleasures she could when they were offered.

And in the end it had cost her. One of her love rivals – Denise Roberts – was already dead, while another had just had her house razed to the ground while she took a bath. Every punch, every clipped ear that Sharon Jackson had given Naomie had been paid back with interest, and though she would never betray this in print, Emilia felt a sneaking regard for the young woman who'd refused to take her punishment lying down. Her mother would rue taking her daughter's submission for granted.

Emilia typed fast, the adrenaline of a big story driving her on, helping to craft the story by instinct rather than forethought. It was all taking shape very nicely and had played just as she'd hoped. She had been the first one to speak to Naomie and, though she couldn't locate her now, she would ride that connection for all it was worth. This coup had been the result of clever investigative work – something she prided herself on – and she was pleased to see that her coverage of the arson attacks had already engendered a sea change in relations at the *News*. The national dailies had picked up on her interview with Naomie, she'd been on the radio discussing it and was due to appear on TV later today in an interview with BBC South – all of which had helped raise the paper's profile and massively boosted sales. Her editor had certainly changed his tune – offering her a bonus and hinting at promotion. It had all worked out well, and though she had sacrificed her good relations with Helen Grace in the process, it had been worth it. Her career was on the up at last and she was happy to weather any fallout that was coming her way.

'Bring it on,' Emilia thought to herself, as she continued to type.

118

The battle was over. They had survived.

Mandy Blayne was swaddled in an emergency blanket and being loaded into an ambulance. They would need to check her out at the hospital – principally for the effects of smoke inhalation. But the initial tests conducted by the paramedics had been encouraging and Helen knew that she would be fine – shaken up, but fine. During the course of the paramedics' examination Mandy had admitted she was in the early stages of pregnancy, a revelation that hit home with Helen. They had been so much on the back foot in this investigation that it felt good to have saved not one, but two of Naomie's intended victims. Did the fact that Mandy was pregnant have anything to do with the attack? Did Naomie know about it? Did she feel threatened? It was a bleak picture that was now emerging.

Helen submitted herself to the paramedics' attention but refused a hospital visit, despite the fact that her whole body was racked with pain. Her bruises from her beating were still livid and her heroics in rescuing Mandy had only added to her injuries. She had never really liked the phrase 'walking wounded' but she was the very definition of it now. Still, she was determined to lead from the front so, having obtained a couple of painkillers from the paramedics, she joined Gardam and Sanderson in conference outside Mandy Blayne's house.

Gardam was solicitous, offering to run the show for her if she needed rest, but Helen dismissed the idea out of hand. She could tell he had news and wanted to know what it was.

'We've had a sighting of Naomie Jackson,' Gardam told her. 'A train driver reported a bizarre game of chicken he'd played with a young girl who refused to get off his tracks until the very last second. He was pretty shaken up by it and caught site of Naomie's mugshot on the local news as he was resting up back at base. He's convinced it's the same girl.'

Helen digested this, then said:

'Ok, let's get everyone out – the whole of MIT as well as uniform. How long ago was this?'

'An hour or so?'

'Where?'

'Northam Junction.'

'Ok, let's focus on her known haunts near there. We must presume she's seen the publicity about herself so won't be returning home any time soon. Her mother mentioned a few places she likes to go – the city library, the pubs on Oakland Street, the Common, the skateboard park, the WestQuay centre. Let's concentrate our fire on those sites nearest Northam and scroll out from there. If we're in luck, she'll still be in the neighbourhood.'

'Good,' Gardam replied. 'In the meantime, we're liaising with the Transport Police, it's not impossible she might try to run.'

'Maybe, but she seems very committed. I think she'll see this through to the end, so we should check out old friends, former schoolmates, anyone who might be sheltering her in the local area. Only those who know her well will want to shield her now.'

Which was exactly what was worrying Helen. She didn't say this to Sanderson or Gardam, but the simple fact was that Naomie didn't have any friends. So what would she do – now that her latest attack had been foiled? Would she ever contemplate giving herself up or would she be in this to the bitter end? Privately, Helen feared the latter. The question was how it would play out. And, more importantly, who would she take with her?

119

Charlie walked along the quiet path, her eyes ranging over the bleak expanse of Hoglands Park. By day, the large swathe of green was a pleasant enough city centre picnic spot, complete with cricket ground, a skateboard park and a small kids' playground. But no sensible person came here at night, when the drug dealers and sex workers drifted in. Now it was a desolate, threatening place, full of shadows and menace. Charlie suddenly felt exposed, pounding the paths alone at this hour.

There were uniformed officers in nearby Sussex Place and Houndwell Park, plus she had her baton to defend herself if need be, but still there was something about the feel of this place after dark that affected you. Charlie's mind took flight across town to Jessica – Steve would be putting her in her bath now – but she pushed the thought away. No point making herself more unhappy by thinking about where she really wanted to be.

It had been a strange and unsettling day so far. She had attended Karen and Alice Simms's funeral, which was why she was still dressed in her dark, charcoal-grey suit that seemed so out of place amid the dope-smoking kids who were now making their presence felt in the park. She had been there to support the family in a professional capacity, but like everyone there had been deeply affected by the ceremony. It was positive and celebratory, but you couldn't escape the fact that the Simms family had been rent in two, a deeply loved mother and daughter snatched from Luke and Thomas in the most horrific of circumstances. Nobody mentioned the fire – it was the elephant in the room – but it pervaded everything, from the carefully worded euphemisms of the vicar to Charlie's own presence at the service. Just when you got lost in the happy family memories, it would hit you again – somebody did this to this family. Somebody wanted Karen and Alice Simms to die.

Charlie walked on, her mind twisting around this notion, attempting to settle on a reason why they might have been targeted. She was so lost in her own thoughts that she stumbled on the group of skateboarders lounging in the grass before she saw them. They were amused by her – assuming she was just a dimwit suit who'd lost her way – but the sight of her warrant card shut them up. As soon as she pulled it from her pocket she felt the mood change and immediately clocked that more than one of those present flicked their eyes nervously towards another, smaller group of dope smokers, idling by the main skateboard ramp.

Instinct took over now and Charlie didn't stop to ask questions, marching instead towards the small knot of kids who were only fifty odd feet away. Her approach was fast – she was forty feet away, now thirty – but not fast enough, for as she neared the group, one of them took off at speed. The lighting wasn't good in this part of the park, but Charlie could make out the frizzy hair and bulky form and she knew immediately that she had stumbled on Naomie Jackson.

Charlie wrenched her radio from her pocket as she ran. She was wearing long boots and her tight suit trousers were irritatingly restrictive – she now regretted her lack of gym time since returning to work. But still she hoped to have the edge on Naomie, who had never been much of an athlete.

'Pursuing suspect through Hoglands Park in the direction of Kingsland Place. I need back-up and officers on South Front, Kingsway Place. I'll cover Hoglands if she tries to double back.'

Charlie clicked off – it was hard to run and speak – and picked up her speed. If Naomie was smart she'd dart across Kingsway Place and into the City College, whose many buildings and walkways offered decent hiding places. But instead Naomie was heading straight for the northern exit of the park – she was in full flight now, panic driving her forward. She was surprisingly fast and Charlie laboured to keep up with the fugitive. Her breathing was already short and painful – her lungs burning – and she realized how long it had been since she'd been in an all-out sprint. In her early days it had been a feature of day-to-day work, but now it was an unpleasant anomaly.

'Requesting back-up and officers on Kingsway Place and South Front,' Charlie gasped into her radio, before clicking off once more. Nobody had responded and she was suddenly gripped by the fear that Naomie might escape her. This girl who had done so much damage, who'd done such terrible things. Charlie could stop her tonight – but only if she could get to her in time.

They were reaching the edge of the park now. And suddenly Charlie realized what was happening. There was an industrial estate just beyond North Front – a depot and a couple of warehouses surrounded by ageing chain link fences. Did Naomie know this terrain? Did she already have a specific escape route in mind?

Naomie was nearly clear of the park now, despite Charlie's efforts to chase her down. Charlie strained to keep up, but she could feel her pace slowing. Only fractionally but it would be enough to ensure Naomie's escape.

Then suddenly and without warning, it was over. Two uniformed officers appeared at the mouth of the park just as Naomie reached it. Her forward momentum was too great now and even as she tried to turn back, the officers pounced. By the time Charlie finally caught up with her, she was already being read her rights.

As Charlie got her breath back, she looked down at Naomie – and she was surprised by what she saw. She'd been expecting anger and defiance, as their killer fought to preserve her liberty. But Naomie was exhibiting none of these emotions. Her head was pointing down, her chin almost touching the floor and, instead of directing any hostility towards her captors, she was simply crying quietly to herself.

120

'Do you self-harm, Naomie?'

It was a strange question for Helen to ask, but one she hoped would get a reaction. So far Naomie had just sat there, slumped in her chair, flanked by a pernickety brief and an earnest social worker, refusing to offer anything except the standard 'No comment'. The usual questioning – why, when, how – would get them nowhere, Helen sensed – Naomie wasn't that kind of collar. As she ran the rule over their prime suspect once more, Helen took in the unkempt hair, the muffin top, and the fresh scarring on her left palm. It had been obvious from the start that Naomie had chronic self-esteem issues and Helen had decided to confront these head on.

For the first time in their interview Naomie looked directly at Helen, before dropping her eyes to the floor once more.

'I'm not judging you, Naomie, or asking you to tell me your life story. I know what it's like. I know that sometimes things get so bad that you feel you have to hurt yourself. And that it can feel like a release, when you can't see a way forward, when the world seems determined to hurt you.'

Naomie shrugged, which was progress of sorts, so Helen pressed on.

'That cross on your palm. It doesn't look accidental. Did you do that?'

'Yeah, I did it,' Naomie mumbled.

'How?'

'With a lighter.'

'And did it make you feel better?'

'For a bit.'

Helen let that settle, then:

'Can you tell me why you did it? Was it something your mother did? Your father?'

'My dad does nothing. Never has.'

'But you still love him?'

'Maybe,' she replied, shrugging once more. 'Do you love yours?'

It was such an unexpected response that for a moment Helen was speechless. How much did Naomie know about her past? It had all been in the press of course, but that was a few years back and Naomie didn't look like much of a reader. On the other hand, the internet is a repository of everyone's misdemeanours and Helen suspected that there was more going on with Naomie than people expected – perhaps she was seeing some of that now.

'No, I don't think I do. But perhaps you already know that.'

Naomie looked briefly at Helen, then looked away. Sanderson shot a glance at Helen – she seemed keen to step in – but Helen shook her head gently. She wanted to stay on this.

'How did you feel when your dad went AWOL for long periods?'

'What do you think?'

'Did you ever talk to him about it? Ask him to stay?'

'He wasn't interested in talking to me. To him, I was just a stupid, fat kid.'

'How did your mum react when he moved on?'

'She used to follow him at first. Have it out with the other women. Then he put a stop to that.'

'What then?'

'You've seen the state of me – take a guess.'

'She beat you?'

'After she'd had a drink.'

'How many times has she beaten you over the years?'

Helen knew this would be manna from heaven for Naomie's defence team, if and when this came to trial, but this was about more than the mechanics of justice now. Helen wanted to get to the truth.

'Twenty, thirty, I don't know. But that wasn't the worst of it. After she'd finished, she just ignored me, wouldn't say two words to me.'

'So who did you talk to?'

Naomie shrugged again, her defiant pose suddenly deserting her.

'Did you talk to schoolfriends, teachers, neighbours?'

'I left school when I was thirteen, didn't I? And as for the neighbours, have you seen the state of our place?'

Helen nodded, but said nothing. She had seen the graffiti that had nearly been scrubbed clean from the Jackson family home. The sentiments weren't pleasant and most of them were directed at the overweight young woman. Many of them had nasty racial overtones.

'And is that why you self-harm?'

Naomie said nothing, picking now at the scar on her hand. Helen noted that her stronger, right hand remained clear of injury, presumably because she needed it to carry out her attacks.

'Naomie, I've already said that I'm not judging you, I just want to understand. Why do you hurt yourself?'

'It's just my thing, innit? I just like to *feel*.'

'Where do you do it?'

'In my room. Mum never comes in, so what's to stop me?'

Naomie's defiance had returned again, but her eyes were glistening, and despite everything Helen felt a sharp stab of sympathy for their firestarter. Naomie had been belittled, ignored, assaulted, and as Helen looked at the slumped teenager she was gripped by a strong sense of the crushing loneliness this young woman must have felt day after day. While it didn't excuse her actions, it certainly made sense of them. When the world offers you absolutely nothing, is it any surprise that you turn on it?

'Did you want your dad to come home? It seems you didn't get on that well.'

'Still my dad though. And she was much nicer when he was around. There were some times that were ok, y'know? But it would never last – she knew he would never stay.'

'Is that why you burnt down Denise Roberts's house? To deny your father that bolthole?'

'Maybe,' Naomie answered in non-committal fashion.

'And Mandy Blayne? Did you want her off the scene too?'

'You tell me.'

'Naomie, please. Do yourself a favour here. We're testing the clothes we picked you up in, but I'm reliably informed that the sleeves and the pockets stink of paraffin. We also have a box of matches among your possessions. We can place you at the scene of at least two fires – the Simms house and the Harris house – and probably more besides. You have motive, opportunity and means and I note for the tape that you've not *once* denied your involvement in these crimes. Now you're not a stupid girl, so start talking to me, because despite appearances I'm your only friend here.'

Naomie looked up once more, hurt and anger playing out in her expression.

'I just wanted my dad back,' she said eventually, despite the advice of her brief to say nothing. 'That's not a crime.'

'No, it isn't. And what about the Simms house? And the Harris family? Why did you target them?'

This was what Helen really wanted to know, the question she'd been building up to over the last two hours.

'No reason.'

'Don't take me for a fool, Naomie. Everything you've done has been planned down to the last detail.'

Naomie looked directly at Helen once more, seeming to size her up before she replied:

'I just wanted what they had.'

'Which was?'

Naomie breathed out heavily, the fight seeming to go out of her at last, before she muttered:

'A happy family.'

121

'So do we charge her?'

Gardam dispensed with the formalities, getting straight to the point. Helen could tell he was wound up, so forgave him his unusually brusque manner. There was a lot riding on this call.

'I don't think we've got enough yet.'

'I'm not going to teach you to suck eggs, Helen, but if we press charges then maybe she'll realize there's no virtue in continuing to hold out on us.'

'But if we go too early we might lose her. Too many people have had their lives ruined by these attacks to let the perpetrator escape justice. We owe it to them to proceed carefully.'

'I accept we don't have chapter and verse but she has *confessed*. The interview was handled in exemplary fashion with a "thumbs up" from both the attending brief and the social worker. There can be no question that she was coerced. She *confessed*.'

'So why the urgency to charge her? She's not going anywhere. Let's take the time we've got to continue questioning her and see if we can find more robust connections to the two fires she called in.'

'What are you thinking?'

'I want to know more about her connection to the Simms and the Harris families. She says she envied them, wanted what they had. But why them specifically? Why choose their homes above all others?'

'She could have chosen them at random.'

'But they are in such different areas of the city. She wouldn't have passed these properties on a day-to-day basis and they were staked out with such precision, such patience. All of these attacks feel *personal* to me. The intent to kill was so clear. I can't believe they were random. Can you?'

Gardam said nothing. He didn't look happy, but he didn't refute Helen's arguments either.

'I've sent Charlie to the Simmses and Sanderson to the Harrises to see if we can unearth a tangible link to Naomie Jackson. In the meantime, I'm going to ask Meredith Walker to go back to the sites of the second and fourth fires. Naomie had a clear motive to attack these properties, but as yet we have no tangible forensic evidence linking her to the crime scenes. There's no witness statements placing her there, nor did she call them in. Why change her MO for the second and fourth fires? It doesn't quite fit and I won't be comfortable until it does.'

'Then we keep on it. But after another twenty-four hours we'll have to make the call. We can't give the impression of drift on this one.'

'Understood.'

'So let's find the evidence we need and bring this one to a close, right?'

Helen left Gardam's office shortly afterwards, his gentle ultimatum still ringing in her ears. The team had clear lines of enquiry to pursue now and she hoped in time this would yield the breakthrough she felt they needed. She would be on it too, but not for the next hour or two. It was pushing midnight now and she had told the team to go home and get some rest. She craved sleep too, a moment's peace, but there was somewhere she needed to be.

Or, more accurately, there was someone she needed to see.

122

It was late now and Charlie wasn't welcome. She hadn't expected Thomas Simms to answer the door and she had her speech ready, justifying her intrusion on this most difficult of days. But it was cutting no ice with Thomas Simms's sister, who seemed determined to deny Charlie access, despite her insistence that her business here was both professional and urgent.

'Mary, it's ok. I know her and it's fine.'

Just as the stand-off had threatened to become vocal, a visibly exhausted Thomas Simms intervened, ushering Charlie into the house. Luke was still up, chatting to his grandmother, who seemed to be running the show in a kind and caring manner. Charlie felt bad having to wrench him away from her, but she had no choice. This was too important to duck, despite the terrible timing.

Charlie quickly brought father and son up to speed but, not for the first time, Thomas Simms just looked stunned by the latest developments.

'I've never heard of Naomie Jackson.'

'Are you sure you haven't seen her? Hanging around? Walking past the house? Have another look at the picture.'

'I don't recognize her,' Thomas replied wearily. 'I don't know the part of town where she lives . . . I just don't know her.'

Charlie nodded and handed the photo to Luke.

'How about you, Luke?'

Helen had dispatched Charlie straight to the Simms house following the conclusion of her interview with Naomie Jackson. Charlie knew that across town Sanderson was asking the exact same questions of the Harris family. The case against Naomie looked good, but their weak spots were the Simms and Harris fires, where there seemed to be no specific motive beyond jealousy and spite. Any extra bite that the Simms or Harris families could give them now would pay dividends later. They needed a more concrete link than the fact that Naomie had called in both fires.

Luke Simms looked at the photo intently, then his expression lifted and he handed it back to Charlie, shaking his head.

'I've not seen her before.'

'Are you sure, Luke?'

'Do you think I wouldn't tell you if I did? Do you think I want whoever did this to go free?'

His tone was suddenly harsh, but immediately he retreated.

'I'm sorry, it's been a tough day . . .'

'I know.'

'I just . . . I just don't recognize her. I wish I did.'

Charlie had been hoping for more than this, but she believed him. She believed both of them. Which left Charlie with an uneasy feeling. What were they missing here? And what would it cost them?

123

The heavy door opened and a man exited at speed, his coat pulled up around his face. The door swung slowly forwards, then began to roll back towards the frame. Helen didn't hesitate, darting from her hiding place in the shadows and jamming her foot into the shrinking gap.

Charging up the stairs, she came to a first-floor door and knocked on it, with a swift, familiar rat-a-tat. Moments later, the door opened to reveal Max Paine. He looked like he was expecting it to be his recent client, who'd forgotten something perhaps, and the blood drained from his face when he saw who it actually was. He moved to slam the door on Helen, but she was expecting this and shouldered it roughly open, sending Paine barrelling back into the room. Helen shut the door firmly behind her, locking them both in.

'What the fuck do you want?' Paine demanded angrily. Despite heavy make-up, his bruising was still obvious and unsightly. His eyes darted this way and that, searching for something to defend himself with.

'I just want to talk,' Helen replied calmly.

'So talk.'

'I want to know what you intend to do.'

Max Paine eyed her warily, then replied:

'Worried I'm going to report you, *Helen*?'

Helen regarded him for a moment, before responding:

'You obviously know who I am. And the awkward situation I find myself in. I wouldn't blame you for reporting me – what I did was wrong – and you could probably get me thrown off the Force if you tried hard enough. But here's why you're not going to do that. Because I'm a good officer. Because I'm in the middle of a major investigation. And because, if you do, I'll be forced to tell the investigating officers what a sadistic, cocaine-snorting, woman-hating little shit you are. I'll be pushing for attempted murder, but I'd settle for GBH or even ABH at a push. Any one of those would land you in jail, Max.'

She said his name with the full contempt she felt for him. He glared at her, but said nothing in return.

'So here's what's going to happen. You're going to go back to your life and I will go back to mine and we'll pretend it never happened. Deal?'

As Helen walked away from Paine's building, having gained his begrudging acquiescence, Helen felt her spirits rise. She had been under so much pressure, so hemmed in on all sides, that it felt good to be finally taking positive action. She had messed up big time, but the fault was primarily his and she was damned if she was going to be brought down by the likes of Max Paine. A surge of adrenalin coursed through her now – Helen suddenly felt as if she could take on the world and win, that everything would be ok, and she smiled to herself at this sudden burst of optimism.

A blast of icy wind roared over her now, as if in defiant response to her improving mood, but even this couldn't dampen Helen's spirits. It did, however, remind her that she'd forgotten to check whether she had left her much missed scarf at Paine's flat, as she rather suspected she had. Too late now. Helen had bigger fish to fry and she couldn't exactly return and ask Paine for it, so she would have to make do without. Pulling up her collar to ward off the chill wind, Helen lowered her head and walked away towards her bike.

124

'What the fuck do you want?'

The girl's nose was wrinkled up in mock disgust, as if the mere sight of a police officer turned her stomach. It was done for effect and it worked – Charlie already wanted to slap her and they'd only been talking for a few seconds. But Charlie swallowed down her irritation, refusing to be deflected from her purpose.

She had risen early after a sleepless night. A worrying thought had kept turning and turning in her head and now she needed to find out if her concerns were justified – or if she was just going mad. She hadn't known where to find her quarry, except that she lived somewhere near Naomie Jackson. Charlie was on the streets of St Mary's by 8 a.m. She didn't expect to find Naomie's mate up and about then – didn't look the type – but she couldn't discount the possibility that she had a job or went to college and would be on the move early.

Predictably, however, there was no sign of her and after an hour Charlie had begun to wonder if she was wasting her time. Then suddenly she saw her – dressed comically in pyjama trousers, fake Ugg boots and a puffa jacket, meandering her way to the corner shop. Moments later, she emerged clutching a carton of milk and began to make her way home.

Charlie approached her at speed. They had last met the

day after the Denise Roberts fire, when the ratty little ringleader of a gaggle of girls had pushed Charlie towards Naomie Jackson, claiming her friend had seen their runaway arsonist.

'Nice to see you again too. What's your name?'

'What's it to you?'

'Name.'

'Danielle Mulligan.'

'That's better – see, you can be nice when you want to.'

'What's this about? I can't stand here like this –'

'You'll stand there until I've finished with you. Got it?'

Danielle shrugged, seemingly determined not to give Charlie the satisfaction of her full acquiescence.

'Talk to me about Wednesday night.'

'What about it?'

'According to Naomie, you all went to a pub near the Common. Which one was it?'

'The Green Man.'

'When did you get there?'

'Around nine, I think.'

'And Naomie was with you?'

'Course.'

'What time did she leave that night?'

'I don't know, do I?'

'She said she left early to go home, is that right?'

'If she says so.'

'What do you say?'

'Yeah, sure, she left early.'

But she didn't sound sure and Charlie knew she had to press further.

'When did you leave?'

'Midnight. Half past maybe. They had a lock-in, so . . .'

'And did you see Naomie leaving?'

'No, I was drinking, having fun with my mates, wasn't I?'

'Did you take any pictures that night? On your phone?'

'Dunno.'

'You said you were mucking around with your friends so . . .'

Suddenly Danielle looked evasive and Charlie followed up quickly.

'Give me your phone.'

'I haven't got it on me . . .'

'Your hand's been clamped in your jacket pocket since you left the house. I know you've got it and I'd like to see it. And before you kick off, I'm happy to do this at home with your folks, if you'd pref—'

'All right, all right,' Danielle said scowling, as she delved into her pocket and dug out her phone. 'Knock yourself out.'

Charlie took it from her and opened up her photos. Quickly she scrolled back through the days before alighting on Wednesday's date. Predictably there were dozens of photos. Danielle was part of the generation that lived their lives in public and Charlie was amused to see photos of Danielle's painted toes, her tattoos, several trial hair-dos, plus a cheeky shot of her mum in her dressing gown among the snaps Danielle had posted that day.

But Charlie was interested in the evening photos and flicked to them now. The gaggle of girls had been in high spirits and there were plenty of stupid, drunken poses. Naomie Jackson was there, not quite in the thick of things but present and enjoying herself, it appeared. Charlie moved through them more carefully now, checking the times that each photo was taken. 10.30 p.m., 10.47 p.m., 10.49 p.m., 11.12 p.m., 11.13 p.m., 11.25 p.m., 11.38 p.m. . . .

And it was with this last one that Charlie had the evidence she needed. Naomie had previously said that she'd left the pub early and headed home, encountering the fleeing arsonist en route, a few minutes before 11.30 p.m. And yet here she was, pictured in the pub with her mates at 11.38 p.m. She had never left the pub – had stayed with them almost to the bitter end, it appeared.

If the timings on Danielle's phone were correct – and there was no reason to doubt that they were – then it was clear that Naomie had spun them a story about her movements that night. She had been lying when she said she encountered the arsonist. More importantly, she had been lying to them when she said she started the fire in Denise Roberts's house.

125

McAndrew stopped in her tracks the moment she saw him.

She'd visited the hospital first thing to speak with Mandy Blayne's care team, who'd confirmed that mother and baby were doing fine. Satisfied and relieved, McAndrew had decided to visit the ward briefly before leaving. Mandy didn't have any family locally and, given what she'd been through, McAndrew was keen to spend a few minutes with her before getting back to work. But as she approached her bedside, she realized that Mandy was not alone.

A man in his forties was sitting with her, holding her hand and talking earnestly to her. Normally she would have withdrawn – their conversation was intense and intimate – but this time she had no intention of leaving. There was something familiar about this guy, even though McAndrew was sure she'd never seen his face before. The dark jeans, work boots, puffawaist coat – *this* was the man whom they had caught on CCTV jogging away from Denise Roberts's house. It was Naomie Jackson's father, Darren Betts.

'Why didn't you come forward?'

McAndrew had hauled Darren Betts out of the ward and now sat opposite him in a junior doctor's office. She'd have preferred to interview him back at Southampton Central, but she had no grounds to arrest him – yet.

'You must have known it was you in that CCTV footage.'

'I don't know what you mean.'

'Don't take me for a fool, Darren. The whole of Southampton has seen that footage. Just like they've seen mugshots of your daughter, thanks to her role in these arson attacks.'

'Kids, eh?'

'Why were you running away from Denise Roberts's house the night it went up?'

'I had *nothing* to do with that. I like Denise.'

'When it suited you. Did you know that your daughter hated her?'

'Of course not, I would have straightened her out if I'd known.'

'Tell me about your relationship with Callum Roberts.'

The sudden change of subject seemed to unnerve Betts and he said nothing in reply.

'He hated you, didn't he? And I bet he made his feelings plain. Did you want to teach him a lesson?'

'I don't go about setting people's houses on fire. If Naomie's coughed for that, it's her business.'

Looking at him across the untidy desk, McAndrew felt nothing but contempt for Darren Betts. Even now that his daughter was facing a life behind bars, he accepted no responsibility for her actions, nor did he seem to care what became of her.

'What about Mandy Blayne? Getting too clingy, was she? Trying to trap you into being a babyfather?'

'You're way off beam, petal. I love these women. I love them too much. That's always been my problem.'

'Which is why I find it surprising that you didn't come forward after Denise Roberts was murdered?'

'You think I'd willingly come and talk to you lot?' Betts laughed.

'I would if I was in the frame for murder.'

'And give your mob the chance to fit me up? You clearly didn't have a clue who was behind it and I know how you coppers work when you're in a fix –'

'Can you tell me where you were on the night of Tuesday, 8 December?' McAndrew interrupted, changing tack again. 'The night the Simms house was attacked? I'm going to need you to account for your movements.'

Darren Betts stared straight at McAndrew. The good humour he'd displayed thus far now vanished in the blink of an eye. His expression was cold and unforgiving. And when he finally spoke, his tone was distinctly hostile.

'Now you listen to me, girl, and listen *good.* I've had it with these questions. My daughter is responsible for this madness – not me – and nothing you do or say is going to change that. So either you arrest me *right now* or you let me go back to my Mandy.'

He fixed her with a withering stare:

'This conversation is over.'

126

Naomie Jackson had a rich internet history. Hunched over her laptop, Helen was climbing inside her other life now and was pretty depressed by what she saw. There were the usual celebrity and reality TV websites, Amazon, Netflix, but darker elements too – suicide websites, the Samaritans, ChildLine and posted pictures of her injuries, shared with teenagers in similar predicaments.

It was the latter that interested Helen the most and she had zeroed in on Naomie's online 'friends', starting with those she had chatted to most recently. There were scores of acquaintances – people she'd never actually met but seemed happy to converse with about matters trivial or grave – but their conversations were sporadic at best, there was no stand-out friend or confessor.

There was, however, one unusual pattern: a cyberfriend whom she had chatted to repeatedly over the last six months, before suddenly dropping them three weeks ago.

Helen looked at the username. Naomie's correspondent went by the handle of 'firstpersonsingular' – no first name or surname was ever referred to in their chats. It was an intriguing choice – implying a sense of difference, a unique quality perhaps but also showcasing a high level of education and exhibiting a degree of wit and sophistication in choosing a grammatical pun as their user name. This immediately concerned Helen – Naomie was not educated, not massively bright per se, whereas this person clearly was – given their vocabulary and the considered, acerbic style of their insults and character assassinations.

As a disturbing thought took hold, Helen searched for other sites or postings linked to firstpersonsingular. There were a few to choose from, but Helen homed in on a blogsite that had been recently added to.

> 'When people come to judge me, they will see that none of this is my fault.'
>
> 'Whatever, it's important that you know I'm not mad, or bad. I'm just reacting to circumstances. Actions have consequences, my friends . . .'
>
> 'They told him he was a worm, a germ, a piece of shit who should never have existed. But he did more than any of them.'
>
> 'I saw what people said about the fire at the Millbrook – they said it was hideous, ugly, an abomination. But not to me. I thought it was beautiful.'

The posts had all been written in the last four days – *after* the spate of arson attacks had begun. Firstpersonsingular's interest in the fires was telling, as was the fact that there had been no formal break-off in their online friendship with Naomie Jackson. What had happened? Had they met at some point? Decided face to face to drop online communication to attempt to conceal their connection?

Suddenly it all made sense. The reason why they couldn't find a motive for the Simms and Harris fires. And why they couldn't place their prime suspect at the Roberts and Blayne fires. She had hidden it pretty well, but now it was as plain as day.

Naomie Jackson had a partner in crime.

127

'Can I just double-check these timings? So there's no mistake in your statement?'

Helen was back in the interview suite, flanked by Charlie, who had just arrived back from St Mary's. Helen had asked her to sit in, tasking Sanderson with chasing down the mysterious 'firstpersonsingular'. It was a slight break in the chain of command, but Helen wanted Charlie's input and, besides, it felt good to have her old friend back at her side as the case reached its climax.

'So on Wednesday night, you left the Green Man around eleven-ish and made your way home?'

Naomie looked tired and wrung out, the product of a sleepless night in the cells. Part of Helen was pleased – it's harder to keep your guard up when you're exhausted.

'More or less.'

'I'm going to have to press you, Naomie. You left the pub around eleven, walked to Denise Roberts's house and then what?'

'I set the fire, like I said.'

'So that would have been around eleven fifteen p.m.?'

'Right.'

'Wrong. Because you were in the Green Man with your friends,' Helen replied, all the warmth suddenly evaporating from her tone.

Naomie's brief shot a concerned look in her direction, but Charlie leapt in before she could intervene.

'I've spoken to Danielle this morning. I've seen the photos, placing you there until gone midnight. We've also had a little look at your movements on Friday – the day Mandy Blayne's house was targeted. The movement of your mobile signal suggests you didn't go near St Denys.'

Charlie could see Naomie was about to kick back, so carried on quickly:

'That doesn't prove anything of course. You might have lost your phone or had it stolen. However, we have tallied your mobile movements with street cameras and guess what – they match.'

'I'm now showing the suspect some CCTV stills time-coded to the hours between two and four p.m. on Friday,' Helen said, taking over. 'Your face can be clearly seen in a couple of them, in spite of your cap. I take it you're not going to deny that it's you?'

Helen pushed the stills across the table towards Naomie and her brief, but the former refused to look at them. She looked ashen.

'Look at them,' Helen barked, her voice suddenly harsh. 'Are you going to deny that's you?'

Naomie glanced anxiously at her brief, but received nothing in return – it clearly *was* her in the photos. Now Naomie's eyes started to fill. Helen could see that the young girl was panicking, clearly torn as to what to do next. Helen cursed herself for ever having believed this scared, downtrodden teenager was the mastermind behind the arson attacks.

'I know this is not what you wanted, not how you

hoped things would pan out, but believe me this is good news, Naomie. There's a simple reason you can't provide any clear motive for the fires at the Simms and Harris households – because they weren't *your* victims. Your accomplice wanted to hurt them, while you wanted to get at Denise Roberts and Mandy Blayne. Credit to you both, you played it smartly. You set the first and third fires, your accomplice the second and fourth. You had no personal connection to the victims you actually targeted making it virtually impossible that you'd be identified as a suspect.'

Helen let her words hang in the air. The brief looked shocked, whereas Naomie just looked beaten.

'Now I know you're a capable girl,' Helen continued. 'But an elaborate scheme like this, well it doesn't feel very *you*, does it? You've been hurt, neglected and belittled more than any girl should be and you're angry with your dad, your mum, with the world. But ultimately you just want your family back together, don't you? You don't want to burn this town down, do you?'

Naomie just stared at her through tear-filled eyes, but didn't commit either way.

'All that planning, the endless scouting, the diversionary fires, was that really your idea?'

Helen could tell Naomie had to think for a moment to work out what diversionary meant and in that instant she knew she had her answer.

'And the idea of putting yourself forward, to sell us the big lie about seeing a guy with a Fire and Rescue tattoo? You came up with that, did you?

Naomie faltered, then replied:

'Sure. Like I said –'

'I'm going to discount what you've told me so far, as you have already lied to me on tape on a number of occasions, but there is something I'd like you to tell me the truth about. Who is firstpersonsingular?'

Naomie's reaction was hard to miss. She looked like she'd been caught with her hand in the till – initial astonishment morphing into a desire to disengage, to retreat. She picked hard at the scar on her hand, wanting to be anywhere but locked in a room with her accusers.

'We know you're close,' Charlie went on, more softly. 'That you feel loyalty to this person, that perhaps they even control you a little bit. But it's our view that this person is principally responsible for these fires, so it would be in your best interests to tell us who they are.'

Naomie shook her head vigorously but refused to look up at them. Helen felt a strange mixture of sympathy and contempt as she looked at the shambolic teenage girl who still clung to the person – to the 'project' – that made her feel special.

'We will find out, Naomie. Make no bones about that,' Helen said. 'And this is your one chance to help us bring this to an end. It could make all the difference when this goes to trial.'

Now Naomie did look up and Helen caught the fear in her eyes.

'You've nothing to fear. If you need protection we can arrange that. And you don't need to go back to your old life, once you've done your time. We can set you up somewhere new – new name, new place, new future. But only if you help us now. Who is firstpersonsingular?'

'I won't help you,' Naomie said suddenly, before receding into herself once more.

'Then I'm calling time on this interview. I've done all I can and I would urge your lawyer to use the break to talk some sense into you. Cooperation is your only option.'

'I'll never give him up to the likes of you,' Naomie spat back bitterly.

'So firstpersonsingular is a "he"?' Helen returned quickly. 'Well that's a start, I suppose.'

The blood drained from Naomie's face, as she felt the guilt of her first betrayal.

'We *will* find out his name, Naomie. It's only a matter of time. So now you have to ask yourself if you're brave enough to speak up or whether you want to spend the rest of your days behind bars for something that *wasn't your fault*.'

And with that Helen left, Charlie following close behind.

128

'Let's take this from the top, shall we?'

Helen had pulled the entire team into the incident room and they crowded round, keen to hear the very latest developments.

'Naomie Jackson has a male accomplice, whom we strongly suspect of having been the instigator of the recent arson attacks. He goes by the online moniker of "firstpersonsingular". DS Sanderson has put together a short profile of everything we know about FPS, which includes his most recent posts on the net, social media and so on. He is male, appears to be local and is probably in his mid-to-late teens.'

Immediately a buzz went round the room – this was not the standard arson profile, which commonly placed offenders in their twenties or thirties.

'He makes several references to schooling or teachers. He doesn't give specifics but the incidents he refers to seem to be recent and would put him in GCSE year or slightly above. He could of course be lying to gain Naomie's trust, but the overall tone of his posts is one of teenage anger and rebellion, infused with deep cynicism and bitterness, particularly towards his parents and authority figures in general. He types much less fluently than Naomie, which is curious. Is he a man of few words or is his access to unsupervised computers limited?'

The team were passing the sheets around now, but their eyes were glued to Helen.

'We're trying to trace his IP address, but if he's using a tablet with 4G or similar, then this may be a dead end, so for now let's keep focused on his character. His posts reveal clear evidence of depression, but also strong feelings of superiority. He craves control and seems to relish the effect that the fires have had. He seems to be calling the tune. So we are looking for a teenage male who until recently has been powerless, overlooked or neglected.'

'What's the tenor of their relationship? FPS and Naomie?' McAndrew asked. 'Were they lovers?'

'Looks that way,' Sanderson interjected. 'They communicated every day during the summer and well into the autumn. He makes great play of idolizing her – calling her "Angel" repeatedly – and is always trying to boost her self-esteem. She in turn is very protective of him – seemingly worrying if he'll come to any harm – though whether at his own hands or someone else's is unclear. She keeps referencing the first time they met as if that explained the root cause of her anxiety.'

'Had they been intimate?' DC Lucas asked, to a few quiet sniggers.

'Tough to say,' Sanderson answered. 'It's hard to imagine they haven't been but there is no mention of sex or intimacy in their communications.'

Sanderson continued her dissection of their relationship, but Helen's mind was already arrowing away in a different direction, hidden connections forming now. Without warning, she walked away from the group, marching towards her desk. She picked up her files and searched through them quickly, until she'd located the hospital reports from the fires' survivors. She flicked through them until she came to the page on Ethan Harris. Her eyes ran over the text, words and phrases now leaping out at her: 'cerebral palsy', 'persistent shaking of the left hand', 'historic burn injuries'. Suddenly Helen knew why Agnieszka Jarosik had been singled out for special treatment. She knew why their arsonist had fumbled the matches during the second and fourth attacks. And she knew where she had seen Naomie's scar – the burnt cross on the left palm – before.

Most importantly, she knew why Naomie had called 999 twelve minutes before anybody else after the Harris fire started. It wasn't fear or excitement that motivated her to call too early that night. It was love.

129

Blog post by firstpersonsingular.
Saturday, 12 December, 10.30

She was a funny-looking angel. But she was beautiful to me.

Her sad face was framed by that crazy, afro hair and the shadow of a black eye haunted the left side of her face. Her face was so close to me, I could feel her breath and at first I was confused. Who was this person? What did they want with me? I thought I was seeing things – she had a kind of aura that framed her head, her voice was smooth and comforting – but later I knew I had seen right. She was an angel. More than that, she was my angel.

It's funny how things work out. How you can swallow abuse, neglect and more, but can be undone by a simple act of kindness. Others might have walked past me but not her. She raised me up that day and made me what I am. Together we are more than the sum of our parts.

But things have changed now. We can't be what we were. So it's time to remember the good times as we prepare to finish the job. People will castigate us for what we've done, but all we've done is show them in their true colours and, boy, have they done that. I didn't know whether to laugh or puke when my parents were giving their interviews after the fire. Saying how much they loved me, how relieved they were I was ok. That rhyme kept going round my head: 'Liar, Liar . . .'. I was their 'accident' – my dad actually said it to my face once. How can someone be accidental??? But it's not him I blame really.

They wished I didn't exist. Farmed me out to nannies, who did the minimum required, then ignored me. I was an embarrassment to everyone, a guilty secret. They would either beat me or sedate me into submission and if that didn't work they'd scream at me. I used to like those moments – the flecks of spit landing on my face as they ranted and raved – at least then I existed in their world.

Well, I exist now. And before I'm done I will have made them both famous. This is my last post, Mum and Dad. My last offering to you. My last offering to you all. My name is Ethan Harris and I am the firestarter.

130

Helen took the stairs three at a time, as DCs Lucas and Edwards struggled to keep pace behind. Sanderson was busy organizing a perimeter cordon, in case Ethan Harris tried to escape, but Helen was determined to deny him the opportunity. After the fire, the Harris family had moved into a rented apartment in Upper Shirley, supported by a new carer, Anastasia Teplova. It was amazing how soon normal life re-established itself in the Harris family. Both parents were already back at work, leaving the care of their son to paid help.

Helen quickly reached their apartment on the third floor. She had wasted too much time chasing shadows on this case, when the solution had been under her nose all along. There had definitely been something 'off' about the way the Harris family behaved together and Helen now realized it was because they were acting – pretending to be a loving family. Ethan had been acting for many months now, cloaking his plans and later his nocturnal activities from his parents and carers. The one thing he wasn't able to conceal was the burn mark on his left hand. When she'd glimpsed it at the hospital, Helen thought it had been sustained in the fire, but now the cross-shaped pattern was plain to see. Firstpersonsingular had referenced burning himself in his blog – was this the pact that he and Naomie had sealed, testing their commitment to each other through fire?

As DC Edwards joined her, Helen didn't hesitate, ordering him to break down the door. She had considered using the concierge or even knocking on the door herself, but she couldn't sanction even the tiniest delay. Edwards took a run up then launched himself at the door. The latch tore from the woodwork with a satisfying scream and the door swung open. Helen was through it in a flash, to be confronted by a very surprised-looking Bulgarian, who was playing Fruit Crush on her phone, rather than attending to her duties.

Anastasia Teplova stammered some protestations in broken English, but shut up when confronted by Helen's warrant card. The young woman was barely older than her charge and clearly had a very basic command of English. Just how uninterested were these parents in their son?

'Where is Ethan?'

Anastasia just stood there, still speechless with shock, so Helen gestured to Edwards and Lucas to start searching. Then she approached the home help, putting her warrant card away.

'You're not in any trouble, but I need to talk to Ethan. Is he here?'

There was another long pause, before she finally said:

'He's in his room.'

With that she gestured to a small, ancillary bedroom towards the back of the apartment. Helen ran towards it now and, throwing open the door, stepped inside.

To find an empty room.

Nothing on the walls yet. Nothing on the bedside table. Just an old laptop, closed and powered down, sitting next to a dirty coffee mug on the table. Ethan clearly had been here but, as the open window by the fire escape revealed, he was long gone now.

131

'Can I ask what it's regarding?'

She was a new receptionist – not one he'd seen on his fleeting visits before – but every bit as snotty as her predecessors.

'It's regarding her son. That's me, by the way.'

Ethan Harris enjoyed watching the expression change on her face. His mother ran a prestigious architects' firm in Ocean Village and generally hired beautiful but flinty young women to guard the gate. They were practised at dealing with salesmen, tardy couriers and freeloaders. Had this new one mistaken him for the latter? As she first took in his face, his limp arm, his stooped posture, her look had belied a curious mixture of distaste and awkwardness. But when she realized who he was, her strangulated expression wrenched itself round to an unconvincing smile. Just one more reason to hate her.

'One moment, please,' she purred, ringing up to the penthouse office. Ethan watched her intently, picking at the scar on his left hand all the while – it had become a nervous tic of late. Moments later, she handed him the phone. Didn't that say it all? Any other parent would have just told her to send him up.

'What's going on, Ethan? Is everything all right?'

'Everything's fine. I'm just bored and thought I would pay you a visit. I can visit my own mother, can't I?'

There was a brief pause before she responded:

'Ok, but I've got a meeting at twelve, so it'll have to be quick.'

'It won't take long,' Ethan replied, before handing the receiver back to the earwigging receptionist. His hand quivered more than usual, making the handover clumsy and awkward. Funny how even now he felt embarrassed by these small things.

The receptionist buzzed him through and he walked towards the lifts. Here he paused and as the phone on the front desk rang once more, he took advantage of this timely distraction, diving past the lifts and through the fire stairs that led to the basement. He had no intention of seeing his mother.

Indeed, if he had his way, he would never see her again.

132

For a moment Luke Simms was unable to speak, the blood draining from his face. Charlie hadn't expected such a strong reaction to her question and now put her arm on to Luke's, worried the young boy was about to faint.

'If you don't feel up to this, I can wait, but it would be useful to know at –'

'He was only there a term. I hardly knew him.'

Luke had regained his speech, but not his colour. His father watched on, confused, anxious and not a little scared.

'What's this about? Who is Ethan Harris, for God's sake?'

'He's a person of interest in our enquiry,' Charlie replied evenly.

'And you know him, Luke?'

'I did. A bit. I mean he was at school for such a short time before he had to leave, but we were friends for a bit. He visited me in hospital after the fire, for God's sake. He sat at the end of the bed and offered me his sympathies . . .'

The devil's in the detail, as Helen had often told Charlie. Scrolling through Ethan Harris's educational background she had alighted on the coincidence of him attending the same posh secondary school in Millbrook as Luke Simms. Harris had been at the school for less than eight weeks – the reason for his sudden departure was not yet clear – and his stay there was so brief it hadn't grabbed anyone's attention in their initial enquiries. But now it seemed supremely relevant, especially after Luke had revealed that Harris had visited him in hospital after the fire. Helen had been right – their killer had been inserting himself into the narrative from the off.

'How would you characterize his time at your school, Luke?'

'Unhappy' was Luke's bleak reply. 'He was a tricky character – hostile, suspicious, quick to take offence if anyone mocked him. And there were plenty of people who were happy to do that. You know what school's like.'

'Why did people mock him?'

'Because he was different.'

There it was. Charlie had read Ethan's hospital report on the way over. In addition to an assessment of his burns and the various tests done to determine the effects of smoke inhalation, there was a small, dispassionate summary of his past health issues. It noted drily that Ethan had suffered from Foetal Alcohol Syndrome since birth. This was caused by his mother's heavy drinking during pregnancy and had affected the development of both his brain and his limbs. While intelligent and articulate, Ethan had had many health problems as a result of his FAS, not least mild cerebral palsy and epilepsy. It was some inheritance to gift to your child.

'He just looked different to everyone else,' Luke continued. 'His features were softer, like . . . you know . . . like they weren't quite formed. And people used to take the piss.'

'Did you mock him?'

'No . . . No, not at first. I *liked* him, for God's sake.'

'Why?'

'Because he was good at writing. Creative writing, comprehension, reviews – all that stuff. He could do it standing on his head. And he helped me – I've never been good at that stuff. He would have done mine for me if I'd asked him to. We got along.'

'So what happened?'

Luke hesitated now, his breathing becoming short. Charlie gave Thomas Simms a quick look, but he gently gestured to her to proceed. Like her, he was desperate to know what Luke was going to say next.

'Luke?' Charlie prompted gently.

'Some of the other lads – the football guys – they didn't want me hanging around with him. Told me to cut him off. I refused, so they cut *me* off. Out of the school team, out of their gang, out of *everything*. I stuck it for a while but . . .'

'But then you wanted back in?' Charlie finished for him.

'Yes, so they set me a challenge. A test . . . and I bloody did it.'

Now tears came, coursing down his cheeks.

'They told me to humiliate him. I wanted my old life back so . . . the next time he came up to me – it was in the canteen – I told him I didn't want him talking to me. When he asked me why . . . when he asked me why, I told him it was because he was a fucking freak . . .'

Luke broke down now, the full import of his actions finally making itself felt. His father rocked him back and forth in his arms, trying to stem the tears. Charlie stayed for ten minutes more but there was little she could do now and she felt that her presence was neither helpful nor welcome. She would keep an eye on them of course, but this was something they had to face alone. Luke had done something unpleasant and mean-spirited and had been repaid in savage fashion by a boy unable to cope with the slingshots life constantly threw at him.

It was an awful retribution out of all scale to the crime and Charlie hoped that in time Luke would come to see this and learn not to blame himself. Some hope, Charlie thought to herself, as she walked disconsolately back to the car, Luke's cries still ringing in her ears.

133

He had never been in the basement before, which added to the thrill. He had seen it on the building's plans, which he'd 'borrowed' from his mother's home office, but he had been wary of scoping it in advance for fear of drawing attention to what he was up to. It was unheard of for him to turn up at his parents' place of work unannounced.

It was pitch dark and no amount of fumbling could locate the light switches, so Ethan pulled the heavy torch from his rucksack and clicked it on. As he did so, a broad smile spread across his face. Sometimes the apples really did fall into your lap. There were several pieces of discarded office furniture – mostly desks and chairs – which would provide adequate fuel, but the real gift was the huge amount of shredded paper that lay on the floor in loose plastic sacks. They would help to get the fire going and after that . . .

Ethan quickly set about moving the old bits of furniture to the centre of the room, using his hips to shove the heavier pieces in the right direction. He knew from his mother's plans that the base of the lift shaft was located here and that's where he intended to make his fire. The flames would leap up the shaft, spreading quickly to upper floors while also taking the lift out of action as a means of escape. This fire would be the biggest one yet and he couldn't wait to see it. He could feel his fingers tingle as the excitement grew.

When he'd first rehearsed this climax to their project with Naomie, she had raised objections. Too much collateral damage – meaning the seven other businesses that occupied this sizeable building. But that made it all the better in his view. By the time the dust settled, *everybody* would know that his parents were to blame. These deaths would be on their conscience and while his father mourned his mother, he would have plenty of time to contemplate *that*.

As planned, there would be no diversionary fires today. There would be no warning of this attack. Ethan walked back now to gather the shredded paper, then suddenly jumped like he'd been shot. A piercing alarm rang out, long and loud, echoing around the dingy brick basement.

'What the fuck . . . ?'

This had to be a joke. It *had* to be. They couldn't be having a fire drill today. He'd checked his mother's diary. Fire drills were on the first of the month, regular as clockwork. What cosmic fuck-up could make them have one today . . . ?

Now a thought seized him. There was a chance, of course, that this alarm wasn't a coincidence. That somehow they *knew*. Naomie wouldn't have said anything – he was sure of that – and he had only posted his most recent offering an hour or two ago, but even so . . .

Now Ethan was on the move. Something told him that Helen Grace was here. That for the first time since this started she was ahead of him. And now he wasn't thinking of fire.

He was thinking of flight.

134

'Everybody out. We need to get everybody out.'

The alarms were still wailing but the flow of office workers exiting the building was still just a steady trickle. It was what Helen had expected but still it infuriated her. Why did office workers assume every fire alarm was a drill or a mistake? Did it never occur to them that the fire might be real, that the nightmare which had visited several other families in the run-up to Christmas might be visiting *them*?

Helen grabbed the fire officers as they presented themselves, urging them to get people moving faster. She couldn't smell burning, but instinct told her that Ethan Harris was here somewhere, plotting his final move in the game. McAndrew had alerted Helen to Ethan's latest and possibly final post as 'firstpersonsingular', and as soon as Helen read the text of it, she knew that his mother would be his last victim.

Jacqueline Harris was a workaholic and reading between the lines probably an alcoholic too, so unless he was going to burn down her favourite bar, there was one obvious place to strike. The business she had spent twenty years building up. The realization had sent a chill down Helen's spine: the number of innocent victims from a fire in this building would be pushing a hundred – and Helen was determined not to let that happen.

The human flow seemed to be picking up pace now and Helen scanned the faces that went by. If *she* were Ethan, where would she go? What would be the best place to start a fire? Ethan had taken the lift up, according to the receptionist, but had never arrived at his mother's office. So where? The floor beneath? Possible but that was an open-plan office – how easy would it be for Ethan to talk his way in there and start a fire?

Something told Helen that that was too localized anyway, not grand enough for Ethan's finale. And as her mind turned on this, her eyes alighted on the lift bank. That was more like it. The fire would spread quickly that way, fanning out on to the other floors. If you started a decent enough blaze at the bottom . . .

The basement. If he was smart, he would have gone to the basement. Helen's eyes moved to the left of the lift bank, then to the right. And there it was. A simple, unassuming door marked 'Staff Only'.

Helen took a step forward, but suddenly cannoned backwards. Immediately, she raised her arms to defend herself – but it was just a tearful PA racing for the main exit. The mood in the building had changed now, as the fire wardens scoured the floors, accompanied by uniformed officers, urging people to leave. The sight of a police presence had obviously spooked the building's occupants – perhaps now they were making the connection between this alarm and the spate of recent fires. They looked scared, confused and very keen to be elsewhere.

Now Helen was fighting a torrent of humanity, surging past her, knocking her this way and that, as she fought her way towards the basement door. She did her best to let them pass, but instinct told her to move fast, so she dodged the fleeing workers as best she could, stumbling as she went. She was so involved in the fight, so determined to get through the human barrier in front of her, that she didn't see the young guy, dressed in the dirty overalls and cap of the building's maintenance team, gliding past her on his way to the exit and liberty.

135

'Where is he?'

Naomie looked from Helen to Sanderson, then back to Helen again. Was she looking for a soft touch – a place of sanctuary? She wouldn't find one today. Helen had her on the back foot from the moment she revealed the real name of her lover and accomplice – she could see Naomie trying to work out how they had cottoned on to Ethan when she'd given them nothing – and Helen was determined to press home her advantage.

'His name's in the press now. We've put out an All Ports Warning. He's got nowhere to run. He's obviously not going to go back to his parents, so tell me where he might go.'

'I don't know,' Naomie replied, shaking her head vigorously.

'Yes, you do, and if you care for him, you'll tell us now.'

'Forget it.'

'Do you have any idea what will happen to him, if we don't get to him first?' Sanderson interrupted. 'The people out there are angry and scared. What if they spot him, confront him. What if others pile in? You've seen what happens to paedophiles on estates, you know what mob justice looks like? Do you want that for Ethan?'

It was an unpleasant line of questioning, but for the first time the recalcitrant Naomie looked like she was considering offering them something, so Helen seized the opportunity.

'I know you have feelings for Ethan. That's why you called the fire service so quickly after you set light to his parents' house, isn't it?'

Naomie hesitated, then offered a brief, reluctant nod.

'You love him and you wanted to save him.'

'And I did the right thing. Neither of us thought it would spread that fast.'

'So help us to help him. Only we can guarantee his safety now.'

Naomie was teetering now between her loyalty to Ethan and the force of Helen's logic. Helen tried one last throw of the dice.

'Despite everything, I know that you're not a bad person. I know you have goodness in you. We found a half-built bonfire in the basement of his mother's office block today. Ethan was about to put the lives of a hundred people in danger. Did you really sign up for that?'

Naomie shrugged, guilt playing across her features.

'Of course you didn't,' Helen conceded. 'But Ethan did. And we stopped him. And I'm very worried about what he'll do now that we've stopped his little game. I know you've felt powerless and overlooked in your life, but it is now in your gift to help us. So I'm asking you to do the right thing. Help us bring your Ethan in safely.'

Naomie hung her head and sobbed quietly.

'Think about it,' Helen told her, determined to make one last push. 'Think about what you've done. Karen Simms, Denise Roberts, Agnieszka Jarosik and little Alice Simms. She was just a little kid, Naomie. Six years old, her whole life ahead of her. You stole that from her – you and no one else. And I think you owe it to her family and all the families you and Ethan have hurt to end this now. I can't have any more deaths on my conscience and neither can you.'

There was a long pause, during which Naomie continued to stare at the floor. Helen looked at Sanderson – had she even heard what she'd said? – then Naomie suddenly spoke, muttering a single word that changed everything:

'Ok.'

136

He brought the cup of coffee up to his lips, but his hand was shaking too much and he put it back down with a clank. The sudden noise made the café owner look up briefly from his work, before he returned his attention to the business of pushing fatty bits of bacon and sausage round a pan. The smell of the grease made Ethan want to vomit and he was very tempted to get up and go, but caution carried the day. This down-at-heel greasy spoon in Nicholstown was a good little hideaway. The only people who came here were dossers and Polish builders, both of whom had enough problems of their own to worry about him.

He cut a ridiculous figure in his dirty overalls, but it couldn't be helped and came in useful now. The TV that hung from the café wall broadcast Sky News round the clock and Ethan was both alarmed and amused now to see his parents sitting behind a table at Southampton Central Police Station, flanked by DI Grace.

The volume was turned down low, so Ethan shuffled his chair a little closer, straining to hear. He refused to miss this little pantomime.

'If you can hear this, Ethan, please get in touch. We love you, son, and we just want to know you're safe and well.'

How much must this be costing them? The lies must

stick in their throat but that wasn't the best bit. They must be cringing inside, being paraded to the world as the parents who bred a killer and never had a clue. Although they had always tried to deny it, he was their flesh and blood. And he would make them pay for that, as they had made him pay.

'There is a number you can call free of charge . . .'

His father continued in his familiar stumbling way. Had he been drinking this morning? He wouldn't put it past him. If he and Jacqueline were ever to acknowledge the extent of their problems, they would probably classify themselves as high-functioning alcoholics. What a misguided label that was. They were successful professionally but there was nothing high-functioning about them. They were cold, cruel and self-absorbed.

He had always strived to get their attention, and when he didn't get it, he screamed louder. And when that didn't work, he resorted to more desperate measures. Abuse, petty acts of violence and later some firestarting. These had always been chalked up as acts of characteristic clumsiness, as the truth was rather harder to swallow. They had tried to control him through medication and later through bitches like Agnieszka, who'd shout at him then lock him in his room when she became bored of his behaviour. Still, good things come to those who wait. They had all been repaid in fine style.

His mother, still stunned from her 'brush with death' had now taken centre stage and was in the midst of a lachrymose appeal. Who, he wondered, was she crying for? Herself? Her marriage? Her life? Or were they tears of regret for her son? That was the only emotion he had ever inspired in her. Not love, not compassion, not even pity – just regret. For one drunken, unprotected screw that had cost them all dear.

Ethan's eye drifted away from the screen to find the café owner staring at him once more, curious no doubt as to why his attention was fixed so raptly on the screen. The man dropped his eyes as soon as Ethan looked over, but it made Ethan think. There was one more thing to do – one last act. How long could he move undetected, now that the city was looking for him? How long before someone became suspicious? Or, worse, recognized him?

Things hung in the balance now. They were so close to the end and as Ethan turned his gaze once more to his pitiful parents, he vowed that he would not be beaten. If Naomie held her nerve, then all would be well. It was only a matter of time now, until the circle was complete.

137

'How did you two meet?'

Now that Naomie was talking, Helen was determined to get chapter and verse.

'I found him.'

'What do you mean?'

'I was walking home and . . . I found him. He was lying face down in the street. I saw a couple of other people walk round him, like he was a drunk. But he didn't look that way to me.'

'He was having a fit?'

Naomie nodded.

'He'd been out late, walking the streets. And he can feel these things when they come on – he gets a tingling in his hands and feet, his vision goes funny – but that doesn't mean he can stop them. He'd fallen, hit his head. So I put his head in my lap and looked after him until an ambulance came. He felt he owed me, but I never felt like that.'

'And you became friends?'

'Didn't have anyone else, did we? His parents liked to keep him inside, boss every second of his life, but he found his way out at night and we used to meet at the same time, same place – we used to joke that it was our ten o'clock shot. A kind of fuck you to my mum and his folks, who thought we were tucked up in bed. Not that they ever bothered to check.'

'What did you get up to?'

'Talked, smoked, walked a bit. We just liked being together.'

It was said so sweetly that in other circumstances Helen would have smiled. It was hard to believe that Naomie and her lover were multiple murderers, with four deaths on their conscience. Even now that didn't seem to faze Naomie as much as it should. She seemed more concerned about her boyfriend.

'Was it his idea? The fires?'

'I'm not saying anything about that. You'll have to ask him yourself.'

'I'd very much like the opportunity, but I'm going to need specifics. Where did you go with him? Where would he go now when he needs time and space to think? Where does he go at night?'

Naomie looked at Helen. She could tell even now that Naomie was torn – she'd never thought she'd be in the position of having to betray her lover. So it was softly and with some regret when she finally said:

'Itchen Bridge – there's a spot under that where we used to go. Sometimes to Pear Tree Garden. Mayfield Park. The pitch and putt by Weston Hard. Chamberlayne leisure centre. Millers Pond. He'll be at one of those tonight.'

The fight had gone out of Naomie now and for a brief moment Helen felt relief. She was sure she had been the junior player in their deadly enterprise.

'Thank you, Naomie. You've done the right thing.'

'Well, it's all you're going to get from me. I've done more than enough already,' she said, rising suddenly. 'I want to go back to my cell now.'

'Sure.'

'I want some hot food and another blanket, it's bloody freezing in there.'

'I'll see what I can do.'

Naomie was staring at Helen with real hostility now – it was amazing how quickly her mood could change. Was she angry with Helen for making her give up her boyfriend? Or did her attitude mask her fear of what might happen next? Either way, Helen was glad she had pushed her. They had the information they needed and, at long last, the end was in sight.

138

'Let the others go, we need you here.'

Gardam said it gently, but firmly, leaving Helen no choice but to comply. Her first instinct as always had been to lead the search, but Gardam had argued that someone senior needed to stay at base to coordinate proceedings. The locations Naomie had listed covered a wide area of the city in Itchen, Woolston and Weston. They would throw all the resources they could at it and it was easy in these situations for the search to become diffuse and unfocused. They would need to do it square mile by square mile, guiding those on the ground from Southampton Central, ensuring no stone was left unturned.

Privately, Helen wondered why Gardam didn't take point on this one – he seemed to be spending enough time in the incident room to do her job for her. He had a peculiar gift for becoming your shadow, monitoring your every move without ever actually intervening. Helen still couldn't work him out. Perhaps he didn't trust her instinct after all, despite all his words to the contrary? Perhaps he was just a voyeur, uncomfortable at being excluded from the heart of the action? Or perhaps he was just the wrong guy in the wrong job? Helen feared the last option the most. She had never needed or wanted a chaperone.

The hours flicked by – 6 p.m., 7 p.m., 8 p.m. The team on the ground had covered half of their allotted grid and still there was no sign of Ethan Harris. With each passing minute, Helen's fears grew. Had Naomie told them the truth? Was she really prepared to collude in the capture of the guy who was her 'family' now? How strong a stranglehold did he have on her?

Gardam was a calming influence, moving around the incident room with coffee and words of encouragement.

'Do you think he'll come quietly?' he said to Helen, seizing a lull in operations to pick her brains.

'That depends on how much he loves Naomie,' Helen replied. 'If he really cares for her, then he won't leave her to face this alone. But if he's been using her for his own ends, if he only truly believes in himself and his own destiny, then he could become violent. He might want to make one last stand – he's got a lot of prison time ahead of him. But the guys on the team know how to handle it – they'll allow him to think he's surrendering on his terms.'

Even as she said it, Helen wished she was on the ground with them. She knew Sanderson and Charlie could handle it, but there was something in her that was never comfortable taking a back seat. That's why she had never taken the promotions that had been regularly offered her. She was a front-line soldier, never the general on the hill. Even now she itched to get out there with the team, but she did her best to disguise it, answering Gardam's probing questions patiently, before returning to direct operations.

Still nothing. Not a sniff of their fugitive. It was getting late now – 9 p.m. had come and gone – and in the darkness it would be easier for Harris to hide. Helen's anxiety rose a notch further – where the hell was he? What was he planning?

Should they send the chopper up? Would that help to panic Harris and flush him out? It seemed a ham-fisted option and Helen wondered if Ethan could be rattled in that way. She was still pondering this when DC Lucas hurried up to her.

'Possible sighting, ma'am,' she said quickly.

'From the team?'

'No, from a member of the public. A young woman saw a man walking through Palmerston Park wearing overalls like those we mentioned in the press release. She went to challenge him, but he brushed her off and continued to walk towards the Esplanade.'

Helen's mind reeled. That was completely the opposite side of town to where her team were now searching.

'She lied to us,' Helen said, as much to herself as to Lucas. 'Naomie deliberately sent us in the wrong direction to aid his escape.'

'Escape?'

'If he's heading towards the Esplanade, then there's only one place he's going,' Helen replied. 'He's making for the train station.'

139

Helen was on the street in under a minute. Central Station was close to their base and Helen knew that she could cut off Harris's escape if she was quick. Gardam was calling ahead to the British Transport Police, alerting them to his movements, but something in Helen told her that wasn't enough. Harris had been a wily adversary, capable of hiding in plain sight, and she wasn't prepared to leave anything to chance. Trains left regularly from Central Station and there would be many possible avenues of escape if he made it that far.

Sprinting up Southern Road, she paused momentarily before throwing herself across the six lanes of Mountbatten Way. Despite the late hour it was still very busy and the trucks and cars roared past, buffeting Helen with their tail winds. Horns blared and drivers shouted, but Helen kept on going. She was making good progress and was nearly at the other side now, but as she made her final lunge towards the pavement, Helen realized she'd misjudged the speed of an oncoming van. The driver saw her and slammed on his brakes, but it was too late. A horrible screeching sound filled the air as the van skidded towards her.

At the last minute, the driver wrenched the wheel round and the van lurched violently to the left. It clipped Helen hard, sending her flying towards the pavement, before toppling over itself and sliding along the road on its side. Helen hit the concrete hard, bouncing beyond it and into the safety barrier at speed.

An odd moment of silence, of blank shock, then Helen was scrambling to her feet. Her head was swimming, a piercing noise filled her brain, but she struggled upright nevertheless. Her first instinct was to run to the van, but pausing, she turned to look at Central Station Bridge. If Harris was coming from Nicholstown, he would have to cross it to get to the station.

And there he was, turning on to the bridge and moving swiftly across it. He was only fifty feet from Helen now and she didn't hesitate, limping into a run and heading fast away from the bemused motorists. Moving was pure agony – she had caught her knee badly and she could feel blood running down the side of her face – but she kept on going. Harris was making good progress, he was nearly halfway across, but as yet he hadn't seen her. It was now or never.

Suddenly a gap opened up in the traffic and Helen ran across both lanes, vaulting the pedestrian fence on the other side. She landed with a bump and at that moment, Ethan Harris turned. He recognized her immediately and turned back to run across the remainder of the bridge, in the direction of the train station. But as he did so, two British Transport Police officers moved into view, cutting off his escape route.

Helen moved forward quickly, determined to capitalize on his confusion. Harris spun once more, his eyes scanning the other side of the road.

'Don't even think about it, Ethan,' Helen warned as she continued her approach.

The sound of sirens was growing louder now. Perhaps they were attending the traffic accident or maybe they were coming their way – whichever it was, Helen was prepared to use them to her advantage.

'You're a few hundred yards from Southampton Central. We've got every officer on the Force heading this way right now, so do the smart thing.'

Harris looked straight at her and Helen was surprised to see that he appeared to be neither panicked nor particularly disappointed by the situation he found himself in. His mind was turning on something, Helen sensed, but what kind of calculation he was making she couldn't say.

'I was hoping it would be you,' he said, casting another half-glance over his shoulder to check on the progress of the uniformed officers. 'What did you say to me at the hospital: "We'll get whoever did this to you."'

Helen didn't give Harris the satisfaction of a reply.

'But are you sure you're ok, Helen? You look a little off.'

She must have made a pretty sight – blood clinging to the side of her face, her suit battered and torn, but she was determined not to be mocked.

'All the better for seeing you,' she countered, wiping the blood from her face with her sleeve. 'But I'll be even happier when we're both in an interview suite.'

'How did you know I'd be here?' Harris asked, ignoring Helen's suggestion.

'Someone spotted you in Palmerston Park and, well, it's the obvious place to head for if you need to get away but don't own a car.'

Harris nodded but said nothing, casting another nervous glance over his shoulder. Helen took a step closer to him, but as she did so Ethan seemed to sense her movement and shifted away. There were only thirty feet between him and the other officers now – time was running out for him, but still he made no move to surrender.

'I hope you won't think too badly of me, Helen. I don't think you liked your folks either, did you?'

Helen said nothing, refusing to get drawn in.

'Doesn't leave you with much, does it? If your own flesh and blood despise you. Funny thing is, I used to want their love at first. When they went out – as they did every night – I used to sneak out too. I used to wander the streets looking for them, hoping they'd see me, hoping they'd *want* me – but it never happened. So after a while I gave up looking, but I continued to walk the streets anyway. I liked the anonymity that darkness gave me. Can you understand that, Helen?'

Helen nodded and took a small step forward. There was no question that Ethan was different – with his soft, Asiatic features, shortened arm and stooped posture – but that would have been fine, Helen thought, if he'd had people who loved him for who he was. His mother clearly hadn't realized she was pregnant – with a baby she'd never wanted – when she'd been drinking herself under the table every night. But that didn't excuse her horrendous treatment of her own son, a son she deemed both ill-formed and unwanted. Helen refused to have sympathy for Ethan, given what he'd done, but his pure, aching loneliness struck a chord with her and inwardly she raged at his parents for their casual cruelty and selfishness. They were the true architects of this carnage.

'I know exactly what you mean. Darkness can be a friend.'

'I thought you'd understand. But then again you've suffered – the whole world knows how you've suffered – so perhaps you do know how *I* feel.'

'It doesn't excuse what you've done, Ethan. You murdered four people.'

'If you can call them that.'

'They were human beings. With husbands, children, friends –'

'They were evil – all of them. Haters who thought nothing of belittling and abusing others for their own entertainment.'

'Luke Simms was "evil"?'

'Well, I guess you had to be there to know what it felt like – the whole school joining in with his taunts. My only regret is that Luke Simms didn't burn with the rest of his family.'

For a moment Helen was speechless. Under the bridge a train rattled through noisily, its metal wheels grinding unpleasantly against the rails. It was the perfect accompaniment to Helen's rising anger and anxiety.

'Agnieszka was no better. She beat me *and* abused me. Thought a poor, damaged kid like me wouldn't fight back. Did Naomie tell you I was in the room when she set that bitch on fire?'

'She told me that and a lot more besides,' Helen lied.

'I'm sure she did.'

'She told me every little detail of your thoughts, your plans. But do you know what the most surprising thing she said was?'

'I don't like playing games –'

'She told me she loved you.'

For once Ethan had no response. Was it Helen's imagination or did he suddenly look a little less cocksure? The assisting police officers were very close to Ethan now, but he seemed to have forgotten about them, so focused was he on Helen.

'Which means you've got something over me.' She was keen to press home the advantage. 'I've read your blog, Ethan. I know how you met, how you feel about her. You called her your "angel".'

'She is.'

'Why?'

'Because she has beauty. And goodness. And serenity. Because she's the only person I ever met who didn't dismiss me before I'd even opened my mouth.'

'I get all that, but here's the thing. Naomie's just a stone's throw away, Ethan. Sitting alone in a police cell. And right now she's carrying the can for your crimes. I think you owe her a little more than that, don't you?'

Ethan said nothing in response. Helen watched his face closely for signs of guilt, signs of surrender, as she carried on:

'She's lonely, she's scared, she needs you. So if you value her as much as you say you do, then let's end this now. You can make the difference, Ethan. Tell the world it was your idea, that you duped her, that you controlled her. You can still be the hero in this story – you can still *save* her. But you have to come with me. And we have to do this now.'

Underneath the bridge, the passing trains provided a

tense, rumbling accompaniment to their confrontation. Helen stared at Ethan for what seemed like an eternity, willing him to respond, then finally he nodded. Helen felt the tension seep from her body and she took a step forward, pulling the cuffs from her belt.

'Did Naomie tell you how we met?' he said suddenly.

Helen nodded, taking another small step forward.

'Did she tell you *where* we met?'

'No,' Helen answered, unnerved by the tone of his voice.

'Here,' he said, gesturing to the bridge. 'And we've met here pretty much every night since.'

And now Helen realized that Ethan *hadn't* been heading for the train station after all. He'd been heading for this bridge.

'Ethan, you have to come with me –'

Helen was moving forward quickly, all pretence at caution now gone, but Ethan seemed unconcerned by her approach.

'Our special place. Our ten o'clock shot.'

Helen could hear the train getting closer and knew exactly what Harris was intending to do. He darted towards the safety barrier and Helen went with him, determined to cut him off before he could jump. With one fluid movement, he swivelled up on to the wall, but just as he flipped himself over the edge, Helen managed to grab hold of his coat. The train was almost upon them, rattling over the tracks at speed, but Helen refused to let go, dragging Harris back from the brink. This was one fight she was not prepared to lose.

Then suddenly it was *Helen* was who falling backwards.

As she hit the kerb, she realized that Harris had slipped out of his coat and was free of her grasp. She made one last, desperate attempt to stop him, but was left clutching at thin air. Seconds later, she heard the dull crunch as his body smashed into the metal tracks and immediately after that the desperate, anguished cry of the train's horn, as the driver realized too late what was happening.

Helen turned away, unable to watch. Why hadn't she realized what he was planning? Why hadn't she stopped him? But even as she lacerated herself with these futile thoughts, something made her pause and look up. A sound. The sound of church bells marking the time.

And now Helen realized the enormity of her mistake. Ripping her mobile phone from her pocket, she punched in some numbers and began a desperate sprint back in the direction she'd just come from.

140

DC McAndrew raced down the stairs, barging her startled colleagues aside. Helen had just rung off and was haring back to base, but there was no time to lose. Pushing through the double doors, McAndrew sprinted into the custody area.

'Cell three. I need it open now.'

The custody sergeant looked up, aggrieved at this sudden intrusion.

'NOW!' McAndrew roared.

And now he didn't hesitate, snatching up his keys and marching with her towards the third cell on the left. Without hesitating to open the viewing hatch, he turned the key and wrenched the door open. McAndrew didn't wait for the standard invitation to enter, pushing past him aggressively.

But she was too late. Naomie Jackson had made full use of the extra blanket she'd requested, fashioning an impromptu noose from which she now swung. Screaming, McAndrew climbed up on to the toilet seat, pulling frantically at the knot, but she knew it was hopeless. Naomie was already dead.

At the end, the lovers would be together in death.

141

It was Christmas Day. A day Thomas Simms had been dreading.

It was less than a fortnight since he'd buried his wife and daughter and the idea of enjoying some Christmas cheer seemed both unreal and obscene. Karen had loved the festive season, Alice too of course, and he knew that even in years to come, when the wounds were perhaps a little less raw, he would always struggle at this time of year. It would remind him of all he had lost.

Fresh on the back of the funeral they'd heard the news that those responsible had taken their own lives in a pre-arranged suicide pact. This was the final blow as far as Thomas was concerned and for days he'd raged at the police, reporters, family – anyone who'd listen – furious that the family had been denied justice. He felt nothing for the perpetrators and their death provoked no sense of triumph in him, just a sense of emptiness and deflation.

Luke felt the same – he knew that. Thomas's son said very little these days – he was a far cry from the chatty, optimistic teenager he'd once been – but Thomas could tell that he too seethed with anger and frustration. Luke was furious with the world, furious with Harris and Jackson, but most of all he was furious with himself for the part he thought he'd played in the family's misfortune.

It had never occurred to Thomas to blame his son. As

far as he was concerned, they had been visited by someone else's madness. But try as he might he couldn't get Luke to see things his way. The boy was intent on blaming himself, even though there were others who were far more culpable in his view. Jacqueline Harris had actually written to them – the letter arriving three days before Christmas – clumsily expressing her remorse and guilt. But Luke wasn't interested and Thomas had torn up the letter before he'd got to the end of the first page. It was clear she was seeking absolution – and he wasn't going to give her that.

There was nothing to celebrate this year, but Christmas had arrived anyway, unbidden and unwelcome. There was no tree, of course, no decorations, no turkey or presents – none of the trappings they used to enjoy. There *were* cards, however. These had arrived in a trickle at first, then by the dozen, then in great armloads, as relatives, friends and total strangers felt moved to send Luke and Thomas their fervent hopes for brighter days ahead. Luke didn't want to look at them, so Thomas spirited them away to his bedroom, where he could read them in private.

Some of them made him cry, others made him smile. But all of them were valuable. None more so than the one from Charlie Brooks, who had kept a discreet but vigilant eye on them since the conclusion of the investigation. She had her own issues to deal with – had her own family – but her concern and affection for Thomas and Luke was not in question. And as Thomas read her card for a third, then a fourth time, he realized why her card – and many others like hers – had given him such comfort.

Because they reminded him that despite all the darkness out there, there is goodness too.

142

Jessica tore the wrapping paper off and peered at the gift inside. Intrigued, she pulled out the Peppa Pig Carousel and showed it to her parents, before returning her attention to the shiny silver paper. Helen suppressed a smile. Her experience of children was limited, but she knew that toddlers were always more interested in the boxes and paper that contained their presents than the gifts themselves.

'Sorry, she will play with it, but needs to spend some quality time with the wrapping paper first,' Charlie said, grimacing.

'Don't worry,' Helen responded quickly, 'I just like to see her enjoying the day.'

And it was true. At first, Helen had been unsure whether to accept Charlie's offer to join them on Christmas Day. She didn't want to be anyone's charity case and, besides, she had her own little rituals at Christmas that had stood her in good stead thus far. However, the temptation to spend the big day with people who cared for her had proved too strong in the end – and Helen was glad to have exchanged her standard Murgh Zafrani with extra coriander for Steve's roast turkey with all the trimmings.

She'd wondered if it would feel odd to spend Christmas with someone else's family but actually she'd had a great time and she chided herself now for her unnecessary fears. The icing on the cake had been the news that Richard Ford had found a new post with a sister fire service in the States and was due there soon. One less thing on my conscience, Helen had thought when she received Gardam's text. She was sure Adam Latham had swung this for his former colleague and, caught up in the Christmas spirit, Helen felt herself softening towards the man who'd tried to destroy her reputation. For all his faults, he was a leader who looked after his own. Just as she had done, Helen reflected, with Charlie.

'Helen?'

Helen snapped out of her thoughts to find Steve and Charlie staring at her, amused expressions on their faces.

'Sorry, miles away.'

'This is for you,' Charlie continued, handing Helen a present. 'And before you open it, I'd just like to say thank you.'

'For what?'

'For everything. I . . . well, we've all found it hard, me going back to work, and I think I'd have probably walked if it wasn't for you.'

Helen accepted Charlie's gratitude, playing down her role in her decision to stay – the latter was far stronger and more determined than she ever gave herself credit for. But, in order to fend off Charlie's protestations to the contrary, Helen now opened the present and was surprised and pleased to find that it was a new scarf – a replica of the one she'd lost.

'I heard you mislaid the last one, so here's No. 2. Try not to lose it this time, eh?'

Helen smiled and uttered a brief thanks, suddenly

choked with emotion by this thoughtful gift. Wrapping it around herself – much to Jessica's amusement and delight – Helen vowed that she would take very good care of this one, because of what it meant to her.

For the first time in ages, Helen didn't feel alone.

143

Christmas was over for another year. The turkey had been eaten and presents exchanged, and the clean-up operation was in full swing. Christmas Day in the Gardam household was always a big deal – Sarah taking it upon herself to up the ante each year to keep the horde of relatives, friends and plus ones entertained. She always complained about it, but Jonathan Gardam knew that secretly she loved it – the excitement, the preparation, and that contented feeling afterwards when you knew it had all gone well.

The TV was on, but nobody was really watching it. Sarah and the kids were playing a board game and his mother was slumbering quietly in the easy chair. Jonathan took this as his cue to slip away. He enjoyed Christmas as much as the next man, but the claustrophobia of it sometimes got to him and then he liked to escape to his office – or his sanctuary, as Sarah labelled it – at the top of the house.

Hovering in the office doorway, he listened for any signs of pursuit. But nobody seemed to have noticed his departure, judging by the raucous and good-humoured accusations of cheating among the board game participants, so he pushed the door to gently and turned the key in the lock. This was probably overkill and might arouse suspicion, but he didn't want to be disturbed.

There had one been gift to himself that he'd been looking forward to all day. Something special, something secret that nobody but him would appreciate.

Seating himself at his desk, he switched on the light and opened the top drawer. It was stacked full of files as usual, but Gardam lifted these out now, placing them carefully on the nearby coffee table. Beneath them in the drawer was a small plastic bag and within that was his prize.

Gardam slipped his hand inside and was immediately excited by the feel of the material. It was a guilty pleasure for sure – a gift that he had stolen rather than been given – which made it all the more enjoyable. He smiled to himself now as he pulled Helen Grace's scarf from the drawer.

He held it to his face, breathing in her scent, before gently brushing it against his cheek, revelling in its softness. He closed his eyes and for a moment was transported away from work and family, away from all the things that were as much a duty as a pleasure, to the real centre of his affections.

The enigmatic but compelling DI Helen Grace.

He just wanted a decent book to read ...

Not too much to ask, is it? It was in 1935 when Allen Lane, Managing Director of Bodley Head Publishers, stood on a platform at Exeter railway station looking for something good to read on his journey back to London. His choice was limited to popular magazines and poor-quality paperbacks – the same choice faced every day by the vast majority of readers, few of whom could afford hardbacks. Lane's disappointment and subsequent anger at the range of books generally available led him to found a company – and change the world.

'We believed in the existence in this country of a vast reading public for intelligent books at a low price, and staked everything on it'
Sir Allen Lane, 1902–1970, founder of Penguin Books

The quality paperback had arrived – and not just in bookshops. Lane was adamant that his Penguins should appear in chain stores and tobacconists, and should cost no more than a packet of cigarettes.

Reading habits (and cigarette prices) have changed since 1935, but Penguin still believes in publishing the best books for everybody to enjoy. We still believe that good design costs no more than bad design, and we still believe that quality books published passionately and responsibly make the world a better place.

So wherever you see the little bird – whether it's on a piece of prize-winning literary fiction or a celebrity autobiography, political tour de force or historical masterpiece, a serial-killer thriller, reference book, world classic or a piece of pure escapism – you can bet that it represents the very best that the genre has to offer.

Whatever you like to read – trust Penguin.